Gasoline

and

Bad Decisions

By

Mark Royer

Chapter One

My morning started off like any other — a routine bathroom trip and a fairly uneventful bowel movement. Yes, I know, probably too much information. But trust me, it's about to get worse, so we might as well dive right in.

Everything seemed normal, and I went on my merry way. After wrapping up in the bathroom, I headed to the manufacturing shop to "discuss" the so-called vital matters at Chester Forge. Spoiler alert: there are no vital matters. My job is boring as hell. But at least a few of my coworkers make it bearable.

To pass the time, I usually shoot the shit with some of the union guys. And this morning was no different — until, mid-conversation, I felt something ominous brewing deep inside. I had to make a hasty exit.

I made my way to the front of the manufacturing building, fully committed to making another bathroom deposit. Twice, I was forced to stop, desperately clenching my ass cheeks in a last-ditch effort to avoid catastrophe. I managed to hold the line — for the moment. But things were escalating fast.

By some miracle, I reached the manufacturing men's room. I grabbed the handle, pulled, and — screwed. Locked.

Now in full-blown crisis mode, I had no choice but to sprint across the street, through wet grass, my shoes picking up an impressive collection of lawn clippings along the way.

For those unfamiliar, our forge shop is graced with a unique individual named Greg. Greg is responsible for cleaning the bathrooms, taking out the trash, and mowing the grass. Every Thursday, rain or shine, Greg mows — because in his world, skipping a week is simply not an option. It had rained its ass off the day before, but Greg was undeterred. And that's how my shoes ended up looking like a makeshift Chia Pet.

Greg's quirks don't end with obsessive lawn care. He also enjoys slipping staples into my work shoes, leaving smeary fingerprints on computer monitors, and, on one unforgettable occasion, prancing naked through the test lab. To this day, no one knows why. And honestly, no one wants to ask.

Back to our story. I burst into the office building, bee-lined to the bathroom, dropped my trousers, and let nature take its violent course. What an explosion! But relief washed over me — I had narrowly avoided a catastrophic disaster in my pants. Feeling considerably better, I admired my accomplishment in the bowl and flushed with satisfaction. That's when I realized something was very, very wrong.

Fifteen minutes of aggressive plunging later, it became painfully clear — this was no ordinary clog. Try as I might, that toilet refused to cooperate. The bowl brimmed with a deep, dark, watery slurry, and each thrust of the plunger did nothing but send foul tidal waves splashing onto the walls, floor, and, regrettably, my shoes. Panic set in. I had no plan. So, I did what any self-respecting person would do—walked away and left it for the next unfortunate soul.

But guilt gnawed at me. A few minutes later, I returned to assess the damage. It was worse than I remembered. Horrified, I plunged again. Splashed again. Failed again. Oh well. We all have to recognize our limitations, so I washed my hands, closed the door, and pretended nothing had happened.

Eventually, I had to own up to my crime. Maintenance was called in, and it took four grueling hours and a pipe snake to resolve the situation. One coworker, after surveying the wreckage, remarked that it looked like a water buffalo had unloaded in there—judging by the sheer volume, the scattered grass clippings, and the apocalyptic fecal splashes decorating the room.

And so, I was crowned "Crapmaster." As if that weren't enough, I had to sit through a mock seminar on bathroom etiquette and was even awarded a plaque commemorating my... achievement. Honestly, I could think of worse nicknames. And, in a way, this one kind of fits.

You see, pooping disasters are something of a recurring theme in my life. Take the U2 concert, for example—the night I dropped acid for the first (and only) time. To this day, I'm not sure if it was the LSD, the sloe gin, or the Heineken, but the result was me stripping naked, using a patch of relatively clean underwear as toilet paper, and flinging the remains out the window — all while my friend drove aimlessly around Veterans Stadium's parking lot.

Now, at forty-five, I'm a husband, a father of three, and somehow, I still manage to have two or three incidents a year. Let's be honest — we've all been there. You think it's just a harmless fart, but then... surprise! Something extra tags along. At my age, though, I should have better bowel control. For Christ's sake.

Now, that infamous plaque — with two plungers crossed like battle swords — hangs on my wall, a reminder of my legacy.

As I leaned back in my chair, those same plungers pressing into my spine, I mindlessly responded to another pointless email. That's when the phone rang. And that's when everything changed.

"Rogden," I answered. Not "Mike Rogden, how can I help you?" Just "Rogden." I don't know when I adopted that as my official phone-answering style, but looking back, it might need some work.

"Wooooob," came the slow, exaggerated reply, the "ooob" drawn out like some sort of ominous chant.

Shit. I knew exactly who it was. And I knew it meant trouble.

For context, my nickname, Woody, has been around for years. It originated in my parents' basement during a hash-fueled smoke session when my friend Steve, in a moment of deep stoner philosophy, asked, "Would he...?" Which, apparently, sounded like "Woody." And just like that, the name stuck. I've been Woody ever since.

I knew the caller immediately—both from his voice and his butchered attempt at my nickname. I had no idea why he insisted on twisting it, but I was fairly certain it involved a combination of weed, alcohol, and poor decision-making.

"What's up, Finster?" I answered.

His real name was Walter, but his uncanny resemblance to Baby-Faced Finster—the pint-sized, cigar-smoking bank robber from *Bugs Bunny*—earned him a nickname he despised.

"Fuck you, asshole. How many times have I told you? Stop calling me that."

"Fin," I said, pausing dramatically after the first syllable.

"Stop calling—"

Before he could finish, I dragged out the rest of his hated name in one long, breathy crescendo.

"Sterrrrrrrrrrrrrrrrrrrrrrrrrrrrrrrrrrrrrrr."

I lived for this. He was too easy.

Silence. He was trying to punish me with the silent treatment. So I gave it right back. We sat in mutual stubbornness for nearly a minute before he caved.

"Are we done now? Can I talk?"

Yes! Victory! "Sure, Finster. What's up?"

He sighed, clearly exasperated, but ignored my final jab. "I'm in jail, man. Can you come pick me up? I need a ride."

"Jail? What the hell happened? Why can't Betty pick you up?"

Betty. A walking, talking bar fight in heels—and probably a slut. Also, his wife.

"I got another DUI. Can't you just pick me up, please?"

"Dude, what the fuck? First off, I'm at work. Second, I'm not lifting a damn finger until you give me the full story. And isn't this, like, your *fifth* DUI? How the fuck do you still have a license?"

"Jesus Christ," Finster groaned. "Alright. Here's the deal. I stole my parents' car and went to Duggy's Bar. You know, that dump over by Five Points?"

"Yeah. Keep going."

"I was only there for a couple of hours. Didn't even drink that much," he lied.

"Yeah, right." I'd heard that one before.

"No, seriously. I was fine. Anyway, when I left Duggy's, the cops say I hit another car and took off."

I sat up. "What do you mean *the cops say* you hit a car? Don't you remember it?"

"Not really. To be honest, I don't even remember leaving the bar. Maybe I was a little buzzed. Next thing I know, I'm getting hauled off to jail."

"Where'd they bust you?"

"In front of my parents' house. I was passed out in the driver's seat. The car was running, the door was wide open, and Ozzy Osbourne was blaring at full volume. My parents are livid."

"I guess so, what with your *fifth* DUI and all."

"It's my *sixth*."

Of course it was.

"Not only that, their car speakers are completely fucked, and I... well... I pissed all over the front seat. Must've happened when I passed out."

That did it. I lost it.

Five minutes later, Finster was genuinely pissed — probably more than when he wet himself.

"It's not funny, douchebag! Stop laughing! Just pick me up, *asshole!*"

I wiped the tears from my eyes, but the image of Finster pissing himself in his parents' car was just too much. Trying to suppress my laughter, I changed the subject.

"What about Betty?"

A long pause.

"*We're getting a divorce.*"

His voice cracked, and I could hear him starting to sob.

"Just pick me up, man. Please?"

Chapter Two

On the way to jail, I wavered between laughter and sheer annoyance. Sure, this was hilarious, but how many times was I going to bail this idiot out? And to make matters worse, he had the audacity to interrupt my busy work schedule—aka internet porn surfing.

Still, against my better judgment, my sympathetic side kicked in, and I went to pick his sorry ass up.

With him finally in my car, I decided to pry."

"So, what's the deal with Betty?"

"It's a long story, dude. I don't want to get into it."

"Come on. Tell me, man." I sniffed the air. "Hey… do you smell something?"

"Nah, I don't smell anything. And seriously, I don't want to talk about it."

"Finster, you know I'm not letting this go. Just give it up."

"Stop calling me Finster. Alright, fine. But if I tell you, you have to swear to keep it to yourself."

"Sure. No problem," I lied.

"She caught me having phone sex, and now she wants nothing to do with me."

"What? How the hell did she catch you? Wait a second… Jesus, it *reeks* in here." I pulled the car over, gagging at the stench.

"What the hell is that? It smells like p—" I stopped mid-sentence as realization dawned. "Finster… tell me you're not wearing the same pants you had on last night."

Silence.

"Shit! Get the fuck out of my car. Now!"

"My bad," he muttered. "I forgot."

I popped the trunk, grabbed two blankets, and tossed them at him. "Lay one on the seat. Wrap yourself in the other. Then *maybe* I'll let you back in."

Once he complied, we climbed back in, rolled the windows all the way down, and I resumed driving.

"By the way, where am I taking you?"

"To my parents' house. I left something in their car."

"Fine. Now spill it—how the hell did you get busted for phone sex?"

"Okay, okay. I was just curious, you know? I had a few drinks, waited for Betty to fall asleep, and gave it a shot."

I stared at him. "That's it?"

"Not really. She found me the next morning—naked, passed out on the living room floor. The TV was still playing porn, and next to me were a bottle of corn oil and a pile of tissues. Oh, and I almost forgot—the phone was off the hook, and my credit card was right there next to it. Pretty sure she put two and two together."

"I'll say," I choked out between fits of laughter. "Where the hell did you even get the phone sex number?"

"That's the thing. I had *Black Booties* circled in my *Penthouse*, along with my password. I left it open. On the kitchen counter."

I stared at him. "Password? I thought you *just* wanted to try this phone sex thing out. How many times have you actually done this?"

He shrugged. "No idea. Betty says I racked up $750 in the last three months. That's why she's so pissed."

Chapter Three

Okay, I admit it—I've whacked off more times than I can count. I've even given phone sex a shot. Twice.

But holy shit, Finster was on another level. I mean, put the goddamn corn oil away, man.

Some lessons in life are non-negotiable:

LOCK THE DOORS. ERASE ALL MASTURBATION EVIDENCE. NEVER GET CAUGHT.

As Finster rambled on, my mind drifted back to a defining moment of my teenage years. I was fifteen, and back then, *anything* could set me off—the *Sears* catalog, a local news anchor, even a particularly well-formed cloud.

But my true obsession? Channel 35.

If I fine-tuned the cable box just right, I could catch a grainy, soundless glimpse of *Playboy Television*. My parents had gone shopping. Game on.

Unfortunately, my parents forgot their checkbook and returned home to see their only son, pants around his ankles, kneeling in front of the TV, furiously going at it.

I think they wanted to pretend it never happened.

They never said a word.

But I *know* they remember.

And from that moment on, I mastered the art of locking a door

I shook myself from my masturbation-induced trance to find Finster sobbing uncontrollably.

"Betty. Betty. I love you, Betty! Please come back to me. Please, Betty, please!"

Not only was he crying, but he was rocking back and forth, and in the process, had managed to wiggle free from the only thing keeping the piss-stench at bay.

Just like that, my car smelled like a gas station urinal.

"Finster. Come on, man. Cheer up. You'll find another girl," I said, half-heartedly, as I tried to re-wrap him in the blanket with one hand while steering with the other.

"Yeah, but she gave *world-class* head. She had this technique where —"

"Okay, okay. She gave good head."

"No, you don't understand. She would take the tip and"

"FINSTER. I DO NOT WANT TO HEAR ABOUT BETTY'S BLOWJOB TECHNIQUE. EVER."

He sighed dramatically.

"The point is, there are other girls out there," I continued, "and you need to move on. Maybe you could hook up with someone from *Black Booties*?"

"Screw you, Woody. I'm serious. She gave the best hummers, man."

Chapter Four

We pulled into Finster's parents' house next to their car. When he got out, I was incredibly tempted to just leave him there—not only because he was a royal pain in the ass but also because my ball sac was really bothering me. It had been bothering me for a couple of days now. Not my nuts, just the sac—on the left side, along the four-week-old vasectomy scar. It should have healed by now, so I was envisioning an infection. Not the most pleasant of visions—a pus-filled sore on your most sensitive region. Whatever it was, I needed to check it out, and soon.

After grabbing a bag from his parents' car and throwing it in my trunk, Finster opened the car door and started to get in.

"Yo," I hollered. "You're not getting in my car with those piss-pants. Go change."

"What the hell, man? This is my parents' house. I don't have any clothes here. What do you want me to do? Besides, I don't feel like dealing with Mom right now. They're still pretty pissed about their car."

"No shit, they're pissed. Their new Toyota Highlander must smell like a urinal. But you're just going to have to suck it up and go say hi to Mommy. Because you're not getting in my car smelling like that. I don't care if you wear your mom's dress."

I rolled up the window, locked the door, turned up the radio, and reclined in the driver's seat. If that didn't signal the conversation was over, closing my eyes for a quick catnap certainly did. A few seconds later, I looked up to see Finster walking toward his parents' front door. Although I could only see the side of his face, I was pretty sure he was pouting.

A couple of minutes later, my brief snooze was interrupted by the sound of a door slamming and Finster running toward me, naked, shouting, "Open the door! Open the door!"

I rolled down the window and asked him what the fuck was going on when a man exited Finster's parents' house—a gun in his hand. Although I had no clue what this was all about, I did know I wanted to get the hell out of there, and quick.

I unlocked the door and yelled at Finster to hurry up. Just as his naked ass plopped onto the passenger seat, a bullet shattered my side window. Neither one of us was hit, but I sure wasn't waiting around to give this lunatic another chance.

As we sped away, I glanced in the rearview mirror. The man with the gun was chasing after us on foot, pistol raised. Man' didn't feel like the right word—he was pint-sized, decked out in full clown regalia, with shocking green hair sprouting from the sides of his balding head. Terrifying."

Turning the corner, I heard the sound of metal puncturing metal—presumably as a bullet entered the rear of my car.

While the man with the gun was no longer visible, I opted not to slow down as the odometer approached eighty.

"Wood, you need to slow down, man. We can't get pulled over by the cops," Finster implored.

"What do you mean, slow down? We're being chased by a freakin' clown psycho. I don't know about you, but I sure as hell don't feel like getting shot. And what the hell are you talking about—don't get pulled over by the cops? Cops are exactly what we do need right now. As a matter of fact, hand me my cell phone. It's in there, in the glove compartment."

"Wood. Just wait a second. And slow down, please. Look," he paused. "If we get pulled over right now, we're both in some serious shit. Besides the fact that I'm naked, we also have five kilos of coke in the trunk of your car."

Chapter Five

What the fuck is your problem, Finster?! How the fuck do you always get tangled up in this kind of bullshit?" I shouted. "And more importantly—why the hell did you drag me into it?

I'm assuming that's why that asshole was shooting at us, right? You screwed him over somehow, and now he's after you.

Correction—he's after *us*, not just you, since I was dumb enough to pick your ass up. Well, if we survive this, you can bet your life it won't happen again. I'm done bailing you out. *Done.*

And Jesus Christ, if I had a dick that small, I sure as hell wouldn't be letting it flop around in the open. Cover yourself up, man.

Oh, and one more thing—why the fuck was that guy dressed like a clown?"

Finster sighed. "Long story. For another time. But I'll give you a clue—it involves clown pornography."

Finster then launched into the details of how we ended up in this mess. But before we get into that, you need a little background information.

Fact: Finster is a cokehead, an alcoholic, a compulsive liar, and a phone-sex addict.

Fact: Finster is convinced he's destined for rock stardom. This belief is in no way supported by his barely passable guitar skills, painfully predictable songwriting, or his unmistakably god-awful voice.

Fact: Although he does have a certain charm — mostly as the target of ridicule — he is, for all intents and purposes, the village idiot.

When he's sober, he's merely annoying. When he's coked up, he transforms into an absolute menace — mouth running at full speed, jabbering endlessly. And during those rare moments of silence, he grinds his teeth or performs a bizarre chewing motion, minus the food.

Not a pretty sight.

At a particularly legendary party, Finster earned the nickname *The Tester*. A keg-and-grain-alcohol affair. Thirty-plus drinks, each in need of a taste test. Finster took it upon himself to oblige.

Unfortunately, his final test landed him face-first in the Breyberne River. His scream faded into the distance as he tumbled down the hill. Several of us ran to help, eventually pulling his half-drowned, booze-soaked body from the water. His face still bears a two-inch scar from that night.

That's not even his worst injury.

Once, he sprinted headfirst into a telephone support cable. His body kept moving. His legs went airborne. For a brief, beautiful moment, he was suspended — parallel to the ground, five feet in the air. Then he crashed. Hard.

We ran to help, but we also couldn't stop laughing.

That was Finster.

On the bright side, he did invent *The Brown Finger*.

The rules were simple. Stick a finger up your ass. Hook an unsuspecting victim's nose. Watch in delight as they inhale pure horror.

I, too, was a victim. But my revenge was spectacular.

11th-grade English. *Hamlet*, Act 1, Scene 1. Finster sitting in front of me. No one behind me. No one beside me.

I had time.

I went deep. *Real* deep.

When my masterpiece was complete, I jammed my finger up Finster's nose and held it there. No one noticed.

Except Finster.

To make matters worse, we were *high as shit*.

Now, as we sped along in silence, I debated my next move.

Option one: Drive straight to the cops.

Option two: Brown Finger him *again* for dragging me into this disaster.

Option three: Pull over, throw his naked ass — and the coke — onto the side of the road, and leave him to fend for himself.

Decisions, decisions.

Before I could finish this thought, Finster interrupted.

"Yo, man. Do you smell gas?"

I sniffed. Sure enough, the familiar scent of gasoline hit me — coming from the back of the car. Concerned that the car might explode, and that authorities would soon discover my charred corpse next to a naked Finster, I immediately pulled over. We jumped out, and as soon as I spotted the bullet hole, I knew.

"Shit. There's fucking gasoline everywhere."

Earlier that morning, I'd filled up at QuickStop — fuel for the car, plus a five-gallon container for the lawnmower. Now, thanks to a stray bullet, my errand had turned into a crime scene.

"Oh, no. No, no, no."

Finster's voice cracked.

"My coke!"

He threw the duffel bag onto the ground, tore it open, and started rocking back and forth, whimpering like a kicked puppy.

The bullet had ripped through both the gas can and his duffel. Five kilos of cocaine—drenched in gasoline. Gone.

What remained was a half-empty Ziploc bag. Plenty for Finster to enjoy a few highly flammable lines, if he was feeling adventurous.

And he was.

I watched in disbelief as he snorted a fat, gas-soaked rail.

Then, predictably, he lost his shit.

"WHY THE FUCK DID YOU HAVE A CONTAINER OF GAS IN YOUR TRUNK, ASSHOLE?!"

Before I could respond, he shoved me—hard. My reaction was pure instinct. I punched him in the face. Harder than necessary Probably harder than I should have. Maybe some of that was years of pent-up frustration. Maybe it was just long overdue. Either way, the result was the same—Finster writhing on the ground, hands clutching his now-broken nose, blood leaking between his fingers.

"You broke my fucking nose!" he wailed.

Then, as if this situation needed another twist—

A police cruiser pulled up behind us.

Chapter Six

I don't know why I lied. Maybe if I'd just told the truth, things would have turned out differently. But that's not what happened.

"What's going on here, boys?" the officer asked.

"Uh, nothing, officer," I stammered. "Just cleaning up a little mess, that's all."

The cop said nothing. Just looked around. I followed his gaze. And that's when I saw Finster. Sitting on the ground. Hands covered in blood. Naked. The blanket he'd been wrapped in had unraveled at some point—probably while he was rolling around in pain.

At that exact moment, I became painfully aware of my own predicament. My ball sac throbbed. Again. Getting to the bottom of whatever the hell was going on down there had just moved up on my priority list.

Unfortunately, I couldn't exactly drop my pants in front of a cop. I already had enough explaining to do. Finally, after what felt like hours, the cop spoke again.

"Let's try this one more time. What's going on?"

"It's a long story," I said.

Here's the thing about lying: you never stray too far from the truth.

You tweak a few details. Omit the important parts.

Like, for example, the fact that, until recently, there had been five kilos of cocaine in the trunk of my car.

Or the real reason there was a bullet hole in my backseat.

Instead, I went with this:

I picked up my idiot friend, who had pissed himself. Naturally, I made him change. But since he didn't have any clothes at his parents' house, he wrapped himself in a blanket. So now I had a naked passenger. On the way home, he had a meltdown over his failed marriage.

I pulled over to calm him down. That's when another car pulled up. (Sorry, officer, I don't remember what the driver looked like. Or the car, for that matter.) The guy must have thought our roadside hugging session was something more because he immediately launched into a string of anti-gay slurs.

Finster, being Finster, reacted in the only way he knew how. He Brown Fingered the man. And things real escalated fast.

Mr. Shit Nose pulled a gun. One shot through the window. Another through the trunk. (You can see the damage for yourself, officer.) Then he sped off.

And in my rage-fueled frustration over my now-bullet-riddled car, I did what any rational person would do. I punched Finster in the face.

End of story.

"Wait a minute." The cop held up a hand. "You stuck your finger up your ass and then shoved it up this guy's nose?"

He stared at Finster in disbelief.

"What the hell possessed you to do that?"

"I don't—"

Before Finster could dig his own grave, I cut him off, steering the conversation back to my carefully constructed lie.

Instead, I gave the officer a brief history of the Brown Finger.

The cop listened. Blinked. Then shook his head.

"You are one sick puppy," he said, wagging a finger in Finster's direction.

"You know what? As far as I'm concerned, you guys got off lucky. Stick shit up *my* nose? The car wouldn't be the only thing that got shot."

He let that sink in. Then he sighed.

"Since there's no one here to press charges, and nobody's hurt—well, besides your friend's nose—I'm just gonna act like this never happened."

With that, he turned and walked back to his cruiser.

Just before climbing inside, he called out:

"Put some clothes on and get the hell out of here."

Then he looked me dead in the eyes.

"You might want to consider getting a new friend. This one's nothing but trouble."

"Thanks for the advice, officer," I said. "I've thought about that myself."

As the cop drove away, Finster finally spoke.

"What do you mean by that, Wood? You don't mean that, do you?"

I sighed. "Just shut up, Finster. And get in the car."

Before he could drop his bare, disgusting ass onto my seat, I threw up a hand.

"WAIT! Wrap yourself in that goddamn blanket first!"

Chapter Seven

We drove in silence toward the nearest Burger King. I was starving, but more importantly, I needed to hit the bathroom. Not because I was living up to my *Crapmaster* name, but because my aching ball sac had just jumped to the top of my priority list.

I pulled into the back lot and stepped out of the car without bothering to ask Finster if he wanted anything. Before I could leave, he grabbed my arm.

"Did you really mean that? What you said to the cop?"

I looked at him. His face was a bloody mess, but his eyes — his *stupid, pathetic* eyes — looked hurt.

Tough shit.

"Finster." I sighed. "How many times have I bailed you out? This one takes the cake. You got me shot at and almost arrested for *cocaine possession*. I'm married. I have three little girls. The last thing I need is to end up in prison as Bubba's personal fuck toy."

I turned and walked away.

As I reached the door to Burger King, Finster called out, "Hey, can you grab me a cheeseburger and large fries? I don't have any money. Oh, and a vanilla shake. And a cup full of ice for my nose. It's freakin' killing me."

I didn't turn around. Just shook my head and walked inside.

Priorities. Food or nut check?

Easy decision.

I headed straight for the men's room.

The only stall was occupied, so I stood at the urinal, unzipped, and did my best to act casual. If anyone walked in, I'd just pretend I was taking a leak.

Then I looked down.

And there it was.

A pus-filled boil the size of a marble.

Hunching over, I pinched it between my fingers and gave it a solid squeeze.

Jesus Christ.

The pain was instant. Blinding. Nearly blacked out right then and there. And while passing out in a Burger King bathroom would be humiliating enough, doing so with my *junk out* would take things to a whole new level of embarrassment.

I needed a better angle.

Scooting over to the mirror, I steeled myself for another go.

Now, while this wasn't quite as bad as *masturbation*, I had no intention of being caught staring at my own dick — or, more specifically, my scrotal region — in the mirror. Should anyone enter the bathroom or exit the stall, I was confident I could zip up fast enough to make it look like I was just washing my hands.

I took a breath. Planted my feet.

One. Two —

Before I could get to three, the bathroom door slammed open.

Chapter Eight

In one motion, I zipped up and turned around.

"Yo, man, we need to get the fuck out of here. Now," Finster hissed.

"What the hell's going on out there?" a voice from the stall called.

I ignored him and turned to Finster, who stood wrapped in a blanket, shirtless, barefoot, bloody nose, and looking like a complete mess.

"What now?" I asked.

He lowered his voice. "Those dudes that shot at us? They're here. Just pulled into the parking lot. There's no way they're gonna miss your car."

"Finster, you're on your own, man. I'm not doing this anymore." I turned to leave.

"Wood, wait a second." He grabbed my arm. "These guys aren't fucking around. They'll shoot you just as fast as they'll shoot me."

"The difference is, I won't be with you. Like I said, you're on your own."

I pushed open the door and stepped outside. Finster followed close behind, and the second we exited, we locked eyes with the guy standing in the cashier line. The same guy who shot at us. His eyes widened. His hand went to his waistband.

Without hesitation, he pulled out his gun and opened fire.

The restaurant erupted into chaos. Customers screamed, chairs crashed, and Finster and I bolted for the side exit as bullets tore through the air.

Outside, another man stood beside my car. It wasn't just the grotesque tattoo across his face that made him alarming — it was the gun pointed right at us.

Trapped between them, we ran in the only direction we could — across the grass and down a side street.

"Feeenstaaaa," one of the gunmen called out, dragging Finster's name like he was taunting him. A shot rang out, nearly missing my left leg.

"We're coming to get you, Feeenstaaaa."

"Fuck you, Bozo," Finster snapped as we ran.

The two of us barreled down the street, our pursuers close behind. Up ahead, a pickup truck sat at a red light. Just as we reached the back of the truck, the light turned green.

Neither of us needed to say a word. We sprinted harder, pushing forward with everything we had. The truck rolled forward, slowly accelerating. I reached the tailgate first, caught the edge with my fingers, and hauled myself onto the bed.

"What the fuck?" the driver shouted.

"Just drive! Those guys are trying to kill us!"

The driver turned, saw the gunmen closing in fast, and floored it.

Finster had just reached the tailgate when the truck lurched forward, sending the tailgate crashing open.

His hands clung to the edge as his legs dragged along the pavement.

"Aaaaaah! Fuck!" he screamed, his bare feet scraping against the asphalt.

I lunged forward, grabbing his wrist, trying to haul him up, but the loose gravel covering the truck bed made it nearly impossible to gain any footing. Gripping the side of the truck, I yanked as hard as I could, managing to pull his upper body onto the tailgate.

Then the blanket flew off.

For a brief, horrific moment, Finster's completely naked ass was on full display, bouncing with every jolt of the road.

The wind snatched the blanket and sent it flying — right into the face of the tattooed gunman, who I later learned was named Beetle. He staggered, arms flailing, momentarily blinded by Finster's airborne toga.

Bozo, however, didn't miss a beat.

He stopped, took careful aim, and fired two quick shots — straight into Finster's bare ass.

Chapter Nine

Once again, I found myself standing on the side of the road with my naked friend—only this time, we had company.

"Well, that sure was interesting," the driver said. His name was Lee, and he was built like a damn grizzly bear. The guy had to be six-five, with arms that looked like they belonged on a silverback gorilla. He had at least a hundred and fifty pounds on me, and most of it wasn't fat.

I considered myself in decent shape for a forty-five-year-old—minus the extra fifteen pounds of beer gut—but standing next to this guy made me feel downright scrawny.

To make things more unsettling, Lee had a habit of standing just a little too close. He'd stare at me with an unreadable expression, rub his groin absentmindedly, and lean in just enough to make me wonder if I should start running.

I didn't think he was actually coming on to me. More likely, he just enjoyed fucking with people. At least, I hoped that was the case, considering we were stranded in the middle of nowhere, and he could snap me in half like a twig.

"Here, put this on," Lee said, tossing a giant pair of oily overalls at Finster.

Finster sniffled as he held them up against his body. "These won't fit."

The poor bastard looked rough. His nose was broken, he had two bullets lodged in his ass, and the tops of his feet were shredded from being dragged along the pavement. I couldn't blame him for crying at this point.

"Don't got nothin' else, Bud. Take it or leave it."

Lee turned his attention to me. "Your partner's got a little dick, you know that?"

I sighed. "Yeah, Lee, I know."

"Bet yours is plenty big, though." More crotch rubbing.

"Uh, yeah. Sure," I said, desperate to end this conversation. "Anyway, thanks again, Lee. We'd both be dead without you."

"Yeah," he said, giving me a long, unreadable look. "Seems like you owe me something." Rub, rub, rub.

I reached for my wallet. "I don't have much cash, but you can take whatever I've got."

Lee shook his head. "Nah. I was thinking we get butt naked and wrestle in the swamp."

He pointed toward the marshy area near the Breyber-ne River—the same river Finster had drunkenly tumbled into years ago. "Cover ourselves in chicken grease. May the best man win."

I forced a smile and nodded. "Gonna have to pass on that one, Lee."

Chapter Ten

I was starting to like this guy. Lee's twisted sense of humor was something I could appreciate, given my own history of questionable antics.

Back in college, I worked construction now and then. For reasons I can't fully explain, I took great joy in strategically dropping surprise turds around the jobsite, just to see which poor bastard would stumble across them. One particularly impressive specimen had my boss convinced a Great Dane had been roaming the area. Just another reminder that I am, without a doubt, *The Crapmaster*.

Things escalated to the point where I once took a dump straight out the window of a half-built second-story house. Just as I was mid-position, a coworker yelled, "Yo, Wood! Pull your damn pants up!" I ignored him. A few moments later, their horrified reactions had me doubled over with laughter.

I can't exactly pull off that level of depravity in my current job, but I still enjoy a good prank. Like taping photos of male models on the wall of an openly homophobic coworker. Or slipping sticks and stones into the quality manager's inbox. Or installing a program on an engineer's computer that randomly swapped his cursor with a middle finger. Not quite the same as airborne shit bombs, but you work with what you've got.

Sitting on Lee's open tailgate, I ran through the events that had led us here. He found Finster's story particularly amusing, especially the part about how he ended up with five kilos of cocaine. I explained Finster's coke habit and how he constantly worked his jaw in that bizarre, twitchy chewing motion when he was high, but I let him tell the rest himself. Since I already knew the details, I wandered off into the woods, hoping to finally deal with my aching ball sac.

Finster's story was as predictable as it was stupid. He'd gone to his dealer for coke, stuck around to party, got wasted, and—in a moment of drunken brilliance—decided to swipe five kilos while the dealer was taking a leak. Proud of himself, he stopped at a bar, got even drunker, hit a car, fled the scene, pissed his pants in his parents' SUV, and got arrested.

Classic Finster.

Meanwhile, in the woods, I was losing a battle against my own body. No matter how hard I squeezed, I couldn't pop the damn thing. The swelling had grown to the size of a small plum, and at this point, I was starting to think I might need actual medical attention.

Frustrated and in pain, I trudged back to the truck, only to be met with a truly shocking sight. I'd seen a lot of disturbing things in my life, but this was right up there.

Bent over the tailgate was my small-penis friend, once again naked, while Lee knelt beside him, one hand gripping Finster's ass and the other holding a pen knife.

I picked up my pace, the throbbing in my pants making every step a reminder that I had my own problems to deal with.

"You guys having fun?" I asked.

Lee, face dangerously close to Finster's bullet wounds, inspected the situation with the focus of a jeweler examining a diamond.

"I can't go to the hospital," Finster whined, still half-sobbing. "They have to report gunshot wounds to the cops. There's no way I want them investigating this whole mess."

"You know, he's got a point," Lee said, nodding in agreement. "Oops. Almost forgot to sterilize this." He waved the pen knife at me like a magician about to perform a trick.

Then he stood, strolled around to the front of his truck, and reached into the glove compartment.

That's when the police cruiser pulled in behind us.

Chapter Eleven

Doesn't this look familiar? You're Mike, right? And Mr. Little Dick here is Finster. How's it going, Lee?"

The cop's name, I would later learn, was Bill Daylay. Turns out, he was married to Lee's sister. I could only imagine what she looked like. If she bore any resemblance to Lee, that poor bastard had my deepest sympathy.

"Not bad, Bill," Lee answered. "I just asked my friends here if they wanted to go wrestle in the swamp. You interested?" He gave his crotch a good rub for emphasis.

"Maybe later, you little bitch."

Bill strolled up, spat at Lee's feet, then, without warning, stuck his arms out like airplane wings and started running in circles.

"Way to go, punk," Lee muttered.

I had absolutely no clue what the hell I had just witnessed, but judging by their smirks, this was some kind of ongoing game between them. Also, watching a cop pretend to be an airplane made me wonder if Officer Daylay might actually be more unhinged than Lee.

"Alright," Bill said, coming to a stop. "Now that we've got that out of the way, who wants to explain what the hell is going on? More specifically, why is Mr. Little Dick butt naked again? And what the fuck happened to your feet?" He nodded at Finster.

Before Lee or Finster could open their mouths, I jumped in.

"Nice seeing you again, Officer. Mind if I call you Bill? I mean, at this rate, we're getting pretty familiar. You finding me and my naked friend on the side of the road seems to be turning into a regular thing."

Bill smirked. "Sure. Call me Bill. After all, we're all friends here. Right, Lee?"

He spit at Lee's feet again.

Lee didn't say a word. He just lifted his shirt, exposing an enormous, hairy beer gut, and thrusted his hips forward like some kind of deranged mating ritual.

"Anyway," I continued, trying to ignore whatever the hell was happening between those two, "after our little visit with you, we grabbed some food. We came back outside, and my car wouldn't start. Lee offered us a ride — on the condition that Finster rode in the back. Something about not wanting a naked man in his front seat.

We're driving along when suddenly, I hear Finster screaming. I turn around, and there he is — naked, hanging off the tailgate, feet scraping the pavement. Turns out, when he hopped in, his blanket got caught in the tailgate. Once we started moving, the wind yanked it away, leaving Mr. Little Dick completely exposed — again.

So Finster tries to grab it, realizes it's jammed, and opens the tailgate to set it free. Instead, he loses his balance, loses his blanket, and ends up dragging the tops of his feet along the pavement. Hence, the bloody feet."

I motioned toward Finster, who sat there looking like a broken man.

Bill stared at him for a long moment, then shook his head. "Jesus Christ."

"That's pretty much it. We pulled over, Lee gave Finster his overalls, and now here we are." I nodded at Finster. "Feel free to actually put some clothes on at any time."

Bill turned to Lee. "You got anything to add, Bitch?"

Lee shrugged. "Nah, that about covers it, dickface. Except for the five kilos of coke, the bullets in Little Dick's ass, and, oh yeah, the guys shooting at us."

So much for my little story.

Chapter Twelve

Seems like you left out a few important details, Mike. That place where you 'grabbed something to eat' wouldn't happen to be the Burger King over in Chadsville, would it?

Because funny enough, we got a call about a shooting over there not too long ago. Witnesses say two men were firing all over the damn place, chasing after two other guys. And one of them? Wrapped in a blanket.

Kind of a coincidence, don't you think?"

Bill gave Lee's truck a long look. "Come to think of it, a witness did mention something about a beige pickup."

I had no idea what to say. I just stared at Lee, pissed off that he'd just destroyed my perfectly crafted story.

Lee noticed. "You got something to say, punk?" He rubbed his crotch like a jackass. "First off, I just met you. Second, this douche bag here is my brother-in-law. Third, I don't lie. Fourth, even if I *did* lie, I wouldn't get myself mixed up in *this* bullshit.

And fifth, as much as I disrespect this queer," he said, motioning to Bill, "he *really* doesn't like being fed a line of crap. Ain't that right, Bill?"

Bill smirked. "Gotta hand it to you—your first story was solid. Almost had me. But something about it didn't sit right. Especially considering the way *your* friend was acting." He nodded toward Finster. "I was convinced you were lying. Or at the very least, leaving out some important details. But since I didn't have anything solid, I let it go."

He folded his arms. "Still, my curiosity got the better of me, so I did some digging at the office. Turns out your buddy here has quite the history of DUIs. Even had some minor cocaine possession charges."

I turned to Finster. "I didn't know about that."

He just kept staring at the ground, looking thoroughly defeated.

Bill sighed. "And now I find you *here,* and I can smell the bullshit from a mile away. Like I said—your first story was better."

I let out a long breath, knowing I was screwed. "Look, I'm sorry for lying, okay? I have a wife and three kids. I didn't want to get caught up in this mess."

Then, for the first time, I told the entire story—start to finish. No spin, no bullshit, no omissions.

When I was done, I apologized again and practically begged Bill for mercy.

Bill turned back to Finster, shaking his head. "Are you a *moron?* What the hell possessed you to outright steal *five kilos of coke?* You didn't think your dealer would notice?"

All of us stared at Finster.

He didn't move. Just kept looking at the ground.

"Answer him, Finster! Answer me!" I yelled.

"I don't know. I was fucked up, man. Figured I'd do a couple lines and sell the rest. You see, I'm saving up for recording studio time. Gonna make a hit record."

Then, as if on cue, he burst into song. "I don't like Mondays, no Tuesdays, no Wednesdays, no Thursdays..."

Finster went full rock star—eyes closed, head tilted back, strumming an invisible guitar like his life depended on it.

The rest of us just stared.

Finally, Lee sighed, walked over, and smacked Finster on the ass—right where a bullet was still lodged.

"AAAH!" Finster howled. "What the fuck was that for?!"

"Got you to stop singing that god-awful song, didn't it?"

"He's right, Finster. The song sucks. And let's be honest—you can't sing for shit."

"It's gonna be big, man. You'll see."

"Uh-huh. So that's why you stole five kilos? Studio time? Dude, the song is garbage. Nobody likes it. Nobody."

"You're just not listening to the lyrics, man. They're deep."

He took a dramatic breath. "I don't like Mondays, no Tuesdays…"

Lee smacked the other ass cheek.

Chapter Thirteen

S o, what now?" I asked.

"Hang on. I think I hear my radio." Bill turned and walked toward his car. "I'll be right back."

Lee and I sat on the tailgate, watching Finster. His borrowed overalls were around his ankles again as he twisted and turned, trying to catch a glimpse of his bullet-riddled ass cheeks in Lee's side-view mirror.

Lee shook his head. "So, how'd you meet this loser?"

Before I could answer, Bill's cruiser pulled up beside us. He rolled down the window.

"Lee, take these guys back to your place. Have Mary patch up Mr. Little Dick as best as she can. I'll be back later — there was a break-in over in West Gornin."

I sat up straighter. "Wait. I live in West Gornin. What was the address?"

I already knew. I felt it.

My chest clenched like it was caught in a vise, my pulse pounded, and my mind flooded with images of my family. I couldn't breathe. I just knew.

Bill glanced at me. "1416 Fairbank."

Oh God.

Chapter Fourteen

I have no idea how long the ride to my house lasted, but it wasn't fast enough.

I kept begging Bill to speed up, but no matter how quickly we drove, it wouldn't be quick enough. My mind was already there—at home, with my family. I didn't know what I would find when we arrived, but I feared the worst.

I couldn't lose them.

I loved them all so deeply, it hurt.

Suzy. My wife. My best friend. The mother of my children. What would I do without her? Even then, in the backseat of Bill's cruiser, I was apologizing to her in my mind.

I was sorry for nagging her about bullshit. Sorry for not communicating better. Sorry for not telling her every single day how much I loved her. Sorry for not appreciating *everything* she'd done for me.

When we first met, I don't know if it was love at first sight, but it was definitely lust. Suzy was beautiful. She *is* beautiful. And I was sorry for that too — for not telling her often enough how stunning and special she was.

And my kids. Halle. Lynn. Janie.

Each of them so completely unique, so completely *themselves*. No one without children can truly understand the depth of a parent's love. It's impossible to even *imagine* life before them.

I had been ready for fatherhood, excited even. But I'd also been scared. People told me that you love your kids more than your spouse, and that thought terrified me. I didn't *want* to love anyone more than Suzy. It felt like a betrayal.

But it turned out to be true.

And that car ride only made it clearer.

I loved my kids more than I loved my wife. And I apologized to Suzy in my mind for that too.

Think about it — would you give up your life for anyone? Do you love anyone *that* much? Your parents? Your wife?

Loving someone like this forces you to ask those questions. And the truth is, as much as I loved my parents, I wouldn't die for them.

I was almost certain I would die for my wife.

But for my kids?

There was no doubt. No hesitation. None.

If I had to give up my life to save them, I would. If I had to cut off my own leg to save them, I would.

A father doesn't hesitate.

It's funny, the things you think about in life. When I was young, I used to believe that if I were ever in an accident that left me paralyzed, I would rather die. Not now. Not ever.

God forbid it should ever happen. But if it did—if I were trapped inside my own body, unable to move, but still able to see my kids, hear them laugh, joke with them, nurture them, love them—then let me live. *Let me live, dammit.*

I don't pray often, but I did then. I begged—pleaded—that if anyone had to suffer, let it be me. *Not my kids.* My mind spiraled into the worst places: abduction, rape, murder, torture. The kind of horrors we hear about every day.

This was why I had feared having children in the first place, because I *knew*—deep in my bones—that I wouldn't survive losing them. The thought alone was unbearable, making me want to curl up, arms around my chest, shielding myself from the world, bracing for the worst. But there was still hope, and that was the only thing keeping me together.

"Bill," I whispered. "Please… drive faster."

Chapter Fifteen

My heart sank as we rounded the corner, my drive-way coming into view. Two police cruisers were already there, but more importantly — more ominously — so was an ambulance. Before the car even came to a full stop, I threw the door open and ran toward the house.

"Mike! Hold on," Bill called out behind me.

I ignored him and kept running.

I reached the front door just as a stretcher was being wheeled out. My breath caught in my throat. A body bag.

"Who is that? Who the fuck is that?" I stammered, reaching for the bag.

"Hold it. Just hold it," one of the EMTs said, placing a firm hand on my chest.

"Who's in the fucking bag?" I shoved his hand away, my voice raw.

"Mike? Is that you, Mike?"

Suzy's voice. From inside the house.

Relief and terror hit me at the same time.

"Suzy? Are you okay, honey? Where are the kids?" I yelled, pushing past the EMT, knocking him aside as I sprinted toward her voice.

"They're fine, babe! They're at the neighbor's. I'm fine."

She ran toward me, and we collided in the dining room, locking each other in a desperate embrace.

"You're sure everyone's alright?" I asked, gripping her tightly.

"Yes, honey. Everything's okay."

"Halle?"

"At the neighbor's."

"Lynn?"

"At the neighbor's. Janie too. The kids are fine."

I pulled back, cupping her face in my hands, needing to see it for myself. "And you?"

"I'm fine too, honey. We're all okay."

I kissed her hard, held her tight, and whispered that I loved her, refusing to let go. When I finally pulled back, I asked, "What the hell happened?"

She exhaled shakily. "I took the kids to the Mason's so Jenny could watch them. I wanted to get some grocery shopping done. Oh, and I just called Jenny—she's keeping them a little longer. I didn't tell them anything yet."

"Okay. And?"

"I got back from the market and found this man lying on the kitchen floor. I called 911, and that was that."

"Jesus," I breathed, shaking my head. "Thank God no one was hurt. Did you ever see this guy before?"

"Never."

"What the hell is going on?" My mind raced, struggling to piece it together. But now wasn't the time. I shook it off and took her hand. "Never mind that now. Let's go get the kids."

Chapter Sixteen

Before we could get our daughters, Bill stopped us. "Mike. Can I see you a second? Follow me."

He led me over to the ambulance, unzipping the body bag just enough to expose the face inside. I felt my stomach tighten. It was Beetle—the same prick who had been shooting at us at Burger King, the same one who had been tangled in Finster's blanket as we sped away.

The reason I knew it was him was simple. That face was hard to forget. A thick, black tattoo, sprawling across his skin like something out of a Mike Tyson fever dream.

I stared down at the corpse, my mind still trying to process everything.

As Finster told me, and as I now relayed to Bill, Beetle and Bozo were both cronies of Eddie Bretz, Finster's drug dealer. Although not entirely relevant to the situation at hand, I've always found nicknames fascinating, so I figured I'd pass along the origins of our gunmen's monikers.

Beetle's was simple enough—his last name was Bailey. *Beetle Bailey*, straight out of the old-school comic strip. Bozo, on the other hand, had a more colorful backstory. Apparently, he had a thing for hookers who indulged his fantasy of dressing in full Bozo the Clown attire, complete with makeup. At his, shall we say, *penultimate moment*, he would honk a bicycle horn and scream, *"Bozo's coming! Bozo's coming!"* while cackling like a lunatic. To top it off, he even started a website where he sold streaming videos (and DVDs, for the old-school perverts) showcasing his bizarre escapades—all for the low price of $24.95, plus shipping.

As I stood over Beetle's lifeless body, my brain still playing an unwanted mental loop of *"Bozo's coming! Bozo's coming!"*, my attention was drawn to his crotch. Not in a sexual way, but it was impossible to ignore the bloody stain spreading across the fabric, along with a noticeable missing patch from his trousers.

"What the hell happened, Bill?"

"Well, as far as we can tell, Beetle here broke into your house and was promptly attacked by your dog. Judging by the damage to his dick, I'd say that's one tenacious guard dog you've got."

Bill was referring to our fifteen-pound Jack Russell, Jake. I beamed with pride at the thought of my fearless little dog taking down an armed intruder. At the same time, I couldn't help but wince, imagining my *own* dick being subjected to such brutality. Instinctively, I reached down to adjust myself, which only made me groan in pain.

"Aaah," I yelped.

Bill eyed me suspiciously. "What the hell's the matter with you?"

"Uh, nothing," I lied, though I briefly considered hitching a ride in the ambulance just to finally get my swollen ball sac checked out. The only thing stopping me was sheer embarrassment.

"You were saying?" I prompted, eager to change the subject.

He gave me another look but continued. "Yeah. Anyway, your dog must have had a death grip. There was broken glass and overturned chairs all over the place."

I glanced over and spotted another officer acting out the incident, gripping his crotch with both hands and staggering backward in a dramatic reenactment of Beetle's struggle. In a final flourish, he jerked back, collapsed onto the ground, and played dead. His fellow officers erupted into laughter.

"So that's what happened?" I asked, nodding toward the scene.

"Basically, yeah. Old Beetle must've pulled back something fierce, trying to get Fido off his pecker. Can't say I blame him."

"It's Jake," I corrected.

"What?"

"Jake. Not Fido."

Bill waved me off dismissively. "Whatever. Anyway, he lost his balance, fell backward, and cracked his head on your kitchen tile. Dead."

Before I could respond, the front door swung open, and out came Jake, sprinting toward me at full speed. The moment he appeared, every cop in the vicinity scattered. One even jumped onto the hood of his car. I crouched down and scooped Jake into my arms, showering him with praise.

"Good boy, good boy."

Bill smirked. "If I were you, I'd keep an eye on that dog. Don't they say once an animal gets a taste for human blood, it wants more? You might wake up with Fido snapping at your dick."

"Screw you, Bill," I said, shoving him lightly.

"Maybe you want to coat your nether region with pepper. Dogs hate pepper, right?"

"Yeah, I'll get right on that, Bill." I mocked him as I pantomimed shaking pepper onto my crotch.

The second I moved, a sharp pain shot through me.

"Ouch! My goddamn throbbing ball sac!"

Chapter Seventeen

As we walked back to my house, Bill asked me to confirm the name of Finster's dealer.

"Yep. Eddie Bretz. You got it," I answered.

"That name sounds familiar. I'll check with narcotics. Oh, by the way, I'll talk to the Medical Examiner. Name's Tsong, but we call him Quincy. Real original, huh? I bet seventy percent of MEs in the country are called Quincy."

"Yeah, you're probably right," I said, briefly recalling the TV show from my youth—Jack Klugman as Dr. Quincy, the forensic pathologist.

"Anyway, he's a great guy. You should see him at a titty bar. He's freakin' nuts."

I smirked, remembering my own experiences in similar establishments.

"What I'm going to do is ask him to leave out the injury to Beetle's pecker. Reason being, you don't need the bullshit. If that shows up in his report, next thing you know, Animal Control will be all over your ass, trying to claim Fido's vicious. And honestly, they'd probably have a pretty strong case," he said, nodding toward the ambulance.

"He's harmless." I glanced over at the flashing lights. "I take that back. He's harmless *if* you're not trying to kill me, my wife, or my kids. If you are, look out—because Jake's coming for your ass."

Bill chuckled. "Like I said, I'll take care of it. But if it were me—" he shook his hand up and down near his crotch.

"I know. Coat it with pepper."

"Damn right. But seriously, we need to talk. Your wife, too."

"Sure."

We walked into the dining room and sat down next to Suzy. I shifted in my chair, leaning to the side to avoid putting any pressure on my left ball.

"Look," Bill started. "I just met your husband today, Mrs. Rogden, and under the circumstances, I'd rather let him explain." He held up his hand like a stop sign, preemptively blocking any reaction from my wife. "Rest assured, he's not in any trouble and he didn't do anything wrong. Except maybe in his choice of friends. You know Finster, right, ma'am?"

Suzy sighed, shook her head, then turned to me with an exasperated look, rolling her eyes in disgust as she muttered something under her breath.

"What did that asshole get mixed up in now?" Suzy asked.

"We'll talk about it later," I replied.

"Yeah, that's a good idea," Bill added. "Because what I've got to say is more important right now. See, you guys have a problem here. It's obvious you're guilty by association in this dealer's eyes."

"Dealer?" My wife's eyes narrowed. "What dealer?" Before Bill could answer, the realization hit her. "Oh, I get it. Of course it's drugs. I should have known. When the hell is Finster gonna grow up?"

"I don't know, babe. He probably never will."

"After what I witnessed today, I'd say you're right," Bill interjected. "Anyway, like I was saying—because of your buddy, you're now mixed up with some bad people. I know we just met, Mike, but I happen to like you. You seem like a pretty cool guy. And Mrs. Rogden, I'm sure you're a very sweet lady. Bottom line, I'd hate to see anything happen to you."

Suzy and I exchanged uneasy glances. Without thinking, we scooted a little closer on the couch, instinctively reaching for each other's hands.

"What I recommend," Bill continued, "is that you get out of the house for a while. Just until this thing blows over. Take some vacation time, get out of Dodge."

"Sure," we both said in unison.

"Alright. You guys have a safe place to go?"

"We should go to my parents', don't you think, Suze?"

She nodded. "Yeah. That sounds good to me."

"It's about three hours away, Bill. Out in the boonies. Even if these guys wanted to come after us, they'd never find it."

"Great. Why don't you come with me, Mike? I'll take you to get your car. The techs finished checking it for evidence—they didn't find a thing. It's still parked over at the Burger King. I'll drive you over."

He turned to Suzy. "Ma'am, why don't you pack some things up and get ready to leave? I'll keep Rochester here to watch over you." He gestured outside toward the cop standing guard, then started his *Jake-on-the-crotch* imitation with his hands.

"Oh, the wannabe actor?" I asked.

"Yep. Which reminds me—" he pretended to shake pepper on his crotch.

"Sure. Like I said, I'll get right on that," I shot back, dripping with sarcasm.

Suzy just stood there, watching us, shaking her head at our immaturity.

Chapter Eighteen

Before we left for Burger King, I ducked into the bathroom, then called my wife in a moment later.

She walked in to find me kneeling on the sink, pants around my ankles, studying my privates in the mirror.

"What the hell are you doing?" she asked, closing the door behind her. Then, "Oh my God! What the hell is that?"

"A fucking boil, I guess. I don't know. It freaking hurts," I yelped.

"I bet it does. Look at the size of that thing," she said, her face a mix of awe and revulsion.

It hadn't grown much, still plum-sized, but it had hardened under the growing pressure.

"See what I did for you?" I teased. "It's right on my vasectomy scar, which, by the way, is *also* still a little tender."

"Grow up. Try giving birth. *Three* times." She rolled her eyes and turned to leave.

"Wait, wait, wait," I pleaded. "I need your help. Can you pop it?"

"What? Are you crazy? I'm not touching that thing." Her expression turned from disgusted to horrified.

This wasn't the first time my wife had to deal with some rather unpleasant issues. Considering I was the Crapmaster, she'd already endured more than her fair share. The asshole, after all, is just *not* designed for the sheer volume my body unfortunately produces. At times, the result could be... painful.

One particularly bad episode had left me trying to ex- amine my own butthole with a handheld mirror. When I couldn't get a good enough look, I swallowed my pride and asked my wife to assist. Amused, she had agreed. I got on all fours, doggy-style, while she took a closer look. After her review, she had even sympathetically applied ointment to my, uh, affected region.

With that humiliating memory in mind, I turned back to my current problem.

"Please, honey. This thing is killing me. Just *look* at it."

She shook her head, vehemently refusing.

I wasn't giving up. "I'm begging you. Please. I tried to do it myself, but I just *can't*. Maybe if you get a better look, you'll have better luck. I just can't deal with it any- more. *Please?*"

"Jesus Christ, Mike. Let me see."

I hopped off the bathroom sink, standing there with

my pants and underwear pooled around my ankles. Suzy hunched over, eyeing the grotesque lump with a mix of concern and disgust.

Shaking her head, she asked, "You ready?"

I gritted my teeth and gripped the towel rack for support. "Yeah."

"Okay," she said, pinching the lump. "One. Two. Three."

"Aaaaaaaaahhhhhhhh!"

The pain shot through me like an electric current. I reeled backward, slamming my head against the tile wall, then lurched forward, toppling onto my wife.

As I rolled off her, we both froze at the sound of Bill's voice from outside the bathroom door.

"Everything okay in there?"

"Yeah. We'll be out in a minute," Suzy called back, sounding only slightly winded.

Lying on the floor in the fetal position, I groaned, the pain radiating from my sac overpowering the dull throb in my skull.

Suzy sat up, brushing herself off. "You know your boil didn't pop, right? Don't you think it's time you went to the doctor?"

The only reply I could muster was a low, guttural groan.

Chapter Nineteen

W hat the hell happened in there?" Bill asked. "Strange time for a little quickie, huh?"

I ignored him and hobbled beside him, opening the passenger door of his police car and easing myself in. As I leaned back against the headrest, I finally noticed a fresh lump throbbing on the back of my skull—the result of my head slamming into the bathroom wall when Suzy tried to pop my damn boil. I rubbed it gingerly and winced, the pain still secondary to the throbbing in my groin.

"How long before my family and I can come back home?" I asked.

"I don't know. Three or four days. A week, tops. Shouldn't take long to track down this Bozo guy. Once we nail him, I think we'll be able to link this whole mess to Finster's dealer—the infamous Eddie Bretz."

Still rubbing my head, I glanced over at Bill. "So what's going to happen to Finster?"

Bill frowned. "You alright, man? You don't look so good."

"Thanks. Yeah, I'm fine. Just bumped my head in the bathroom."

"I *told* you it was a strange place for a quickie," he said with a smirk. "And what about the limp? You were walking fine before you went to the john."

"Don't worry about it. Finster?"

Bill shook his head. "Something *definitely* went on in that bathroom. But anyway—Finster? Yeah, he's got a problem. Not sure what we're going to do yet." He shot me a look. "Why? You *still* concerned about that loser? I told you, you need to distance yourself. He's trouble."

"I know. But I've known him since eighth grade. I'm not saying I want to stay friends with him, but I don't want to see him go to prison for twenty years either." I exhaled. "I always hoped he'd grow up someday. If he does, I'll be there for him. If not, I'm staying the hell away."

Bill nodded. "Sounds like a plan. But I wouldn't hold my breath. I know I just met him, but Mr. Little Dick has *a lot* of changing to do, and I don't know if that's possible at this point in his life."

"No, you're right. I mean, Jesus Christ. The guy's fortty-five years old and still acts like he's eighteen."

We pulled into the Burger King parking lot, stopping beside my car.

"Thanks for all your help, Bill. I appreciate it."

"Hey, no problem. It's my job. And like I said, you seem pretty cool. We should hit up Hooters sometime — catch a game, check out the other sights, of course."

I smirked. "You asking me out on a date? What, are you gay? Not that I care, but I'm married, dude."

"Screw you, Mike."

I opened the door to leave, but Bill grabbed my arm. "Seriously. What the hell happened in the bathroom? Come on, you can tell me."

I laughed. "Fuck off."

Shutting the door behind me, I gave him a final wave. We exchanged cell numbers and agreed to keep in touch.

Chapter Twenty

Driving home, I felt an immense sense of relief. My insane, batshit adventure was finally over — except for a few loose ends, none of which I wanted to be involved in.

Honestly, I was even looking forward to my forced vacation. Work had been stressful as hell. Our forge shop was teetering on the edge of bankruptcy, and a fair number of high-ranking assholes had wormed their way into positions of power. Basically, I needed this break.

I pulled onto the shoulder to make a few calls. First, I left a message for one of our company's top-tier assholes — my boss. Told him there was a family situation, I'd be out for about a week. Blah, blah, blah. Then, being the dedicated employee that I am, I listened to my voicemail and responded as needed.

Fifteen minutes later, with work officially out of the way, I called Suzy to let her know I was heading home.

I put the car in drive and checked the rearview mirror for oncoming traffic — but instead of the road, I saw my trunk door wide open.

I frowned and threw the car back into park.

The hell? I was positive the trunk was closed when I picked it up at Burger King. And I was equally sure it hadn't popped open during the drive. Frowning, I slammed it shut, yanked on it to make sure it latched, then sighed. Weird. Making a mental note to keep an eye on it, I headed back to the driver's side door.

Just as I slid into my seat, I caught movement out of the corner of my eye. The passenger door was open.

Too late. Gravity had already taken over—I was inside before I saw who had opened it.

Bozo.

Gun pointed at my ribs, he scowled. "Do you have any idea how freaking hot it is in there?" He jerked a thumb toward the trunk. "Those goddamn gas fumes were killing me."

I exhaled sharply. "Wow. Sorry I couldn't make it more comfortable for you." I glanced at the gun. "But actually, I think the fumes were your fault, weren't they? Seeing as you were shooting at me a couple of hours ago?"

"Smartass," he answered, jabbing my arm with his gun. "Let me just warn you. I'm not in the mood for jokes. I don't feel so good. Now turn the key and start driving."

I started the car and pulled off the shoulder. I was truly scared shitless, not sure what this lunatic would do next. As I drove, I stole furtive glances at my kidnapper. He was indeed a startling sight. Although he was sitting, I was sure he stood less than four feet tall. His nose was tremendous in both size and shape, hook-like and reminiscent of an eagle's beak. At the same time, his nostrils were excessively exposed, and unfortunately for me, the left side contained a very prominent booger, forcing me to stare at this region.

"What the hell are you looking at?" he asked, jabbing me with his gun. "Keep your eyes on the road."

"Nothing. Nothing. Sorry," I stammered. But I couldn't help myself. I just had to look. And it wasn't just the booger, it was his entire appearance that served as a visual magnet. In addition to his nose and height, his hair was ridiculous, a classic example of male pattern baldness — except the sides were permed and dyed fluorescent green.

To lighten up the situation, I quipped that I should do my hair like that, but Bozo missed the insincerity and took it as a compliment.

"Yeah, I like it. I used to wear a wig, but it didn't look too good in my videos. This is much more natural," he said, proudly touching his hair. "The only problem is shaving the top. Sometimes I get razor burn. See?" he asked, pointing to his skull.

"Yeah, a little bit. Nothing some concealer wouldn't hide."

"You're right. Turn on the damn AC," he ordered as milky white sweat rolled down his face, presumably colored by remnants of his clown makeup. "I'm still not feeling too good here."

I reached over and cranked on the air conditioner, then asked Bozo where we were going.

"Just keep driving. I'll tell you where to turn. Hey, do you know anything about websites?"

"Not me. My wife does, though." I immediately regretted mentioning her.

"Your wife, huh? What's she look like?"

"I think she's beautiful, but she struggles with self-confidence," I lied. "She's got this thyroid problem and gained a lot of weight. I still love her, though," I added, hoping Bozo's clown fetish didn't extend to plus-sized women.

"She's fat, huh? There might be a market for that. I'll have to look into it. See, right now, I pretty much cater to the mainstream of the clown fetish community. You got some weirdos out there, though. Maybe I could —"

"Bozo," I interrupted. "Where are you taking me?"

"Just keep driving," he snapped. "I told you. I'll let you know when to turn. Does this fucking AC work?" He wiped another chalky trail of sweat from his face.

Even on his best days, Bozo was a hideous sight. But now, after marinating in gasoline fumes and baking inside my trunk, he looked downright pathetic. Still clutching the gun, he was swaying in his seat, eyes unfocused, teetering between nausea and unconsciousness.

"Pull over," he groaned. "I'm gonna be sick."

For a split second, I actually felt bad for him. I'd been there—too much booze, stomach lurching, head spinning, regretting every decision that led to that moment. But sympathy didn't stop me from slamming the brakes and pulling onto the shoulder.

Unfortunately, rapid deceleration wasn't what the doctor ordered. Bozo lurched forward, and before I could react, he unleashed a torrent of vomit, hitting me square in the face.

Maybe it was the puke dripping down my chin. Maybe it was the sudden realization that Bozo was weak—vulnerable. Either way, instinct took over. I lunged for his gun.

The little bastard was freakishly strong. As we wrestled for control, he suddenly shrieked, "Bozo's coming! Bozo's coming!"

Horrified that I might, in some way, be assisting in his climax, I recoiled—just for a second.

Big mistake.

Bozo seized the moment, throwing all of his weight onto me, gnashing his teeth like a rabid dog. His breath reeked of vomit and gasoline. His yellowed teeth clamped down on my shoulder with such force that I felt the muscle tear in his mouth.

And then, with a clown hanging off my shoulder like a goddamn facehugger from Alien, I passed out.

Chapter Twenty One

When I came to, I was in the passenger seat, my arms bound behind my back, while the clown freak was now in the driver's seat. My head throbbed, my shoulder felt like it had been set on fire, and despite everything, I was still acutely aware of the damn boil pulsing on my ball sac.

"It's getting late, Bozo," I said, glancing at the clock. "I called my wife three hours ago and told her I'd be home soon. The cops are at my house—they'll be expecting me too. Hell, they're probably already out looking for me." I shifted slightly, testing my restraints. "Why don't you just pull over, let me out, and take the damn car? Just get the hell out of here. I swear, I won't say anything about what you look like. I won't tell them shit. Just let me go."

"Shut the fuck up!" Bozo snapped. Then, suddenly, he took both hands off the wheel, grabbing his head as if trying to crush his own skull. "Goddamn headache! You got any aspirin?"

"Bozo, watch the road!" I yelled.

Too late.

The car veered toward a telephone pole. At the last second, Bozo jerked the wheel, but the overcorrection sent us spinning. The rear end slammed into the pole before we careened off the road, plowing through the marshy land leading up to the Breyberne River.

I was lucky—Bozo had actually buckled my seatbelt. But my hands were still tied behind my back, so I had no way to brace myself. I was thrown around like a goddamn ragdoll, my ribs slamming into the doorframe as we finally skidded to a stop.

Bozo wasn't so lucky. He hadn't bothered with his own seatbelt. Now he was slumped over the wheel, moaning, a slow trickle of blood running down his forehead.

I took a moment to assess my ever-growing list of injuries. Let's see—still had the pus-filled ball sac boil. Added to that, a throbbing lump on my head (courtesy of my failed attempt to pop said boil), a bite wound on my shoulder, multiple bruises from getting jabbed by Bozo's gun, and now, a gash above my right eye and even more bruises from the crash.

There'd be time to lick my wounds later. Right now, I needed to get the hell out of there.

With Bozo still groaning, I worked quickly. Twisting my wrists, I managed to wriggle my hands under my ass, then hunched forward and pulled them under my legs. My shoulder screamed in protest, but I didn't stop until my hands were finally in front of me.

The bastard had ripped up my brand-new Penn State football jersey—straight out of the shopping bag in the backseat—and used the strips to tie me up.

That was it.

Fury took over.

I clenched my bound hands into a fist and brought them down on Bozo's face. Once. Twice. Three times.

I loved that fucking shirt.

After my brief moment of insanity, Bozo was out cold. I took a deep breath, trying to calm the lingering rage before focusing on the next problem—I still needed to free my hands.

Leaning over, I fished my keys from the ignition. Attached to my keyring was my trusty Swiss Army knife. People always gave me shit for carrying it—"Why do you even have that?" or "When are you ever gonna need it?" Well, this was my moment of vindication.

I fumbled through the attachments, first opening the useless can opener, then the awl, before finally finding the tiny scissors. Awkwardly bending my wrist at a painful angle, I sawed through the shredded remains of my brand-new Penn State jersey. Once my hands were free, I calmly closed the knife, set it on the seat beside me... and punched Bozo square in the face.

The sight of my ruined jersey reignited my fury. If I haven't mentioned this already, I LOVED THAT FUCKING SHIRT.

At my feet lay Bozo's gun. I snatched it up, along with my cell phone and keys, then climbed out of the car. Behind me, Bozo was stirring, groaning like a dying animal. He sounded weak—no immediate threat—but I wasn't taking any chances.

As I trudged toward the road, my feet squelching in the mud, a thought hit me. I didn't want to be caught with the gun if a trigger-happy cop showed up. I turned back, and without a second thought, hurled it into the river.

That's when the pain hit.

I realized my mistake the instant I drew my arm back, but momentum took over before I could stop myself.

White-hot agony ripped through my shoulder, and I collapsed forward, face-planting into the mud with a scream. Jesus Christ. Aside from the ball sac incident earlier that day, this was easily the worst pain I had ever felt.

Minutes passed before I managed to drag myself upright. Muddy, bleeding, sore as hell, and in an absolutely miserable mood, I limped my way toward the road.

Behind me, Bozo's cries were getting louder.

I ignored him, sat down on the shoulder, and called home.

Chapter Twenty Two

After updating Suzy on my predicament, I called my new cop friend, Bill. He told me to stay put—someone would be along to pick me up soon.

I hung up and glanced back at my car. Jesus. It was a wreck.

Now, I wouldn't call myself a car enthusiast, but I liked my car. It wasn't anything fancy—an eight-year-old Subaru Legacy—but it had served me well. More than that, though, it held memories. Like the day we brought our oldest daughter home from the hospital. How could I not think about something like that?

As I sat there, debating what new car we'd need and how the hell my insurance would handle this mess, Bozo's wails grew louder. Every few minutes, his cries of pain would break into unintelligible mumbling, then back to wailing again.

The longer I waited, the weirder it got.

His ramblings cycled between agony and full-blown conversation, like he was arguing with someone who wasn't there. Curiosity got the better of me. Since I had nothing to do but wait for my ride, I started making my way back toward the car.

Without his gun, I was fairly confident I could kick the shit out of the clown freak—though my mangled shoulder and the very real memory of his rabid-ass bite reminded me this guy was nuts.

Just in case, I scanned the ground for a weapon. Finding a hefty stick, I tightened my grip and crept closer.

At first, his words were too garbled to make out, but as I got within ten feet, the nonsense took shape.

Bozo was having an imaginary argument with an irate customer.

"No sir. You ordered Clown's Pack, which is our current monthly special. It includes *Bozo's Revenge* and *Clown Affair*. If you want *Clowns Gone Wild* and *Clowns Gone Wild II*, they can be ordered for $24.95 each, plus shipping. As a special offer, we'll include *White Make-up and Pink Vagina*, an internet-only stream, for just $14.95 more."

His head lolled back, his body twitched, and he let out another broken howl of pain before launching into the same spiel all over again.

Jesus Christ.

Between the gas fumes, heat exhaustion, my punches, and the car crash, the clown freak was completely fried.

"No, sir. You ordered 'Clown's Pack,' which is our current monthly special. It includes 'Bozo's Revenge'…"

I turned away in disgust, my curiosity thoroughly satisfied. Unfortunately, I wasn't nearly as quiet leaving as I had been approaching.

"Hey! Get back here!"

I turned to see Bozo struggling to haul himself out of my wrecked car. Deciding that putting more distance between us was the best plan, I turned back toward the road and picked up my pace.

"I said get back here! I'm going to keeeel you! Bozo's coming! Bozo's coming!" he shrieked, his voice teetering between rage and delirium.

I risked one last glance over my shoulder but kept moving. Just as I reached the road, a familiar truck screeched to a stop beside me.

"Hop in, dickwad."

It was Lee.

Not the cop I was expecting, but at this point, I'd take whatever I could get. I scrambled inside.

"Thanks for the ride, Lee."

"No problem. Who's the clown?" he asked as Bozo stumbled toward us, still screaming.

"I'll tell you later. Just drive!"

Lee didn't hesitate. He hit the gas, and the truck lurched forward.

Behind us, Bozo's cries grew more frantic.

"Stop! Stop, you bastard! Bozo's coming! Bozo's coming!"

Lee glanced in the rearview mirror, watching the clown freak flail wildly in the middle of the road. He shook his head.

"That's one sick sonofabitch," he muttered, rubbing his crotch.

"You got that right," I agreed—instinctively mirroring his motion.

Fuck! My damn boil!

Chapter Twenty Three

So why'd you pick me up, Lee?"
Right before you called, I was out riding around looking for Finster. After you talked to Bill, he called me and asked me to grab you."

"Wait a minute—looking for Finster? Where the hell is he?"

Lee shot me a look. "If I knew that, dickwad, I wouldn't be looking for him, now would I?"

Fair point. I nodded, acknowledging my own stupidity, and he continued.

"I took your friend over to see Doc Wills, a vet over in Thursndale. He wasn't exactly thrilled about patching up a grown man's ass, by the way. But he dug the bullets out, stitched him up, cleaned and dressed his feet, then gave him a shot. Fixed him up with some painkillers and antibiotics."

"Okay," I said, waiting for the inevitable "but."

"Me and Doc were in the next room shooting the shit while Mr. Little Dick went to the bathroom. Next thing I know, he's gone. Stole some cat tranquilizers, too."

"What an asshole," I said, shaking my head. "He's got a real talent for stealing drugs. That's how this whole mess started."

"Yeah, I caught the irony too."

I sighed. "So now you know how I ended up needing to be rescued. What's the plan for finding Finster?"

Lee shrugged. "We'll figure it out. But first, you wanna explain what the hell was up with that weirdo back there? You know, he kind of reminded me of a clown. Slap some white makeup on him, and boom—instant sideshow act. Sure, I've seen plenty of kids with green hair, but that dude wasn't a kid. And he was practically bald. I don't get it."

"Neither do I."

I relayed everything I knew about Bozo, including his website and twisted clientele, though I left out the part where he showed an unsettling interest in my wife joining his production team.

"You're telling me that freak was one of the guys shooting at us?" Lee asked. "I don't remember him having green hair."

"Really? Kind of hard to miss, but I guess with all the chaos... Anyway, he said he got it done right before the Burger King shootout." I paused. "Apparently, wigs don't look natural on film. He needed a fresh dye job before kicking off production on *Anal Clown Play*."

"Huh."

That was all Lee could manage.

We drove in silence for several minutes. I wasn't sure what Lee was thinking about—aside from his usual crotch-rubbing routine—but I had a feeling he, like me, was trying to wrap his head around how someone even gets into a clown fetish. Sure, I had my own preferences, most of them involving the lesbianic variety. But clowns? That was some next-level weird. Then again, I didn't understand the appeal of golden showers, feet, or—God help us—fecal fixations, either.

I figured as long as it wasn't hurting me, I didn't really care. My personal grievances with Bozo had nothing to do with his niche audience and everything to do with the fact that he shot at me, kidnapped me, crashed my car, and bit a chunk out of my goddamn shoulder.

As for my own fantasies? Let's just say I was still working on convincing my wife to consider a ménage à trois.

My fantasy goes like this: Suzy and I rent a room. We go out for dinner, have a few drinks, then return to our hotel. A couple more drinks, some making out, and then—a knock at the door. Who could it be? Perhaps the *previously arranged* brunette escort with long legs and a great ass? Yes, that would be her.

This dark-haired beauty poses as a masseuse I hired to relieve my wife's aches and pains. Naturally, I step out to let the two of them get acquainted. *I won't be gone long, of course.*

When I return, Suzy is naked, the "masseuse" kneeling behind her, hands gliding over her ass. A brief, awkward pause—then I ask if I can join. Before long, the three of us are tangled in a blissful tangle of soft skin, mouths, and pleasure. And that's just the beginning.

But I digress.

"Yeah, I sure don't understand that clown stuff," Lee muttered.

"Me either," I said. "To each their own, I guess."

"I guess," Lee added, though he didn't sound convinced. "Which way do I go up here? Bill told me where you live, but I'm not exactly sure."

"Take a right onto Lamper Lane, then another right. First house in the cul-de-sac on the right."

"Right, right, right," he said, confirming.

"Right," I replied, playing along with his idiotic repetition.

With that brilliant display of humor out of the way, we pulled into my driveway. I thanked Lee for the ride, said goodbye, and walked up to my front door. I was exhausted, in pain, but grateful this ordeal was finally over.

Or so I thought.

Chapter Twenty Four

After greeting my wife for our second joyful reunion of the day, Bill and I stepped outside to talk. When I'd called him about my latest predicament with the asshole clown, he decided to come over and wait for me. I was starting to like this guy more and more.

Walking across the lawn, I filled him in on everything—my run-in with Bozo, the destruction of my car, the bite wound, the whole nine yards. We talked about Finster—where he might be, how they'd try to find him, and what sort of trouble he'd inevitably stumble into next. Finally, we agreed it would be best if my family and I stayed with my parents for a few days. Bill promised to keep us updated and let us know when it was safe to return. I thanked him, waved goodbye, and headed back inside.

Finally alone with my family, I played with the kids for a few minutes, grateful to be home. Then I glanced at the clock—8:30 p.m.—and realized I hadn't eaten since that morning. I would have grabbed something at Burger King, but, well… we all know how that turned out.

Starving, I raided the fridge, stuffing myself with pepperoni, chocolate, and assorted junk. My wife asked if

I wanted to go to the hospital, but I waved it off. "Fuck it. It can wait till tomorrow." I was just too exhausted to deal with it now. Besides, I figured the odds of developing gangrene in my shoulder were relatively low. As a precaution, I downed a beer, some Advil, and whatever antibiotics we had lying around from God-knows-what past ailment.

We packed up the kids, buckled them in, and hit the road for my parents' house. A true testament to how drained I was? I rode in the passenger seat while my wife drove. Anyone who knows us knows that never happens. The reason? My wife is a terrible driver, and I can't stand being in the car with her behind the wheel.

But exhaustion won. I was out cold before we even hit the highway and didn't wake up until we pulled into my parents' driveway.

Chapter Twenty Five

Eddie Bretz was a sadistic sonofabitch. Some blamed it on his upbringing—his mother had a particular fondness for corporal punishment and outright torture. But odds were, there was a genetic component to his fucked-up behavior too.

One of the more infamous examples of Eddie's cruel childhood happened when he came running home, his face a bloody mess. He'd been playing basketball—one of the rare times he was allowed out of the house. With his team up by four, he drove to the hoop for a layup. Unfortunately, one of the rusty "S" hooks holding the chain net had come loose, dangling right in the path of his descent. The ball went in. So did Eddie's right nostril—right into the hook.

His shot had counted, but so had the damage.

The look on his friends' faces told him something was seriously wrong. Reaching up, his fingers met blood and shredded cartilage where his nostril had been. Panicked, he sprinted the five blocks home, leaving a crimson trail in his wake.

He should have known better than to expect sympathy.

This was the same woman who had beaten his bare ass with a hot curling iron for leaving a candy wrapper on the floor. The same woman who forced him to sit on the kitchen floor for a week, eating from the dog's bowl as punishment for spilling its water. The same woman who dunked his head in the toilet for forgetting to flush.

"What the hell happened to you?" she screamed the moment he stepped inside. "Look at you! And you've been crying—I can see it!"

"No, I wasn't, Mom," he stammered. "I was just—"

"Don't you fucking lie to me, you little baby," she snapped, grabbing his hair and yanking him forward. Dragging him through the house, she shoved him into the bathroom. "Stay there. Don't move."

Eddie stood frozen, blood dripping down his chin.

When she returned, she ordered him to kneel up on the bathroom sink and look at himself in the mirror. Then, stepping behind him, she wrapped her arm tightly around his shoulders, locking him in place.

Her lips brushed his ear as she whispered, "I'm going to teach you a little lesson about symmetry. S-Y-M-M-E-T-R-Y. Symmetry."

Eddie's mother, a second-grade English teacher, liked to use her punishments as vocabulary lessons. Like the time she smashed his finger with a hammer to illustrate the word contrast.

"See, you little baby?" she sneered, holding up his trembling hand. "See the contrast between the finger I smashed and all the others? How it's swollen, bruised, and bleeding, while the rest are completely normal? That's contrast. Definition: To compare in order to show unlikeness or differences. C-O-N-T-R-A-S-T. Contrast." She wrenched his hand closer. "Just look at your fucking finger, you little bastard."

Now, she had another lesson in mind.

"Symmetry is defined as 'the correspondence in size, form, and arrangement of parts on opposite sides of a plane, line, or point,'" she lectured, gripping Eddie's jaw with one hand. In the other, she held a kitchen knife.

"Let's draw a line down the middle of your face," she murmured, pressing the blade to his forehead and dragging it slowly downward—over the bridge of his nose, across his lips, stopping at the point of his chin. A thin red line followed, marking the center of his face.

"See?" she said, smiling. "You have a right half and a left half."

Eddie sat frozen, terrified to move, terrified to breathe. He had no idea what she planned to do with that knife, but he wasn't about to find out the hard way. He nodded, eyes wide.

"Now, let's forget about your nose for a second," she continued, voice syrupy sweet. "See how everything else is the same on both sides? One eye on the right. One on the left. One ear here. One there. The shape of your chin— perfectly mirrored. That's symmetry. You understand?"

Another nod.

"But if we include your nose," she said, tilting her head in mock pity, "it's all wrong, isn't it? You're un-symmetrical now. It's not the same on both sides, is it?"

Eddie barely had time to register what was coming before the blade flashed.

A sharp, wet sting. The world went red.

"Unsymmetrical," she said as she sliced through his left nostril to match the right. "Symmetrical."

She left him there, crying and bleeding, the knife clattering onto the sink. When he finally calmed down, Eddie bandaged himself as best he could. Going to the hospital wasn't an option. It never had been.

Years later, long after the wounds had scarred over — thick, ugly, permanently misaligned — he decided it was time to teach his mother a lesson about irony.

I-R-O-N-Y.

He found her in the kitchen, curling iron in hand, the same one she had so often used to sear his skin. As he loomed over her, she looked up, half-smiling, as if she knew what was coming.

"See this fucking thing, you miserable cunt?" Eddie snarled, brandishing the iron in front of her face.

Her smile didn't waver.

Then he raised his arm high above his head.

The last words she ever heard:

"How about this for irony? I-R-O-N-Y."

Chapter Twenty Six

Eddie Bretz was another case study in the classic nature versus nurture debate. But whether his cruelty was genetic or learned, the end result was the same — he truly enjoyed inflicting pain. Perhaps even more than his mother.

And that was very unfortunate for Raymond Pierce.

"Ray," Eddie said, his voice almost gentle. "How many times have I had to repeat this to you?" He let the question hang, then twisted Ray's ear between a pair of pliers, reopening the fresh wound there. "Is it eight? Nine? Or maybe thirty fucking seven?"

"I don't know, boss. I'm sorry. Please stop," Ray whimpered.

Eddie let go of his ear and stepped back. "Get up." He kicked Ray's lunch tray across the floor. "And get me my goddamn sandwich. Ham. Cheese. Nuked for thirty seconds. No fucking mustard. Understand?"

"Yes, sir," Ray mumbled, eyes downcast.

"Good. Now get the hell out of here."

Just as Ray reached the door, Eddie called after him. "And clean this shit up when you get back." He gestured toward the mess of broken glass and scattered sandwich.

It was not a good day.

Aside from the morning BJ from his whore-of-the-month, everything else had gone to shit. That asshole Finster had stolen his coke—not just any coke, but his experimental batch. In a mocking tribute to his dead mother, Eddie had named his new blend *Irony*—four times more potent than the best stuff on the market and six times as addictive.

More importantly, it had other uses.

A mere sprinkle applied to the right sensitive areas had already proven... thrilling results.

Under normal circumstances, Eddie would have written off the loss and hunted down the thief at his leisure. But *Irony* was different. It was the only sample of its kind, and to make matters worse, Eddie had—perhaps prematurely—shot and killed his research chemist in a fit of rage over production delays.

And now?

Now he had one goal—find that idiot Finster and get his fucking coke back.

It got worse.

No question—Eddie was a vital cog in the East Coast cocaine distribution network. But he was also a rising star within The Seed, the syndicate controlling the trade. Under his leadership, drug sales in Pennsylvania, Maryland, and Delaware had nearly tripled. There were even rumors that he'd soon take over operations in New Jersey, maybe even New York.

But that all hinged on the success of *Irony*.

If *Irony* failed — or worse, if word got out that it had been stolen and that Eddie had killed its inventor — there would be hell to pay. Everyone in the cartel was watching. They knew the potential of his new formula. And no matter how successful Eddie had been up to this point, if he lost control of the situation, there was only one possible outcome.

Death.

Not that Eddie feared dying. He didn't. But he did fear the method of his execution. That had been made clear to him when he first joined The Seed.

It had been a swift rise.

Not long after he put his mother in the ground, Eddie made a career move. He saw how a local dealer flaunted his wealth and had an epiphany. So, one night, he stabbed the man to death, took over his operation, and transformed it into something far more lucrative. His blend of business acumen and unrelenting brutality made his territory flourish.

But Eddie had violated the chain of command.

The higher-ups took notice. He was beaten, dragged from his operation, and thrown in front of Alan "The Praying Mantis" Leeds, CEO of The Seed.

"I don't know what to do with you, Eddie," The Mantis mused. He leaned back, as if considering the question with genuine curiosity. "See, normally, the penalty for killing one of my employees is death. But I'm conflicted."

He smiled. A slow, thin-lipped expression, the kind a man like Eddie should have feared.

"You see," The Mantis continued, "I'm a hands-on kind of guy. I like to know everyone in my organization personally. I think that's important. Don't you, Eddie?"

Eddie, bloodied and kneeling, barely restrained by two enforcers, glared up at him. "Sure. Whatever."

The slap came fast. A sharp, backhanded strike that snapped Eddie's head to the side.

"We'll have to work on that tone when you speak to me," The Mantis said. "I require a certain level of respect. Not to be arrogant, of course, but a man in my position demands it. Right, Eddie?"

Eddie said nothing.

A swift kick to the stomach knocked the wind out of him. He coughed violently, doubling over as the enforcers kept him from collapsing.

The Mantis sighed. "We'll continue working on your attitude — if our relationship moves forward."

He strolled around Eddie, slow and deliberate, like a predator circling its meal.

"This man you killed? J.J. Simmons. I didn't like him." He gave a casual shrug. "Frankly, the amount of coke he moved was pathetic. He was lazy. A liar. He would've been removed soon enough. You just sped up the process."

He knelt down, placing a hand on Eddie's shoulder.

"But we have rules in this organization, Eddie. Which leaves me with a dilemma. "

Eddie started to speak, but another slap silenced him before he got a word out.

"That was a rhetorical question," The Mantis corrected. "Do you know what rhetorical means?"

Eddie nodded. His mother had taught him that long ago. The lesson had involved a waffle iron.

The Mantis smirked. "Good."

He stood up, dusting off his suit.

"Since your little... coup, sales in that region have improved significantly. And after meeting you, aside from your general lack of respect, I see something in you that might be useful to The Seed."

He waved a hand.

"Bring him this way."

The two men lifted Eddie off the ground and forced him forward, following The Mantis down a dimly lit corridor. The air thickened with the scent of damp concrete and old sweat. At the end of the hallway, a heavy steel door loomed. The Mantis unlocked it with an old-fashioned key, its metallic scrape against the lock the only sound in the suffocating silence.

Inside, the room was cold and clinical. A single padded table stood in the center, fitted with chain restraints. The walls, lined with soundproofing foam, swallowed sound whole.

"Strap him in," The Mantis ordered, his voice as casual as if he were requesting a cup of coffee.

Eddie fought, but his captors were stronger. They forced him onto the table, bending him forward, securing his wrists and ankles with iron cuffs that left no room for movement. He sucked in sharp breaths, his muscles tightening against the restraints. He'd learned long ago how to brace for pain.

The Mantis stepped around him, slow and deliberate, a predator savoring the moment before the kill. His gloved fingers traced along Eddie's back, appraising him.

"You know why they call me The Praying Mantis?" he asked, almost conversationally. "It's because I enjoy devouring my prey. Breaking them. Making them beg."

Eddie ground his teeth, refusing to give this bastard an ounce of satisfaction.

"I'll be honest with you, Eddie," The Mantis continued. "You impressed me today. Most people in your position would already be screaming. I like that you're holding out."

His hand suddenly gripped Eddie's hair, yanking his head back.

"But let's see how long that lasts."

Eddie barely had a moment to brace before a sharp, blinding pain exploded across his lower back. The Mantis had pressed something cold and jagged against his skin—a blade. He dragged the tip along Eddie's spine with unbearable slowness, not deep enough to wound, but enough to set every nerve ablaze.

"You took something that didn't belong to you," he murmured, leaning in, his breath hot against Eddie's ear. "And now, I'm going to take something from you."

The room was silent except for Eddie's strained breathing.

The Mantis chuckled. "Don't worry. I'm not a savage. I believe in patience. In drawing things out. I like to savor my work."

Eddie kept his jaw clenched, his mind retreating to that cold, dark place where pain meant nothing. He would not give this bastard the satisfaction.

The Mantis sighed. "You'll break eventually. They always do."

A brutal fist crashed into Eddie's ribs, then another. The impact rattled his bones, forcing a choked gasp from his throat. The Mantis stepped back, wiping his gloves on his immaculate white shirt.

"That's enough for tonight," he said, signaling to his men. "We've got all day tomorrow—and the day after that."

"Unstrap him."

The chains loosened, and before Eddie could react, a boot slammed into his stomach, sending him crashing onto the cold, unforgiving floor.

He lay there, gasping for air, his body a raw nerve, his mind already calculating his next move.

The Mantis crouched beside him, gripping his face in one strong hand. "This was just a taste," he whispered. "Next time, I'll take something you can't get back."

And then, he was gone, leaving Eddie sprawled on the floor, his body screaming, his mind already planning his revenge.

Chapter Twenty Seven

Recalling that first meeting with The Mantis, Eddie felt bile rise in his throat.

Sure, he had an employee with a clown fetish, but gay shit? Now that was fucking disgusting.

Thankfully, he hadn't been penetrated by The Mantis. The thought alone made his skin crawl. God only knew the damage Long Dong Silver would've done to his insides. But he hadn't escaped unscathed. The Mantis had still left his mark, masturbating all over him before sinking his teeth into his ass — deep enough to scar.

The threat had been clear: step out of line again, and Eddie would find himself back in that same hellish room. Only next time, he wouldn't just be restrained. He'd be broken. Violated. Left for days at The Mantis' mercy. And when The Mantis finally grew bored? A slow, inventive, agonizing death.

Eddie shuddered.

The Mantis was even more sadistic than he was.

Maybe he needed a blowjob to clear his head.

Before speed-dialing his regular, Eddie tried Bozo again. Still no answer.

Where the fuck was that clown?

He had been calling since last night, ever since his informant told him about Beetle's death. Not because he gave a shit about Beetle or Bozo, of course—compassion wasn't part of his wiring. But his own ass was on the line. If he didn't recover *Irony*, The Mantis would come collecting.

For a fleeting second, he almost blamed himself for killing his chemist.

Then, just as quickly, he shoved that thought aside. The chemist had been too slow. Too careless. And Eddie sure as hell wasn't about to take responsibility for this mess.

No.

This was Finster's fault.

That pathetic little junkie had stolen from the wrong man, and he was going to pay for it.

Eddie snatched his phone off the table and called his informant.

"Where's Bozo? Where's Finster?" he barked. "I need my fucking coke!"

The voice on the other end stammered something that didn't satisfy him.

"I don't want to hear that shit! Get me Finster. Now! And find out what the fuck happened to Bozo!"

A weak excuse came in reply.

Eddie clenched his teeth. His grip on the phone tightened.

"Listen to me, motherfucker. What I did to that chemist? That was quick. Painless. What I'll do to you if you don't get me answers—" He let the sentence hang in the air, his silence more menacing than anything he could say.

The man on the other end swallowed hard.

Eddie hung up without another word.

Now, about that blowjob.

He dialed his hooker.

"Storm? It's Eddie. My dickie-dickie's ready for another suckie-suckie. When can you come over?"

Chapter Twenty Eight

I woke up at my wife's parents' house feeling like complete shit. Every inch of me ached, like I'd been worked over with a baseball bat. And then, of course, there was the goddamn tumor on my ball sac.

Groaning, I swung my legs over the bed and stood up, unsure how I'd even made it there the night before. I hobbled toward the bathroom like an old man.

Unzipping carefully—because jostling that lump was the last thing I wanted—I took a long, painful piss. After washing my hands and splashing cold water on my face, I dried off and headed to the kitchen.

"Morning, Mom. Morning, Dad." I called them that not just out of custom with in-laws, but because I truly loved them—more than my own biological parents. My relationship with them was troubled, to say the least.

They were both sitting at the table with Suzy. I walked over, kissed my wife, did the same to Mom, then gave Dad a hug before collapsing into a chair.

Everyone immediately started in with questions about my health. Naturally, they all wanted every last detail of what the hell had happened. I assured them I was fine—more or less—but I needed directions to the nearest hospital. This ball-sac disaster needed professional intervention, along with the bite wound on my shoulder and the rest of my assorted injuries.

As I shoveled bacon into my mouth, I walked them through everything—Finster, Lee, Beetle, Bozo, the stolen coke, the gunfire, the kidnapping. When I was done, I wiped my mouth and finally thought to ask where the kids were.

"They're over at Grammy's, playing with their cousins," mom said.

Dad shook his head. "How many times have I told you, son? Keep away from that Finster. He's nothing but trouble. Goddamn cokehead."

I didn't argue. He was right.

Dad kept going. "Does he still drag that stupid guitar everywhere he goes?"

"Yeah. Unfortunately."

Suddenly, Dad sat up straight, slung an imaginary guitar over his shoulder, and started singing in a ridiculous voice:
"I don't like Mondays, no Tuesdays, no Wednesdays, no Thur-days..."

We all lost it, laughing at Finster's expense.

Between the laughter and the smell of bacon, my stomach reminded me how empty it was. Suzy offered to fix me a plate. Everyone else had eaten hours ago, and as I glanced at the clock, I realized it was already 11 a.m.

With three kids, I wasn't sure when the last time was that I'd slept this late.

As I devoured pancakes loaded with bananas, several slices of bacon, and copious amounts of coffee, Mom spoke up.

"There's no way you, Suze, or the kids are going back home until I say it's okay. Do you hear me, Mike? I don't give a shit what anybody else says. You listen to me. Promise me," she demanded, her voice thick with emotion.

I got up, walked around the table, and wrapped my arms around her. She was crying.

"Promise?" she asked again.

"I promise."

Holding her close, I felt the depth of her love for me, and in that moment, I realized how much I missed my own kids. It felt like ages since I'd last seen them.

After a brief argument, I agreed to go to the hospital—but only after we stopped at Grandma's to see the kids. My wife and I said our goodbyes, assured Suzy's parents we'd be back for dinner, and headed out.

On the drive over, I shot Suze a grin. "Quickie?"

She rolled her eyes. "Not with that pimple," she said, nodding toward my crotch.

"It's a boil," I corrected.

"Pimple. Boil. Whatever it is, you're not getting near me with that."

"Why not? I've got my red wings, don't I? If I can chow down on you when you have your period, then you can certainly have sex with me now."

She wrinkled her nose. "You're disgusting."

Chapter Twenty Nine

Heeeey! How are my little girls?" I called out. "Dada!" my oldest shouted, racing toward me.

I bent down to squeeze her in a hug, wincing slightly. "Careful, guys. Daddy's a little sore."

Lynn, our second-born, was next, charging straight for me. I barely managed to shield my groin before she collided into my legs.

"Up-a," she demanded, reaching up with grabby hands. "Upee, Daddy!"

"I can't, Sweets. Daddy's not feeling too good," I said, then grinned. "I need to go to the doctor's. You have to come too—to get a shot!" I teased, pretending to jab at her with an invisible syringe.

"Nooo!" she shrieked, giggling as she bolted away.

I turned to Gram's, giving her a kiss, then looked at our baby girl, just nine months old. The second Janie saw me, her whole face lit up. I smiled right back, tickling her, kissing her soft little cheeks, just soaking in the moment.

God, they were growing up too fast. Nine months had disappeared in an instant, and soon, Janie wouldn't be a baby anymore. She'd be toddling, talking—hell, dating and marriage couldn't be far behind.

It was easy to think that way, looking at Halle. Seven years old already. First grade. Getting so damn big. Every year passed faster than the last, the seasons flashing by like a time-lapse video.

Had it really been over five years since I turned forty? Had we really blown through two decades of the new millennium? It felt like yesterday the world was panicking over Y2K, convinced computers would self-destruct the moment the clocks struck midnight. Now, here I was, picturing myself at seventy—old, irrelevant, wondering what I'd regret.

But one thing was certain.

My daughters would always know how much I loved them—more than anything, more than anyone. I'd kiss them, hug them, play with them, hold them, be with them as long as time allowed.

And no matter what, I'd cherish each and every day—forgive the cliché—as if it were my last.

Chapter Thirty

We sat around catching up, my grandmother and I. We talked about the kids, her health, and reminisced about the time I lived with her while going to Penn State.

Afterward, I played with the kids a little more, kissed them all, and turned to my wife. "Alright, I'm heading to the hospital."

"Wait a minute. You're not going anywhere," Suzy said. "I'll drive."

"No, really, honey. I'm fine. What are they going to do? Stitch up my shoulder, maybe give me a shot, some antibiotics. Take care of things down low, I hope."

"What's wrong with your pecker?" Grammy chimed in.

"Nothing, Grams," I lied. "I was just kidding."

"Then why the heck were you pointing at your dick? I'm not blind yet, Mikey."

"I know, Grams. Just forget about it. Please? And watch your language—you want your grandkids saying that?"

"Aahh, they can't hear me. Watch—dick, dick, dick, dick, dick." She pointed her thumb at the kids, who were completely oblivious, lost in their own little world. "See what I mean?"

"You better watch it, Grams," I teased. "Or I'll wash your mouth out with soap."

"You just try it," she warned. "I can still put you across my knee. Remember when I spanked your bottom with a wooden spoon?"

"I remember."

"Good. Anyway, Suzy and I will talk about your dick when you're gone. She'll fill me in."

I looked at my wife, who was nodding. I shook my head no, but I already knew it was a lost cause.

After a final, brief argument, Suzy relented. She would stay with the kids while I drove to the hospital. I kissed everyone again, said my goodbyes, and left.

Chapter Thirty One

I didn't think anything of the car behind me. Figured he was just riding my ass because I was driving too slow — which, to be fair, I was. Between the bruises, the shoulder bite, and the boil on my sac, I wasn't exactly NASCAR material.

When I stopped at a red light, the car behind me bumped my bumper. Gently, but still. My wife was going to be pissed. First the Subaru, now her car too?

Cursing, I opened the door to check the damage. The driver behind me got out as well, and we started walking toward each other. That's when I saw him raise a gun.

And just like that, I knew — I was back in the shit.

"Get in the car, Mr. Rodgen," the man said calmly, gesturing toward his vehicle. "Driver's seat, please."

"Aww, c'mon," I groaned, already heading toward the car. "What is this, more Finster bullshit? I'm guessing this is about the stolen coke?"

"Yes, sir. Drive, please."

Despite being taken hostage by a man with a gun, I wasn't scared. Not really. Just tired. And angry. Angry at

Finster for dragging me into this ongoing disaster of a week.

"Look, man," I said as I drove. "I've got nothing to do with this. I didn't steal the coke. I don't know where it is. And I definitely don't know where Finster is. I can't help you. Just let me go back to my boring-ass life. You go find your coke, and we can both move on."

Then I slammed on the brakes and veered onto the shoulder, struck by a sudden realization.

"Mr. Rodgen, what are you doing?" the man asked, still level, still polite. "I asked you to drive. I'm trying to keep this as civil as possible, but I do have a job to do. If you—"

"Wait, wait, wait!" I cut him off. "I misspoke earlier. I *do* know what happened to the coke. Or at least... where it *was*. But you're not gonna like it. It's gone. Washed away."

He stayed silent, so I kept going. I walked him through the whole sorry story—Finster, the gas can, the bullet hole, the soaked duffel bag.

And while I was talking, something weird happened. I started really *looking* at this guy.

Now, don't get me wrong—I wasn't attracted to him or anything. I'm just saying, the dude was *stunning*. Movie-star level. Brad Pitt had nothing on him.

Meanwhile, I felt like I'd just crawled out from under a boulder. Dirty, swollen, bleeding, reeking of painkillers

and gasoline. It was hard not to feel like Quasimodo behind the wheel.

"You say it's gone, Mr. Rodgen? Everything? All five
kilos?"

"Yep. All gone. Well… maybe not *completely* gone. If
you're lucky, you could probably scrape up a couple of
lines. I'm no coke expert, but what could that be worth?
Twenty-five bucks?"

"Mr. Rodgen, that 'couple of lines' is worth considerably more. I'm going to have to ask you to drive us directly to your car. Now. Please."

"I don't get it," I said, pulling back onto the road.
"What's so special about this cocaine? And why do I have
to take you there? I can tell you exactly where it is. Route
50, just past — "

"Mr. Rodgen." He turned slightly, just enough to let
the muzzle of his gun brush my side. "Please. Drive."

I did as he asked, glancing over at him. "Alright then.
But can you at least tell me who you work for?"

"I'm not at liberty to say. But I *can* assure you, he's a
reasonable man — as long as you don't lie to him. And if
the story you told me is accurate — which it *is*, right, Mr.
Rodgen?"

"Yes. It is."

"Good. Then you shouldn't have anything to worry
about. We'll retrieve what we can from the car, and once

my employer hears your explanation, I imagine you'll be on your way. Back to your family. I promise."

He was calm. Too calm. It wasn't a threat, exactly — but the way he said it, the cold neutrality in his voice… it chilled me. For the first time, I was genuinely afraid.

I nodded, silently praying he wasn't full of shit.

"Since we'll be together for a little bit," I said, trying to sound casual, "can I at least get your name?"

"Sure. Clint. Clint Mercer. But if we can speed things up, I'd appreciate it. The faster we finish this, the faster you get your life back."

That earned a dry chuckle from me. "No argument here."

And Clint Mercer… Jesus, of course that was his name. With a face like that, he should've been in a movie, not holding me at gunpoint. Still, I had more pressing concerns than being overshadowed by my own kidnapper's cheekbones.

Like the fact that my balls were still throbbing in boiling, pus-filled agony. If someone didn't drain this thing soon, I was seriously considering surgery with a pocketknife and a bottle of whiskey.

Chapter Thirty Two

After ditching Lee and the veterinarian, Finster decided it was time to get happily high on his stolen cat tranquilizers. He plopped down beneath a tree, popped a few pills, and closed his eyes. While he waited for the drugs to kick in, he leaned his back against the rough bark and sighed. Even though it was still technically summer, the night carried the chill of early fall. More than anything, though, Finster just liked to snuggle—and without his blanket, it wasn't the same.

It didn't take long for the high to hit. That woozy, disconnected buzz washed over him—like being drunk, but floatier. As the pill-fueled warmth spread through his limbs, he heard shouting in the distance. Curious, he struggled to his feet to investigate. Big mistake. The moment he stood, the world tilted. He wobbled, stumbled, and collapsed back to the ground in a heap.

Undeterred, Finster crawled toward the nearest tree and used it for support, swaying as he dragged himself upright. Holding onto the trunk like it was the mast of a ship in a storm, he peered through the darkness.

He couldn't see the shouter, but just beyond the trees was a road—maybe twenty yards away. Even though he felt like a sack of wet laundry, he let go of the tree and staggered in that direction.

He didn't make it far.

Three-quarters of the way across the field, he collapsed again. As he pushed himself up, he spotted a pickup truck pass in front of him. It looked vaguely familiar, but in his current state, Finster couldn't place where he'd seen it before.

Then came the real show.

Charging down the road behind the truck was, quite possibly, the strangest person Finster had ever laid eyes on: a borderline midget with fluorescent green hair, a beak-like nose, and a truly unhinged expression. He was yelling—screeching, really.

"Bozo's coming! Bozo's coming!"

Even through the haze, Finster recognized him. One of Eddie Bretz's goons. The same psycho who had been shooting at Mike and him earlier. It took a second, but then it clicked—this was Bozo. Although Finster had no memory of Bozo having green hair before, which was weird. Maybe the dude had gotten a makeover. Clown makeover. Hell if he knew.

Despite being blissfully high, Finster had enough sense to stay put. He crouched low in the tall grass, eyes wide, and watched the freak pass by. Once Bozo was out of sight, Finster figured it was time to do the smartest thing he'd done all day: run in the *opposite* direction.

Running wasn't easy. He fell twice and nearly face-planted three more times before he finally stumbled across a parked Subaru. At first, he wasn't entirely sure it was Mike's. But when he saw the Penn State decal on the rear windshield—and, more convincingly, the bullet hole in the trunk—he grinned.

Yep. This Subaru had Finster written all over it.

He wasn't sure how the car got there, but at that point, he didn't really care. He just wanted to lie down for a while. Climbing into the back seat of Mike's Subaru, he briefly mourned the loss of the blanket that had wrapped his naked body in Lee's pickup. *So that's where I remember that truck from,* he thought, just before drifting off to sleep…

Chapter Thirty Three

Bozo wasn't answering his phone—and for good reason. He was too busy huffing gasoline.

The high he'd gotten while hiding in the Subaru's trunk was unlike anything he'd ever experienced. Better than nitrous. Better than clown sex.

After his failed pursuit of Mike Rogden and the man in the pickup truck, Bozo had wandered back to the Subaru, drawn by an overwhelming urge to recreate the ecstasy of that first inhalation. As his phone rang somewhere in his pocket, he hunched over the open gas fill pipe, lips sealed tight against the nozzle, greedily sucking in the fumes. Still unsatisfied with the vapor density, he jammed a stick into the valve to prop it open and inhaled again, deeper this time.

That's when it hit him.

During his first gasoline stupor in the trunk, Bozo had a revelation. All his life, he'd been someone's lackey. Someone's stooge. But lying there, awash in fumes, he'd finally seen a way to be in control. The clown porn business had given him purpose, sure—but something had always felt missing.

Then he'd opened the duffel bag.

Now, with what remained of *Irony* in his possession, everything had changed. He knew the chemist was dead. He knew the drug's potency. And he knew that the only surviving stash — however degraded — was right here, right now, in his hands.

Why shouldn't it be me? he thought, eyes glassy, lips glistening with gasoline. *Why shouldn't I be the one to benefit?*

Maybe this was his turning point. Maybe he could retire somewhere warm. Find someone who shared his... sensibilities. Get married in Vegas — him in a tux, his bride in a lacy gown, both of their faces painted in custom-designed clown makeup for the ceremony.

He even imagined kids. Little squeakers with red noses and rainbow suspenders. He wouldn't *push* the lifestyle, but he wouldn't hide it either. Clown sex was beautiful, dammit. And he was done being ashamed.

A voice cut through the haze.

"Hey! You alright, mister?"

Bozo turned from the fuel nozzle, dazed, slack-jawed, and gave the stranger the finger.

"Fuck you too," the man shouted before driving off.

Bozo took one last pull from the nozzle, wiped his mouth, and climbed into the driver's seat.

In addition to his many talents, Bozo was adept at hot-wiring cars. Moments later, the Subaru sputtered to life. Lucky for him, the all-wheel drive handled the marshy terrain surprisingly well, and soon he was back on the road. The exterior was a mess—shattered windshields, a dangling bumper, a crushed quarter panel—but somehow, the Japanese engineering held. Sure, there was a violent vibration and a shrieking metal-on-metal wail coming from somewhere in the undercarriage, but Bozo, blissfully baked, paid it no mind.

His gasoline haze made driving... challenging. The clown began to swerve, steering with lazy, drug-numbed limbs. For a few terrifying seconds, he blacked out entirely, snapping awake to find himself drifting into the wrong lane—staring down an oncoming police cruiser. Bozo jerked the wheel hard and swerved just in time, his head slapping against the side window as he floored the accelerator.

Through the mirror, he saw the flashing lights ignite behind him. The cop was attempting a U-turn, but the winding road slowed him down. Giddy with relief, Bozo slapped himself across the face, then again, shaking his head like a boxer in the corner trying to stay conscious.

Still high and now paranoid, Bozo kept the gas pedal mashed to the floor. The car screamed like a tortured banshee as it hit sixty. Ahead, the light turned green just in time—but his twitchy reflexes and mangled coordination sent the car fishtailing through the intersection. He overcorrected, spinning a full 360 before coming to a stop, miraculously facing the opposite direction.

And just to his right? Salvation: the vast, gray emptiness of a Walmart parking lot.

He gunned it toward the entrance, nearly mowing down an elderly woman pushing a cart stacked with enough cat food to survive the apocalypse. It occurred to him—belatedly—that maybe a lower profile was wise. Easing off the gas, he cruised through the lot, scouting for a spot.

He saw one—perfect—and cut off another shopper who'd been waiting patiently for it. As she leaned on her horn and cussed him out, Bozo calmly parked, turned off the engine, stepped out, and called her a bitch.

Still passed out in the backseat, Finster remained blissfully unaware of the chaos unraveling around him.

Bozo didn't notice the gawking stares. Not the ones aimed at his neon-green, male-pattern-balding hair. Not the ones fixated on the smeared clown makeup or the unmistakable whiff of gasoline wafting around him. No, Bozo had a mission.

He needed teriyaki beef jerky, a bag of M&Ms, corn chips, and a six-pack of Cherry Coke.

Inside Walmart, high as a kite and humming to himself, Bozo wandered the aisles like he was browsing an art museum. Somewhere along the way, he wondered if gasoline gave you munchies. But really, what didn't?

Eventually, he found his treasures and made his way to the checkout, whistling like a man without a care in the world. No fear of police. No guilt over the bag of experimental cocaine in his possession. And no idea that someone else was out cold in the back seat of the stolen car.

With *Irony* in his bag and gasoline in his lungs, Bozo was on top of the world.

At the front of the store, something in the football tailgate display caught Bozo's eye. He grabbed it, then doubled back to the food section to snag a six-pack of Cherry Coke. From there, he wandered over to the hardware aisle, muttering to himself until he found what he needed. Twenty minutes later, he finally headed to checkout.

"How are you doing today, sir?" the cashier asked automatically, eyes still on the register.

"Just great. Now hurry the fuck up."

She looked up—and froze.

Her voice caught in her throat as she took in the spectacle before her: a man with smeared clown makeup, dyed green tufts of hair sprouting from an otherwise bald head, and the wild, twitching eyes of someone clearly not right.

"Didn't you hear me, stupid?" Bozo snapped. "Let's move."

The girl said nothing, but her trembling hands resumed scanning. She focused intently on the items, doing everything in her power not to make eye contact. Still, she flinched with every word he muttered, every erratic movement he made.

"That'll be $24.17," she finally whispered.

Bozo handed her a crumpled wad of bills. "Keep the change, bitch," he said with a mocking grin.

Then he leaned in close. Uncomfortably close. The girl tried to keep her eyes down, but curiosity — or fear — got the better of her.

She looked up.

Bozo barked like a rabid dog, baring his teeth and snapping them inches from her face.

The girl recoiled, letting out a small yelp. Bozo laughed, turned on his heel, and strutted out the automatic doors like a man who owned the place.

Chapter Thirty Four

Bozo popped open the front passenger door, tossed his bag of supplies onto the seat, and slammed it shut. He trotted around the back of the car, but just as he reached the rear driver's side, something struck him—an idea. He doubled back.

With a giddy little skip, he stopped beside the gas cap. Glancing around to make sure no one was watching, he unscrewed it, dropped to one knee, and clamped his face over the opening.

He inhaled—deeply—four, five times, eyes fluttering in euphoria. Satisfied, he screwed the cap back on, exhaled in a dreamy sigh, and scampered to the driver's side door.

But something was dangling from the handle.

Bozo grabbed it absently, assuming it was some Walmart flier or trash left by a bratty kid. Then he looked closer.

"What the fuck?!" he shrieked, hurling the bloody tampon across the parking lot like it had bitten him.

"What the *hell* was that all about?" he barked into the open air.

His answer came in the form of a note tucked beneath his windshield wiper: "That's what you get for stealing my parking spot, ass-hole!"

Bozo crumpled it in his fist, trembling with rage.

"That bitch!" he roared. "That *fucking bitch!*"

He thought about storming back inside the store to find her—but decided instead on another hit of his favorite new drug. He unscrewed the gas cap once more, took a few deep pulls, then returned to the driver's seat, sparked the ignition wires, and pulled out to cruise the lot.

He had no idea what the woman drove. But she *felt* like a Ford Explorer type.

Spotting one, Bozo swerved beside it, opened his door, unzipped his pants, and let loose a steaming arc directly onto the driver's side.

"Yeah, bitch! Take *that!* Wooooooo!" he howled, pumping his fist like he'd just scored a touchdown.

Then he floored it out of the lot—one clown, one car, and one very stoned, very unconscious stowaway curled up in the back seat.

Chapter Thirty Five

As Bozo carried on in the front seat like a deranged ringmaster, Finster stirred from his foggy slumber. For a moment, he wasn't sure where he was. The last thing he remembered was curling up in the back of Mike's Subaru, high on stolen cat tranquilizers and dreaming about grilled cheese sandwiches.

As the drugged haze slowly lifted, Finster recognized the voice coming from the front seat—and it sure as hell wasn't Mike's. That hooting, snarling, sing-song shriek could only belong to one person: Bozo.

Shit.

Not wanting to announce his presence, Finster stayed perfectly still. Maybe if he pretended to be unconscious—or better yet, dead—Bozo wouldn't notice him. As quietly as possible, he adjusted his position, trying to slow his breathing and melt into the upholstery.

Up front, the clown was fully immersed in snack time. Bozo reached into his crinkling Walmart bag and cracked open a can of Cherry Coke, draining it in a few noisy gulps. He flung the empty on the floor, fished out another, and took a more leisurely swig before dropping it into the dashboard cupholder. Jerky came next. Gnawing on it like a wild animal, he followed it with a generous handful of M&M's, polishing off half the bag in one go.

When he finished the second can, he let it drop to the floor with a metallic clatter, oblivious to the muffled groan it triggered from the back seat.

He glanced at his palm, now smeared with sticky brown residue. "Melts in your mouth, not in your hand, my ass," Bozo grunted, before licking his fingers clean with cartoonish gusto.

The car came to a stop. Finster, still flat on his back, had no visual cues, but the smells and sounds gave it away: gas station.

Bozo cut the engine, shoved the empties into his bag, and hopped out. Finster heard the nozzle click free. Then came the familiar slurp of gasoline flowing—followed by a few deep, voluntary inhalations from Bozo.

Of course.

Bozo, momentarily satisfied, topped off the tank. Then, unable to resist temptation, he pulled the two empty soda cans from his bag and began carefully filling them with gasoline.

Halfway through the first, a voice crackled over the intercom:

"Excuse me, sir. You're only permitted to fill fuel into an approved container. Please stop."

Bozo didn't even flinch. He kept going, tipping the pump just so, as if nothing could come between him and his precious vapor cocktail.

"Sir! If you don't stop, I'm calling the cops! Sir!"

Bozo ignored him. But before he could finish topping off his makeshift stash, the fuel cut off from inside the station. The clown looked up, flipped the guy off, packed up his supplies, and hopped back in the car.

The attendant burst out the door, still shouting, but Bozo just cranked the engine and tore out of the lot. As he pulled into traffic, he rolled down the window and hollered, "Screw you, douche bag!"

Now truly delirious with excitement, Bozo jerked the wheel left and right, sending the car (and the barely-conscious Finster) careening back and forth across the lane.

"Woooooooo! Yeah! You can't stop Bozo! Nobody can stop Bozo! Bozo's coming! Bozo's coming! Wooooooooooo!"

In the back seat, Finster groaned and clutched his stomach. The nausea was bad enough from all the swerving, but the gasoline fumes swirling through the cabin made it almost unbearable. He gagged when he heard Bozo inhale deeply, sucking in the noxious vapors like they were his personal brand of oxygen.

"Wooooooooooooo! Yeah! Fucking-A right! Who's the man?! Who's the man?!"

Still swerving like a lunatic, Bozo reached for the construction helmet on the passenger seat — his Walmart trophy. He jammed it onto his head and connected two plastic tubes, one from each gas-filled soda can mounted on either side. The other ends disappeared into his nostrils.

Letting go of the wheel for a moment, he steered with his knee while tearing off a strip of duct tape. He fastened the tubes to his face like a DIY oxygen rig from hell.

Bozo inhaled deeply, eyes fluttering in euphoric approval.

"Oh, yeah," he whispered in a low, trembling voice. "Bozo's coming. Bozo's coming."

Chapter Thirty Six

Finster couldn't believe his eyes. It took every ounce of willpower not to ask the clown what the hell he was doing. Everyone knew Bozo was a freak, but this? This was a new level of unhinged. *Yeah, like clown porn ever made sense,* Finster thought.

Shaking his head in disbelief, he wondered how the hell he was going to survive this. Any hope of staying undetected vanished when an ambulance appeared behind them, lights flashing and siren wailing.

Bozo glanced in the rearview mirror and eased to the shoulder to let it pass. But as he checked the mirror again to merge back into traffic, something caught his eye. He focused on the reflection—and there they were. Two pairs of eyes locked together.

Smiling wide, Bozo turned and said, "Hi, Finster. How are you today?"

On the verge of tears, Finster whispered, "Stop calling me Finster."

Bozo cackled—and with the laughter came a deep, involuntary inhale. He snorted in a lungful of gasoline fumes and immediately began coughing, his nostrils burning like fire. He clamped a hand over his face and shook his head, trying to ride out the burn.

"Wow," he gasped, blinking. "What a rush. What a *freakin'* rush! Wooooooooooo!"

In the chaos, he'd forgotten Finster was even in the car. But once it clicked again, Bozo threw the car in park, jumped out, and yanked the poor bastard from the back seat. He barked at Finster to drive, then climbed into the rear himself.

Now in the backseat, Bozo closed his eyes and pondered his options. There wasn't much *Irony* left. And honestly, he didn't *need* Finster. But he didn't have a good reason to kill him either. And now that Beetle was dead, maybe it'd be nice to have someone around. Even if that someone was a twitchy, nose-whistling twerp with terrible taste in music.

"I've decided to let you live," he muttered, glancing around for his gun. When it didn't turn up, he shrugged. *Doesn't matter. I could strangle him with one hand if I had to.*

"But on one condition," he continued. "No singing. That *'I don't like Mondays, no Tuesdays'* bullshit? That song sucks. I don't want to hear it again. Got it?"

"Sure," Finster muttered. "But you watch—one day that song's gonna be a hit. Just you wait."

"Whatever," Bozo said. "Like I said: *no singing.* Stick to that, and we'll get along just fine."

"Okay, Bozo. No problem."

"Great. Now drive us over to that Days Inn in Marlton. We need a room."

Finster's eyes widened. "Bozo, please. I'm not into... y'know, clown stuff. And I'm straight. Please don't—"

"Jesus Christ," Bozo snapped. "Don't flatter yourself. I'm exhausted. I need sleep. Maybe a few more hits first, then sleep." He leaned his head back and gently inhaled through one of the tubes dangling from his face.

"Bozo? Can I ask you something? What the hell is that contraption?"

"Don't knock it till you try it," Bozo replied. He removed one of the cans from his head and offered it forward. "Want a hit?"

Finster hesitated. "I mean... that can't be good for you, right?"

Bozo shrugged. "You only live once."

Finster shrugged right back. "Ah, what the hell. If I can take cat tranquilizers, why not huff gas from a clown hat?" Still watching the road, he pressed the can to his mouth and inhaled.

"Cat tranquilizers?" Bozo perked up. "You got any more?"

"Yeah, hold on." Finster took a couple more drags from the can, then reached into his pocket. He popped a pill for himself—*just one*, he decided, in the interest of staying upright behind the wheel—and handed the bottle back to Bozo.

"Cool," Bozo said, swallowing three without hesitation. "Where'd you get these?"

Finster described the veterinary heist, complete with Lee, the overalls, and his own feet being shredded on the road. Bozo filled in the rest of his day, including the hair dye, the Walmart run, and the custom-built huff rig strapped to his head.

"So that's why you dyed your hair green, huh?"

"Yeah. Like I said, wigs don't look right on camera."

"Huh. I guess I can kinda see that. Hey, you got any all-girl videos? No offense, Bozo, but I don't need to see you banging anybody. But, like... lesbian clowns? That might be interesting."

Bozo's eyes lit up. "Wait a minute. That's fucking *brilliant!*"

Or at least, that's what he *meant* to say. What actually came out was: "Wey-a meen... hash fughy breen!"

And then he passed out cold.

Still behind the wheel, Finster was barely holding it together. He swerved into a trio of mailboxes, bounced up over a curb, and miraculously corrected himself. Moments later, the glowing sign of the Days Inn came into view like a heavenly beacon.

He pulled into the lot, turned into a space, and only remembered to hit the brakes after the car hopped over the cement parking stop with a heavy *clunk*. He turned off the ignition.

And joined Bozo in unconscious bliss.

Chapter Thirty Seven

The next morning, both Finster and Bozo were rudely awakened by the sound of someone banging on the driver's side window.

"Hey! Hey, douchebags! Wake up! Wake the fuck up, assholes!"

They groaned in unison, blinking into the sunlight as the hotel manager loomed outside the car, red-faced and shouting.

"What the hell are you two doing in there? Roll down the window. *Now!*"

Still dazed, head pounding, Finster fumbled for the window switch. When nothing happened—dead ignition—he gave up and opened the door.

Unfortunately, he didn't think to warn the manager.

The door cracked into the man's shin, causing him to stumble back and land hard on the cement parking stop, ass-first.

"Aww, dude, I'm *sorry*," Finster muttered, cradling his throbbing skull. "It was an accident, man."

"Jesus Christ!" the manager bellowed, rubbing his tailbone. "You're lucky I didn't break my damn back!"

He pointed furiously at Finster's crooked parking job. "What the hell is this?! And what's that *smell*? Your car reeks of gasoline!"

"Yeah, we had a little... accident," Finster said vaguely. "Alright, we'll get out of here. Sorry to bother you."

He started to climb back into the driver's seat.

"Wait a minute! Give me your name and number. I'm going to a doctor to get my ass checked out, and *you're* paying for it!"

Finster ignored him and cranked the engine. He slammed the car into drive and floored it.

The chassis shrieked as the undercarriage scraped over the cement barrier. The back wheels bumped free, launching the car forward — directly toward Room 121.

Finster yanked the wheel hard to the left. The car veered, but not fast enough. The right rear quarter panel smashed into the motel room's front window.

Inside, Mr. Keen and his secretary had just reached the *downstroke* of their illicit missionary rendezvous when the crash sent shards of glass across the room and brought everything to a screeching halt.

Back outside, Finster sped along the sidewalk, ignoring the manager's curses and limp pursuit. He turned the car sharply, bouncing off the curb, fishtailed through the lot, and tore out into the street.

Behind him, the manager was still rubbing his ass and yelling into the wind.

"That was some impressive driving, Finster."

"Thanks, man. I learned it watching *Fast & Furious* reruns." He held up the gas-filled soda can. "Dude, that shit's potent."

"Yeah, no kidding. My head feels like it got stomped by a marching band. But hey — you know what they say, *hair of the dog*. Don't Bogart that thing. Hand it over."

"Whataya mean?" Finster took another drag from the can. "What about yours?"

"I must've spilled it all over myself," Bozo said, sniffing his shirt with appreciation. "We'll have to score more. But for now, we share."

"No problemo, mi amigo," Finster replied, passing him the can.

Bozo took a long hit, then exhaled slowly. "You know, Finster... I'm starting to like you. To be honest, I always thought you were an asshole. But maybe it was just that song of yours."

Finster nodded and started humming the tune — careful to follow Bozo's *No Singing* rule.

"Yeah, *that* one," Bozo said. Then, as if unable to help himself, the clown began singing. And somehow, despite his ridiculous face and rubbery voice, it came out... beautiful. Raw. Soulful.

Finster's foot eased off the gas. He pulled the car over to the shoulder.

"What's the matter?" Bozo asked.

Finster turned to him, eyes glistening. "Dude," he whispered. "That was freaking *awesome*. That's exactly how the song was meant to be sung. Like... when Hendrix did *All Along the Watchtower* and made it his own. You just did that to my song. That was fucking brilliant."

He held up his hand. Bozo slapped it.

"Really?" the clown asked, beaming. "You really think so, man?"

"Hell yeah! Fucking *brilliant!* Wooooooooooo!"

They both broke into hysterical laughter, high-fives flying, whooping and yelling as they passed the gas can back and forth.

Twenty minutes later, the laughter finally died down, giving way to deep, chemically-fueled inspiration.

"You know," Finster said, "we should totally start a band. I'll play guitar, you sing. We'll be unstoppable."

"I like it," Bozo said, nodding with conviction.

"I've got another idea, too. Ever heard of *Insane Clown Posse*? They wear makeup, do rap-metal stuff. We do something like that—but our own version. Full clown outfits. Paint. Wild stage shows. Tie it in with your whole clown porn thing. Which reminds me—remember that idea I had last night? All-lesbian clown video? Whataya think?"

Bozo's eyes went wide. "Holy shit! I *almost forgot!* Woooooooooo! We're gonna be *rich,* Finster!"

Finster joined him with a "Wooooooooooo!" of his own.

Their dreams of musical stardom and clown-themed porn riches echoed through the car, both men giddy and high on gasoline. Hopped up on fumes and fantasies, neither of them noticed — or remembered — the duffel bag of *Irony,* what little remained, still stashed in the trunk of the stolen car.

Chapter Thirty Eight

"Did you find my coke yet?" Eddie Bretz barked into the phone.

"Not yet. We're working on it. We haven't been able to find Finster or Bozo, but we shou—"

"Listen to me." His voice dropped to a growl. "What did I tell you last time? No more excuses. Find my coke, or start saying your goodbyes."

He slammed the phone down before the man could respond.

"Damn it—watch the teeth," Eddie snarled, smacking Storm on the back of the head.

"Sorry," she mumbled, never missing a beat.

Eddie prided himself on being a master multitasker—especially during oral sex. He saw no reason to pause productivity just because someone had their mouth on his dick. Typing emails, taking calls, eating lunch—it all continued uninterrupted. In fact, he once insisted a previous escort keep going while he sat on the toilet. Not out of kink, just... time management. Efficiency mattered. Granted, his divided attention tended to drag things out, but his girls were always well compensated for their patience.

Now, with Storm still diligently at work, Eddie fired off one last email, then stood and—without breaking rhythm—guided her across the room toward the closet. Tonight was the Twelfth Annual Seed East Coast Christmas in July Party. All the major players would be there, and Eddie intended to look sharp.

Tilting her head—still firmly attached—Eddie held up a navy suit with a paisley tie.

"You like this one?"

"Mmhmm. Loogs grah," Storm mumbled around him, nodding in approval.

That was all it took.

"Ohhh yeah. That's it. Nod again. Keep nodding. I'm coming!"

He buckled, collapsing forward with a groan—then immediately scrambled off her, inspecting the damage.

"Shit! My suit!" he barked, lifting the crumpled outfit from the floor. "Fucking wrinkles."

He hung the suit back up, then gave Storm a pat on the head.

"Nice work, baby. I like that technique. You should trademark it. Call it the *nod job*. You know—*nod job*. Get it?"

"Yeah, Eddie. Hilarious. Now where's my money?"

He strolled to his desk, pulled open a drawer, and grabbed a thick wad of bills. With a flick of his wrist, he tossed them at her feet—his preferred method of payment, purely for the humiliation it inflicted.

"What a gentleman," she muttered, bending over to scoop up the cash. No goodbye, no thank-you. Just business. She was gone a moment later.

Alone, Eddie leaned against the desk, already running through the lies he'd need for The Mantis that night. He'd have to deliver an update on *Irony*, and the truth just wouldn't cut it. He needed something convincing. Something airtight. The Mantis wasn't the type to chase people down—but if he smelled bullshit, he'd make you bleed for it.

Eddie winced, remembering their first encounter. The panic. The restraints. The slow, deliberate violation that followed.

And the worst part? It didn't end when the pain became unbearable.

It ended when The Mantis decided it would.

That was the real torment—being completely under his control.

Chapter Thirty Nine

As I drove, I glanced briefly at my abductor sitting beside me.

"Clint, can I ask you something?"

"Yes sir, Mr. Rodgen."

"How does someone like you end up in a job like this? I mean—have you looked in a mirror lately? You could be a movie star or a model. Hell, even a male stripper, for Christ's sake. Why get caught up in something like this? A guy like you... I don't even want to think about what prison would do to someone who looks like that. And the thing is—you seem like a decent guy. Smart, even. But what you're doing? It's just plain stupid."

Clint paused before responding, his voice steady but low.

"I appreciate your honesty, Mr. Rodgen. But the truth is—I don't really have a choice. I've made some bad decisions along the way. Got in with the wrong people. And now... this is where I've landed."

He turned to look at me, the conviction in his eyes softening.

"I'm sorry for putting you in this position. I really am. When this is over, you'll be back with your family. Safe. That much I can promise. Because I know what a family means to a man."

I looked over at Clint again. He was staring out the window, his mind somewhere far away. I sensed he wanted to stay there, so I let him be. We drove in silence.

And during that time, I found myself reflecting on my own life. How had I ended up in this mess?

It's strange. During that drive, my thoughts were scattered — drifting from childhood, to my parents, to old friends, regrets, hopes, dreams... but always, they came back to my wife and kids.

It's hard to describe such a jumble of memory and emotion. But I started at the beginning.

I thought about my childhood — about how much I'd changed. My brother and I were raised in a typical white American household. Normal, in the worst kind of way. Casual racism wasn't just tolerated; it was baked into our everyday lives. We were taught, either outright or through implication, that most of the world's problems were somehow the fault of Black people.

My great-grandfather lived with us for a time. I still remember the way he'd sit in his recliner, watching *Family Feud*. If a Black family appeared on screen, he'd start muttering under his breath — rubbing his chin and repeating, "Goddamn niggers," shaking his head with a slow, disgusted rhythm, as if the mere sight of them confirmed something broken in the world.

We grew up in an economically depressed, racially mixed area. When I was seven, my nine-year-old brother and I were both beaten up—badly—by a group of Black teenagers. That one moment seemed to confirm everything I'd been taught: that Black people were nothing but trouble.

And I held onto those views for years. Through high school, through college. I'd argue with my roommates—and my future wife, too—though never with my childhood friends, because they hated Black people just as much as I did. I'd rattle off statistics like they were gospel: *Look at the prisons. Look at the crime rates. Look at the slums.* I thought I was making a point.

Then I got my first "real" job—in a lab where, for the first time in my life, I was the minority.

It didn't take long before everything I thought I knew fell apart. These were some of the kindest, smartest, most decent people I'd ever met. They told me what it felt like to be profiled, to be pulled over just for existing in a white neighborhood, to be passed over for jobs because of the color of their skin.

That job changed my life. They changed my life.

I felt ashamed of who I'd been—but grateful, too, that I had the chance to unlearn it. I promised myself I'd teach my kids what I never knew growing up: that everyone is their own person. And yes, it's a cliché, but it's true—you can never judge a book by its cover.

And as I drove, held hostage by a stranger, I promised myself something else: I'd get back in touch with those coworkers. I'd thank them—for their patience, their honesty, and for showing me a better way.

But I didn't hate my parents for what they believed. That's how they were raised. These kinds of prejudices can take generations to fade. And if I hadn't crossed paths with the people I did, I might've passed those same lies down to my own children. That's a terrifying thought.

The truth is, I didn't love my parents. Not really. I don't think I ever did.

We occasionally talked, sure—but only about the weather, or what we had for dinner. Never anything real. Never anything that mattered. There was no closeness to drift away from—just a lifelong pattern of silence, control, abuse in all its forms, and resentment dressed up as family.

I didn't have a happy childhood. Not by a long shot. And while I made plenty of my own mistakes later in life—hanging out with people like Finster, for starters—those mistakes didn't come from nowhere. They came from growing up in a house where fear passed for discipline, silence was mistaken for stability, and affection didn't exist—not even as a bargaining chip.

People talk about unconditional love between parents and kids like it's a given. Like it's something you're born into. But for some of us, that love was never there to begin with. Just rules, punishments, expectations—and never, ever the sense that we were enough.

So when I think about my own daughters, about the kind of father I want to be, the kind of love I want to give... it's not about recreating what I had. It's about building something entirely new. A different legacy.

One that starts with me.

And then my thoughts drifted to the mistakes I made growing up—the alcohol, the acid, the hash, the lines of coke—and whether that kind of chaos might somehow find its way into my daughters' lives. Not because I've exposed them to it, but because patterns have a way of echoing through generations. During that ride, I made a promise: to break the cycle. To take responsibility for my own past, and to raise my kids with the love, safety, and truth I never had.

That promise brought with it a flood of memories—reminders of just how far off the rails I'd gone. Of how easy it is to lose your way when no one's really looking out for you.

One night, I passed out from alcohol poisoning. I almost died. It was one of the coldest nights in Pennsylvania history—two degrees. I didn't have a coat, and I lay unconscious outside, on the concrete slab by the sliding glass door. The only thing that saved me was our dog. He barked and barked until a neighbor woke up and found me.

Another time, I told my parents I was going to hang with a friend, two houses away. They said fine, just be home in three hours. It was a school night after all and I was only fifteen. Sure Mom. Sure Dad. No problem. Three hours was more than enough time to get plastered on vodka and Kool-Aid.

When I returned home, I knew I was too drunk to see them. So I just yelled downstairs, said I was home, and went to my room. I couldn't even make it to my bed before I vomited all over my room, spewing spiked red punch and spaghetti remains on the new carpet. While I laid on the bed, my mom came into the room. I pretended to be sick, but she knew the truth. Still, she didn't ask questions. She just told me to get up—then yanked me out of bed and hit me. First with her fist, then with a belt buckle. And like a dog being punished for an accident, she shoved my face into the mess and kicked me hard in the stomach. That was the pattern. No questions. No comfort. Just punishment. There would be many more times like that. And worse.

I don't know if my alcohol and drug use was a form of escape—but whatever it was, I excelled at it.

When I was seventeen, I got wasted on PCP and weed in the middle of the day. I was inside a 7-Eleven, laughing my ass off—loud, manic, completely out of control. Then my mom walked in. She'd come to pick me up, just like we'd planned earlier. We agreed to meet there, and I showed up obliterated. I didn't even try to cool off beforehand.

That was the thing: even though I knew the beating that would follow, I didn't care. Not even a little. I'd get shitfaced five minutes before walking through my front door. No fear. No shame. Just pure, self-destructive recklessness.

Another shining childhood moment: the day Dad found my rolling papers. Today, that might not raise an eyebrow. But back then, it was a serious offense. I tried the classic excuse—*I'm just holding them for a friend*—but he wasn't buying it. He knew.

They never caught me with actual weed in those early years, but the signs were all there: bloodshot eyes in the middle of the day, the lingering stench of smoke on my clothes. If they were ninety-nine percent sure back then, any lingering doubts disappeared when, at twenty-one, they found a joint in the refrigerator.

They didn't say a word.

They just put it back—right on top of the iced tea pitcher—where I couldn't miss it. Like a warning. Or maybe a quiet acknowledgment. Either way, the message was clear: they knew. They'd always known. And though I wasn't beaten for that one—I was old enough to fight back—they smashed my guitar. The one I'd saved up for, for over a year.

The list continues. I got drunk and called my mom a bitch. Punched my brother and called him a motherfucker—in front of both of them. Put holes in the ceiling during a party while they were out of town. Got caught skipping school and heading to the Jersey shore. Got bailed out for underage drinking. On and on.

But it wasn't about rebellion or making a statement. It was chaos—just me, crashing into the world the only way I knew how. My parents didn't give a shit about me—they cared about appearances. Embarrassment. A blow to their pride, maybe. They were pissed. Ashamed. Maybe even scared—scared someone might find out what kind of house I really grew up in. Scared the mask might slip.

As an adult, I wasn't looking for their forgiveness. I didn't want it. I just hoped—*prayed*—my daughters wouldn't end up walking the same fucked-up road I did.

Eventually, I couldn't take the weight of my own thoughts anymore. I broke the silence.

"Clint? Tell me about your family."

Chapter Forty

Clint glanced at the road. "I have a wife named Mariet-ta. We've been married five years. We have a five-year-old boy named Tommy. Our daughter, Amy, died four months ago."

"Ah, Jesus Christ. I'm sorry."

"She was a great kid. So brave—right up until the end. Brain cancer."

"Fuck. I don't even know what to say, Clint. That's... awful. I really am sorry."

And I meant it. Even though this man had taken me from my family at gunpoint, it was impossible not to feel for him.

"Thanks. I appreciate that, Mr. Rodgen. I still can't be-lieve she's gone. Life's just not fair. Everyone loved that girl. She was our firstborn. Our little angel. Every day with her was a gift. When she'd come running into my arms to greet me... there's no feeling in the world like that."

He paused, his voice thick.

"People ask how you get through something like this. The truth is, I don't think you do. Will a day ever go by that I don't think of her? Not a chance in hell. The only thing that keeps me going is knowing I still have a son who needs his father. And trying to be grateful. I know it sounds twisted, but—she could've died five years earlier. Or a week earlier. Or even an hour earlier. I cling to that. Because if I don't... I think I'd lose my mind."

He covered his face with his hand and started to cry.

Looking back, I guess I could've used that moment to grab the gun. But I didn't.

I didn't even think about it.

I just reached over, placed a hand on his shoulder, and squeezed. I didn't say anything. What was there to say?

Eventually, he wiped his eyes and looked at me. "Cherish every day with them, Mr. Rodgen. Every damn day."

I nodded, smiling just enough to let him know I understood.

"Mr. Rodgen? Would you mind if I called you Mike? Seems more fitting now, after my little breakdown here."

"Sure, Clint. I was about to say the same thing. And seriously—how'd you get to be so damn polite, anyway?"

"My upbringing, I guess. Ya know, I just thought of something—who the hell am I to lecture you on cherishing every day with your kids. Meanwhile..." he lifted the gun slightly, giving it a little wave, "I'm the one stealing you away from them."

"Now that you mention it, yeah... that is a little hypocritical," I replied, only half-joking.

"You're right," he said with a sigh. "But I meant what I said. I'll get you back to them. Very soon. You hear me?"

"Okay, Clint. I'll trust you on that," I said, glancing over and locking eyes with him.

"I think I owe you a better explanation," he added after a pause. "About how I ended up in this mess. You deserve that much."

I nodded. "Yeah. I'd like to hear it."

"Three and a half years ago, I started working at Culligan & Finleys—you know, the big accounting firm in Feltzer?"

"Yeah, I think I've heard of it."

"I was a CPA there. One of the accounts I was assigned to was this company called Future Growth. Supposedly, they sold agricultural products—fertilizer, seeds, heavy machinery, the whole deal. But when I started running the numbers... something didn't add up. Not even close. I figured maybe I was missing something, so I brought it to my division boss—just trying to do the right thing, ya know? I laid it all out for him, thinking maybe I'd made a rookie mistake. But he looked through the paperwork and agreed something was off. Then he told me to leave it all with him, said he'd take it from there."

"Can I interrupt you for a second, Clint? Why the hell did you go into accounting? You're more handsome than freakin' Brad Pitt, for Christ's sake."

"Thanks. You're pretty sexy too," he joked.

I laughed. "Seriously though."

"I don't know," he said with a shrug. "I've always liked numbers. Accounting just seemed like the right thing to do at the time."

He paused a moment before continuing. "Anyway, I kind of forgot about that whole Future Growth thing until about a week later, when I ran into my boss. I asked what the story was, and he told me it was just an error on their part, said the situation had been resolved. But something about the way he said it—it didn't sit right. You know what, though? I didn't really care. As long as it wasn't my problem anymore, I let it go."

"Two weeks later, we were all called into the conference room. The president announced that my boss had committed suicide."

I let out a low whistle. "Holy shit."

"Yeah. When I got back to my office, I sat there trying to convince myself Jim was capable of killing himself. It didn't feel right. And then the phone rang. The voice on the other end told me to keep my mouth shut about Future Growth... or I'd end up like my boss."

I stared at him, stunned. "Jesus."

"That was just the beginning. The phone calls kept coming. Threats. Sometimes at work, sometimes at home.

And they weren't just aimed at me—they mentioned my wife, my son, even Amy. I started getting pictures in the mail. My house. Me at the grocery store. My kids at school. This was before Amy got sick."

He paused, his voice catching a bit before he continued.

"Then one day, I was walking into the supermarket when a car pulled up. A guy jumped out and forced me into the backseat. Sitting next to me was another man... holding all of the paperwork I'd turned over to my boss. He handed it back to me and said, 'Fix it. Don't ask questions.'"

I could feel the chill settle into my bones as he went on.

"I've been doing it ever since. Almost three years now—fudging the numbers, making it all look legit. I've learned more than I ever wanted to about Future Growth. It's not a real company. It's just a front. The real operation is a cocaine cartel called The Seed."

"That's cute," I said. "Future Growth. The Seed. Nice little play on words."

"Yeah. Real cute," he muttered. "They're out there selling coke to kids, and I'm helping them keep the books clean."

"Can't you go to the cops?"

"Not a chance. My house is wired. My office too. They've got me by the balls, Mike. And this thing with you? It's just another layer of control. Just another way to make sure I stay in line."

He looked over at me.

"I'm sure you didn't notice them, but when I took you? There were cameras. They filmed everything. So even if I wanted to go to the cops, they'd just hand over the footage. Blackmail. Insurance. I'm trapped."

I shook my head, trying to wrap my brain around it. "That's a hell of a story, Clint."

"If only it weren't true," he said quietly.

Chapter Forty One

After their fourth attempt, Finster and Bozo finally found a hotel willing to rent them a room. The three previous clerks had refused service—partly because of their obvious doped-out condition, but mostly because Bozo just plain scared the shit out of them.

Before walking into this last place, they agreed it would be best if Bozo stayed in the car. The only other option was for him to remove his gas-carrying construction hat—and for the clown, that simply wasn't on the table.

Even without Bozo in sight, any halfway sensible clerk would've turned Finster away. The only reason they lucked out was that the desk clerk was stoned out of his mind.

Proudly strutting out of the lobby, Finster jingled the room key in the air.

"Wooooooooooo!" Bozo yelled from the car window.

Finster spun around, paranoid the clerk might've heard. But no—the guy was now fast asleep, face planted on the countertop.

"Yo, man," Finster said as he climbed into the car. "We gotta keep it cool. I think that guy was lookin' at me funny."

"Sorry, bro. You're right," Bozo said, throwing the car into reverse. "I'll wait to get rowdy until we're back in the room."

"Fuckin'-a right," Finster grinned, raising his soda can and clinking it against Bozo's hardhat. Gasoline sloshed out, spilling down the clown's face.

"Dude! You gotta be careful. You're wasting that shit." Bozo wiped his face, then stuck a finger under his nose and inhaled deeply. "Phew," he muttered, eyes fluttering. "That was a hell of a hit."

"You're welcome," Finster replied.

"Screw you, moron," the clown laughed, and smacked Finster's can in return.

"Yo! You got it all over my shirt," Finster groaned, then lifted the soaked fabric to his face and breathed in. "Talk about *me* wasting it."

A beat passed, then Finster's eyes lit up.

"I got an idea."

"What kind of idea?"

"Just wait. I'll show you when we get to the room."

They spent the next ten minutes ambling through the parking lot, struggling to locate Room 277. Eventually, they pulled up next to a hotel cleaning lady and asked for directions.

"277," she said, eyeing the two of them warily. "There is no 277."

Finster dug into his pocket, pulled out the key, and squinted at the number. "How about 211?"

She pointed three doors down. "It's right there."

"Wooooooooooo!"

"Shut it, Bozo," Finster hissed, giving her a sheepish wave. "Thanks!"

The woman stared a second longer, then spun her cart around and hustled off toward the front lobby.

"Real smooth," Finster muttered.

"What? Screw her if she can't take a joke. Let's party!" Bozo yelled after her.

Finster watched the woman glance back again, shaking her head.

Bozo parked the car crooked, taking up two spots like a drunk bowling pin, and killed the engine. They both stumbled out and wandered toward the room.

Inside, Bozo yanked the drapes shut. "So what's this big idea of yours?"

"Oh yeah. Check this out." Finster pulled a pillow off the bed and shook out the case. Holding the empty sleeve in one hand, he started looking around the room.

"What are you doing?" Bozo asked.

"Need something sharp. You got anything?"

"No. Why? What're you tryin' to do?"

"You'll see. Chill."

Finster rummaged in the nightstand, came up with a ballpoint pen, and jabbed at the pillowcase. A few minutes later, he held up a makeshift hood—complete with rough eye holes and a jagged slit for a mouth.

"I don't get it," Bozo said flatly.

Finster didn't answer. He slipped the hood over his head, grabbed his gas can, and poured a stream onto the fabric under his nose.

"I know it's not as good as yours…"

"Got that right," Bozo said, tapping his gas-hat proudly.

"…but it works."

"So *that* was your idea?" Bozo snorted. "Man, that blows. Let's just go to Walmart and get you a real setup. I could go for more M&M's anyway."

"Let's just chill, bro. This works fine." Finster jabbed a thumb toward his hood.

"Whatever. Still think it's dumb."

"Screw you, clown boy. What about my *other* ideas? Do they suck too? Lesbian clown pornos? The clown band? Huh?" He started humming. "I don't like Mondays, no Tuesdays…"

"Don't push it."

"Wait a minute! I'm the singer, remember? *I don't like Mondays...*"

"Woooooooooo! Sing it, Bozo! Sing it!" Finster screamed, thrashing on air guitar.

"...no Tuesdays, no Wednesdays, no Thursdays..."

"Woooooooooo!"

"Woooooooooo!" Bozo echoed, as they launched into a chaotic slam dance, bouncing off each other like deranged pinballs.

"Wait, wait, wait, wait, wait!" Finster shouted, grabbing Bozo's shoulders to steady him. "The gas, man. *The gas,*" he said, pointing at the wet stain spreading on the carpet.

"Shit."

Both dropped to the floor, shoving their faces into the gasoline-soaked fibers. As Bozo tilted his head for a deeper inhale, more of the precious fluid spilled from his can.

"Fuck! Dammit!" he yelled. "Guess it's all yours, dude," he added, pushing himself to his feet.

"Cool," Finster mumbled, his nose still pressed to the floor.

"Yo—got any more of them pills?"

Without lifting his head, Finster stuck a thumbs-up in the air.

"Woooooooooo!"

Finster returned a muffled *woooooooo*, barely audible through the shag, his face glued to the fumes-soaked carpet.

Chapter Forty Two

So what the hell are we going to do, Clint? The Seed's got you by the balls, and they're not gonna stop until they get their coke. Wait a minute—why is this particular batch so important? There can't be more than a couple lines left in that duffel bag, right?"

Clint told me all about *Irony*. Once I heard the details, it was easy to understand why the Seed valued it so highly—especially with its ultra-addictive properties.

"I get why they'd want a high-potency, high-addiction formula. It's marketing genius. Stronger coke means more appeal to first-timers. The addiction means more loyal customers. Which means more money. I'm with you there. But one thing I don't get—how the hell did they figure out it worked as a sexual stimulant? You said 'topical,' right? What is that, you rub it on your dick and it gives you a boner?"

"I guess," Clint replied. "I think it works on women too. I didn't ask a whole lot about that part. It wasn't something they designed intentionally—it was just a freaky side effect. If I had to guess who discovered that? Clown-boy. That guy's a goddamn weirdo."

We both laughed at the reference to Bozo, and I launched into a rundown of the various injuries I'd sustained since meeting that green-haired lunatic. My thoughts, inevitably, circled back to my swollen testicle — which I felt compelled to share with Clint.

"Damn," he said. "That doesn't sound too pleasant."

"No shit, Sherlock. You ever had a boil on your sack? I was on my way to the hospital to get it checked out, remember? I—SHIT!"

I yanked the wheel hard left, barely avoiding an Amish horse and buggy that rolled onto the road without warning. As we settled back into our lane, I checked the rearview mirror.

"Check that out," I said. "Isn't that against their religion?"

Clint turned to look. "Guess not. Hey, if he can do it, so can I," he said, flipping the bird.

"Well," Clint said, watching the buggy disappear in the mirror. "*That* was interesting. Anyway—I'm real sorry about your ball sac, and I'm real sorry I'm keeping you from getting the medical attention you so obviously deserve."

His words might've sounded sincere if he hadn't delivered them in full-on baby talk.

"Screw you, Clint. You want to see this thing?" I said, reaching for my zipper like I meant it.

"Go ahead," he said. "I've got a penknife. I'll take care of it for you right now."

"No thanks. I'll pass."

Looking back, it was kind of weird—joking around with my kidnapper like that. But there was a strange connection between us. Maybe because, in some twisted way, we were in the same boat. Both being forced to do something we didn't want to do—all because of that goddamn special blend of cocaine called *Irony*.

What really sealed the bond, though, was the simple truth that we were both just trying to stay alive. And at the heart of it? We just wanted to make it home. Back to our families.

Chapter Forty Three

We drove in silence for a while longer, but not for long. As we got closer to my car, the weight of what was coming pressed down on both of us.

"Seriously, Clint. We need a plan. Let's say we get *Irony* back—what then? You promised to return me safely to my family, and I believe you want to—but do you *really* have any control over that? What if The Seed decides I'm a loose end? And what about you? Are you just going to keep living like their puppet? What happens when they don't need you anymore? Are you the next loose end?"

"You're right," he said. "We're fucked."

"Wow," I muttered. "Such language from the gentleman kidnapper."

"Sometimes the F-word is the only word that fits," he said with a shrug. "Anyway, I don't know what we're supposed to do. But once this 'mission' is over, we lose whatever control we've got left."

"Then maybe we don't finish the mission," I said. "Right now, the only leverage we have is *Irony*. If we still have it, they can't just erase us. Hand it over, and we're screwed. They can do whatever the hell they want."

"I get that," Clint said. "But what do we *do* with it? Keep it forever? Delay the inevitable? They'll come for it. Eventually, they'll come for us."

"I haven't figured out the endgame yet," I admitted. "But for now, delay *is* the game. We get the coke, and then we decide. That's all we can do."

Clint let out a slow sigh. "You're not wrong. It's the only card we've got left."

We didn't talk for the next fifteen minutes. Instead, we cranked up the music—first Nirvana, then the Foo Fighters, then Radiohead. As "Creep" ended with the haunting line *I don't belong here,* I turned down the volume.

"It should be just down this road," I said, pointing to the right. "Feeley Road."

A few moments later, we reached the spot where Bozo and I had careened off the road.

"What the..." I murmured, trailing off as I pulled onto the shoulder.

"What's the matter?" Clint asked.

"Remember our brilliant plan to grab the coke first and *then* decide what to do?" I pointed to the empty field. "Yeah. My car's gone."

We both got out and walked through the tall grass to where my Subaru had been the day before. No car. No duffel bag. Just some deep tire tracks leading back out to the road.

"Huh," I muttered. "I thought it was totaled. Guess not."

Clint scanned the area, hands on his hips. "Damn. Now what the hell are we supposed to do? We *have* to find that coke."

He checked his watch, then let out a groan. "I'm due to give a status update. What the hell am I going to say — 'Sorry, sir. I lost your top-secret super-coke. No idea where it is, no clue how I'll find it. But hey, trust the process!' That's not going to fly."

I stared at the tracks, then back at Clint. "Looks like it's time for Plan B."

"Do we even *have* a Plan B?"

"We do now."

Chapter Forty Four

As Eddie Bretz stepped into his car to head to The Seed's East Coast Christmas in July Party, he made a call. The update was useless. Still no sign of Irony. He gritted his teeth, hurled the phone onto the passenger-side floor, and stomped on the accelerator.

But rage only took him so far. He needed something else to take the edge off. A distraction. Another call.

Fifteen minutes later, he pulled up to a quiet corner, and Storm slipped into the car with a sly grin.

"Busy day, huh?" she said, raising an eyebrow.

Eddie didn't answer right away. The truth was, his monthly tab for her services already clocked in around three grand, but even he had to admit—three visits in a single day was pushing it.

"Do I get a frequent flyer discount?" he asked.

"Standard rate, Eddie," she replied dryly, massaging her jaw. "You're lucky I don't charge extra for repeat trauma."

He smirked, already unbuckling his belt. "Then let's not waste time."

Eddie adjusted himself in the seat and unzipped his pants. "Go to town," he muttered, slipping the car into drive.

As Storm got to work, Eddie steered with one hand and dialed with the other, weaving through traffic while juggling phone calls and misplaced priorities. He barked orders, threatened underlings, demanded updates—never once acknowledging the woman kneeling at his side like she was anything more than an accessory to his ego.

At one point, he asked her to grab his phone off the floor. When she hesitated, he pressed a hand to the back of her head, a silent command to stay put. Storm blindly fumbled for the device, finally passing it up to him without breaking rhythm.

Twenty minutes and three phone calls later, with the Seed party fast approaching, Eddie glanced at the clock, then down at her.

"C'mon," he said, tapping her head. "Give that *nod job technique* another go."

With Storm's rhythmic motion intensifying, Eddie suddenly jolted upright, a sharp gasp escaping his throat. The angle was off—painfully so—and for a moment, it felt like something might snap. But he didn't stop her. Not yet. The discomfort twisted into something else—raw, overwhelming, almost pleasurable in its own way.

Then it hit him. His whole body tensed, hands gripping the wheel tighter than ever before. Instinctively, his foot slammed the brake, and the car lurched to a stop—

Storm thrown to the floorboard in a tangle of limbs and curses.

"What the hell, asshole!"

"Ahh, quit whining," Eddie muttered, zipping up and easing back into gear.

Five minutes later, they pulled up to the party. Eddie threw the car into park and jumped out without a word.

"Hey! What about my money? And how the hell am I supposed to get home?"

He reached into his pocket, peeled off a few bills, and tossed them onto the pavement without looking back.

"There. That covers the ride—and maybe a tip. Now beat it," he said, already halfway to the entrance.

Chapter Forty Five

Eddie's first stop was the bar, where he ordered a Tanqueray and Tonic.

"Hey, dickhead. Don't be so stingy with the limes," he snapped at the bartender.

When the extra wedge arrived, he downed half the glass in one go. His hand drifted to his waistband, reflexively adjusting himself with a wince. It had been a busy day.

That's when The Mantis strolled up behind him.

"Keep rubbing, big boy," he purred. "You're turning me on."

A chill crept down Eddie's spine as The Mantis approached, triggering the memory of their first encounter.

"How are you doing, Mantis?" Eddie asked, trying to sound casual.

"Just fine. Looks like you had yourself a good time. Couldn't bother to clean up a little though?"

"What do you mean?" Eddie asked, eyebrows raised.

The Mantis pointed at the stain on Eddie's pants — front and center.

"Oh. That. I must've spilled something," Eddie muttered.

"Uh-huh. Sure." The Mantis leaned in, voice dropping. "Now tell me about *Irony*, Eddie. I'm very curious."

Eddie hesitated. Just for a beat. But it was enough.

"Is there something wrong, Eddie?" The Mantis's tone softened into something almost paternal — *almost.*

"No. Not at all," Eddie said quickly. "What makes you think that?"

"You just seem... tense," The Mantis replied, his gaze unblinking. "Maybe you're worried about something you haven't told me yet."

Eddie forced a laugh. "I've just had a lot on my mind. Actually, if you want to know what's been occupying me — " he pointed toward his lap " — I had a little roadside entertainment on the way here. Let's just say the woman's got a signature move."

"Oohh. Continue, please," The Mantis said, licking his lips.

Eddie pushed through the revulsion building in his throat and kept talking, describing the drive over like it was just another crude anecdote. If he could distract The Mantis — even for a moment — it might buy him time.

When he finished, The Mantis smiled. "Sounds delightful. Maybe you can try that *nod job* on me sometime."

Eddie didn't answer. He downed the rest of his drink in one gulp, gestured for another, and prayed the conversation would shift. It did.

"What about *Irony*?" The Mantis asked, casually now. But the weight in his voice was unmistakable.

"We're on schedule," Eddie lied. "The trial run's almost wrapped. Once we confirm the results, we'll be ready for full-scale production. With any luck, we'll be pushing it on the street inside a month."

"Very good," The Mantis replied, brushing invisible lint from his jacket. "Keep me updated."

Then, pausing before he walked away, he added, "And Eddie—maybe clean yourself up a bit. Or should I help with that, too?"

"Very good. Very good. Keep me informed, Eddie." The Mantis turned to leave, then paused. "Oh—and show some class. Clean the cum off your pants. Or would you like me to do it?"

Eddie shook his head and headed straight to the men's room, not daring to look back.

Chapter Forty Six

Finster lifted his face from the floor as the blackout ended with a bang—literally. Someone was pounding on the door. Under the bed, Bozo jerked awake and smacked his already throbbing head on the box spring.

"Excuse me?" came a muffled voice from the hallway. "Mr. Smith? It's the front desk. I'm going to have to open the door if you don't answer." Knock knock. "Please, Mr. Smith?"

"Okay, okay!" Finster yelled, stalling. "Just give me a second—I'm getting dressed!" Total lie, but they needed time.

Bozo whispered from under the bed. "What the hell is this about?"

"I don't know. And what are you doing under the bed?"

Before Bozo could answer, the voice outside interrupted again: "Mr. Smith? Are you coming?"

"In a minute, I said!"

"Mr. Smith, huh?" Bozo muttered. "That was the best you could come up with?"

"Fuck off, Bozo. We're lucky I got us this room at all. Just gather our shit and get in the bathroom—we might have to bolt."

While Bozo scrambled around the room, Finster checked the peephole. The glassy-eyed front desk clerk stood swaying on the other side. Just as Finster leaned in, another knock rattled the door—and his skull.

"Shit!" he winced.

Opening the door a crack, Finster tried to look mildly inconvenienced. "Yeah?"

"Sorry to wake you, Mr. Smith," the clerk said, eyes half-lidded. "But the guests next door are complaining about a strong gas smell coming from your room."

The clerk sniffed the air theatrically. "Phew. What's going on in there?"

"Oh. That. Sorry. I work at a refinery," Finster improvised. "Clothes reek. You get used to it. I'll stuff some towels under the door—should fix it."

"Cool," the clerk nodded slowly, clearly not all there. "I don't know how you live like that."

"Yeah. Me either," Finster said, then shut the door in his face.

"You can come out now," he called out. "He's gone. Everything's cool. Who's the man?"

"Nice job, Mr. Smith," Bozo grinned, emerging from the bathroom. "Hey—since we're up, let's hit Walmart. You still need one of these hats," he said, tapping his jerry-rigged gas rig. "And I need to top off," he added, pointing at his head. "I must've spilled some."

"Yeah, probably under the bed. Why *were* you under there, anyway?"

"Beats the shit out of me," the clown answered as he walked towards the door. "Let's go."

"Wait a minute," Finster said as he walked into the bathroom. Moments later, he returned with a dripping wet towel, rolled tightly and ready for action. He crouched down and shoved it along the base of the adjoining door. Then, standing up, he banged on it with his fist.

"Listen, you motherfucker! Don't you dare call the front desk again! I'll fucking kill you! You hear me?!"

Giggling at his own performance, he sprinted for the door, waving Bozo to follow.

"Now we can go. Woooooooooo!"

"And you were telling me to settle down," Bozo muttered as they jumped into the car. "Let's go score some gasoline," he added, hot-wiring the ignition.

They rolled down their windows and screamed in perfect harmony—"Woooooooooo!"—as the battered car lurched out of the lot, still screeching from yesterday's damage.

Back in Room 210, the terrified couple who'd lodged the complaint peeked out from behind their curtain, then scrambled to pack their bags and get the hell out.

Chapter Forty Seven

After talking things over, Clint and I agreed on two things. First, we were starving and needed food. Second, when it came to finding *Irony*, we didn't have the faintest idea where to start.

"Where do you want to go?"

"Anywhere but Burger King," I said. "Actually... I could go for a beer. A Dogfish Head 60 Minute, to be specific. How about George's Pub? Pretty solid roast beef sandwiches. It's about a quarter mile past the Walmart — right-hand side."

"Yeah, I know George's," Clint nodded. "Sounds good. Maybe a beer'll help us think straight."

On the drive over, we chatted about politics, sports, and babes. Right in the middle of breaking down the Sports Illustrated Swimsuit roster, I saw it — my car.

"Holy shit! That's my freakin' Subaru!" I yelled.

We both watched it fly past us in the opposite direction. The Doppler Effect was in full swing, but it wasn't just engine noise — there was a high-pitched metallic screech and what I could only describe as the unholy sound of two maniacs yelling, "Woooooooooo!"

Clint and I looked at each other, wide-eyed, as I stomped the gas and searched for a place to U-turn. At a break in the median, I whipped the wheel hard—momentarily forgetting we were in an SUV. The driver's side wheels actually lifted off the pavement before slamming back down, miraculously not flipping us.

"Jesus Christ," Clint muttered as we roared forward.

We gained on them fast. Within seconds, my car came into view.

"There! Right lane!" I pointed, heart pounding.

We pulled up beside the Subaru. Clint rolled his window down and shouted, trying to get their attention.

The driver turned and looked.

Bozo.

Wearing a goddamn hardhat.

In the passenger seat—Finster. Also wearing a hardhat. And both of them, grinning like lunatics.

They recognized us, too. Because a second later, Bozo jerked the wheel and veered off-road, launching the Subaru into a nearby field, while Clint and I flew past, still on the street.

"Shit! That asshole's crazy," I yelled.

"Turn around—there!" Clint pointed.

I yanked the wheel again, but this time slowed down, remembering the SUV's tendency to tip like a drunk cow. At the next light, I pulled one last U-turn and then shot off-road, following the fresh tire tracks my Subaru carved through the grass.

"Do you see them anywhere?" I asked.

"No, but they couldn't have gotten far. Your car sounded like it was dying."

"I know. That prick," I snapped, suddenly pissed about the abuse my car had taken. "He's gonna pay for that. And what the hell was with those hardhats? Were those beer helmets?"

"Yeah, but with gas cans. And those tubes? Right up their noses. Did you see the duct tape holding it all together?"

"I don't even want to think about what kind of Frankenstein setup they've got going. I just want to find them, get the coke, and figure out our next move."

"Agreed. Now where the hell are they?"

"I don't know. Just follow the tracks."

Less than five minutes later, the tire marks ended—right at the edge of a street.

"Shit," we said at the same time.

I looked over at Clint. "Well... which way do we go now?"

Chapter Forty Eight

We decided to go right, for no other reason than it just *felt* like the way to go. After about ten minutes of driving, we looked at each other, silently acknowledging the obvious.

"How about we get that beer?" I suggested.

"Might as well. The clown's long gone." Clint glanced over. "Who was that guy in the passenger seat, by the way?"

"A friend of mine. Former friend."

I gave him the rundown on Finster—our history, his idiocy, and his theft of *Irony*.

"Oh. So *he's* the idiot," Clint said. "He just strolls out of there, coke in hand, no fear of getting hunted down? Your friend's not exactly a genius, huh?"

"*Former* friend," I corrected. "But yeah, that about sums it up. Finster's life is basically a case study in bad decisions."

"Then why'd you stick around so long? I mean, come on—he's the reason you're caught up in this shitstorm in the first place."

"I know. I guess... I don't know. Maybe I felt loyal? Maybe I thought he'd eventually grow up. But I should've figured that wasn't happening. Hell, I even forgave him after he pricked me over at a Pearl Jam concert—left me stranded in downtown Philly without a ride."

"So I'm guessing I've got a pretty good shot at forgiveness, huh?" Clint grinned. "I mean, if you can stay friends with *that* moron, surely we'll be cool after this is over. All I did was kidnap you."

"Kidnap me? Eh, I can live with that. What I *can't* forgive is you screwing up my hospital visit. I did mention my ball sac, right?"

"About twenty times now, you freakin' baby."

"Speaking of my balls," I said as we pulled into George's lot, "maybe a beer will ease the pain. You have no clue, Clint. I'd love to see how *you* act with a plum-sized boil down there." I pointed at my groin for emphasis.

He got out of the car without a word. Then, as we headed toward the entrance, he looked over, sucked his thumb, fake-cried, and said, "Waaaaaah. Freakin' baby."

"Screw you."

He pushed the door open to George's, and I followed closely behind. We briefly debated where to sit, eventually deciding on a booth instead of the bar. Sure, we both needed a beer—but we also needed a little privacy. Discussing *Irony* and the largest East Coast drug cartel didn't seem like barstool conversation.

We slid into the most secluded booth we could find. Before long, a waitress wandered over. We both ordered Dogfish and asked for menus.

While we waited for our drinks, we started hashing out a plan. Surprisingly, it didn't take long to come up with a basic outline. We fed off each other's ideas, tweaking and sharpening them as we went. Maybe it was a good thing our waitress was incompetent — although she never brought our beers, at least she didn't interrupt us either.

Fifteen minutes later, the conversation hit a lull — and so did our patience.

I flagged her down. She gave a flustered apology and hurried off to fetch our beers. Five minutes after that, she returned, breathless, placing two Dogfish Head pints in front of us.

"Menus?" I asked, as she apparently forgot those too.

"Sorry! Be right back, sir!"

As she disappeared again, Clint leaned back in the booth and said, "Wow. She might actually be less competent than Finster. Or even our president."

"Enough politics, Clint. Please," I groaned.

"Alright, alright." He lifted his glass. "Anyway, I think this could actually work. Maybe we can both get out of this thing alive."

The waitress returned, plopping down two menus before vanishing again.

"But first things first, right?" Clint continued. "We've gotta find that coke."

"I might have an idea," I said. "That cop I told you about earlier? Bill? Maybe he can help us out. I'll give —"

I cut off mid-sentence as both of us turned our heads toward the front door, watching a scene start to unfold.

"Sir, I told you," the manager said sternly. "I can't allow you in here, especially with that thing on your head. And you reek like gas. I'm going to have to ask you to leave. Now, please."

"I'll jusht wun a seex peek," Finster slurred, pointing toward the takeout refrigerator.

"No! Sounds like you've had enough, sir. You're not getting a six-pack. Now leave," the manager snapped, giving Finster a hard shove out the door.

Clint and I looked at each other — then quickly threw some cash on the table and bolted from the booth.

"Sirs? No food?" our waitress called after us as we hurried to the exit.

"No thanks. Maybe next time," Clint said over his shoulder as we pushed through the door, rushing to search for Finster.

Chapter Forty Nine

To our surprise, as we walked out to the parking lot, we spotted Finster stumbling toward my car, where Bozo waited behind the wheel. Clint and I ducked behind a nearby minivan, not wanting to draw any attention. As they started to pull away — the Subaru protesting loudly — we rushed to our SUV.

"Well, whatd'ya know? How fucking lucky was that?" I said, still in shock at the sight of those two idiots.

"I know. Crazy," Clint said. "After all the shitty luck we've had, maybe things are finally turning our way. Why don't we just follow them for now? See where they go. We saw what happened last time — we tried to chase them and they damn near killed us. Who knows what this douchebag'll do to get away. Maybe he'll cut across the street or drive down the wrong side of the road. I'm not getting killed over this. Let's just tail 'em and wait until they stop."

"For a kidnapper, you're pretty smart."

We pulled out slowly and kept several car lengths behind them, watching the Subaru swerve like it was driven by a couple of toddlers.

A few minutes later, they stopped at a gas station. We pulled onto the shoulder to watch.

"What the hell are they doing?" I asked. "Are they filling up those cans?"

"Sure looks like it," Clint said, his face a perfect mixture of disbelief and awe.

When they finished, they jerked the car back onto the street, both of them screaming out the windows.

"Wooooooooo!"

"Wooooooooo!" they echoed back and forth like drunken maniacs.

We could hear them clearly even from where we were.

"Those guys are fucking crazy," Clint muttered.

I just nodded, still trying to process what we'd seen at the gas station.

We stayed a few car lengths behind them for about twenty minutes. Honestly, the distance was probably unnecessary. Given their condition, I'm pretty sure even if we'd climbed into the back seat, they wouldn't have noticed.

Unbelievably, they managed to pull into the Liberty Inn without killing themselves. They drove around in circles a few times—Clint and I had already passed this same hotel three times ourselves—and eventually managed to park. We pulled into a space about fifty feet away.

From our car, we watched as they got out, left both doors hanging wide open, and staggered toward their room. They fumbled with the key for a while, then finally stumbled inside.

Clint and I waited a couple of minutes, hoping they might come back outside. But we couldn't wait any longer—the pull of getting our hands on *Irony* was just too strong.

We crept toward the car. As we got closer, we saw the doors still open, the interior lights still on—and unbelievably, the engine still running. I crouched beside the driver's side door, then glanced over at their hotel room. I motioned to Clint, who stood near the trunk, to look. The lights in the room were off, but the door was slightly ajar.

I reached for the steering column, trying to turn off the car, then remembered: Bozo had hot-wired it after I took the keys. Forgetting the ignition, I switched off the interior lights instead.

One more look toward the room—still dark, still quiet. Then I popped the trunk and signaled Clint. He opened it, and I darted around to join him.

"Yes," Clint whispered. "Yes."

We quietly high-fived, then sprinted back to his Jeep. Once inside, we flipped on the dome light and unzipped the duffel.

"You were right. Not much left."

"Blame the clown," I said. "He's the one who shot a hole through my trunk."

Clint nodded. "Still, this little bit of coke just might save our lives—and our families' too."

We stared at the bag in silence, both of us feeling the weight of what we held. Finally, I looked over at Clint.

"I need another beer. Let's go back to George's. Hope we get a new waitress this time, order some food, and celebrate."

Clint nodded, started the car, and began backing out.

"Wait. This is killing me. I have to know what's going on in that room. They could be dead for all we know."

"Who cares," Clint said flatly.

"I'm just curious. You saw how they were driving. If they spot me, there's no way they're catching me—not in their condition."

Clint waved a hand. "Fuck it. Go for it."

I walked over to the hotel while Clint waited in the car. As I reached their door, the stench of gasoline hit me like a slap. Peering through the darkness, I spotted Finster sprawled face-down on the bed. A couple of feet from the doorway, Bozo lay passed out on the floor.

I stepped inside and crouched next to the clown. With that ridiculous hat on his head and tubes duct-taped into his nostrils, I already knew what was inside the cans. But just to be sure, I removed one from the side of his helmet. The intensifying reek of gasoline confirmed it.

Standing up, I shook my head in disbelief and turned to leave. I guess removing the can jarred Bozo awake—

sort of. He started mumbling, incoherent at first. I paused, curiosity getting the better of me, and leaned in closer.

"Beezeel kalmeen. Beezeel kalmeen," he slurred.

It took me a minute—several, actually—to decode what he was trying to say. But when it clicked, I slapped a hand over my mouth to muffle the laughter and bolted out the door.

I didn't stop running until I was back inside Clint's car. And then I completely lost it.

"What the hell's wrong with you?" Clint asked.

I doubled over, tears in my eyes, laughing uncontrollably.

"Bozo's coming! Bozo's coming!" I howled.

Chapter Fifty

After cleaning himself up, Eddie Bretz stepped out of the bathroom and made his way back to the bar. He downed his third gin and tonic in one long gulp and slammed the empty glass on the counter.

"Make it two more," he barked, not bothering to look up.

Double-fisting his fresh gin and tonics, Eddie strolled across the hall toward the buffet. He locked eyes with The Mantis, who gave a slow, deliberate glance at Eddie's pants, then nodded in approval—clearly noting the absence of the earlier stain. He licked his lips with theatrical flair. Eddie offered a nervous half-smile and kept moving.

At the buffet, Eddie heaped his plate with crawfish scampi, ginger beef, blackened tuna steak, and scallops lejon—skipping the vegetables entirely, just in case they ran out of the "good stuff." Not that it was likely. The Seed always knew how to throw a party.

Unable to juggle both drinks and his overloaded plate, Eddie downed one of the cocktails in three big gulps. Now officially buzzed, he grabbed his plate and remaining drink and hunted for a table far from The Mantis. With a slight wobble in his step, he spotted a seat and dropped into it without bothering to check if it was taken.

"Hey, sexy. Ever give anyone a nod job?" Eddie asked, grinning over the rim of his glass.

The redhead across from him looked at him with pure disgust and swiveled her seat away. She wasn't one of the Seed-supplied prostitutes—just The Mantis's sister.

With a wad of crawfish still in his mouth, Eddie mumbled, "Whatsa matter, babe? It's not like you haven't sucked a dick before."

She didn't reply. Just gave him one last withering look, stood up, and walked away—fast.

As he turned around—food still in his mouth—Eddie shouted, "Bitch!" loud enough to turn heads. Then, unfazed, he went back to inhaling what was left of his plate. Within minutes, he finished, stood, and spun around to grab more.

Standing directly in front of him was The Mantis.

"Eddie," he said, voice calm but cold. "We seem to have a problem."

"Whataya mean?"

The Mantis didn't blink. "You see that beautiful redhead who was sitting across from you a moment ago?"

"Oh yeah. She ignored me. Can you believe that bitch?"

"That 'bitch', as you so eloquently call her, happens to be my sister." Mantis said coolly.

Eddie froze mid-swig. He set the glass down and fumbled for words.

"I... I didn't know. Seriously, Mantis—I'm sorry. If I'd known, I never would've said anything. Please."

The Mantis took a step closer. "I love my sister, Eddie. Did you know that?"

Eddie shook his head.

"I don't take kindly to anyone who disrespects her. Now, tell me—do you think your comments hurt her?"

"I didn't mean to. I swear."

The Mantis's voice dropped, deliberate and cold. "Do you remember what happened last time you stepped out of line?"

Eddie nodded slowly.

"And do you remember what I said I'd do if it ever happened again?"

Another nod.

"This? This was close, Eddie. Very close."

Eddie swallowed hard.

"Be careful," Mantis said, his tone even but full of menace. "Next time, you won't get to apologize."

Eddie nodded.

"You will apologize to her. Now. And you will never speak to her again. Right, Eddie?"

He nodded quickly.

"Good. Have a nice night, Eddie."

The Mantis turned to walk away. A few steps later, he paused and looked back.

"One more thing, Eddie. Don't fuck up *Irony*. Kindly excuse my language. But do I make myself clear?"

"Yes, Mantis."

"Good. Because you know the consequences... don't you?"

"Yes, Mantis."

"Good."

He walked off into the crowd. Eddie exhaled, then made a beeline for the bar.

Chapter Fifty One

After his encounter with The Mantis, Eddie polished off two more drinks and went outside. He hopped in his car to get some privacy, then dialed his cell phone.

"Storm? I need you. Now," he slurred.

"Jesus, Eddie. It's late. I'm sleeping. It'll have to wait until morning."

"Please, Storm! I'm desperate. Please," he begged.

"No, Eddie. I'm going to sleep. Goodbye, Eddie."

"Wait, Storm! Wait! How about some phone sex? I'll pay you your normal rate. Please?"

There was a long pause. He could practically hear her rubbing her temples on the other end.

"Eddie... I swear. You're lucky I need rent money. But here's the deal—you've got ten minutes, max. If you're not done by then, I'm hanging up. And yes, I still get paid."

"Deal," he said, already fumbling with his zipper. "And can you pretend you're, like, Eastern European or something? You know. Mysterious."

She sighed. "Fine. But I'm not doing that weird elf voice again."

"Fair enough."

He leaned back in his seat, eyes half-closed, trying to conjure something sultry out of her bored, vaguely Slavic intonation. It was all going reasonably well — until he caught sight of The Mantis and his sister walking toward the car.

Panic surged. He scrambled to cover himself, knocking over his gin in the process. The ice cubes bounced onto his lap, but the cold shock barely registered. He slammed the phone face down on the seat and grabbed the steering wheel with both hands, grinning maniacally like a man just enjoying the air conditioning.

"Eddie," The Mantis said, tapping the window. "You remember my sister?"

Eddie rolled it down halfway. "Yes, of course. And I want to apologize — again. Very sincerely. It was the gin talking. And maybe a little bit of deep-rooted insecurity. But mostly gin."

The Mantis stared at him for a long moment, then smiled.

"Good boy," he said. "Just remember — we all slip sometimes. But some people fall a lot harder than others."

The Mantis' sister gave Eddie the finger, told him to "fuck off" and walked away.

"As you can see, my sister is still very upset, Eddie."

"I really am sorry, Mantis."

"I'm sure you are." The Mantis held his stare for a long moment, then added, "I expect to hear from you tomorrow regarding *Irony*." With that, he turned and walked away, his sister close behind.

Eddie slumped back into the driver's seat and exhaled, relieved.

When he was confident the coast was clear, he reached for the phone to resume his conversation with Storm.

Too late.

"Time's up," Storm said flatly, then hung up.

"Wait, bitch! Wait," he screamed. But it was too late. He tried calling her back several times, but each time, all he got was a busy signal.

"Pick the fuck up when I call," he shouted at his phone, then hurled it onto the passenger seat. Frustrated and drunk, he slumped back, lifted his thigh, and tried to calm himself down.

But the quiet was deafening. The cold air outside did little to cool his temper — or his thoughts. Eddie closed his eyes and let out a long breath, trying not to spiral any further. Furious and in need of some relief for his blue balls, he angrily yanked on his swollen Johnson.

Recalling his last session with Storm, he realized that a little penis pain was a good thing. Each tug was progressively harder than the last, resulting in groans of both pain and ecstasy. As he surveyed the parking lot for potential witnesses, he smiled, realizing he was about to achieve release.

With a final exuberant jerk, a loud popping noise emanated from his groin. Eddie screamed in pain and promptly passed out as his fractured penis shot copious amounts of semen all over his brand new suit.

Chapter Fifty Two

Returning to George's to finally get something to eat, Clint and I drank beer, skimmed the dinner menu, and discussed our next move.

"First priority: call our families and get them to safety. My parents' house is out—thanks to you kidnapping me," I added, shooting Clint my best *thanks-a-lot* glare. "In fact, I need to get my parents out of there too. If The Seed can't get to my wife and kids, they'll have no problem using my parents for leverage."

"Good point," Clint nodded. "And you're right. Irony doesn't do us a damn bit of good if they've got us by the balls."

"My parents have an RV. I'll tell them to take a little road trip. Disappear into some random campground for a while."

"Just make sure they're not being followed."

"Obviously," I said. "And if they are, then we're already screwed. Plan's dead on arrival. We just have to cross our fingers and hope The Seed isn't watching our families right now."

"Yeah. But honestly? I doubt they are. They already know where our families are—they can get to them anytime they want. And they've got no reason to suspect either of us would ever double-cross them."

"If they only knew," I said, raising my beer in a toast. "By the way, I'm getting the roast beef."

I flagged down our slightly-more-competent waitress and we both ordered sandwiches, fries, and another round of drinks. Once she left, Clint answered my earlier question.

"My wife's friend, Elle. She's got a farm in Maryland—one hundred and twenty-five acres. They can go there. It's safe. Nobody knows the location, and Elle's a paranoid sonofabitch. Full security system, bodyguards, stockpile of weapons... the works. In this situation, paranoid's not such a bad thing."

When our food finally arrived, we dug in. The roast beef lived up to the hype—tender, juicy, and slathered in horseradish, just the way I liked it. The fries were crisp, the beer cold, and for the first time in a while, I almost felt normal.

I pushed my empty plate away and raised my glass to signal another refill.

"One more beer, then let's get out of here. I'm beat. I guess we need to find a room," Clint said.

"Maybe we could crash with Finster and Bozo," I offered. "Bozo didn't seem to be using his bed anyway. He preferred the floor."

"Yeah, some people are like that," Clint said, dry. "You don't think it had anything to do with the gasoline huffing, do you?"

"Nah. He just had a long day," I shot back with equal sarcasm. "Besides, who are we to judge? We drink beer. They huff petroleum. Everyone's got their thing."

"I guess."

Our refills arrived, and we each took a long, satisfying pull. It's strange how a few sips of beer can make the world seem a little more manageable. We talked a while longer—nothing important, just nonsense—and I made a conscious effort to avoid any more talk of politics. Eventually, we drained the last of our drinks, paid the tab, tossed a tip on the table, and headed for the door.

Outside, the air had a crispness to it—the first hint of fall. It felt good on my face. I took a deep breath, savoring the clean, cool oxygen as it filled my lungs. When we climbed into the car, I rolled down the passenger window and looked up at the night sky.

As Clint drove, something about the stars reminded me I wasn't insignificant—not really. It would be easy to feel that way, staring up at the endless dark. But no. In the grand scheme of things, sure, maybe my life didn't register. But in *my* world? To the people I loved? It meant everything.

I glanced over at Clint. "I'll be glad when this is over."

"You and me both."

Chapter Fifty Three

Moments after passing out, Eddie snapped awake to a blinding bolt of pain. The six gin and tonics he'd downed dulled the edge, but not enough to ignore the throb radiating from his groin. Wincing, he realized walking was out of the question. Grunting, he started the car and coasted up to the front entrance. Rolling down the window, he barked at the valet standing nearby.

"Two Tanquerays and tonic. Heavy on the lime. Chop chop."

The teenager blinked, unsure if he'd heard right. "Uh… are you sure you need another?"

Eddie narrowed his eyes. "Do you know who I am, kid? Just get the damn drinks."

"Okay, okay," the valet mumbled, backing away. "Be right back."

While waiting for his drinks, he finished the last of his gin and tonic, took a deep breath, and finally forced himself to look down at his crotch.

"Oh my God! What the fuck? Jesus Christ, what the fuck happened?" he screamed. Tears welled in his eyes—

not just from the pain, but from the grotesque sight below. At the point of fracture, his penis was swollen to the size of a baseball. The entire shaft was black and blue, with a slow trickle of blood escaping the tip.

Eddie rocked back and forth, wailing. Then he froze, forced himself to look again, and started huffing in disbelief — half panicked, half mesmerized by his own destruction.

"You did this, you bitch!" he howled. "You and your fucking nod job! Look what you've done to me!"

"Sir? Excuse me, sir... Holy shit — what happened to your dick?" the teenager blurted as he returned with Eddie's drinks.

Eddie snatched them from his hands. "What the hell does it look like, genius? Never seen a broken dick before?"

"A broken dick?" the teen echoed, eyes wide. "Jesus. How'd that even happen?"

Eddie didn't answer. He downed half a drink, slammed the gear into drive, and peeled away from the curb.

He knew damn well he shouldn't be driving — between the gin and the busted anatomy, he was in no shape to operate a vehicle. But calling an ambulance wasn't an option. The last thing he needed was to be the punchline of The Seed's next party.

As he drove with one hand and drank with the other, Eddie felt reasonably sure he was heading in the right direction for the hospital. At a red light, he polished off his first drink and tossed the glass out the window, where it shattered across the sidewalk.

A window slid open in a nearby apartment.

"Hey! Hey, you! What the hell are you doing?" a man yelled. "You better get your ass out of that car and clean up that mess!"

"Screw you, douchebag!"

"What did you just call me?!"

"You heard me!" Eddie shouted. "Douchebag! Did you hear that?!"

Just then, a police cruiser pulled up beside him.

"What seems to be the problem here?" the cop asked.

"This asshole just threw glass all over the sidewalk!" the man in the window shouted down.

Eddie didn't wait for more questions. He slammed the accelerator, tearing through the intersection and making a hard right onto the next street. Seconds later, flashing lights filled his rearview mirror.

The cruiser gave chase, sirens blaring, but Eddie floored the gas pedal, pushing his BMW past a hundred miles per hour. The gap between him and the cop started to widen.

As the road crested a hill, Eddie blew through a stop sign and barreled down the other side. Ahead, a railroad crossing came into view—cars lined up, waiting for the train to pass.

"Shit."

He slammed the brakes, tires screeching and smoke trailing behind. With the cruiser fast approaching, he yanked the wheel hard left and veered onto the dirt shoulder, skimming past the waiting cars.

Now he was racing alongside the train, kicking up dust, heading in the opposite direction. The police car didn't hesitate. It followed.

Eddie cleared the end of the train and, seeing an opening, yanked the wheel hard to the right. The car jolted over the railroad tracks and bounced violently onto the other side. In his drunken confidence, he truly believed his Beemer could handle a U-turn at seventy.

He was wrong.

The back end fishtailed wildly on the loose dirt, and the car flipped. It rolled—once, twice, then a half—before landing roof-first with a brutal crunch. Eddie's world turned upside down, literally, as the car skidded nearly forty feet before finally coming to a groaning stop.

Hanging from his seatbelt, dazed and bleeding, Eddie blinked through the fog of alcohol and shock. Disoriented, he struggled to release the belt, grunting as pain shot through his body. A flashlight beam suddenly flooded his eyes.

"That was impressive," the officer said, dry as dust. "You haven't been drinking, have—holy shit. What the hell happened to your dick?"

Chapter Fifty Four

Damn. My wife's going to be worried sick," I said to Clint as we pulled into the hotel parking lot. "I completely forgot to call. She probably has no idea what the hell's going on. I left for the hospital twelve hours ago. Can I borrow your phone?"

"Nope," Clint replied. "What kind of self-respecting kidnapper would I be if I just handed that over?"

"Come on. Give me the freakin' phone."

He tossed it to me as we walked toward the room.

"Honey?"

"Mike? Where *are* you? I called the hospital—they had no record of you. Are you okay? What's going on?"

I told her everything. Not just about the kidnapping, but the bigger mess—the drugs, the danger, the need for everyone to disappear for a little while. Clint and I had originally planned to explain things to our families in the morning, but there didn't seem to be any point in waiting.

"What the hell are we mixed up in, Mike?" Her voice cracked. She wasn't scared for herself—that much I knew—it was the kids.

We talked a little longer while I tried to calm her down. In the end, we agreed: they needed to leave. Lay low. Get far away. Before I hung up, I told her I loved her and promised to call again as soon as I could.

"Did I mention I'll be glad when this is over?" I said, handing Clint his phone.

"Yeah. Ditto," he replied. "I think I'll wait till morning to call my wife. No point waking her up just to tell her to worry."

"Agreed. Let her sleep."

We found our room, went inside, and collapsed on our beds. It had been a long, chaotic, nerve-wracking day. We didn't even bother undressing—just shoes off, covers on. I said goodnight. Clint said it back. Silence.

Then, a few minutes later, Clint spoke.

"Yo, man?"

"What?" I groaned. "I'm trying to sleep."

"You wanna go get some gasoline? Do some hits?"

I laughed, told him to shut up, and drifted off to sleep.

Chapter Fifty Five

The next morning, Bozo and Finster were roused from their slumber by the sound of a voice.

"Excuse me, sir? Sir? Are you okay?" the hotel cleaning lady asked.

Bozo lifted his head off the carpet and squinted at the woman standing above him. Then he groaned, shut his eyes again, and tried to go back to sleep.

"Sir! You can't lie here with the door wide open! Sir!"

Grumbling, Bozo hauled himself to his feet, muttered something obscene, and slammed the door shut. He stumbled to the bed and flopped down with a groan.

"Hey… you awake?" he mumbled.

"Yeah," Finster replied, his voice gravelly. "That shit packs a wallop. Do you remember anything after Walmart?"

"We went to Walmart?"

"Check out my head," Finster said, pointing to his construction helmet. "Ring any bells?"

Bozo stared blankly. "Huh."

"So you don't remember either?" Finster asked, massaging his temples. "Man, maybe we need to chill today. I don't think my skull can take much more of that stuff."

"Pussy."

"Fuck off, Bozo. You feel fine?"

"I didn't say that. I feel like I got hit by a damn bus. But hey—no pain, no gain."

Finster groaned. "What about the clown pornos? Maybe we actually work on that today. I'm not saying we don't party a little, but you remember those ideas? Lesbian clown pornos? The clown band? Let's do it! Keep it to gasoline only—those cat tranquilizers wrecked me."

"Fine, fine. But you're still soft. Let's just see how the day goes, alright?"

They both rolled out of bed slowly, rubbing their eyes and cradling their heads.

"Let's get something to eat," Bozo said. "Then refill," he added, tapping the empty canister taped to his helmet.

They stepped into the sunlight, wincing as if it were personal. After a moment of squinting and shuffling, they climbed into the car—Bozo behind the wheel, Finster riding shotgun.

The clown reached under the dash to hot-wire the engine.

Nothing.

"What the fuck! We're out of gas?" Bozo shouted, staring at the dashboard. "We had half a tank last night. You're right, Finster — those cat tranquilizers are potent as hell. We must've driven all over the place."

He didn't realize, of course, that he'd simply left the car running all night.

"Damn. I guess we're walking," Finster groaned, stepping out of the car. He paused and pointed at the back seat. "What the hell is all that?"

Bozo leaned in for a better look. "Looks like we went on a shopping spree."

He reached in and grabbed a few Walmart bags.

"Let's go see what we scored," Finster said, grabbing the rest and following Bozo back to the room.

Once inside, they dumped the bags onto the bed and surveyed the loot.

Their haul:

- Six bags of M&M's
- Three bags of beef jerky
- A three-pack of ChapStick
- A 500-count bottle of aspirin
- An assortment of clown face makeup
- Four bras
- And a karaoke machine.

Finster scratched his head. "I mean... it's not the worst emergency supply kit I've ever seen."

"Woooooooooo!"

"Wooooooooo!" Finster screamed back as he ripped open the karaoke machine box with manic glee.

"Hold up," Bozo said, grabbing the face makeup. "Priorities. First things first."

"Yeah, yeah—you're right," Finster replied. "But I need to eat something before I do anything else. And kill this headache while I'm at it."

They scarfed down handfuls of M&M's, tore into the jerky, and chased it with five aspirin apiece. Then, they stumbled to the bathroom to transform their faces.

"Alright," Bozo began, taking on the tone of a seasoned artist, "you start with the white base. Get it smooth. Then add your colors—this is where the expression happens. Now, normally I go for erotic. Seductive clown. But for the band, I'm thinking something darker. Sinister. You feel me?"

"Yeah. That fits the vibe of the song."

"Exactly," Bozo said, already dabbing on the white. He began to hum, then broke into an impromptu chant: "I don't like Mondays... no Tuesdays, no Wednesdays, no Thursdays..."

And just like that, *Clownophobia* was born.

Chapter Fifty Six

After calling his wife the next morning, Clint headed down to the hotel lobby and grabbed a copy of the local paper. He spotted the complimentary continental breakfast and helped himself to a coffee, a bagel, and a Red Delicious apple. Skimming the headlines as he walked back to the room, he frowned at the latest chaos unfolding in the Middle East.

As he opened the door, the sound of running water greeted him—along with my passionate shower performance.

"Give it a rest, Mike!"

"Feeeelings... nothing more than feeeelings... trying to for-geeet myyyy —"

"I said shut it!" Clint shouted, banging on the bathroom door.

"Yeesh. No appreciation for art," I muttered, rinsing the shampoo from my hair.

"You call that art?"

I turned off the water, carefully patted dry — paying extra attention to my still-tender ball sac — and threw on some clothes.

"Anything good down there?" I asked, eyeing Clint's breakfast.

"Hotel breakfast. You've got the imagination — use it. Maybe grab a napkin for your ego while you're at it, Sinatra."

"You're just jealous of my vocal chops."

"Yeah," he said dryly.

"I'm gonna head down and see what's left."

"Cool. Maybe serenade the crowd."

"Jealousy's an ugly trait," I called over my shoulder.

"Wait, wait," Clint said between chuckles. "Listen to this headline: '*Man With Broken Penis Charged With DUI After High-Speed Chase Ends at Railroad Tracks.*' I didn't even know you could *break* a penis."

"Yeah? I didn't know you could get a boil on a vasectomy scar either. But between the two," I said, pointing to my crotch, "I'll stick with the plum-sized ball."

I walked back toward him as he read aloud from the article.

"'In West Nerbery last night, a high-speed chase culminated at the Breyberne Railroad crossing, about half a mile south of Fork Road. The pursuit began at approximately 10:30 p.m. in Marlene and reached speeds exceeding 100 miles per hour...'"

"Eddie Bretz was... Holy shit! Eddie Bretz," Clint said, eyes wide. "Eddie *freaking* Bretz!"

"Oh my god," I echoed, staring back at him in disbelief. Then we both dove back into the article, hungry to learn how the dealer who had made our lives hell ended up shattering his junk.

When we finally finished reading, neither of us said a word. We just sat there, letting it sink in — especially that one unforgettable line: *'Mr. Bretz was momentarily trapped in his car, hanging upside down, the seatbelt pressed tightly against his broken penis.'*

After a long pause, I broke the silence. "Like I said... I'm gonna grab some food. But after that, I think we should swing by the hospital. See how our good friend Mr. Bretz is holding up."

Chapter Fifty Seven

"You had quite the night, Eddie," The Mantis said as he stepped into the hospital room.

Eddie lay in the bed, handcuffed to the railing—just in case he got any bright ideas about escaping. His right arm was in a cast, his face looked like it had lost a fight with a brick wall, and a catheter ran from beneath the bandages wrapped around what was left of his dignity. On top of it all, his hangover felt like a jackhammer in his skull.

"Yeah, I had a little accident after the party," Eddie croaked. "It wasn't my fault, though. I—"

"Save it, Eddie." The Mantis waved him off and tossed a folded newspaper onto his lap. "I already know the whole story. And something tells me this article's going viral."

Eddie blinked down at the headline and winced.

Man With Broken Penis Charged With DUI

He started reading, his eyes bulging as the words sank in:

In West Nerbery last night, a high-speed chase culminated along the Breyberne Railroad tracks, approximately a half-mile south of Fork Road. The chase began at 10:30 PM Thursday in the town of Marlene, and reached speeds exceeding 100 mph.

Eddie Bretz, a 31-year-old resident of Keel Square, was charged with reckless driving, evading arrest, speeding, multiple counts of failure to signal, and littering. He was also charged with driving under the influence after a breathalyzer measured his BAC at 0.34% — more than four times the legal limit.

The incident began when Mr. Bretz allegedly threw his empty highball glass at the intersection of Walley Road and Pierce Street. A verbal confrontation followed between Mr. Bretz and a local resident who wishes to remain anonymous. This prompted Officer Dennis Halliger to approach the scene.

As Officer Halliger questioned Mr. Bretz, the suspect fled, initiating a pursuit through the town of Derby and eventually leading to the railroad crossing in West Nerbery.

While several cars waited for a passing Tusquena freight train, Mr. Bretz reportedly accelerated along the dirt path beside the tracks, heading southbound. Moments later, after clearing the end of the train — which had been traveling in the opposite direction...

With Officer Halliger close behind, Mr. Bretz attempted to jump the railroad tracks and perform a high-speed U-turn. His BMW failed to execute the maneuver, flipping several times before landing upside down in a ditch.

When Officer Halliger approached the wreckage, he found the suspect inverted, semiconscious, and partially undressed. Most notably, Mr. Bretz's genitalia was exposed, visibly swollen, and bleeding. After reading Mr. Bretz his rights, Halliger arranged for transport to Chaney Hospital.

Mr. Bretz is currently being treated for multiple injuries, including facial lacerations, a fractured arm, and what attending physicians described as a "penile fracture." According to preliminary assessments, the injury to Mr. Bretz's penis appears to have occurred prior to the crash. The circumstances leading to the injury remain unclear.

A full recovery is expected. Upon discharge, Mr. Bretz will be arraigned on multiple charges. No other injuries were reported in the incident.

Eddie slowly lowered the newspaper to his lap and looked up at The Mantis.

"As I said, you had quite the night, Eddie. Now, do you mind telling me how you broke your penis?"

"Well," Eddie stammered. "I..."

"Forget it. I don't actually care," The Mantis cut in. "What I do care about is *Irony*. I won't let your little antics set us back any further."

Without warning, The Mantis reached forward and squeezed Eddie's bandaged groin.

"Do you understand?" he asked calmly.

Eddie's face contorted in agony as he stifled a scream.

"I said—do you understand?" The Mantis repeated, tightening his grip.

"AAAH! Yes, Mantis! Yes!" Eddie cried out.

At that moment, the hospital door creaked open and a police officer stepped inside.

"Is everything alright in here, sir?"

"Yes, officer. Thanks for checking," The Mantis said smoothly, releasing Eddie and heading toward the door. As he passed, he slipped the cop a folded fifty without breaking stride.

At the threshold, he turned back.

"I'll be calling you, Eddie. Please—don't disappoint me."

Chapter Fifty Eight

On the way to the hospital, we made two quick stops—first the grocery store, then a medical supply shop. A few minutes later, I climbed into the back seat of the SUV with a bedpan in one hand and a set of orderly scrubs in the other.

"Eyes on the road, homo," I joked as I started changing.

"Don't flatter yourself, a-hole. If I were gay, believe me—I'd aim a hell of a lot higher than you. I look like a movie star, remember? *You* said it."

"Bite me," I muttered weakly.

Ten minutes later, we arrived at the hospital. I headed for the elevators while Clint walked up to the front desk. Posing as Eddie Bretz's brother, he managed to get the room number—424. We met back at the elevator and rode up to the fourth floor.

The plan was simple: dressed as an orderly and carrying a bedpan, I'd be the one to go in. If there was a cop outside, the disguise would hopefully pass muster. It's not like they'd assign their top talent to guard a busted drunk driver with a broken penis. Clint's role was back-up—there if things went sideways.

As the elevator doors opened, I spotted a directional sign straight ahead: Room 424 to the left. I nudged Clint and we headed down the hall. Twenty feet away, a cop stood near the room. Without missing a beat, Clint peeled off down a side corridor while I continued on.

"How you doing, officer?" I asked casually as I reached for the door handle.

He gave me a silent nod. No questions. No suspicion. Just like that, I was in.

Eddie was asleep in the bed, snoring faintly, his right arm in a cast and his left hand cuffed to the rail. I walked over quietly and moved the nurse call button just out of his reach. No need to be dramatic—he wasn't going any-where.

Carefully, I reached into the bedpan and pulled out a pre-cut strip of duct tape I'd stashed earlier. In one swift motion, I slapped it over his mouth. Eddie jolted awake, eyes bulging.

I leaned in, gripping his face hard.

"Feel that, Eddie? That's me squeezing your face. Now imagine how it's gonna feel if I decide to do that to your dick."

His eyes filled with terror, almost like someone had *already* done that to him earlier.

"That's exactly what's going to happen if you make a sound. Do you understand me, Eddie?"

He nodded.

"Good," I said, straightening up. "We haven't met before, but we know each other. I'm Mike Rodgen—the guy you've been trying to track down."

At the mention of my name, his expression changed. Hatred flared in his eyes.

"Yeah, I figured you wouldn't be a fan. Don't worry. The feeling's mutual. I didn't ask for any of this—I got dragged into it the moment I crossed paths with Finster." That got a reaction. The loathing in Eddie's face twisted even further at the sound of Finster's name.

"Oh yeah. Finster. That little shit," I said with a sneer. "Believe me, I'm not exactly on his fan club mailing list either."

I reached into my pocket and pulled out the baggie Clint and I had picked up earlier—the one filled with baking powder.

"This, Eddie, is what you call *Irony*. Cute name, right? Look, I didn't want to be part of this crap. But I am. And the only way I see out is through this." I held the bag up, gave it a little shake, then walked into the bathroom.

I dumped the contents into the toilet and flushed it. When I returned with the now-empty bag, Eddie looked like he wanted to rip his own arm off just to throw a punch. His left hand gripped the bedrail, white-knuckled with rage.

"That was just a warning. Proof that I mean business."

I moved to the bedside and gestured to the tape across his mouth. "I'm taking this off now. If you scream, I swear the rest of your stash goes straight down the drain. Got it?"

He was still seething, but he gave a tight nod.

"Alright. Here we go."

I peeled the tape off and started walking toward the door. Just before I could open it, Eddie's voice stopped me.

"You just made a big mistake, Mr. Rodgen."

I didn't respond. But something about his tone — calm, cold, certain — followed me out the door and stuck with me all the way down the hall.

Chapter Fifty Nine

"What the heck were you doing with that cop?" I asked as we rode the elevator down.

"You couldn't tell? He was gay. I was flirting."

"Clint? You're married."

"Fuck you, loser. I was distracting him. That was the *plan*, remember?"

"Yeah, but you looked so natural. Like you enjoyed it."

Clint punched me in the arm. "It won't be the arm next time."

"Touchy," I said, rubbing my arm. "Anyway, it worked."

"So how'd he react when you flushed the fake Irony?"

"Oh, he was furious. Like, *terrifying* furious. Just before I left, he said I'd made a big mistake. Honestly, I think he might be right."

"Yeah, well, what else could we do?" Clint sighed as the elevator doors opened. We walked through the lobby and out into the parking lot.

"I know," I said. "Still… the way he said it—it didn't sound like a threat. It sounded like a promise."

"Fuck *him*," Clint snapped, loud enough that a few people turned to look. "I'm sick of this goddamn shit."

He rubbed his eyes, trying to calm down, but his breathing was heavy, his hands clenched.

"Sorry," he muttered after a moment. "This is just getting to me."

"I know," I said. "Me too. But we'll get through it. We *have* to. For our families."

At the mention of our families, Clint looked like he might break. His shoulders trembled, just for a second— but when he spoke again, his voice was steel.

"No. We didn't make a mistake. *He* did—when he fucked with me. And I'm gonna make him pay."

We didn't speak after that. We just got in the SUV and drove.

Chapter Sixty

From the hospital bed, Eddie picked up the phone and dialed Storm.

"Hi, Storm. How's your day going?"

There was a pause. "Uh… fine, Eddie. Why do you ask? Usually you skip straight to demanding blow jobs. What's with the small talk?"

"Believe me, it's not concern. I couldn't care less how your day's going." His voice turned sharp. "But you ought to be real concerned about mine—especially after what you did to me."

"What *I* did to you? What the hell are you talking about?"

"That *nod job* of yours! You broke my goddamn penis!"

There was silence—then Storm dropped the phone and burst out laughing.

"Bitch!!! Bitch!!! Do you fucking hear me?!! I'm gonna kill you," Eddie screamed before he slammed down the phone.

"Excuse me, Mr. Bretz. Is there a problem here?" the officer asked, stepping into the room with a practiced calm.

"Problem? What makes you think there's a problem, Officer Sunshine? Now do me a favor and get the hell out of my room."

"Sure, Mr. Bretz. No problem," the cop said as he pulled out his baton.

"Hey! What the hell are you doing?!"

With a quick flick of his wrist, the officer snapped the baton down on Eddie's pecker.

"Aaaaahhhhh!" Eddie screamed.

"Now I'll get out," the cop said calmly, turning to leave. A second later, he popped his head back through the door. "Oh, and please keep it down, sir. Don't make me use this again," he added, patting the baton for emphasis.

An hour later, Eddie was feeling well enough to pick up the phone again.

"Storm?"

Her laughter rang out immediately on the other end.

"You—" Eddie began to shout, then stopped himself. His voice dropped to a cold, deliberate tone. "Do not mock me. You're going to pay for this."

He ended the call and immediately dialed another number.

"Where is Irony?" he asked, teeth clenched and voice sharp.

"Eddie?" the voice on the other end replied, hesitant. "I just saw the news... someone forwarded me a link. There's a whole site blowing up about you. Brokenpenis.com. I—uh—didn't know a story like that could go viral so fast."

"I said where is *Irony*!" Eddie yelled into the phone.

The cop at the door poked his head in, narrowing his eyes at the outburst. Eddie immediately waved him off, mouthing *sorry* over and over like a desperate schoolboy. The officer stepped back into the hall, but not before holding up a single finger—a silent warning: *one more strike, and you're done.*

Back on the line, the voice sounded flustered. "I've been trying to reach you for an hour. Didn't you have your cell?"

"No, genius. It's probably still in my wrecked car. Now stop wasting time and tell me what's going on."

"We found Bozo and Finster."

"And the coke?"

"We're not sure yet. We were waiting to hear how you wanted to handle it."

Eddie's voice dropped an octave, simmering with disbelief. "*Handle it?* Are you fucking kidding me?" He sat up as far as his injuries would allow. "You grab them. You find the coke. If they don't talk, you *make* them talk. I don't care how. Beat it out of them, bury them in a hole, cut off a goddamn toe if you have to. Just get me back my *Irony*. Now. Is that clear enough for you? Or do you need a translator?"

Chapter Sixty One

When the three officers charged into the hotel room, they stumbled upon the most bizarre scene any of them had ever witnessed — and that included the time Officer Tulber was called to investigate a disturbance at the West Gornin Chapter of the Sadomasochism Society.

Finster and Bozo were in the middle of recording the first half-assed demo tape for their band *Clownophobia*. Bozo was howling into a karaoke mic, while Finster banged on the table and made electric guitar noises with his mouth. Both wore thick face paint, with their trademark construction hats strapped tight to their gasoline-soaked heads.

"Freeze! Hands up! Against the wall, now!" Tulber barked.

"If this is about those tranquilizers, they were for my kitty," Finster said, stumbling. "She's got cancer."

"Shut up and move," snapped Officer Wilson, shoving him toward the wall.

As the officers began to frisk the clowns, a wave of fumes filled the room — pure gasoline, radiating from their heads like deranged air fresheners.

"What the hell is that smell?" Officer Malor asked, recoiling. "You two huffing gas?"

"You want a hit?" Bozo offered, cracking up as Finster joined in with a snort.

"Jesus," muttered Tulber. "Shut up, freaks."

"Yes sir," Finster said meekly, still smiling. "But is there a law against this?" He pointed to his hat.

"There's about to be," Tulber growled. "Now face the wall."

As Officers Wilson and Malor continued frisking them, Tulber gestured to the headgear. "Get those hats off and rip those tubes out of their noses."

"Ow!" they shouted in unison as the duct tape tore.

"I said shut up. I'm not the one who strapped hoses to your faces," Tulber snapped.

"He's clean," Wilson reported after patting down Bozo.

"So's this one," Malor said, stepping back from Finster. He held up one of the reeking helmets. "What do you want me to do with these?"

"Put them by my car," Tulber said. "*Not* in the car. We'll need a bag. That shit'll stink up my ride for a month."

As he turned toward the door, a fourth officer stepped into the room.

"About time you got here," Tulber snapped.

"When you gotta go, you gotta go," Officer Kegin muttered as he stuck a cigarette between his lips.

No one in the room was quick enough to stop what happened next. The moment Kegin's thumb clicked his lighter, the spark ignited not only the propane from the flame but also the heavy gasoline vapors lingering in the room.

A sudden *whoosh* of rushing air filled the space as fire shot out in every direction. The three other officers were singed and staggered back, momentarily stunned—but Kegin took the full brunt of the blast. His forehead practically melted, and he screamed in shock and agony as flames raced up his shirt.

Panicked, he flailed and spun, accidentally igniting the curtains. The others sprang into action, tackling him onto the bed and smothering the flames with pillows, blankets—anything they could grab.

Remarkably, the clowns stood untouched. Bozo and Finster exchanged a glance, realizing at the same time: this was their moment.

Without a word, they slipped into the bathroom. Finster climbed halfway out the small window when he noticed Bozo hesitate.

"What are you doing?" Finster hissed. "Let's go!"

"I'll be right back," Bozo whispered—and vanished.

Back in the flaming chaos of the room, Bozo crept low across the floor, staying just out of sight. The officers were still frantically dealing with the fire. Bozo reached over, grabbed both hard hats, and bolted back toward the bathroom.

Out of the corner of his eye, Officer Malor caught the movement. "Hey! Get back here!" he shouted, giving chase.

Bozo dove for the window, but Malor lunged just in time, grabbing the clown's right foot.

"Help!" Bozo cried as he flailed. Finster, still halfway out, grabbed both of Bozo's arms and pulled. It turned into a bizarre tug-of-war—cop versus clown.

Bozo kicked wildly. One shoe flew off and nailed Malor in the face, snapping his head back. The officer held on, teeth gritted.

Then—*pop!* The shoe slipped. Malor toppled backward, crashing onto the bathroom floor, as Bozo tumbled out the window into Finster's arms.

Outside, gasping for breath, Finster tossed the hard hats to Bozo.

"Jesus, you're crazy."

"Maybe," Bozo said, slipping his hat back on. "But now we're back in business."

Chapter Sixty Two

W hat do you mean they *got away?*" Eddie growled into the phone. "What the hell am I paying you guys for?"

"I'm sorry, Eddie. It was kind of... unavoidable. A cop was on fire at the time."

"*On fire?* What the hell are you talking about?"

The man on the other end hadn't been at the hotel, but he'd heard enough details to give a full account. As he finished relaying the chaos—clowns, gasoline vapors, exploding hats, and a flaming police officer—there was a long pause.

"Eddie? You there?"

"Yeah," Eddie finally answered, stunned. "So you're telling me Finster and Bozo are off somewhere together... huffing gasoline and forming a clown band?" He gritted his teeth. "Goddamn it! I *knew* I couldn't trust that Bozo."

Just then, the hospital door slammed open. The cop on duty stormed in.

"No, no! Please! It wasn't—"

Whack!

The phone hit the floor. On the other end, the caller winced as he heard a sickening thud, followed by muffled groans.

"Eddie? Eddie, are you alright?"

No response — only low, pain-soaked moaning. Several minutes later, the phone was picked up again.

"Jesus Christ, that hurt." Eddie's voice was ragged. "You've gotta get me out of this hospital. That cop is a fucking psychopath."

"What do you mean?"

"Don't worry about it," Eddie snapped. "Just come and get me. *Do whatever it takes*, you hear me? And make it fast. We still haven't found the coke, and I'm running out of time."

Chapter Sixty Three

After Clint's meltdown in the hospital parking lot, I figured it was best to give him a few minutes to cool off. Twenty minutes later, the silence was unbearable.

"Well, we've planted the first seed — pardon the pun," I said, trying to lighten the mood.

Clint didn't bite. "Did I ever tell you I hate puns?"

He was still simmering. I went with calm logic.

"Look, Clint. I know you're upset. So am I. But this thing isn't over — not by a long shot. We've got to hold it together, or we're both screwed."

He nodded, barely.

"I know. It's just..." He stared through the windshield like he was trying to see something he'd left behind. "Being at the hospital... I started thinking about when Amy died. My daughter. And then I thought about my wife, my son. And how I couldn't handle losing another kid."

I opened my mouth, but he stopped me with a hand.

"Don't," he said. "First, it's not gonna help. Second, you're right—we've got to keep our heads. I promise it won't happen again."

I tried again—same result. A raised palm. Silence.

This one only lasted a few minutes. Then Clint, voice lighter, broke it.

"That really was a dumb pun, you know."

"What do you mean? 'Plant a seed'? *The Seed*? C'mon, that's layered."

"Oh, I got it."
"Try not to sound so thrilled."
"I told you. I *hate* puns."
"Even a top-shelf one like that?"
"I'd rather talk politics."
"Alright, alright. No politics, no puns. Deal?"

"Deal." He shifted in his seat, more focused now. "So—'phase two,' huh? I say we give him till tomorrow. Then we visit again."

"Yeah. Let it marinate. He's probably crawling out of his skin already. He strikes me as a control freak. And right now? He's got no control. We're the puppet masters—he's the puppet."

Clint cracked a thin smile. "Let's just hope the strings hold."

"All this over a couple lines of coke."

"But Eddie doesn't know that," I said. "He thinks we've got all five kilos—and that we flushed some of it right in front of him."

Clint grinned. "That's the beauty of it."

"You ever do coke?"

"Sure. Haven't you?"

"Yeah. Tried just about everything once. Coke never really did it for me, though. I've always been more of a weed guy. Still am, now and then."

"Funny you mention that," Clint said, reaching into the ashtray. He pulled out a fat joint, like it was a magic trick he'd been saving for just the right moment.

He held it up. "Spark it. I could use a little unwind."

"Well damn, Clint," I said, grinning. "Didn't have you pegged for a stoner."

"Occasional stoner," he clarified. "Once a week. Twice if the world's falling apart."

"Yeah, same. I gave it up for years, then a friend convinced me I was missing out. He was right. I mean, what's the harm?"

I lit the joint, took a hit, and immediately burst into a coughing fit.

"Still cough when you smoke?" Clint asked, amused.

"Yep. Every time," I wheezed. "Like clockwork. I haven't learned."

We passed it back and forth as he drove, the smoke curling into the air like it had somewhere better to be. By the time we hit the hotel parking lot, only a tiny roach was left. It burned my fingers.

"Ow," I muttered, flicking it out the window.

Clint chuckled. "Man. I am *stoned*."

"Yeah. Ain't it great?"

He gave me that slow, glazed-over nod. "Yep. Sure is."

We staggered out of the car and wandered back to our room. Ten minutes later, the munchies hit like a freight train, so we crossed the street and grabbed a greasy pizza and a twelve-pack of Dogfish IPA.

Back in the room, we demolished the pizza like we hadn't eaten in days.

The beer was a different story. We were both snoring into our second bottle.

Chapter Sixty Four

Finster and Bozo lay flattened beneath a dented Ford Taurus in the hotel parking lot, face-down in an oily puddle, reeking of gasoline and stale fries. From their vantage point, they saw the feet of Officers Tulber and Malor pacing in erratic circles, boots slapping asphalt as they shouted over one another.

"Where the fuck did they go?" Tulber barked.

"I don't know! One second they're at the window, next—they're *gone*."

"Jesus H. Christ. We are *so* screwed. What a goddamn clown show."

From beneath the car, Bozo snorted.

"Shh!" Finster hissed, smacking him.

"At least we got their vehicle," Malor offered. "Hard to miss two clowns wandering around in broad daylight. Somebody's bound to call it in."

Tulber rubbed his temples like he was trying to erase the last twenty minutes of his life. "Yeah, I guess. Not sure how much that'll matter to *you-know-who* back at the station. But sure—small wins."

He pointed toward the parking lot exit.

"Go back to the squad car. Call an ambulance for Kegin, put out an APB on our favorite circus act, and get that Subaru impounded."

"You got it, boss." Malor turned to go, then hesitated.

"Sorry, boss. I really thought I had 'em."

Tulber sighed. "Don't beat yourself up, Chuck. Not your fault."

He swept his arm at the still-smoldering second-floor window.

"What the hell are you supposed to do when a whole goddamn room explodes?"

Chapter Sixty Five

Underneath the Taurus, Finster and Bozo decided it was as good a place as any to catch some shuteye. Before dozing off, they re-secured their plastic hardhats and took one last deep pull from the empty gas cans, inhaling whatever fumes still lingered.

An hour later, their nap ended with a loud *rumble*—the car above them had started to move.

Bozo, half-asleep and fully disoriented, didn't react fast enough. The front tire rolled backward over his right hand.

"AAAAAGH!" he shrieked, instinctively bolting upright—and immediately cracking his forehead on the undercarriage.

Finster startled awake just in time to slam his own skull into the front axle. Both men collapsed back into the puddle of oil and shame, moaning in cartoonish unison.

The car came to a sudden halt. The driver cracked the door open, leaned out while still seated, and peered underneath. What he saw were two grimy clowns writhing beneath the sedan like cursed grease monkeys.

"What the hell?" the driver muttered, eyes wide. "Are you guys... okay?"

Bozo, eyes watering and nostrils flaring, stumbled to his feet with his one good hand and *charged*.

He managed to get both hands — well, one hand and a flailing flipper — around the driver's neck before the man screamed, shoved Bozo back, and pulled the door closed. Tires screeched as the car jerked into reverse, peeling out.

"Freaks!" the driver yelled as he sped off.

Bozo extended a middle finger — left hand, uninjured, proud.

Finster picked himself up and brushed gravel off his face. "So... now what?"

"You check the front. See if the cops are gone. I'll scope out back."

Five minutes later, they reconvened behind the hotel.

"They're gone. So's the car," Finster reported.

Bozo shrugged. "No biggie. It didn't have gas anyway. We'll hot-wire another."

Then he froze. "Oh... shit."

Finster narrowed his eyes. "What?"

"The *Irony*. It was in the trunk."

Finster's face fell. "You *left* it in the trunk?"

"I forgot! I meant to blackmail The Seed with it, but then we started Clownophobia, and, well... I had new dreams. Music. Pornography. Riches."

Finster stared at him.

Bozo smiled like a man who'd just invented fire. "We don't *need* coke to succeed. We've got a kazoo, a snare drum, and an artistic vision."

"Were you ever going to tell me about the *Irony*?"

Bozo considered this. "Eventually. Probably."

"Like I said, I didn't even think abou   t it. We've got a bright future, man. But yeah—if it came to that, of *course* you'd get a cut. How could I screw over the guy who invented lesbian clown pornos? You're my bro."

Bozo's sincerity hit Finster like a freight train. He started to cry.

Bozo joined in.

The two clowns embraced, sobbing in full greasepaint under the midday sun. After a few long, sniffly minutes— during which several bystanders slowed down to gawk— they finally pulled apart, high-fived, and yelled, "Wooooooooooo!"

"Now," Finster said, wiping his eyes, "let's go find us a car."

"Not yet," Bozo replied, fishing a hotel key from his pants. "We've got unfinished business."

They opened the door to their room and froze.

The place looked like it had lost a fight with a flamethrower. Scorched walls, overturned beds, drawers gutted, and debris strewn like a looted circus tent.

But against the far wall, miraculously upright and only *partially* melted, stood the object of Bozo's affection.

"Cool," he said, walking over to pick up the charred karaoke machine. "Let's get outta here."

Chapter Sixty Six

It didn't take long for the clowns to steal another vehicle. Lacking even the faintest concept of subtlety, they hot-wired a bright yellow Hummer.

"I guess we need to find another hotel," Finster said, gripping the oversized wheel like a tank commander.

"Yeah, but first thing's first," Bozo replied, tapping his temple. "Fill 'er up! Wooooooooo!"

"Wooooooooo!" Finster echoed, laying on the horn as they barreled down a residential street doing fifty in a twenty-five.

"Yo, check this out," Bozo said, pointing at the PA system embedded in the dashboard.

"Sweet. Fire that thing up."

Bozo grabbed the handset and twisted the knob. "Testing! One, two, three."

The resulting squawk startled pedestrians and commuters alike. Faces froze. Coffee was spilled. A small dog yelped. The clowns howled with laughter.

When they finally caught their breath, Finster veered to the curb and threw it in park.

"Yo! First gig! *Clownophobia Live!* Let's go! Sing, man!"

Bozo cleared his throat and leaned into the mic. "I don't like Mondays... no Tuesdays... no Wednesdays... no Thuuuuursdays..."

To their astonishment, people stopped. Listened. A few even nodded along.

When Bozo finished, they clapped.

One particularly excited woman—missing a leg—ripped off her prosthetic, waved it triumphantly in the air, and shrieked, "Encore!"

Bozo bowed and launched into a second rendition of Finster's anti-weekday anthem.

By the time he hit the last note, a full crowd had gathered around the Hummer. Despite the greasepaint and construction helmets, most of them were entranced.

"We're Clownophobia!" Finster bellowed, grabbing the mic. "Look for our record soon! That's Clown-o-pho-bia!"

He chanted it.

"Clown-o-pho-bia! Clown-o-pho-bia!"

The crowd joined in. Someone produced a lighter. Someone else started beatboxing.

An obviously stoned teenager pushed forward. "Yo, dude... can I get an autograph?"

"Of course," Bozo said, puffing out his chest. "What's your name?"

"Getty. G-E-T-T-Y. That's my nickname."

"Got it," Bozo said as he signed the package of Joker rolling papers.

"Dude, what's with the hats?" Getty asked. "I get the makeup—kinda cool, really. But the helmets?"

"Gasoline, bro. It's all about gasoline."

"Huh. I thought I smelled something." Getty grinned. "Thanks for the autograph. You guys rock."

He held up a hand. Bozo smacked it proudly.

As the crowd finally dispersed, Finster and Bozo stared at each other in stunned silence.

"Holy shit," Finster said. "Clownophobia, baby. That was *amazing*."

"How did I sound?" Bozo asked. "Was I a little flat on that last note?"

"Are you kidding me? Did you *see* that crowd? They lost their minds."

Bozo beamed. "I *was* pretty good, huh?"

"Good?" Finster shoved him playfully. "You were fucking *awesome*."

Bozo tapped his helmet. "Let's go get fucked up."

Finster grinned and floored the accelerator. The Hummer roared forward, tires screaming. They settled into eighty, riding high on adrenaline and fumes.

Up ahead, a gas station appeared on their left.

"Gas!" Bozo shouted.

They were going way too fast.

Finster slammed the brakes. The Hummer screeched, laying down two thick rubber lines across the asphalt. They overshot the entrance entirely.

"Hang on," Finster muttered.

He let off the brakes and yanked the wheel hard left. The Hummer veered, launched off the curb, caught air, and slammed back down in the parking lot with a bone-rattling thud.

Finster braked hard again, bringing the beast to a stop three feet from the gas pumps.

He grabbed the PA mic. "Fill 'er up, please."

The gas station attendant stormed out of the kiosk, glaring.

"What the hell's your problem, pal?"

Finster clicked the PA again. "No problem here, mi amigo. Eighty-seven octane, please."

The attendant flinched. "Turn that thing off, jackass—I can *hear* you."

"Sorry," Finster said—still through the PA.

"Didn't you hear me? Cut the loudspeaker."

Finster tossed the handset onto the seat. "Sorry, dude. Can you fill it up, please?"

"Cash or credit?" the attendant asked, still glaring.

"Credit!" Bozo shouted, leaning across Finster and waving his Mastercard like it was a backstage pass.

As the Hummer gulped down fuel, the clowns debated how to refill their hats. Past experience told them the guy wouldn't just hand over gasoline for recreational huffing. After a few minutes of deep, possibly brain-damaged contemplation, they landed on a plan.

"One-gallon container?" Finster asked.

Bozo shook his head. "Nah. Go big."

Bozo reached for the PA mic again. "Excuse me, bud—"

Finster slashed his finger across his throat in warning. "No PA, remember?"

Then, to the attendant: "Sorry about that. Hey—you got one of those gas cans? For, uh... lawn mowers and stuff?"

"One gallon or five?" the man grunted.

The clowns exchanged a look.

"Big one," Bozo said. "Fill it up. Put it on the card."

The attendant didn't reply. He just turned and walked back toward the building.

A few minutes later, he reemerged with a five-gallon gas can.

Bozo's eyes lit up. "Dude. We are gonna *par-tay*."

"Wooooooooooo!" he howled—into the PA.

The attendant froze, then shot Bozo a lethal glare. But Bozo stared right back, eyes wild, smile wide. The look of a man who *wants* to be banned from public spaces.

Sensing the guy's discomfort, Bozo leaned into it.

"Hurry up, bitch!" he shouted into the mic. "Don't you know who we are? We're *Clownophobia*! And we're gonna be *huge*! Do you hear me? *HUGE!* Look at me when I'm talking to you! Hey! Hey! I said look at me!"

The attendant didn't respond. He just finished fueling with the haunted efficiency of someone trying to avoid eye contact with a bear.

When he was done, he flung Bozo's credit card through the driver's side window and sprinted back to the building. The door locked behind him with a loud *click*.

Chapter Sixty Seven

At the station, Bill Daylay paced back and forth like a man rehearsing for his own funeral. Three hours ago, he'd broken the news about the explosion at the hotel—and that Finster and Bozo had vanished. Now, after combing through the wrecked motel room and the impounded Subaru, there was still no sign of *Irony*.

He knew the conversation ahead wasn't going to be pleasant. But he picked up the phone anyway.

"Eddie? It's me."

"Yeah? You better have some good news. Where's my coke? And when are you getting me the hell outta this hospital?"

"Unfortunately… we haven't found it. The room and the car were clean."

There was a pause. Then Eddie's voice dropped into that soft, terrifying register.

"Bill. I know I've told you the story of how I met The Mantis. You remember that fucking story, Bill?"

"I do," Bill said quickly. "And I get the message. But we're doing everything we can down here. Give us a break."

"Well your *everything* isn't good enough, is it? Maybe it's time we stopped all those little kickbacks you've been enjoying from The Seed. Hell, maybe we don't need you at all."

"Eddie—"

"If that coke stays missing, the money's gonna be the *least* of your concerns. Your ass is on the line same as mine."

"I know that, Eddie, I—"

"Then what the *fuck* are you doing?" Eddie bellowed.

At that moment, the hospital room door creaked open. A cop stepped inside, smacking his baton rhythmically against his palm like he was warming up for a beating.

"Is everything alright in here, sir?"

Eddie didn't miss a beat. "Just the TV, officer. I shut it off. Sorry for the language."

The cop gave him a skeptical once-over, eyes flicking to the phone. He didn't buy it—but he also didn't feel like starting trouble. He gave a nod and backed out of the room.

Eddie brought the phone back to his ear.

"Bill? Get your ass down here. I told you that three hours ago, didn't I?"

"I've been a little busy," Bill snapped. "Chasing two clown freaks and a drug that doesn't officially exist. You wanna cut me some slack?"

"No, I don't. You're not the one with a broken dick and a rent-a-cop outside the door playing whack-a-mole with a nightstick. And I'm done with the freakin' excuses. You and I are gonna find that coke *together*. Now for the last time—get me the hell out of this hospital."

Chapter Sixty Eight

In the morning, Clint and I each made calls to our families. We kept it vague—no specifics about where they were, just in case The Seed had someone monitoring our lines. But there was no sign they'd been traced. Everyone was safe, sound, and, surprisingly, enjoying their forced vacations.

When we hung up, I turned to Clint.

"Who exactly forced you to kidnap me? And aren't they wondering why you haven't called yet?"

Clint scratched his head. "Yeah... I've kinda been putting that off. Right now, they don't know anything. But once I make that call, the cat's out of the bag. Guess I should probably do it this morning."

I nodded, and he continued.

"As for who's behind it—my contact at The Seed is a guy named Wendall Hanes. Big guy. Looks like he was built out of leftover gym equipment. But he's just the muscle. Everything I've been ordered to do traces back to one man."

He paused.

"A guy they call The Mantis."

I gave him a look. "The Mantis?"

Clint nodded. "Yeah. Want to know how he got that name?"

He told me.

By the time he finished, I had a serious case of the willies. Getting back to my family was still the top priority, but avoiding anal trauma at the hands of a guy called *The Mantis* had now secured a firm second place.

"Well," I said, "now I understand why you've been dodging that call."

"Yeah. And just to make it worse, rumor has it the guy's packing a full foot. Like, *horse-level*."

I blinked. "So what—you're saying you might be able to handle six inches? That's what I've got. Wanna give it a try?"

Clint rolled his eyes. "Screw you, jackass."

"I knew you were a homophobe," I said. "You know a lot of people with that phobia turn out to be closet cases, right?"

"It's just an expression, asshole," Clint shot back. "For your information, I've got no problem with anyone—gay, straight, bi, black, white, whatever. I learned a long time ago you can't judge people by how they look or what goes on in their bedroom. Truth is, what two consenting adults do has exactly zero impact on my life. So why should I care?"

He paused, then added, "And for the record, I have two gay friends. I've even been to a gay bar. *Twice.*"

"Now we're learning something," I said with a grin.

Clint threw up his hands. "I can't win."

"Nope. You can't. But hey, I've had my fun. You making that call?"

Clint flopped back on the bed and pulled out his phone. As he scrolled for the number, my stomach gave an ominous churn. I sprinted to the bathroom.

Thanks to my boss-level shitting efficiency, I was done in under five minutes. When I stepped out, I caught Clint mid-conversation.

"Where have I been?" he snapped into the phone. "I'll *tell* you where I've been—dumping your damn coke down the toilet. Hello?" He paused, frowned. "Hello? Wendall? You still there?"

He glanced at me, confused. "He didn't hang up. But he's not answering."

I shrugged. No idea what to make of it.

Then, a beat later, we both got our answer.

Clint stiffened, lifted the phone again. "No... I don't. I have no clue who you are."

In the next instant, the color drained from Clint's face.

I didn't need to ask, but I did anyway. "What is it?"

Clint slowly placed a hand over the mouthpiece, eyes wide.

"It's The Mantis," he whispered.

Chapter Sixty Nine

"What took you so long?" Eddie snapped.

"Sorry, Eddie. There was an accident on the way," Bill Daylay said, stepping inside. "Didn't think blowing through a crash scene would look great."

"More bullshit. Can we go now?"

"Yeah, I talked to Joey out front," Bill said, nodding toward the door. "We've got everything lined up. You know he's gay, right?"

"What?! That cop's a homo? The same one who's been tenderizing my pecker with a baton?"

Bill nodded just as Joey entered the room.

"Bill, can you get this asshole outta here?" Joey said, deadpan. "I'm tired of coming in just to discipline him."

"Sure, Joey. We're on our way," Bill replied. Joey left without another word.

"Eddie, calm the hell down," Bill said under his breath. "I'm trying to keep this low-profile. We don't need a scene in a hospital."

"What—are you afraid of that fudgepacker? If my dick wasn't broken, I'd beat the living shit out of him."

"Yeah, well... I wouldn't." Bill gestured toward the door. "Joey's a third-degree black belt in Taekwondo. And he doesn't need a baton to put you down."

Eddie scoffed. "Taekwon-don't give a shit. He'll find out how useful that crap is when I shoot him in the face."

"Please, Eddie. Just drop it," Bill said, pointing to the wheelchair. "Let's get you outta here."

"Fine," Eddie grunted, motioning toward the door. "But I won't forget that prick. And I won't forget about Storm either. Fucking nod job."

"I have no idea what you're talking about," Bill muttered. "And I'm not sure I wanna know."

He started to help Eddie up, but hesitated. The man looked like roadkill with a pulse.

"You sure about this, Eddie? You've got a broken arm. A broken... other thing. Maybe stay here a little longer. We *will* find Irony—I promise."

"Put me in the goddamn chair. Your promises are garbage. You haven't found the coke, have you?"

"Eddie—"

"*Now,*" he barked.

The door swung open. Joey stepped in, billy club in hand, his patience clearly gone.

"Bill," he said, voice tight with frustration. "I've had it with your friend. He's begging for another lesson."

"Screw you, faggot!" Eddie screamed.

Joey's eyes narrowed. "What did you say? You think it hurt last time?" He stormed forward.

Bill stepped between them. "Joey—wait. Just wait. The guy's a complete asshole, I get it. But let me get him out of here. He's not worth it."

"Asshole? He's the—"

"Shut up, Eddie," Bill barked. "Just shut the hell up." Then to Joey, calmer: "Come on. Do me a favor."

Joey pointed the baton and backed toward the door. "Five minutes. If he's not out of here by then..." He let the threat hang, twirling the club as he disappeared.

Bill hurried over, scooped Eddie up, and dropped him into the wheelchair.

"Aaaahhhh!" Eddie shrieked.

"Sorry."

"You know my pecker's broke," he whined. "Did you do that on purpose?"

"Of course not," Bill said, lying as he wheeled him toward the exit.

Chapter Seventy

After refueling both the Hummer and their hard hats, the clowns drove to Bozo's house. By the time they staggered through the front door an hour and a half later, they were well on their way to being plastered.

"The video equipment's down here," Bozo said, leading the way into the basement.

"Nice setup. Now we just need a couple of babes. Who do you usually get for your movies?"

"I've got a few regulars," Bozo said. "Faces aren't anything special, but once they put on the clown make-up? Total transformation. Honestly, it's weirdly hot."

"Yeah? But are they into each other?" Finster asked, raising an eyebrow.

"With enough money, they'd probably hook up with a scarecrow," Bozo smirked.

"Guess they already did — considering they slept with you," Finster shot back.

Bozo laughed. "Fair. I know I'm no catch. But hey, speaking of which... you ever think about being in one of these films? I bet you'd do pretty well on camera."

"I dunno. Depends on what these 'actresses' look like. If it sparks anything, maybe."

"Oh, you'll be sparked," Bozo assured him. "Tyler's the real star. Full sad clown aesthetic—tears, smeared mascara, the works. There's something hauntingly sexy about it."

"Huh," Finster said, unsure if he was intrigued or disturbed.

"And then there's Sienna. Her make-up's a mess, but... she's got other talents. Let's just say she's enthusiastic."

"You're painting quite the picture," Finster muttered.

"I'm just saying, I'm getting worked up just thinking about it."

"Cool it, Romeo. You're not aiming that thing anywhere near me."

"No worries," Bozo said, heading toward his bookshelf. He pulled down a DVD titled *White Make-up and Pink Vagina.*

"Yo! If you wanna check out any of those videos, go for it. DVD player's in the other room. If I were you, I'd start with *Clowns Gone Wild II.* Tyler looks incredible in that one. Solid strokin' material."

"Alright," Finster called back. "Might as well see what I'm getting myself into. Though seriously—who the hell still watches DVDs? And hey, if the door's closed, knock first, alright?"

"No problemo, bro. But if I were you, I wouldn't be so modest. You do realize who's gonna be behind the camera, right?"

"I know, I know," Finster muttered, now more unsure than ever about this whole clown porn detour. "Just let me masturbate in peace, please."

Chapter Seventy One

So, what did he say?" I asked as Clint ended the call. He stared ahead for a moment, then looked at me. "The first thing he said was my address. Then my wife's name. Then my boy's. And then... he said, 'You already know what it feels like to lose a loved one, don't you?'"

I didn't respond right away.

"I don't think I would've said much either," I finally muttered.

"I didn't say a word," Clint said. "But he just kept repeating their names. Marietta. Tommy. Amy. Over and over. And his voice—Jesus—it was so calm. Like he *enjoyed* it. It creeped me the fuck out."

"And then you hung up?"

He nodded. "And then I hung up."

I tried to keep things light. "Well... could've been worse."

Clint gave me a hard look. "You didn't hear him, Mike. He sounded like he'd take *pleasure* in killing them. And I'm sure he'd do the same to your family too."

"But we already knew that, didn't we?" I said, more for myself than him. "We knew The Seed would use our families. But they're safe. They're having a decent time, even. We've got the only leverage that matters—*Irony*. We just have to stick to the plan."

"You're right," Clint said quietly. "I know you're right. It's just... his voice. I can't shake it."

"Try. Just for now," I said, patting his arm. "Besides, we need to head back to the hospital."

Clint nodded, and we headed for the door.

In the car, I tried to steer Clint's mind off the doom spiral.

"Hey—ya know what? All these hospital runs and I haven't once mentioned the problem with my ball sac. I must be getting used to it."

"That's great," Clint said flatly.

"No, seriously. It hasn't really hurt the last couple days. Maybe it's healing." Curious now, I discreetly reached down for a little exploratory check.

"*Fuck!*" I screamed.

Clint slammed on the brakes. "What the hell happened?!"

"It's still there!" I winced. "I pinched it. Too hard."

"Why the hell would you *pinch it?*" he shouted.

"I don't know!" I groaned. "It wasn't hurting—I thought maybe it was going away. I was wrong."

"Next time you start inspecting your balls, can you at least wait until I'm *not* in the car?"

"Sure," I said. "But now that we're on the topic—what do you think about me getting this thing looked at after we check in with Eddie? Maybe it's a quick outpatient deal."

"Yeah, I don't care," Clint replied. "I'll swing by the mall, kill a couple hours. Call me when you're done."

"Perfect. Now—Eddie. Just another repeat performance, right?"

"That's the plan. Same song, second verse."

"You know what that means, don't you?" I said, glancing sideways.

Clint squinted. "No. What?"

"Remember the cop? The gay one? This time you might have to do more than flirt. Maybe a little maintenance-closet action. Or a bathroom BJ. Whataya think?"

Clint groaned. "Jesus. Why is *everything* with you about balls and blowjobs?"

"Hey," I said. "We all cope in different ways."

"I think you're an asshole," Clint said.

"Asshole? Whataya mean?" I asked. "Are you saying you wouldn't take one for the team—do whatever's necessary to complete the mission?"

"Enough of your pep talk bullshit. If anyone's blowing that cop, it's gonna be you."

"No can do. Roles are already defined. I'm the orderly—note the outfit and bedpan. *You,* my friend, are the distraction. How you choose to distract him is entirely up to you. I merely offered creative suggestions."

"I've got a suggestion," Clint muttered. "Go fuck yourself."

"Such language. And to think I was so impressed with your manners when you first kidnapped me."

"That just shows how annoying you are. Before I met you, I hardly cursed at all."

We pulled into the hospital lot and parked. As we walked toward the entrance, Clint asked, "You remember the room number?"

"424. Maybe if you didn't smoke so much dope, you'd remember, too."

"What is this, break-my-balls day? Speaking of balls, I hope they cut off more than that pimple on your sac. Wouldn't be a big loss to your wife—*Mr. Teeny Weenie.*"

I was still laughing as we pushed through the sliding doors, but inside, my mood turned cold. Just as Clint had dreaded calling The Mantis, I wasn't exactly thrilled about round two with Eddie Bretz. His last words still echoed in my skull:

"You just made a big mistake, Mr. Rodgen."

As we rode the elevator up to the fourth floor, Clint seemed to pick up on my shift.

"So, honey," he said in an exaggerated lisp, loud enough for everyone to hear, "what time should I pick you up tonight?"

I turned to him in horror. The other passengers stared.

"Do you have a problem?" Clint said, scanning the crowd. "This is a *private* conversation."

No one answered, but everyone turned sharply forward, suddenly fascinated by the elevator door.

"What the hell are you doing?" I hissed through clenched teeth.

Clint stroked my arm and leaned in. "Honey... you're not still mad about last night, are you? I thought you *liked* me on top."

Mercifully, the elevator dinged and stopped at the fourth floor. In what could only be described as either a cosmic coincidence or a massive outbreak of homophobia, every single passenger got out.

Clint and I stayed behind. I gave him a shove and muttered, "Asshole," as I held the door to keep it open.

And that's when I heard a familiar voice call out behind us.

"Hold that, please."

I poked my head around the corner and saw Bill Daylay pushing Eddie Bretz in a wheelchair.

My brain did somersaults. Why the hell was *this* cop—the same guy who was so helpful when I found a dead body on my kitchen floor — escorting *Eddie Bretz* out of a hospital? What was he doing here, twenty miles outside his jurisdiction? None of it made sense.

But I didn't have time to work it out. Before Bill spotted me, I ducked behind Clint, yanking the back of his shirt and pulling him into the corner with me. I threw my hands over my face just as the elevator doors slid open again.

"Thanks for holding it," Bill said casually, pressing the button for the ground floor.

Clint nodded, still processing what he was seeing. He didn't recognize Bill, but Eddie? That face had been splashed all over the tabloids — *Man With Broken Penis Charged With DUI.*

As we descended together, Bill glanced back at us.

"What's with him?" he asked, jerking a thumb in my direction.

Clint slipped effortlessly into character, using his best exaggerated lisp. "My honey? He's a little upset with me. We had a bit of a lover's quarrel."

Bill gave an awkward nod and turned back around.

Eddie, of course, couldn't let the moment pass.

"What is this — a fag convention?" he muttered. "First that baton-swinging cop, now these two queers. Jesus. Get me the hell outta here."

Bill turned again, looking mortified. "Sorry about that. He's... recovering."

Clint didn't miss a beat. "No problem, officer. We're used to it. Comments like that usually come from closet cases. Isn't it about time you came out?" he added, patting Eddie on the shoulder.

Behind him, I jabbed a finger into Clint's back — *shut the fuck up,* I begged silently.

"Are you calling me a homo, you rump ranger?!" Eddie shouted, practically vibrating with rage.

The elevator dinged, and Bill wasted no time wheeling him out. "Sorry," he muttered over his shoulder, pushing the chair faster now, trying to calm the irate drug dealer.

"Was he calling me a fag?! Was he?!"

"No, Eddie. Just drop it, alright? Let's go."

As they veered left, Clint and I slipped out to the right.

"That's the cop I told you about," I whispered. "The one who helped with the body in my kitchen. What the hell is he doing with *Eddie Bretz*?"

Clint didn't answer, but he didn't need to. We both knew something was seriously off.

Then I heard it — my name.

"Mike!"

It was instinct. I turned. Fifty feet away, Bill Daylay was staring straight at me.

The way he looked — the forced calm, the hesitation — it told me everything I needed to know.

"Go," I said to Clint, shoving him forward. "Go, now."

"Mike! Stop! Mike!" Bill called after us.

We didn't stop.

We tore down the hallway, weaving through corridors like rats in a maze. The hospital felt endless, a fluorescent nightmare of linoleum and panic. Finally, we spotted a side exit.

Bursting through the doors, we looked back — no sign of Bill.

Still, we didn't slow down.

Across the parking lot. Through four lanes of traffic. Dodging honking cars and angry drivers. Then into the mall lot, feet slapping asphalt, lungs on fire.

Finally, we reached the entrance.

Sweat-drenched and gasping, we stumbled inside.

Chapter Seventy Two

"Why the fuck did you leave me here?" Eddie screamed. "I told you I wanted out of this hellhole, didn't I?"

Bill Daylay raised a hand, signaling Eddie to be quiet. With the other, he held a phone to his ear.

"Excuse me, officer," said the woman at the front desk. "You can't use that here. Cell phones are prohibited. I'll have to ask you to turn that off, please."

"Go ahead and arrest me," Bill said without looking at her.

He continued talking for several minutes, ignoring both Eddie and the increasingly annoyed receptionist. When he finally hung up, he offered the woman a quick, half-hearted apology.

"Sorry. Life-or-death situation."

Then he leaned down and whispered into Eddie's ear. "It was him. The guy who has Irony — Mike Rodgen."

Eddie looked up and grinned. "Then what the fuck are we standing here for?"

Outside, Bill explained his plan. He'd already contacted the three other officers who were also on The Seed's payroll. Kegin would've helped too, but he was still recovering from the hotel fire.

They didn't know what kind of vehicle Mike and his companion were driving, but Bill was confident they hadn't yet left the hospital lot. With Tulber, Malor, and Wilson's help, they'd check every license plate. Between their access to DMV records, hospital security footage, and the description of the man with Rodgen, Bill was sure they could ID him within the hour.

"So we'll have his name, his vehicle, and a description. That should go a long way toward getting your coke back."

But Eddie seemed fixated on one thing.

"I thought he was married. Are you telling me that guy's a fudgepacker?"

Bill sighed. It took a while, but he finally half-convinced Eddie that it was just an act.

"If you say so," Eddie muttered. "But the way that guy touched me in the elevator? He sure seemed like a queer to me."

Chapter Seventy Three

Back at Bozo's place, the two clowns lounged on oppo-site ends of the couch, breathing heavy and still half-baked. Post-orgasmic and giddy, they debriefed.

"So what'd you think?" Bozo asked.

Finster exhaled slowly. "Gotta admit—it turned me on. Who knew a woman in full clown makeup could be that sexy? I'm a believer, Bozo. I'm a believer."

Bozo grinned. "You saying you might be ready to shoot some pornos?"

"Damn straight. *Woooooooo!*"

"*Woooooooo!*" Bozo echoed. "Then I better make a few phone calls."

"Wait," Finster said. "You know any veterinarians?"

Bozo blinked. "Vets? Why? You tryna get some dogs in the mix? I mean… there's probably a market, but—"

"No, dude!" Finster shook his head. "I want to score some cat tranquilizers. You know, get me in the right headspace for my *debut performance.*" He mimed humping Bozo.

"You're one sick bastard, Finster," Bozo said. "And I like it. Let's go for a ride."

In the driveway, Finster popped the trunk.

"What for?" Bozo asked.

"Need a refill," Finster said, tapping his gas can hat.

"Damn. You're a machine. I've still got plenty left."

"I would too, but I spilled half of it when I was jerking off. Also... pretty sure I melted a patch of your carpet."

Bozo shrugged. "No worries. This dump's a lost cause anyway. Once *Clownophobia* blows up and we've got lesbian clown pornos on every shelf—we'll be living large. I ain't staying in this shithole."

They topped off their cans and jumped into the Hummer.

As they pulled out, Bozo spotted his neighbor bending over for the morning paper. A wicked grin crept across his face.

He grabbed the PA mic. "*Mrs. Grabine... you got a fat ass!*"

Mrs. Grabine—who, it must be said, did indeed have quite the generous backside—snapped upright and spun around. She didn't recognize the Hummer, but Bozo's clown-painted face was unmistakable.

She flipped him the bird without hesitation, then stormed around the back of her house.

While the clowns drove off, howling with laughter, Mrs. Grabine marched into her shed and yanked out a hand truck. She wheeled it to the dog's kennel, slid it under the trash can, and began rolling it down the block — toward Bozo's house.

Her original plan was simple: dump the entire contents of the can on his front porch and be done with it.

But when she reached the door and gave the knob a twist — just for the hell of it — it turned.

She blinked.

Then smiled.

Wasting no time, she wheeled the trash-laden hand truck inside and quietly closed the door behind her.

Chapter Seventy Four

Several miles away, the clowns sped down the road in their stolen Hummer, blissfully unaware of what was unfolding back at Bozo's house.

For hours, their attention had been glued to clown pornography. But once they refilled their gas can helmets, their true passion came roaring back—huffing gasoline like it was holy incense.

Now, they were plowing down the highway at seventy-five miles per hour, swerving across lanes like a demolition derby with no audience.

By some divine glitch in the matrix, no one was killed when the behemoth of a vehicle screeched into a veterinarian's parking lot. The only casualties were a terrified poodle who pissed on the pavement, and his equally terrified owner, who did the same in his pants.

The Hummer finally skidded to a stop in the corner of the lot.

The two gas-huffing lunatics sat in silence, eyes wide, breathing like asthmatic hyenas. Then, slowly, they turned to each other.

"What now?" Finster mumbled.

They babbled for fifteen minutes, trying to piece together the best way to score tranquilizers. Ideas ranged from "breaking into the back" to "seducing the receptionist with a kazoo solo."

Fortunately, fate intervened.

A pimply, possibly feral twelve-year-old boy wandered up to the Hummer, entirely unfazed by the painted faces and construction hats.

"Hey. You guys want some Special K?"

Bozo blinked. "Isn't that a cereal?"

"No, douchebag. It's cat tranquilizers."

"*Woooooooo!*" the clowns howled in unison.

"Yo, assholes! Keep it down. You want the K or not?"

"Hell yes," Bozo said. "How much?"

"Tell you what—give me a ride to the mall, and I'll cut you a deal. How many you want?"

"How many you got?" Finster asked.

The kid reached into his oversized hoodie and pulled out a 500-count pharmacy bottle. "This enough?"

Bozo turned to Finster. "Hop in, buddy. Looks like we're going to the mall."

Chapter Seventy Five

Clint and I sat inside a Chick-fil-A, staring at our food like it might whisper answers. We had no idea what to do next.

What we did know was this: Bill Daylay had to be connected to The Seed. The way he acted in the hospital left no other explanation.

And once that realization hit, the fear really settled in. If *one* cop was involved, how many more were there? A few? Dozens? The whole damn department? The state police? The FBI?

We had no idea — and that scared the living hell out of us. As far as we could tell, there wasn't a single soul left we could trust.

Not even waffle fries and the world's greatest chicken sandwich could cheer us up.

"We're fucked," I said.

"Basically," Clint agreed.

"One thing I don't get," I said, "is why Bill would send me and my family away. If he's dirty, wouldn't it make more sense to keep us close? Easier to keep tabs, right?"

Clint shrugged.

"I remember the second time I met him," I continued. "We were with his brother-in-law, Lee. Total lunatic. Was pulling a bullet out of Finster's ass at the time."

Clint blinked. "Wait—what the hell are you talking about?"

"If you'd let me finish, *douchebag*—yes. While Lee was extracting a bullet from Finster's ass, Bill pulled up on the side of the road."

"I... I don't even know what to do with that sentence."

"Oh, and Lee? Has a habit of rubbing his junk while talking to you. Just casually. Like it's punctuation."

"No. Fucking. Way."

"Swear to God," I said. "Anyway, when Bill saw us, I had to tell him everything—Finster stealing the coke, Bozo and Beetle chasing us, the coke getting washed away when the bullet punched through my trunk... the whole clown-fueled saga."

"So why didn't Bill kill you right then and there? Or at least take the *Irony* and claim it as evidence?"

"Exactly!" I said, throwing my hands up. "That's what I can't wrap my head around."

"Yeah... minus the cock-rubbing and ass bullet, you've got a point."

We sat in silence, trying to untangle the threads.

And then we saw them.

Two absolutely hammered individuals staggering across the food court, arms draped around each other, tripping and laughing like frat boys at a funeral.

Both had their faces painted.

Both wore construction helmets.

They bounced off a pillar, giggled, and made their way toward the Chick-fil-A counter.

Clint leaned forward, squinting.

I didn't need to.

"Of course," I muttered. "Finster."

"What the hell are those assholes doing?" Clint muttered.

"Beats me," I whispered, ducking low in my seat. "Just pray they don't recognize me."

But it was impossible *not* to watch them—just like it was impossible for anyone else in the mall to *not* watch them. All eyes were on the two painted idiots staggering through the food court, giggling, shouting, and somehow still upright.

Everyone except mall security, of course. Because there wasn't any.

Thank God they weren't carrying machine guns.

As they wobbled closer, Finster tripped and slammed face-first into the tile. He popped up with a triumphant wobble, then locked eyes with me.

"*Weeehh! Weeez aah Weeeehh!*" he screeched, sprinting toward us.

"What the hell—?" I stood and held out a hand to stop him.

"*Weeehh! Weeez aah Weeeehh!*" he cried again, throwing up a high five.

I had no idea what he was saying—only later would I decipher the gas-fueled dialect: "*Wood! What's up, Wood!*"

"Finster!" I hissed. "What the hell are you doing?"

I glanced at his companion. Short. Beak-nosed. Familiar in the worst way.

Bozo.

"You've got to be kidding me," I muttered. "*You two? Together?*"

They smelled like an Exxon station on fire.

Clint leaned in close. "Mike, we've gotta go. Now. We don't want mall security—wherever the hell they are—thinking we're *with* these losers. You think the cops would hesitate to cuff the whole group?"

He had a point. The last thing we needed was to get lumped in with two clowns reeking of gasoline and insanity.

We stood and started walking—fast.

We didn't look back.

Until I *did* look back.

They were following us. Arms linked. Staggering. Smiling.

Clint and I picked up the pace, slipping into that awkward, half-run, half-speed-walk gait you only see in Olympic events and urgent bowel emergencies.

When I looked back again, we were finally pulling away. The two clowns had stumbled and were struggling to get up.

Clint and I didn't slow down. We wanted to be *sure* we'd shaken them.

I risked one last glance.

"Shit."

"What?" Clint asked, eyes wide.

I pointed. "Look."

They were sprinting—full speed—heading straight for us. Somehow, the same two lunatics who could barely walk five feet without collapsing were now running like Olympic hopefuls.

They were less than ten feet away and babbling unin-telligibly.

"Weeehh! Wheeck ahh!" Finster screeched. *(Editor's Note: "Wood! Wait up!")*

"Meeehh! Eehh seeggy fee beegy yee!" Bozo added. ("Mike! I'm sorry for biting you.")

We stopped. Not because we wanted to — but because it was clear they wouldn't quit.

Predictably, they didn't stop so much as *crash* — both landing flat on the floor in a heap.

Clint and I sighed and helped them up.

I grabbed Finster by the shirt and shook him. "You *never* cease to amaze me," I muttered.

We slung our arms around their shoulders and dragged them toward the nearest exit. The plan? Get them outside, ditch them, and disappear.

Halfway there, Clint had an idea.

"Wait... we don't have a ride, right? And we can't go back to the hospital. So why not catch a lift with these morons? I'll drive."

I nodded. "Finster, where'd you park?"

"Reeh thee," he said, pointing unsteadily toward a poorly parked Hummer sitting half on the curb, ten feet from the door.

We hauled the clowns into the backseat and climbed into the front.

"Keys?" I asked.

Bozo waved his hand vaguely toward the wheel.

We checked the ignition.

Nothing.

Then we saw the dangling wires.

"You assholes *stole* this, didn't you?" I snapped.

The clowns grinned and nodded in unison.

"Do you know how to hot-wire a car?" I asked Clint.

"Nope."

"Me neither."

Five minutes later—through what could only be described as a series of reckless guesses—we somehow got the thing running and rolled the Hummer off the curb.

Clint looked around, stunned. "Does this fucking mall even have security?"

"Sure doesn't look like it," I said, as we peeled out of the lot. "Either that, or they're just as high as the clowns."

Chapter Seventy Six

The Mantis sat in his office, fingers steepled, eyes unfocused. He was thinking, as he often did, about who would next be "invited" to the sex room.

Eddie Bretz was the obvious choice.

The thought made him smile—thin, reptilian, joyless.

"I warned you, Eddie," he murmured. "And my warnings are never idle."

He picked up a remote and turned on the monitor.

The screen flickered to life, playing a grainy, timestamped feed from one of his earlier sessions. The footage was clinical, catalogued—like a twisted form of data analysis. Since the age of eighteen, The Mantis had kept a record of every encounter. Not out of sentiment, but control.

He leaned forward, eyes locked on the screen. His breathing deepened. Teeth clenched.

To The Mantis, this wasn't arousal. It was ritual. Ownership. Power rehearsed in the dark.

Chapter Seventy Seven

"What the hell are we doing?" Eddie screamed. "I want my *Irony*!"

"I told you—we're trying to find out what car they're driving. Once we get that, we'll know who Mike's accomplice is."

"Big fucking deal! I don't care who that other asshole is. I want my coke!"

"Eddie—"

"*Coke!*"

"Will you just let me—"

"*C! O! K! E!*" Eddie bellowed, pounding the dashboard like a toddler on a sugar crash. "I want my coke! I want my coke! I want my *fucking* coke!"

Bill Daylay didn't answer. He opened the cruiser door, got out, and slammed it shut behind him.

"Get back here! Do you hear me, you—"

The door muffled the rest of Eddie's rant.

Bill pressed the heels of his hands into his eyes and exhaled. A year ago, he never would've walked away from Eddie Bretz. But things were different now.

It wasn't that Irony didn't matter. It still did. But lately, Bill had started to wonder — *maybe Eddie didn't.*

And maybe, just maybe, once *Irony* was found, The Seed wouldn't need a loudmouthed liability with a broken dick and no impulse control.

Maybe they'd need someone smarter. Someone quieter. Someone like Bill.

He chewed on the thought while walking the lot, jotting down makes, models, and license plates. The others were doing the same in their assigned zones. It was only a matter of time.

"Red Hummer," said Officer Malor through the walkie. "License plate DRD-9812. Just pulled in. Second row, south corner."

"Got it," Bill replied, scribbling it into a separate column. No need to include recent arrivals when they ran the plates.

"I'm done with my section," came Officer Wilson's voice.

"Good. Stay put and keep an eye on it."

"How's it going over there, Tulber?"

"Five more cars. Couple more minutes."

"Alright. Call it in when you're finished. I'll be wrapping up soon."

Ten minutes later, all sections were complete. Bill told the others he'd swing by to collect their lists. Once in hand, he'd scan the data into his laptop and begin the process of elimination.

Step by step, they were closing in.

Chapter Seventy Eight

Thankfully, the two clowns were unconscious in the backseat when Clint and I pulled the Hummer into the hospital lot.

"Excuse me, sir," an officer said, approaching Clint's window. "Just doing a routine check. Mind telling me what brings you here?"

"My father's got cancer," Clint snapped. "Do you mind?"

The officer held up a hand. "Sorry, sir. Just need to take down your license plate. Then you're free to go."

"Yeah. Thanks a lot," Clint muttered, dripping sarcasm.

As the officer turned to leave, he paused. "By the way, your car smells like gas. You might wanna get that checked out."

Clint gave a tight nod, and we exchanged a look that said exactly what we were both thinking:

We just dodged a bullet.

Clint pulled into a space near the end of the row.

"Well, at least those two clowns did *one* thing right," I said, nodding toward the unconscious gas-huffers in the backseat.

"Yeah," Clint said. "That cop came outta nowhere. I have no idea how I would've explained *them*."

"You'd figure it out. You've got a real gift for lying."

He smirked. "Not bad, huh?"

"Yeah, but all the lying in the world wouldn't mean jack if that cop had been Bill Daylay. We got lucky. Not sure we'll be that lucky next time."

Clint nodded grimly. "So now what? We need to get to my car and grab the duffel bag. Problem is, there's cops all over the place."

He paused. "Also—guess that answers our question about whether more cops are involved."

I didn't respond. From where we sat, we had a clear view of Clint's SUV.

Unfortunately, we also had a clear view of the police cruiser parked just three spots away.

We sat in silence, weighing our options.

Then—five minutes later—another miracle.

"Look," I whispered. "He's leaving."

The cruiser backed out and rolled past us. As it went by, we saw the face in the passenger seat.

Eddie Bretz.

"Well, this is it," Clint said. "I'm gonna make a run for it. You get out first—make sure the coast is clear."

I nodded. We both hopped out of the Hummer and crouched low, slipping between rows of parked cars, heading toward Clint's SUV.

"I'm going for it," he whispered. "Keep watch."

"You got it. Be careful."

Clint dashed across the aisle. Seconds later, he was at the trunk. No cops in sight. He fished his keys from his pocket—but dropped them, the jingle echoing far too loud in the silence.

He winced, scooped them up fast, and popped the trunk. The duffel bag was out in seconds.

Across the lot, we locked eyes. Thumbs up.

Then the moment shattered.

"*Eeh deahn leehk Meehndeez, nay Tishdeez, nay Weshdeez, nay Thishdeez…*"

I froze. "Shit," I hissed. "It's the fucking clowns."

Clint didn't need a second warning. He bolted across the aisle, duffel in hand, and we hustled back to the Hummer. We slid in just as Bozo slumped between the front seats, the PA mic still clutched in his unconscious hand.

"What the hell was he saying?" Clint asked.

"Finster's song," I groaned. Then, in my best Elvis voice: "*I don't like Mondays, no Tuesdays, no Wednesdays, no Thurdays...* God, I hate that freakin' song."

Clint blinked. "Those are the lyrics? Jesus Christ, that's awful. But honestly... even slurring through gas fumes? That clown's got a damn good voice."

"I know," I said. "Who would've thought?"

"Shit—look!" I pointed to the cop car speeding around the corner. "He must've heard Bozo."

Clint snapped upright. "What do we do? Hide? Or play it cool?"

"Wait till he gets closer," I said. "If it's Bill—we hide. If it's anyone else, we use your world-class bullshit skills."

"Not my best plan, but sure."

The cruiser turned down our aisle.

We ducked—low enough to avoid the spotlight, high enough to maybe catch a glimpse. Neither goal was achieved.

"*Step out of the car, please,*" a voice boomed from the loudspeaker.

A spotlight lit us up from behind.

Bill Daylay's cruiser blocked the road.

"*Fuck!* That was him. I recognize his voice."

"Then we stick to the plan," Clint said, starting the Hummer. "If it's Bill—we run. Right?"

"I guess," I muttered, fumbling for my seatbelt.

"I said, out of the car! Now!" Bill barked from behind.

Clint threw the Hummer into reverse and floored it.

We smashed into Bill's cruiser with a thunderous crunch, shoving it back into a row of parked cars. Bill vanished behind the crash, dazed or pinned—we didn't know. Clint slammed it into drive and tore toward the exit.

"Get him in back!" Clint shouted, nodding at Bozo.

I grabbed the unconscious clown and hauled him onto the floor. As I did, one of the gas cans tipped over. The fumes hit instantly—thick, chemical, choking. The reek was unbearable.

"Jesus," I coughed. "It's like bathing in a refinery."

We rolled down the windows to air it out.

"Fingers crossed," Clint muttered. "Let's hope that cop up front lets us through."

Standing in the middle of the exit lane was the same officer we'd spoken to earlier.

I don't know why I had any hope left—but I did. That somehow we'd get out clean. That I could still save my family.

Looking back, it was probably the dumbest thought I'd had all day.

The Hummer came to a stop. The cop approached Clint's window like nothing had happened.

"How're you doing, sir?" he asked, casual as can be. "Hope your father's alright."

"Uh, yeah. Actually… he seemed better today. Little stronger. We kept the visit short."

"That's good to hear." He glanced at the dashboard. "You two didn't hear any noise back there, did you? Sounded like something over a PA. This rig have one?"

Clint nodded. "Yeah, actually—it does. We heard something too, but couldn't make it out."

The officer nodded. "Well, drive safe. And check that fuel system—the gas smell's stronger than ever. I'm sure your mileage sucks as it is."

"You're not kidding," Clint said, easing onto the gas. "Thanks, officer. Have a good night."

We rolled out onto the street, trailing fumes—and a little more luck than we deserved.

Chapter Seventy Nine

Bill Daylay sat in his battered cruiser, dazed but uninjured. His hands shook as he grabbed the walkie.

"Chuck? If you see a red Hummer coming your way—*do not* let it out. Got that?"

"Shit, Bill... too late. They just pulled out."

"Goddammit! Did you see which way they went?"

"To be honest?" Malor said. "Didn't really pay attention. Sorry."

"*Goddammit!* That fucker just plowed into my car!"

"You get a look at 'em?"

"Nah. Couldn't see their faces. But I've got a hunch it was Mike and his butt-buddy. Tell me—did one of them look like a movie star? Real clean-cut, maybe a little smug?"

Malor laughed. "Now that you mention it, yeah. My wife would've been creamin' her pants."

"And the other guy?"

"Pretty average. Brown hair. Slight receding hairline. Honestly didn't stand out."

"That's them. That's *fucking* them!"

"Well hey," Malor offered, "maybe they'll run outta gas. Smelled like they were leaking all over the place."

"Maybe." Bill exhaled hard. "Alright, get an APB out on that Hummer. I'm gonna finish cross-checking these plates. We'll figure out who Mr. Adonis is."

"You got it, boss."

Bill opened his notebook, eyes darting across the scribbled columns of makes and models, narrowing in on the red Hummer.

In the passenger seat, Eddie Bretz stirred.

"Ahhh," he moaned. "Storm... nod job... *Nod job!* Aaahh..."

Bill flinched. "Eddie? Wake up."

Eddie grunted, still half-lost in whatever nightmare — or fantasy — he was having. "Storm... do that trick again, baby. Not so rough this time, okay?"

"Jesus Christ," Bill muttered. "*Eddie!* Wake the fuck up!"

"Huh?" Eddie blinked, confused. "What'd you say?"

"I think we need to take you back to the hospital, Eddie."

"What?" Eddie snapped, suddenly wide awake. "The *hospital*? Hell no! There's no fucking way I'm going back to see that baton-swinging perv friend of yours. *Not happening*. Got it?"

"Whatever, Eddie," Bill muttered, eyes still scanning the list in his lap.

Eddie's voice sharpened. "You talking to me with attitude now? You forget who's in charge here?"

"Not at all," Bill said calmly. "Just got work to do."

And for the second time that night, Bill Daylay opened the door, stepped out, and slammed it shut — right in Eddie's face.

He paced the lot, breathing deep, jaw tight. Then he pulled out his phone.

First call: his contact at the Department of Transportation.

"List is on the way," he said. "I need a full report ASAP. Every name, every address. Call me the *second* it's ready."

Next call: his own voicemail.

"Hey," he said flatly. "I'll be late tonight. Don't wait up."

He could've called his wife directly — but he didn't feel like hearing her bitch.

Final call: The Mantis.

It was short. Direct. Chilling.

When it ended, Bill stood in the dark for a long moment, phone still in hand.

And now, more than ever, he knew.

Eddie Bretz was expendable.

Chapter Eighty

ell, where the hell do we go now?" I asked. "Driving around in *this* beast isn't doing us any favors. A red Hummer? We might as well slap *'Arrest These Dumbasses'* on the side and do donuts in front of the police station."

"Yeah, we've gotta ditch it," Clint agreed. "Problem is, where are we gonna find another car? We could ask Bozo to hot-wire one, but I doubt he's waking up anytime soon."

"I don't know," I said. "He was semi-conscious earlier—singing that freakin' clown song. Maybe we could rouse him just long enough to do it."

"I really hope you're joking."

"What are you, a moron? *Of course* I'm joking."

"Screw you." Clint shook his head. "Anyway, we can't go to my place. If they don't know who I am yet, they will soon. They were clearly scanning plates back there. And your house is out too."

"Which leaves..." I nodded toward the backseat.

"Bozo's," Clint finished. "Can't be Finster's. His wife kicked him out, remember?"

"Hard to imagine why," Clint deadpanned.

"Oh, it gets better," I said. "She found him passed out naked with porn blaring, a bottle of corn oil next to him, phone off the hook, and a Penthouse ad circled — *Black Booties*. He even wrote his access code right next to it."

Clint blinked. "He spent *seven hundred and fifty dollars* on phone sex?"

"Yep. That's a lot of whacking off."

"So… Bozo's it is."

"We could always ditch the Hummer near our hotel and leave the clowns behind," I offered.

"Yeah, great idea — except we still need a car. And I doubt we can rent one. If the rogue cop brigade has our names, we'll be flagged in no time."

"Right. Forgot about that." I turned and looked at Bozo. "So Bozo it is."

I leaned over the seat and patted him down, found his wallet jammed in his front pocket. The moment I reached in to grab it, Bozo groaned and clamped down on my wrist.

"*Beezees keymey. Beezees keymey,*" he mumbled.

"What the hell is he saying?" Clint asked.

I yanked my hand free — wallet in tow — wiping my fingers on my jeans.

"Bozo's coming. Bozo's coming."

Clint laughed. "And you *pulled* your hand away? You prick. You're gonna give the poor guy blue balls. Let him finish—put your hand back."

"Fuck you, Clint," I muttered, flipping open the wallet. "Okay—1728 Surrey Lane, Brookhaven. You know it?"

"Yeah, about ten minutes from here," he said, pointing ahead.

A few minutes later, I grabbed the PA mic.

"What are you doing?" Clint asked.

"Feelings... nothing more than feelings," I crooned into the mic. *"Trying to forgeeet myyyyy, feelings o-of love..."*

Clint yanked the mic from my hand and, in the most ear-piercing falsetto I've ever heard, belted, *"Feeeelings! Wo-wo-wo-wo feelings!"*

"Clint, stop!" I shouted. "Behind us—cop!"

We both whipped around. Sirens. Lights. A cruiser barreled up behind us... then zipped past in the right lane.

We sat there, frozen.

"I think I'll put this down now," Clint said, calmly mounting the handset like nothing happened.

I nodded, trying to steady my heart rate.

A few minutes later, we pulled into Bozo's driveway.

"You're getting the keys," I said. "I'm not going any-where near him."

"What a baby," Clint grinned, reaching into Bozo's pocket.

The clown reacted exactly the same way he had with me — moaning, grabbing, mumbling. But Clint didn't have my patience.

"Let me go, you fucking pervert," he snapped, and punched Bozo in the face.

Clint dangled the keys in front of me. "Garage time. Wanna do the honors?"

I took them and headed to the front door. Three keys. The first two didn't work. The third slid in — but the knob didn't budge.

Locked?

I turned the key the other way. *Click.* The door swung open.

Turns out it had been *unlocked* the whole time. What-ever.

I stepped inside and instantly gagged.

The stench hit like a punch — dense, sour, and omni-present. Not coming from one room, just *everywhere*.

I didn't want to know. I didn't care. First order of business: get the red Hummer out of sight.

I held my breath and veered left. First door — closet. Second — garage.

I ran my hand along the wall, found the light switch... and just below it, the button for the garage door.

Bingo.

A minute later, the Hummer was tucked away in the garage and the door was down.

"You're not gonna believe how bad it smells inside," I warned as Clint climbed out.

"Can't be worse than in *there*," he said, waving toward the Hummer. "I was two whiffs away from blacking out."

"Okay," I said, heading back toward the house. "Don't say I didn't warn you."

We stepped inside.

"*Ah, Jesus Christ!*" Clint gagged. "It smells like shit in here. *Literally.*"

"I told you. The stench is everywhere."

We flicked on a few lights — and instantly saw why.

Dogshit.

Smeared on the walls, matted into the carpet, crusted on the sofas, streaked across the beds. Every room. Every surface.

It was less of a mess and more of a statement.

My stomach turned.

"Charming," I muttered. "Who the hell did this clown piss off?"

Clint covered his mouth, eyes watering. "You *hope* this was someone else?"

"I mean… Bozo's weird, but this feels personal."

We both stood there, blinking, as the full horror set in.

Someone had declared war.

And their weapon of choice was a shovel and dogshit.

"You're right—this wasn't a prank. It was personal. And considering Bozo's life choices, the suspect list's probably a mile long. Hell, maybe he *likes* the smell of dogshit. Guy's into clown porn and huffing gasoline—anything's possible."

But we got our answer a minute later when I went to the bathroom. Taped to the mirror was a handwritten note:

CALL ME FAT ASS AGAIN AND SEE WHAT HAPPENS NEXT!

"Damn," I said, stepping back. "Think this lady over-reacted a little?"

"You're assuming it was a woman?"

"Yeah. I don't think most guys get that worked up about ass size. Do you?"

"Probably not," Clint admitted. "Although… my wife did jack me up against the wall once."

"What?"

"I was messing around and pinched a roll on her stomach. She flipped. Had her hands around my throat and slammed me against the wall. She's five-four, maybe a hundred ten pounds—damn near lifted me off the ground."

I nodded. "Smart of you to keep your mouth shut since."

"Survival instinct. So... now what? We've got no car, and those clowns aren't hot-wiring anything in their current coma-state. We're stuck."

"I'm not staying *inside* this hellhole," Clint said. "That's not an option."

"How about we find some blankets and sleep outside? It's not that cold."

"Assuming we can find a blanket not crusted in shit."

Twenty minutes later, we'd cobbled together a makeshift campsite on Bozo's deck. We dragged out two mattresses—shit-covered sides face-down, of course—and even rolled the TV outside after wiping dog crap off the screen. Honestly? It wasn't bad. All we needed was some beer.

We flipped a coin.

I lost.

Back inside I went.

The second I cracked the sliding door, the stench punched me in the face like it had been waiting.

I held my breath, beelined for the fridge, and flung it open.

Top shelf.

A single, oversized dog turd.

Right there.

Front and center.

Like it had been *placed* for display.

Although I was disgusted, I still held out hope there was some untainted beer left in the fridge.

The fridge door hung open, the image of that proud little turd on the top shelf burned into my brain.

To stem the urge to vomit, I kept my eyes low and went straight for the vegetable drawer.

Hallelujah. Yuengling Lager.

I pulled the entire tray out and inspected every bottle like I was disarming landmines. No turds in sight. Victory.

I cracked open the freezer, dumped a tray of ice over the beer, then raided the cabinets for pretzels and Doritos before heading back outside.

"Success?" Clint asked.

"Success," I said, holding up the haul like a game show prize. "But double-check your bottle before you drink."

"Why? What's wrong?"

I told him about the fridge surprise from Mrs. Fat Ass. We both agreed—every bottle needed a visual inspection *and* a sniff test before approval.

Once cleared, we raised our drinks and toasted. Half the bottle disappeared in a single gulp.

"That clown's not all bad," I said.

"Mrs. Fat Ass might disagree with you."

We talked more about the carnage inside. Whoever left that mess had gone *full psychopath*. But honestly? Living next to Bozo probably broke her long before the dogshit came out.

We stretched out in front of the TV, munching junk food and channel surfing. For the first time all day, it felt like we could breathe.

Then Clint stopped on *Cops*.

A pair of officers tackled a guy in a wife-beater. Sirens blared in the background.

And just like that, it hit me.

"I have his number," I said, sitting up. "Why the hell didn't I think of that?"

"Whose number?"

"Bill Daylay. He gave it to me back when I still thought he was one of the good guys. What do you say we give him a call?"

Clint grinned. "Hell yeah. Let's go for it."

Chapter Eighty One

W hat's up, Bill?"

"Mike? What's going on? Why'd you run off at the hospital? Is everything alright?"

"Sure—aside from just finding out you're mixed up with The Seed. I thought you were my friend."

"What are you talking about? Of course I'm your friend. You think I'm connected to The Seed just because I was pushing Eddie Bretz in a wheelchair? Talk about jumping to conclusions."

"Save the bullshit, Bill. I—"

"No, *you* save the bullshit," Bill snapped. "You've got some nerve accusing me like that—*after* I helped your family. Or did you forget about that?"

"I know what I saw."

"You saw me pushing a wheelchair, for Christ's sake! Are you really that dumb? If you have to know, I was transferring that asshole to a holding cell. Doctor released him this morning."

He sounded sincere. Almost too sincere. And part of me—*the gullible part*—wanted to believe him. I still couldn't square it with the guy who comforted me in my kitchen. Who promised to protect my family.

But my instincts were screaming. And I'd learned the hard way not to ignore them.

I gave Clint a nod. He stood in the bathroom doorway, hand over his nose, trying not to gag from the dog-shit stink.

I flushed the toilet.

Over the phone: a pause.

"Bill? Hear that? Say goodbye to *Irony*."

"Wait! Just hold on—"

"Too late. That's one bag." *Flush.*

"Wait—stop! *Please!*"

"Why do you care, Bill? You said you're not part of The Seed, remember? Here goes bag number two." *Flush.*

"Alright! Alright! *Stop!* No more games, okay? I'm in. I'm mixed up with The Seed. Just—*please don't flush any more of that coke.* We can work something out."

I hung up.

Then I powered off the phone.

He'd call back. I didn't want to hear it.

"Let's get some fresh air," I said, stepping past Clint and heading toward the sliding glass door.

"That's the best idea you've had yet," Clint said.

"But you know what? We've got something else to handle first—the clowns. I know they're out cold now, but at some point, they're going to wake up. And I really don't want to be asleep with that lunatic roaming free. The bastard bit my shoulder, which still hurts, by the way."

"And the boil on your balls too, right? Jesus, stop whining."

"Both can be true. But you're right. Let's go find some duct tape."

Twenty minutes later, we had both of them secured in the back of the Hummer. Honestly, it was probably over-kill—neither of them had moved or made a sound, not even a moan or a "Bozo's coming."

Still, I felt better knowing Bozo wasn't going to wake up and be standing over me with a gas can and a grin.

Back on the deck, we settled in with our beers and junk food.

"Well... today was something," Clint said.

"You got that right," I replied. "Think it's safe to say we're gonna have to tweak the plan a little."

Chapter Eighty Two

Bill hung up the phone and walked back to his cruiser. He didn't feel like dealing with Eddie Bretz—not anymore. But he told himself he wouldn't have to much longer.

Sure, tonight had gone sideways. But Bill was confident that one way or another, *Irony* would end up in his hands.

And when it did, Eddie Bretz would get a bullet in the head.

Bill wasn't the kind of man to take pleasure in killing. *Except* when it came to Eddie. That one, he'd enjoy.

It wasn't that Eddie hadn't paid well over the years. Bill had made a small fortune working for The Seed. It all started with a traffic stop. Five years ago.

Bill had pulled over a swerving Lincoln on suspicion of DUI. The second he lit it up with his flashlight, he knew this was no ordinary bust.

Behind the wheel was a clearly drunk Eddie Bretz.

In his lap: a prostitute. Still going.

She didn't stop, even with a cop staring down at her.

It was the first of *several* times Bill was forced to witness Eddie receiving oral. Not something he was likely to forget.

There was also a healthy pile of cocaine on the dashboard, sparkling like a party favor.

"Step out of the car," Bill had said, stunned.

Eddie obeyed—but dragged the woman out with him, crouched and still working.

"Get her on her feet," Bill snapped.

Eddie didn't even blink. "Nah, let her finish. I paid for it."

He turned to Bill, calm as ever. "Besides... I think we can come to an understanding."

"Ouch! Watch the teeth, bitch!"

Bill stood there, blinking. In twelve years as a cop, he'd seen plenty of shit—but never a guy negotiate a felony while getting a blowjob.

"What the hell are you talking about?" Bill asked. "You're going to jail. DUI, solicitation, coke. Or should I just pretend I don't see any of this?"

"Not at all," Eddie said. "But I think we can reach an arrangement."

He patted the woman's head. "How much do you make? Thirty-five, maybe forty grand? I can triple that. You just need to forget what you saw tonight."

And that's how it started.

This was a turning point in Bill's life.

He'd been struggling for years on a cop's salary, watching other people get the things he wanted. A boat. A better car. A kick-ass TV. A diamond necklace for his wife. Hockey lessons for his kid. The kind of life you can't finance with pay stubs and good intentions.

And it wasn't like he was new to crossing lines.

Bill had skimmed bills from suspects' wallets. Pawned seized electronics. Flipped small-time dope from evidence bags. Nothing major—but enough to dip a toe into the dirty pool.

So when Eddie Bretz offered to talk, Bill didn't walk away.

"I'm listening," he said.

"Just a minute," Eddie replied. Then to the woman, "Faster. Faster. Ah—ah—AAHH."

He zipped up and tossed a crumpled wad of cash at the woman's feet.

"Thanks, bitch."

Then, cheerful as a sitcom dad: "Now—where were we? Let's have a seat."

He hopped onto the hood of his car like it was a barstool and launched into his pitch.

Eddie described The Seed, his role in the organization, and exactly how Bill could fit in. For a generous cut,

Bill would help recruit fellow officers. They'd all be well compensated, of course. Their job? Turn a blind eye to Seed shipments—and crack down on the competition.

By the time Eddie finished, Bill Daylay was sold.

It wasn't that he wasn't grateful for the lifestyle. He was. But that didn't mean he had to like Eddie.

He hated his smug voice. His constant sadism. His habit of turning every conversation into a blowjob showcase. The way he belittled Bill in public. The way he made him feel like an errand boy.

And Bill was done being anyone's errand boy.

So yes—he'd gladly be the one to pull the trigger.

But for now, he kept his face blank and opened the door to the cruiser.

"What the fuck were you doing?" Eddie screamed. "Get me out of this goddamn car. Now!"

"Relax, Eddie. We'll get you out in a minute."

"In a minute, my ass! I've been roasting in here for an hour with a broken dick. And I still don't have my cocaine!"

"Alright, Eddie. Alright…"

Chapter Eighty Three

We woke up around nine, the warm sun shining down on our faces. Since I was the unlucky loser of yesterday's coin toss, it was Clint's turn to venture back into the house.

Ten minutes later, he returned with two bowls, two spoons, a half-full gallon of milk, and a box of Frosted Flakes — the undisputed king of cereals.

"Yuengling and Tony the Tiger. Bozo's a legend," I said.

"If we were smart," Clint replied, "we would've opened all the windows yesterday and aired out the place."

"Yeah, good point. Let's do it after we eat."

Clint nodded. "Oh, and I checked on the clowns. Still out cold."

"Not surprising, considering last night. Beezees keymey," I muttered, mimicking Bozo mid-orgasm.

Clint tried to hold it in—mouth full of cereal—but failed spectacularly. Milk shot from his nose and dribbled down his chin.

We both lost it.

For several minutes, we laughed like idiots. Him at the memory of Bozo's blissful breakdown. Me at his milky nose geyser.

Eventually we calmed down, wiped our faces, and finished breakfast.

Then it was time to face the day.

First order of business: get a car. For that, we'd need the clowns. Looking back, it's wild how casually we accepted that car theft was part of the plan. But when your life—and your family's—hangs in the balance, morality gets fuzzy fast.

After securing transportation, the next step was scheduling a meeting with The Mantis.

The outcome of that meeting would decide whether we lived or died.

So no, stealing a car didn't exactly keep us up at night.

While the clowns stayed passed out, Clint and I made our morning calls. I talked to my wife and kids. It drained the hell out of me. I missed them so much. And I couldn't shake the feeling that it might be the last time I'd hear their voices.

I stayed upbeat for the kids. I didn't want them picking up on anything.

But when I tried that same fake calm with my wife, she saw right through it.

"What's wrong, honey?" she asked. "I can tell something's not right."

"Nothin', babe," I said. "Everything's fine."

It was a lie. And she knew it.

I felt a lump rising in my throat as I explained everything to her.

She started crying.

And it took everything I had not to do the same.

I was supposed to be the strong one. It's what they say about men, right? That we're hardwired for composure?

Bullshit.

Male or not, I couldn't let myself break. If I started crying, I might not stop. I'd curl into a ball, give in, and disappear into the fear.

And I couldn't afford that.

So I played the role. I told her everything would be okay. I comforted her. Reassured her.

But if I'm being honest, I think she could hear the fear in my voice, too.

When I finally hung up, I sat there for a moment, staring at the phone like it had just pulled a knife on me.

"Whew," I said. "That was brutal."

"I know. My wife was bawling," Clint said. "Yours?"

"Yep."

"I thought I saw you crying too," Clint added, nudging the tension with a weak smile.

"Fuck you," I said.

Then, trying to shift the mood: "Whataya say we open some windows and wake up the douchebags?"

Chapter Eighty Four

The house started to smell marginally better as we opened the windows, but it was still revolting. The stench clung to everything.

We couldn't get out fast enough.

In the garage, we had one last laugh before opening the door. I'd found a heaping pile of dogshit on Bozo's nightstand. Clint found another one mashed into his keyboard.

"How the fuck is he gonna clean all this up?" I asked.

Clint just made a face, clearly picturing it in too much detail.

As he reached for the passenger door, I stopped him.

"Wait. I have a brilliant idea."

Fifteen minutes later, the PA system mounting bolts were off the roof of the Hummer.

The clowns were still lifeless in the back seat. Clint placed the speaker between them while I grinned like an idiot, clutching the handset.

We exchanged a look.

Showtime.

"WAKE UP, CLOWN FREAKS! WAKE UP!" I screamed.

Nothing.

"Are they dead?" Clint asked, poking Finster's chest.

"I don't think so," I said. "Let me crank the volume and try again."

"Hang on," Clint said. "Let's close the door first — no sense blowing out our eardrums."

He laid the speaker on Finster's chest, ran the wires through the door, and gently shut it, trapping them in place.

"Go for it."

I pulled the handset back and screamed from the garage:

"WAAAAAKE UUUUUP! WAAAAAKE UUUUUP!"

The sound echoed through the metal like a demon in a trash can.

Inside, they started to twitch — heads rolling side to side like zombies in slow motion.

We opened the door.

Finster blinked up at me.

"Uuuggghhh," he moaned.

"Rise and shine," Clint said, grinning.

"My arms! I can't move my arms!" Bozo screamed.

"That's because they're tied, douchebag," I said.

Bozo let out a shriek—full volume, top-of-the-lungs panic.

We told him to shut up. He didn't.

So Clint grabbed a mop from the garage and shoved the dirty end in Bozo's mouth.

"There," Clint said. "Now can we have a conversation?"

Bozo nodded, wide-eyed and gagging.

Next to him, Finster just moaned.

"First of all," I said, "your house is a pigsty. Let me guess—did you call someone 'fat ass' recently?"

Bozo nodded again, slower this time.

"Well, payback's a bitch. Your place is covered in dogshit."

Bozo tried to scream into the mop, but Clint calmly palmed his face and pushed it back.

"Settle down, Bozo. Pro tip: don't comment on a woman's weight. Especially one with a vendetta and a dog. Just take it as a life lesson."

I crouched closer. "Now, we need you to steal us a car. Something that doesn't scream, 'Hey, arrest me!' Got it?"

Bozo nodded once more.

"Okay. I'm taking the mop out. But if you scream, it's going right back in—with a fresh scoop of Mrs. Fat Ass's dogshit. Understood?"

This time, he nodded with actual fear in his eyes.

"Good," Clint said, slowly sliding the mop out.

We watched.

No screams.

Just quiet breathing.

Except for Finster, who groaned like a cartoon mummy.

"What's the matter, Finster?" I asked. "Hungover? Maybe if you didn't huff gasoline all night, you wouldn't feel like a human dumpster fire."

"My head," he moaned. "It's freakin' killing me."

And right then, I wanted to choke him.

This was the guy who dragged me into this whole nightmare. While I was trying not to get murdered by drug dealers, he was off turning his brain into soup with gasoline and porn.

I took a deep breath and restrained myself.

But not entirely.

I rapped my knuckles against his skull.

"Ow! What was that for?"

"Think about it," I said. "You'll figure it out."

"Can we get back to the subject at hand, please?" Clint said, shooting me a look before turning to the clowns. "Here's how this is gonna work. We untie you, and we go straight out the garage. You can deal with the dogshit later."

He held up a DVD case: *Bozo Uncut.*

""No screaming. No funny business. And you do exactly what we say. If not..." Clint wiggled the disc between his fingers. "Say goodbye to your old-ass clown porn collection. Who even watches DVDs anymore?"

Bozo gasped like someone had just threatened to burn his family Bible.

"Please, no!"

"Yes," Clint said, waving a mock goodbye. "Straight to hell with it."

He turned to the clown. "What kind of car does Mrs. Fat Ass drive?"

"A black Honda. Why?"

"Sounds good to me. Whataya think, Mike?"

"Sure," I said.

"Congrats, Bozo—you get a small taste of revenge. Although, if I'm being honest, I think she won this round. Wait till you see your house."

Clint pointed toward the back of the property. "You're gonna hot-wire her car and pick us up on the next street over. Easy, right?"

"No problemo," Bozo said.

"You do that, and *Bozo Uncut* lives to see another day. Got it?"

"Let's do it," Bozo said, all business now.

Chapter Eighty Five

Twenty minutes later, Clint and I were crammed into the backseat of Mrs. Fat Ass's Honda. I held the Hummer's license plate in my lap—we planned to slap it on the Honda as soon as we found a quiet place to swap them.

But first, we had to ditch the clowns.

No matter how inconspicuous the car, two grown men in clown makeup riding up front kind of kills the stealth factor.

We pulled behind a grocery store. Bozo gave us a quick and disturbingly confident tutorial on hot-wiring. Then we swapped the plates and ordered them into the backseat.

They didn't argue. Bozo was still laser-focused on protecting his porn stash, and Finster looked like he was one whiff of gasoline away from cardiac arrest.

Clint drove us back to the edge of Bozo's neighborhood.

At the first stop sign, we told them to get out.

"Can't you drive us a little closer?" Bozo whined. "My house is like four blocks away."

"You're lucky we brought you this far," I said.

"Four blocks?" Finster groaned, gripping his head. "I don't think I can make it."

"Out," Clint barked, holding up *Bozo Uncut* like it was a hostage.

"Okay, okay! Just don't hurt her!" Bozo pleaded.

They climbed out, Finster swaying like a seasick giraffe.

"Can I have my DVD back?" Bozo asked, still standing in the middle of the road.

"Sure," Clint said — and chucked it out the window as we peeled off.

In the rearview mirror, I watched Bozo dive for the disc while Finster leaned over and puked on the curb.

"What a pair," I muttered.

"Yeah. Those two really take the cake. And to think — *one of them's your friend.* Kinda makes me question your judgment."

"Don't worry. I've got zero plans to put on clown makeup anytime soon."

I exhaled.

"Anyway... isn't it about time we made that phone call?"

"Yeah, I guess," Clint said. "Why don't you talk to him this time? Here—use my phone. He's in my contacts under 'M'."

"Thanks a lot," I muttered, not at all excited to make this call. But I didn't really have a choice.

I found the name. Tapped it.

The man who answered had the calm, dead voice of someone who'd casually slit your throat just to see if it made a sound.

"Yes."

"Mantis? We haven't met, but... our lives have kind of become intertwined. I'm Mike Rodgen."

"I see," he said, cool as ice. "Yes, Mr. Rodgen. Entwined indeed."

"Not my idea, for the record."

"It's not important *how* we got here. Only where we go from here."

A pause.

"I believe you have something I need."

"*Irony*," I said.

"Of course. *Irony*."

We spent the next few minutes negotiating the terms. One-on-one. Just me and The Mantis. Neutral ground. No funny business.

I didn't trust a word of it.

But I didn't have a better option either.

When I hung up, I turned to Clint.

"We're all set."

"Yippy," he said flatly.

Chapter Eighty Six

The Mantis hung up the phone.

Smiling, he looked up at the two women seated across from him.

"Unfortunately, I didn't get the chance to speak with your husband again, Mrs. Mercer," he said. "But I *did* have the pleasure of speaking with *your* husband, Mrs. Rodgen. A very polite man, I must say."

Neither woman responded.

The duct tape across their mouths made conversation... inconvenient.

Chapter Eighty Seven

Bill Daylay was coming unglued.
Eddie Bretz just would *not* shut the hell up.

Ever since they'd swapped cars with Officer Malor, it had been non-stop whining:

I need my coke. Where's my coke. I'm gonna kill that bitch Storm. Stupid nod job. Where's my coke.

Over and over. Like a cokehead parrot from hell.

But worse than the noise was the sight of him. The way his lip curled when he talked. The way his gums flapped around every stupid thought. For five years, Bill had put up with this jackass. And now, every time he looked at Eddie, all he could picture was putting a bullet through his skull.

It would've been easy.

So easy.

But instead, Bill just kept driving. Kept pretending to listen.

"Hey!" Eddie snapped. "Are you even listening to me?"

"Huh? What's that?" Bill asked, eyes still on the road.

"You didn't hear a *goddamn* word I said, did you? You stupid prick! I should ditch your ass and find someone useful. How'd you like that, fuck-face?"

"Sorry, Eddie. It won't happen again."

"You're *damn right* it won't. Now listen — *listen good.* Got it?"

Bill's hand crept to the grip of his service revolver.

He nodded.

"Good. Here's what we're gonna do —"

And just like that, Bill tuned him out again.

Whatever Eddie said didn't matter anymore. Not really. All that mattered was keeping him alive — for now. That was the job.

So Bill unclenched his teeth. Let go of the gun. Bit his tongue and kept driving.

Trying not to snap.

"Hey! You're doing it again!" Eddie barked. "You missed the freakin' turn! What the hell, man?! Turn around! *Now!*"

Bill didn't pull the trigger.

But he did reach for his baton.

With the same technique Joey used at the hospital, he whipped it into Eddie's crotch with a satisfying *whack.*

"Shut the hell up," Bill said calmly. "And enjoy the ride."

Chapter Eighty Eight

On the way to the meeting, Clint and I smoked another joint.

Probably not the smartest move.

But honestly? We were scared shitless. And at the time, weed seemed like the perfect coping mechanism.

So by the time we turned onto the dirt road leading through the apple orchard, we were *very* stoned.

But the sight of the Jaguar parked under the trees snapped us back to reality.

"Looks like he's already here," Clint said.

"No shit, Sherlock."

We pulled up beside the Jag and stared at it for a moment.

"This is it," I said. "Let's go for it."

We stepped out and started walking toward the trunk. As we did, the car door opened and a man climbed out.

Tall. Six-four, easy. Impeccable tailored suit, built like a linebacker. His eyes—jet black, bottomless—looked like something you'd see on a shark. No emotion. No light.

Just void.

"Gentlemen," he said, extending a hand. "I'm The Mantis."

Clint and I froze.

His presence wasn't just intimidating—it was wrong. Like the air around him had stopped moving.

"Gentlemen?"

"Sorry," I said, swallowing hard. "I'm Mike Rodgen. This is Clint Mercer."

We shook his hand. His grip was firm—not bone-crushing, but very clear: *I could break you if I wanted to.*

"Shall we take a walk?" he said.

"Sure. After you," I replied.

We'd agreed I would do most of the talking—not because I was better at it, but because in a desperate game of rock, paper, scissors, I lost.

I was paper. Clint was scissors.

Lucky me.

As we walked among the trees, The Mantis began:

"I'm sure you understand the predicament you've put me in. That cocaine—*my* cocaine—is vital to our operation. Now, you may not agree with my line of work.

That's fine. Think I'm despicable? Go ahead. I don't lose sleep over what people like you think of me. What I *do* care about is results. And I will have *Irony* back in my possession. That, I can promise you."

"Excuse me, uh... Mantis?" I asked. "Is that how I should address you? Or Mr. Mantis? *The* Mantis?"

"Mantis is fine," he said smoothly. "I'd like to think we can have a civil negotiation, wouldn't you agree? And on that note—may I call you Mike?"

I nodded.

He turned to Clint.

"And your handsome associate here—the prick who's chosen to betray me—may I speak to you on a first-name basis as well?"

Clint locked eyes with him.

"*Betrayal?* You've gotta be kidding me," Clint snapped. "I never *joined* The Seed. You bastards forced me into it. Blackmail, threats against my family— whatever it took. Don't act like I was some loyal minion who suddenly turned. Everything I did was out of sur- vival."

"Okay, okay—time out," I said, raising both hands like a ref breaking up a fight. "Let's not get lost in person- al drama. Can we focus on the reason we're all here? *Iro- ny.*"

"Fair point," The Mantis said. "Let's cut to the heart of the matter."

He stepped closer.

"Return my cocaine. Now. If it's not with you, go get it. You have one hour."

And with that, he turned and began walking away.

Clint and I stood there, stunned. Was that it?

Finally, I spoke. "That's not going to happen," I called out. "At least... not yet. You're not the one in control here. *We —*"

The Mantis stopped. Turned. Raised a hand to silence me.

"I'm afraid *you're* wrong, Mike."

He clapped — once, sharply.

From the treeline, two women emerged.

Our wives.

Behind them, a man held a gun.

"As you can see," The Mantis said, that shark's grin creeping across his face, "*I'm* the one who has control. Wouldn't you agree?"

Chapter Eighty Nine

When Bozo and Finster first walked into the house, neither of them noticed the overwhelming stench of dogshit.

Their clown noses were still rigged with empty gas cans—spilled in the Hummer—but the lingering fumes had them floating just enough to miss the early warning signs.

It wasn't until Bozo opened the fridge that Mrs. Fat Ass's revenge became impossible to ignore.

"What the hell!" he screamed, yanking out a plate and holding it up like Exhibit A. "Is this... is this a turd?!"

Then he sniffed it.

"*That bitch.* That *fat-assed* bitch! She's gone too far this time. She's gonna pay!"

Finster tried to intervene, but Bozo was already pacing the house. And with each step came another discovery: a turd in the laundry basket, one mashed into the couch cushion, and a particularly offensive pile sitting proudly on his bed.

"I'm gonna kill her!" Bozo shrieked, still clutching the plate of poop like a holy relic. "I'm gonna shove this in her dumb fucking face and *then* I'm gonna strangle her!"

"Now just... just calm down."

"*Calm down?! There's shit everywhere!*"

"I know, Bozo, I know. But we can't kill her. That'll screw up everything—Clownophobia, the lesbian clown films, *everything.* You really wanna spend the rest of your life as someone's prison bitch? I'm not saying we don't get revenge. I'm just saying... maybe not *murder.*"

Bozo stood there, breathing heavily, eyes bloodshot with rage.

"Fine," he growled. "You're right. But she *will* pay. One way or another."

Now that he was calm enough to talk strategy, the two sat down and began brainstorming revenge.

First idea: capture a deer and release it in her house.

That one was scrapped quickly when they realized they had no idea how to trap a deer. Or where to find one. Or what to do if it kicked them to death.

Next idea: photoshop her face onto a clown porno DVD cover. But Bozo vetoed it—she didn't meet the high standards of his smut films, and her ass would ruin the brand.

So they decided to stick with what worked: body waste.

Dog poop was passé. Too cliché.

Urine, though? Urine had *potential*.

But it couldn't just be a quick tinkle on her welcome mat. The destruction in Bozo's house demanded something *bigger*.

The plan? Go to the market. Buy twenty gallons of water. Dump it all out. Then slowly refill the bottles... with piss.

How long would it take to collect twenty gallons of urine?

No clue.

But they were prepared to find out.

Step one: hydrate.

"No problemo," Bozo said. "I've got plenty of beer," he added, yanking open the fridge.

When he found the tray empty, his first instinct was—naturally—to blame Mrs. Fat Ass, completely unaware that Clint and Mike had cleaned out his Yuengling the night before.

"That bitch! She stole my beer!"

"Don't worry about it, dude," Finster said. "We'll grab some when we go get the milk. Might as well fill these up too," he added, pointing to his hard hat.

"Woooooooo!"

"Woooooooo!"

Celebration complete, the two clowns staggered into the garage and climbed into the red Hummer—still blissfully unaware that "blending in" was a thing people did.

Bozo hot-wired it like a pro. He looked at Finster, grinning.

"We're gonna get that bitch."

He threw it in reverse and floored it.

Unfortunately, he forgot one small detail.

The garage door.

CRASH.

The Hummer blasted through the door, splinters flying everywhere.

"Holy shit," Finster muttered as they skidded into the driveway.

"Damn," Bozo said, casually brushing woodchips off his shoulder. "I needed to fix that door anyway."

But then he saw her.

Mrs. Grabine.

In the rearview mirror.

Laughing her fat ass off.

Bozo's mood instantly shifted.

He grabbed the PA handset and screamed, "*Bitch! This is your fault! Bitch!*"

Then he floored it—straight toward her.

Mrs. Grabine dove just in time as the Hummer *smashed* through her garage door.

"Take *that*, fat ass!" Bozo shouted over the PA, before yanking it into drive and peeling out.

Mrs. Grabine sat up on her lawn, dazed but unbroken. Her garage was destroyed. Again. But her mind wasn't on the damage.

It was on revenge.

"That asshole's never gonna learn," she muttered.

Five minutes later, her war plans were interrupted by a knock at the door. A police officer had arrived to investigate her stolen vehicle. Which meant her garage door story needed... editing.

It probably wouldn't help to mention the prelude of carefully curated dogshit.

And she certainly didn't mention her very strong hunch about who stole the car.

Half an hour later, the cop drove off satisfied.

Mrs. Grabine stood in the doorway, arms folded, lips tight.

She watched the patrol car disappear down the street. Her jaw clenched. Her mind sharpened.

Then, to no one but herself, she spoke.

"You just fucked with the wrong fat ass, clown boy."

Chapter Ninety

My first instinct was to run to my wife. But before I could take a second step, The Mantis's hand clamped down on my shoulder and stopped me cold.

"Now, Mike," he said, his voice steady and almost gentle. "You don't really want to do that, do you? Things could get a *lot* uglier than they already are, I assure you."

I froze. He didn't need to raise his voice. The weight of his calm was more terrifying than a scream.

"Take a breath. Running to your wife won't help any-one—least of all her. All it'll do is get you hurt. Or worse."

He leaned in closer.

"The solution here is simple. Bring me *Irony*. You have one hour. As we discussed."

Then, with a casual wave of his hand, our wives were led away—escorted back into the trees at gunpoint.

Clint and I stood paralyzed, rage and fear clawing through our guts.

Without another word, The Mantis slipped into his Jaguar.

And just like that, he was gone.

Chapter Ninety One

Obeying The Mantis's instructions, Bill Daylay drove to The Seed mansion.

Eddie Bretz, cradling his broken penis like a wounded animal, glanced nervously out the window. He recognized the place instantly.

"What the hell's going on?" he asked, voice cracking. "Why are you taking me here?"

"Just a little meeting with The Mantis," Bill said flatly.

"You little fucker. You sold me out, didn't you?!"

Bill rested a hand on his nightstick. Instantly, Eddie shrank against the door like a terrified toddler.

"That's more like it. Just settle down, Eddie. Okay?"

"But why?" Eddie whimpered. "What did I do to you? Haven't I been good to you? Haven't I paid you? Why would you do this to me?"

Bill pulled the car into the long circular driveway and parked in front of the mansion.

He turned off the ignition, took a breath, and looked at Eddie.

"Nothing personal," Bill said. Then he paused. "Wait, scratch that. It *is* personal. You're a prick, Eddie."

He stepped out and walked around to the passenger side.

Click.

The door was locked.

Bill sighed and fished out his key fob. He hit the unlock button.

Click.

Eddie slammed the lock down again.

Bill unlocked it.

Click.

Locked again.

They did this five times. It felt like the world's stupidest hostage negotiation.

Finally, Bill hunched over, voice low and sharp. "Open. The. Fucking. Door."

Eddie shook his head like a stubborn toddler.

Bill pulled his service revolver and pointed it straight at Eddie's face.

Eddie blinked. Then slowly — *click* — unlocked the door.

"Smart move," Bill muttered.

He opened the door and gestured.

"Out."

"I can't walk," Eddie whined. "My penis! Remember?!"

Bill groaned and paced. The steep staircase to the mansion loomed like a punishment from God. He had two options: carry this sack of crap himself or get help. Neither appealed to him.

Finally, he reached for his belt.

"Alright, here's what's gonna happen."

He cuffed Eddie's good wrist—just below the cast—then clipped the other cuff to the inside door handle.

"I'm going in to get someone to help. Don't try anything cute, Eddie."

Eddie nodded quickly.

"Good."

Bill turned toward the mansion, muttering, "God, I hate this fucking job."

Satisfied that Eddie wasn't going anywhere, Bill turned and climbed the steps to the mansion.

At the top landing, he glanced back at the cruiser—one last check to make sure the human hemorrhoid was still there—then disappeared inside.

Less than five minutes later, he emerged with a grunt from the mansion in tow.

But when Bill looked down the steps toward the driveway…

The car was gone.

Eddie Bretz — broken dick and all — had vanished.

Chapter Ninety Two

An hour after leaving the house, the clowns had everything they needed: two cases of beer, beef jerky, a giant bag of M&M's, twenty gallons of empty water jugs, and a fresh stash of gasoline for their hats.

When they pulled into the driveway, they were buzzing with excitement over their upcoming revenge mission. That excitement, of course, was only magnified by the steady stream of fumes still coursing through their brains.

Even without the beer, they were already half-wasted. But they had a goal — and that goal was piss.

Inside the house, they sprang into action. The plan was simple: chug beer until the jugs were full of pee. Genius.

Three Yuenglings in and only a quarter-gallon filled, the clowns were wobbling like inflatable tube men.

Any normal human would've realized how absurd this plan was.

But they weren't normal humans.

They were clowns.

So they kept going, guzzling beer like frat boys at a demolition derby.

Twenty minutes later, they were both passed out on the floor—surrounded by empty cans, uncapped jugs, and one very confused cat.

It wouldn't be until morning that they'd discover the newest chapter in Mrs. Fat Ass's ongoing war.

And this time, she had *upped her game.*

Chapter Ninety Three

Eddie was extremely proud of himself. Not only had he managed to hot-wire a car with one hand, but the fact that he was able to drive was truly impressive. With his right hand still cuffed to the passenger side door, he stretched his left leg over to the gas pedal and used his free hand to steer. Naturally, this elongated position was excruciating for a man with a broken penis. But he continued to drive, motivated by the thought of The Mantis mounting him from behind.

But he couldn't drive like this for long. Not just because of the pain, but also because the entire police force would be looking for him. And if he didn't ditch the car, it would only be a matter of time before they caught him.

Unfortunately, he didn't have many options. Because he was such an asshole, he didn't have any friends. And he didn't have any family to speak of, especially since he killed his mother several years ago. Really, the only people in his life were his associates at The Seed. But it certainly looked like they were no longer an option either.

That left Storm. While he did still blame her for his fractured pecker, she was the only one Eddie could turn to for help. So Eddie pulled behind a vacant strip mall and dialed his cell phone.

"Storm?"

"Eddie? How's your dick," she asked between muffled laughter.

"Are you laughing at me, bitch," he screamed. But he immediately realized this was not the way to get her assistance. "Sorry, babe. It's been a bad day. I really need you, honey."

"What?! You're telling me you want a blow job with your dick in a splint?"

"No, you stupid cunt. I mean no, honey. I just need you to come get me. Please. I'll pay you dearly, Storm," he begged. This, of course, was complete bullshit. He had no intentions of paying her a single cent. In fact, Eddie was still going to choke her to death once she freed him from the patrol car.

"Are you ok, Eddie? You don't sound to good."

"I'm not. That's why I need you. Name your price, Storm and you got it. OK?"

"Sure, Eddie. But believe me, you're not gonna like my price."

Ten minutes later, Eddie hung up his phone and Storm was on her way.

Chapter Ninety Four

As Eddie waited for his hooker to arrive, he struggled to imagine a way out of his predicament.

Sure, he fully intended to kill Storm. In his mind, it was only fair—if she hadn't pulled her infamous "nod job" stunt, he wouldn't have jerked himself into a medical emergency. She broke his dick by proxy.

But before he could strangle her with his good hand, he needed her help.

Beyond that? He was clueless.

Bill Daylay had turned out to be a traitor. Which meant The Mantis now knew the truth—*Irony* wasn't in production. There were no trial runs. No progress reports. Just a trail of bullshit and blow jobs.

And no *Irony* meant one thing: Eddie was royally fucked.

Soon to be literally, if The Mantis had his way.

There was no long-term plan. No masterstroke escape. All Eddie had was a single, pressing priority:

Get the fuck out of this police cruiser, and put as much distance between himself and The Mantis' sex dungeon as possible.

Problem was, with one hand cuffed to the passenger-side door and a penis held together with gauze and hope, his options were limited.

Without Storm, he wasn't going anywhere.

Still, Eddie allowed himself one twisted fantasy. Maybe — *just maybe* — he'd get one final blow job before he wrapped his fingers around her throat.

Broken penis or not, he figured it was worth a shot.

Chapter Ninety Five

Standing outside The Mantis' mansion, Bill Daylay was in shock.

Eddie Bretz had vanished.

Still trying to process what had happened, Bill was snapped back to reality as The Mantis' Jaguar purred into the driveway.

The car door swung open. The Mantis stepped out — smiling.

"Bill," he said, adjusting his tailored jacket. "Where is Eddie? As you can see, I'm rather excited to see him."

He motioned downward.

Bill's eyes dropped to the grotesque bulge in The Mantis' pants. Words failed him.

"I'll ask again," The Mantis said, voice tightening. "Where. Is. Eddie? I require immediate... attention."

"Mantis, I—I don't know how to tell you this. He's gone."

"Please explain. Then explain what I'm supposed to do with this erection."

Bill stammered through the story—how he'd hand-cuffed Eddie to the patrol car, how he'd gone inside the mansion for help, how when he returned... Eddie was gone.

"I swear, Mantis. It was five minutes. That's it. Just five—"

He turned to the Seed goon standing nearby. "Wasn't it? Tell him."

The man stayed quiet, waiting for The Mantis to speak.

With a slight nod from the boss, he finally replied, "That's correct. Bill came inside and asked for help. Eddie said he couldn't walk, on account of the, uh… broken penis."

"I see," The Mantis said, cutting him off. "Thank you, Rick. That'll be all."

Rick made himself scarce.

The Mantis turned back to Bill and draped an arm around his shoulders with unsettling ease.

"Let's take a little walk," he said, his voice calm, almost cheerful. "We'll need to figure out a *Plan B* for this erection… won't we?"

Chapter Ninety Six

Finally, Storm arrived.

In reality, it had only been fifteen minutes. But to Eddie—handcuffed inside a patrol car, balls-deep in paranoia, and nursing a shattered penis—it felt like decades. Each tick of the clock stoked his fury. And in the best of times, Eddie Bretz was not a patient man. In these, the absolute worst of times?

Eddie was about to go full apeshit.
Until Storm stepped out of the car.
Damn, Eddie thought. *She looks fucking hot.*
And just like that, the rage melted away.

Despite his predicament... despite the shooting pain from his mutilated member... his mind flooded with one singular, overwhelming thought: *nod job*. The moment she started walking toward him, every angry impulse in his body bowed to the growing tent in his pants.

Fuck The Seed.
Fuck Bill Daylay.
Fuck The Mantis.
Fuck Irony.

All that mattered now was his dick—and the woman who, despite everything, still made it rise from the dead.

He wasn't exactly sure what to make of this emotional whiplash. Ten minutes ago, he wanted to strangle her to death. Now? He was terrified of losing her.

And that... that was the scariest thought of all. Even scarier than getting prison-pounded by The Mantis. Somewhere between humiliation, arousal, and desperation... Eddie had fallen in love.

Had to be love, he reasoned. *What else could explain this boner?*

His dick was barely held together with gauze and Ibuprofen. And yet here it was, trying to salute. Sure, her mini-skirt and belly shirt helped. She was a smoke-show. But what kind of lunatic gets wood with a splintered shaft?

Only someone truly, deeply in love.

Maybe we can make it work, he thought. *Therapy, fresh start, mutual respect.* No more blowjobs while he was taking a dump—unless she was into that. No more throwing money at her feet. No more "bitch" or "cunt" talk.

She deserved better. And for the first time in his life, Eddie was ready to try.

Storm opened the door.

"Eddie, before we get started, let's talk money. I—"

"Shut the fuck up, bitch. I mean, uh—uh—I'm sorry. That won't happen again, sweetie. I think... I think I love you."

"Wait a minute," Storm interrupted. "Did you just call me *sweetie*? What the actual fuck is going on, Eddie? 'Sweetie' doesn't sound like the Eddie Bretz I know. This is... this is fucked. You're acting weird as hell and—"

She froze, eyes wide.

"What the fuck is *that*? Is that a *boner*?! You have a fucking boner? How in the hell..."

"It's because of *you*, Storm!" Eddie shouted, desperate. "I'm acting crazy because of *you*! And yes, I have a boner. A rock hard boner. Because of *you*! And not just because of your nod job—though let's be real, that shit drives me absolutely nuts—but it's... it's more than that."

He stammered, trying to wrestle his emotions into words.

"It's *you*, Storm. All of you. Forget the bullshit, forget the past—I know I treated you like shit. But I'm different now. You've gotta believe me."

"Eddie, what the fuck are you trying to say?" Storm narrowed her eyes. "If it's about the money, I *told* you, this isn't gonna be cheap."

"No, wait—just hear me out. Please." Eddie held up his cuffed hand. "This has nothing to do with money. It's about *you*. And *me*. And us."

"Eddie, I..."

"Storm, I love you," he blurted out. "I've never loved anyone in my life — until now."

There was a pause. A long, awkward pause.

"...Are you on medication?" Storm asked, genuinely concerned.

"Not now. But if you have any, I could use it. This erection is *killing* me."

She stared at him, blinking. Then, slowly, a smile crept across her face.

"I don't have meds, Eddie," she said, reaching into his lap. "But I've got something better. Free of charge."

Chapter Ninety Seven

Despite his status as a police officer, Bill Daylay had no illusions about who was really in charge. The Mantis had made that brutally clear—in his sex room. Like Eddie Bretz and countless victims before him, Bill had been strapped to the infamous table while The Mantis masturbated onto his exposed backside.

An ass that had been savagely bitten, Bill thought bitterly, rubbing his sore buttocks.

As he hurriedly pulled up his pants, two urgent tasks loomed: find Eddie Bretz and recover *Irony*. The Mantis had outlined, in vivid detail, the punishment for failure—and Bill had no intention of returning to that godforsaken room.

He pulled out his phone and dialed Officer Malor.

"Chuck, we've got a situation."

Bill summarized Eddie's deception—the fake lab results, the lie about *Irony's* readiness—and how it had blown up in their faces. Conveniently, he left out the fact that *he* was the one who ratted Eddie out. He also skipped over the part where The Mantis had punished him with what could generously be described as traumatic sexual horror.

As far as Bill was concerned, what happened in the sex room needed to stay buried in the dark.

"How the fuck did Eddie drive outta there? Wasn't he cuffed to your door?" Chuck asked.

"Don't worry about that. The guy's a resourceful piece of shit, apparently. Doesn't matter how. What matters is that you find him. Fast. My cruiser's got a GPS — same as all department vehicles. Track it. Quietly. We can't afford anyone else getting involved or this whole thing blows sky-high."

"You got it, boss. No worries. I'm pretty savvy with the tech stuff. We'll locate the car within the hour — just gotta hope Eddie's still cuffed inside."

"Then get on it. I'm counting on you."

"You got it. And hey — one more thing."

"What?"

"With Eddie outta the picture... does that mean you're moving up? And if you are, any chance you could help a brother out?"

Chapter Ninety Eight

For a few moments, Clint and I stood together in silence. The image of our wives being whisked away — the helplessness, the pure evil radiating from The Mantis — left us in a daze. Not just fear. Not just anxiety. But despair.

We were well and truly fucked.

And yet, the clock didn't care. It kept ticking. Fifty-seven minutes became fifty-six, and no matter how frozen we felt, time marched forward. When the hour ran out, we knew The Mantis wouldn't hesitate. Our wives would be dead — no drama, no mercy, no second chances.

Retrieving *Irony* wasn't the issue. We already had what remained of it in the trunk of Mrs. Grabine's stolen Honda. The problem was what happened *after*. Because once we handed over the coke, any leverage we had was gone. Completely.

Did we trust The Mantis? Of course not. Would our lives return to normal once the deal was done? Highly unlikely. The cleanest path for The Mantis — the one he was probably already planning — was for all of us to simply disappear. Quietly. Permanently.

So like I said—we were fucked.

Don't hand over *Irony*, and our wives die.

Hand it over, and we *all* die.

Clint and I couldn't envision a single version of this ending well.

And the clock kept ticking.

Chapter Ninety Nine

Well," I said, "we've got about an hour to kill. Possibly the last hour of our lives. What say we go have a quick drink?"

"Sure. Why not? One last toast to this beautiful shitshow," Clint replied.

"You know, Clint? If I die, it's all your fault." I shoved him in the back. Maybe it was weird, being so flippant given our predicament—but what was the alternative? Curl up and cry in the fetal position? Not my style.

Stumbling ahead from my push, Clint stopped, turned around, and cocked his fist like he was about to swing.

"C'mon, motherfucker. Bring it," I dared, curling two fingers toward my chest like *Mr. T with a death wish*.

"Aww, you don't want any part of me, you big ol' pussy."

And just like that, the slap fight began.

We lost it—howling with laughter, smacking each other upside the head like deranged middle schoolers. Finally, I wrestled Clint to the ground, pinning him flat on his back.

"Ever been brown fingered?" I asked.

Clint blinked. "What the fuck is that?"

I rolled off him, both of us now flat on our backs, staring at the sky.

"Finster," I said, "used to stick his finger up his own ass… then jam that same finger up someone else's nose."

There was a moment of silence.

"You're shitting me," Clint said, horrified.

"Nope. I watched it happen. My friend Domenic was stopped at a red light, window down. Finster walks up—bam!—fishhooks his nostril with the full-on brown finger. Dom jumps out of the car and chases him through traffic. I laughed so hard I thought I was gonna pass out."

"No shit. Pardon the pun," Clint said. "The depths of that asshole's depravity are fucking impressive."

I nodded, choosing not to mention the time *I* got brown fingered—or the time I retaliated, years later, in the back row of Mr. Farrell's Civics class.

Some stories were best saved for a second date.

Still lying there, catching our breath, I turned my head toward Clint.

"Hey. I'm sure this'll sound crazy. But tell me what you think of this..."

Chapter One Hundred

Slowly — finally — the two morons stirred from their alcohol and gasoline-induced comas.

Finster woke first, groaning as he struggled to sit upright. Though surrounded by dogshit, he couldn't smell a thing — his nostrils had been torched by petroleum fumes.

Sitting up proved too ambitious. With a retch, Finster projectile vomited directly onto Bozo, who, remarkably, did not wake. The clown did groan, however — then opened his mouth and slurped in a bit of puke like it was soup. Smacking his lips contentedly, Bozo continued to sleep.

Though Finster's nausea subsided, his skull throbbed like it was being jackhammered from the inside. He writhed on the ground, moaning in agony — rolling through a minefield of dogshit. At one point, he knocked over a jug of mostly-piss intended for their revenge scheme against Mrs. Grabine. Naturally, he noticed none of this. His entire existence had narrowed to the pain in his head.

Bozo finally stirred. Whether it was the lukewarm urine soaking into his leg or the vomit cooling on his face, something finally did the trick. Unlike Finster, Bozo felt amazing. Rested. Rejuvenated. At peace with the universe. He stretched, yawned, and smiled like a man waking from a weekend spa retreat.

Oblivious to the bodily fluids clinging to him, Bozo popped up and started to sing.

"I don't like Mondays, no Tuesdays, no Wednesdays, no Thurdays..."

"Aww, man, Bozo," Finster groaned. "Keep singing, bro. Keep singing. Your voice is like fucking medicine. My head is killing me."

Bozo dropped to one knee and gently patted Finster's back.

"Time to take some real medicine, my friend." He reached into the beer stash and cracked two cans.

"I *am* kinda thirsty," Finster said, easing himself upright.

"There ya go. It'll soothe what ails ya. Cheers, bro." Bozo clinked their cans and they both took a long drink.

"Damn, that hits the spot. I—" Finster stopped midsentence, eyes locked on the hallway. Hanging from the ceiling was a sign:

HEY ASSHOLES. LOOKING FOR THE REST OF THESE?

Pinned to it: one of Bozo's prized clown porn DVDs.

Bozo's face twisted with rage. "That total fucking *cunt*! That fat-ass wants to fuck with me?! *I'll fucking kill her!*"

"Yeah," Finster said, nodding solemnly. "That is *not* cool, bro. Not cool at all."

"Not cool is right, Fin. I'm serious—I'm gonna kill Mrs. Grabine. Slowly. That bitch fucked with the wrong clown."

Still fuming, the two idiots stomped over to the sign and yanked it down. Big mistake.

A thick brown slurry rained down from above, drenching them from head to toe. They stood frozen in disbelief, blinking shit out of their eyes like confused toddlers at a waterpark. Unbeknownst to them, Mrs. Grabine was a retired science teacher—and a master of pulley systems. This particular system was rigged with a five-gallon dogshit payload.

"Motherfucker!" Bozo screamed, charging toward the front door like a poop-soaked linebacker.

They made it to the middle of the street—then stopped cold.

There she was.

Mrs. Grabine, leaning casually on her mailbox with a pump-action shotgun in one hand. Her dog, Lulu, sat obediently by her side, posture perfect, as if posing for a Norman Rockwell painting from hell.

"I'm gonna kill you, you fucking Fat Ass!" Bozo yelled, taking a step forward.

Mrs. Grabine raised her voice just enough. "Sic 'em, Lulu."

Lulu exploded into motion, crossing the lawn with terrifying speed.

Bozo didn't stand a chance. He lifted his right arm to shield his face—and Lulu went straight for it. Her jaws clamped down with unholy force, shaking him like a rag doll. Bozo screamed and hit the pavement, flailing like a bug on its back.

"Get it off me! Get it the fuck off!"

Finster ran in, heroically stupid, and booted Lulu in the ribs.

Bad move.

The dog yelped, then pivoted and launched at Finster. Seconds later, he was on the ground too—sprawled across Bozo—while Lulu latched onto his upper thigh. Her jaws clenched dangerously close to his nutsack.

"Aaagh! My balls! She's gonna eat my balls!" Finster shrieked, flailing and slapping like a drunk toddler.

"Help! Please!" Bozo screamed, completely pinned beneath the clown pile.

"*Her*, dipshit," Mrs. Grabine corrected, now looming over them with the shotgun slung casually across her shoulder. "Lulu doesn't have a cock. Try to keep up."

She whistled. "Heel, girl."

Lulu released her grip and backed off slowly, tail still wagging with violent anticipation. Her eyes never left the clowns.

Mrs. Grabine stepped closer and cocked her head, looking down at them like someone examining two spoiled bags of meat.

"Bozo, I seem to be missing a car. Black Honda. Ring any bells?"

Bozo didn't answer.

"I already reported it stolen," she continued, "but I figured I'd keep things neighborly and handle our little... dispute... off the books."

She leaned in.

"Don't you think that was generous, shithead?"

"Fuck you, Fat Ass," Bozo growled, still pinned under Finster.

Mrs. Grabine smiled and nodded.

"Sic 'em, Lulu."

The second attack was worse.

Lulu lunged for Bozo's head, teeth sinking into his ear and yanking like she was pulling a stubborn weed. Bozo screamed and clawed at her collar, one hand gripping her snout, the other desperately holding on to what remained of his ear. But the dog wouldn't let go.

She dragged him down the driveway, scraping his back along the concrete like a human Swiffer mop.

"PLEASE! BITCH! CALL HIM OFF!" Bozo shrieked.

"*Her.*" Mrs. Grabine corrected again. "Jesus, you're dumb."

"Well. Let me think about that," Mrs. Grabine said, casually adjusting the shotgun on her shoulder. "Calling me a bitch is *slightly* better than Fat Ass. *Slightly.* Still, when I'm being asked for a favor, I usually get a little more respect."

"Okay, okay! I'm sorry!" Bozo begged, still locked in a desperate tug-of-war with Lulu, the survival of his ear very much in doubt. "Please, ma'am. Please get him to stop!"

"I told you already," Mrs. Grabine snapped, whacking him across the cheek with the butt of her shotgun. "My dog is a *female,* you stupid fuck. Heel, Lulu."

The dog obeyed, reluctantly releasing her grip, but not before one final growl inches from Bozo's face—a guttural warning that she was still on standby.

"Now let's try this one more time," Mrs. Grabine said, stepping back a few feet and fanning the air in front of her face. "Where's my damn car, douchebag? And speak up, will ya? You assholes smell like a landfill. Not sure *why,* but I can't get within ten feet of you."

"You fucking—"

Before Bozo could finish his comeback, Finster elbowed him hard in the ribs. Bozo wheezed and turned his head, but the look on Finster's face stopped him cold.

"Bro," Finster hissed. "The dog is *fucking insane.* Just chill out. We gotta get your ear sewn back on—it's hanging by, like, a goddamn thread. If she gets it again, it's gone. And I don't want her getting another shot at my nuts, either."

Bozo clenched his jaw but kept quiet.

Finster turned to Mrs. Grabine, preparing to throw himself on the mercy of her shotgun-wielding court. He was ready to spill everything—The Seed, The Mantis, the missing coke, all of it—in hopes she'd show a shred of sympathy.

But just as he opened his mouth to explain, her black Honda pulled up to the curb.

The driver's side door opened, and out stepped Clint.

"What the hell's going on here?" he asked, eyes locking on the clowns, the shotgun, the dog, and the sheer absurdity of the scene.

·◦✿◦·

Chapter One Hundred And One

Ahhhhhhh! What the fuck!" Eddie howled. Instead of gently cradling his fractured penis as he'd fantasized, Storm had gripped it with a vice-like squeeze that made him see stars.

Releasing her hold, she looked him dead in the eye. "That's for all the times you treated me like shit. It doesn't make us even—but it's a start."

Woozy from the pain, Eddie wheezed, "I know, babe. I know. I don't even know why I treated you that way."

He paused.

"Wait. Who am I kidding? I *do* know why. My mom was a complete cunt. A real sadistic bitch. You see this scar on my nose?" He pointed. "That was her. She sliced it open to teach me the word *symmetry*."

Storm blinked. "Wait. What?"

"She was an English teacher with a flair for corporal punishment. She smashed my finger with a hammer once to teach me *contrast*. Compared the broken one to the normal ones. Vocabulary lessons by way of blunt force trauma. And that curling iron? Not for her hair. She used to spank me with that fuckin' thing. High heat."

"Aww, Eddie," Storm murmured, her voice softening as she reached over and stroked his head. "That explains a lot. You know, I've put up with a lot of your crap over the years. And it wasn't for the money."

"You love me," Eddie said, half-question, half-statement.

"I do. I have. Since the day we met."

"You remember that day?" he asked, his tone shifting—hopeful now.

"Of course I do. You made me blow you while you were taking a dump."

"I meant the *other* part," Eddie interjected, cringing. "The bar. Before I knew you were a hooker."

Storm smiled despite herself. "You came over and told me I was the most beautiful woman you'd ever seen. Then you had the bartender bring me some ice for my black eye. And then, of course, you had the guy who gave it to me killed."

"How could I *not* fall in love?" she added, smirking.

"I love you too, Storm. I truly do."

They embraced, holding each other tightly. But then Storm pulled back, looking him straight in the eye.

"For this to work, Eddie, things have to be different. I deserve respect. I deserve to be treated like someone you *love*. Not like some piece of garbage you pulled off the curb."

"I know, Storm. I know. I promise, I'll change. No matter how much of a cunt my mother was, that doesn't excuse how I treated you. Never again, Storm. Never again."

"You better not," she said — and squeezed his dick.

"Ahhh!" Eddie yelped. "Okay, okay — I get it, babe. Loud and clear. Now... could you ease up? Not all the way, just... a little."

"Eddie, you're fucking crazy. I think your dick needs time to heal. Don't you think?"

"I — Shit! It's the cops!" Eddie blurted, pointing to the parking lot entrance. "Fuck! He sees us!"

In the flush of their newfound romance, neither of them had addressed a rather urgent logistical detail: Eddie was still handcuffed to the passenger door. Luckily for him, it was his broken right arm that was cuffed, leaving his uninjured left free to grab the shotgun mounted in the cruiser.

"Babe, listen to me," Eddie said, voice low and serious. "We don't have much of a choice here. That fucker's not planning to take me to jail. He's taking me to The Mantis. And there's no way in hell I'm going there alive."

"I'm in," Storm said instantly. "I'm not going back to my old life. I'm done blowing random dudes for money. This mouth belongs to *you* now," she added with a wink. "Let's do it."

"You sure? You can get out now. Run. Start fresh. Forget all this."

Storm put a hand over his mouth.

"Let's do it," she said, then kissed him.

After they pulled apart, Eddie nodded toward the dangling wires under the dash.

"Hot-wire it, babe. I already stripped it. Just twist the red and yellow."

Storm reached under the steering column and sparked the engine to life.

"Alright then," Eddie said, cocking the shotgun. "Buckle up."

Outside, a voice bellowed through a loudspeaker.

"Turn off the car. Hands where I can see them. Step out, Storm. Not you, dickhead—you're not going any-where. But you, Storm, get the fuck out of the car, you whore."

Pedestrians outside the strip mall gasped at the of-ficer's language, but Chuck Malor didn't give a single shit. He had one mission: deliver Eddie to his boss—and by extension, to The Mantis. If anyone had a problem with his bedside manner, they could fuck right off.

"I'm gonna kill that motherfucker," Eddie growled. "Calling you a whore? *How dare he.*"

He gently stroked Storm's hair, his broken dick for-gotten in the rush of adrenaline and love.

"Don't worry about me, Eddie. I've been called a hell of a lot worse."

"I said get the fuck out of the car. Now, Storm!" Officer Malor screamed through the loudspeaker.

"Gun it, babe," Eddie said calmly.

Storm dropped the car into drive and floored the gas.

"Stop the car! Stop the fucking car, you crazy bitch!" Chuck shouted as the vehicle barreled toward him. There wasn't enough time to reposition his cruiser — so he did what any cornered coward would do: emptied his service revolver into the oncoming vehicle.

Bullets tore through the windshield, sending spiderweb cracks across the glass — but miraculously missed both Eddie and Storm.

Just before impact, Storm slammed the brakes.

Eddie raised the shotgun, braced it against his shoulder, and fired through the shattered glass.

The blast caught Officer Malor dead center. He dropped instantly, like a ragdoll tossed from a rooftop.

The recoil from the shotgun was far more than Eddie anticipated. The jolt slammed him back against the seat and sent a lightning bolt of pain directly through his groin.

"Goddamnit!" he screamed. "Holy shit, that fucking *hurt!*"

He hunched forward, clutching himself, on the verge of blacking out.

"Are you alright, babe? I can't believe you did it. That shot was *insane*."

"I'm alive. My dick's not thrilled, but yeah—I told you I was gonna kill that bastard."

"Yes you did, Eddie. Yes, you did," Storm said, smiling like a proud wife in a Tarantino wedding video.

Eddie groaned. "Alright. Do me one more favor, sweetie. See that hardware store over there?"

Storm followed his gaze.

"Run in, grab a hacksaw. We need to lose the cuffs. Then we find a new ride—*fast*."

Chapter One Hundred And Two

"Bill, we have a situation," Officer Tulber stammered. "Chuck's dead. He was shot outside the Brookhaven Strip Mall. Multiple witnesses. It was Eddie. And his prostitute—Storm."

"Jesus Christ," Bill muttered. "Where the fuck are they? Did they get away?"

"We don't know yet. Just got the 911 call. We're en route now. GPS says your cruiser's still at the mall, but whether Eddie's still there? No clue. I'll update you as soon as we get eyes on the scene."

"Motherfuckers," Bill said, rubbing his temple. "Get *everyone* on this. Now. We're gonna have a shitstorm on our hands if this isn't contained. Do you fucking hear me, Tulber?"

"Understood. I'm on it."

"You better be. Or you'll be explaining your failure to The Mantis—*personally*."

He hung up and started pacing.

His mind raced, still raw from the sting of the bite on his ass courtesy of The Mantis' "discipline." Doubt crept in: *Had he miscalculated?* Maybe being closer to The Mantis wasn't the career move he thought it was. With Eddie in charge, at least there was a buffer between him and that sadistic psychopath.

But no—he shook the thought off. He'd made the right call.

Sure, moving up meant more visibility. More responsibility. More chances to be blamed. And yes, a significantly *higher* likelihood of dying in a creatively perverse way. But he was done taking orders from Eddie Bretz and watching him get blown in squad cars like some perverted mob mascot.

No. This was the right decision. He just had to survive it.

Still, Officer Tulber better come through—*fast*. Bill checked his watch.

The Mantis' one-hour deadline for Mike and Clint was almost up.

Eddie might be off the grid, but if *Irony* made its way back into The Mantis' hands, maybe—*just maybe*—his boss would be in a better mood.

And if Bill was really lucky?

He'd avoid another trip to the sex room.

Chapter One Hundred And Three

When Clint and I discussed our plan, we knew the risks. Danger was a given—comes with the territory when you're juggling high-potency cocaine and a drug cartel run by a sociopath.

But factoring in two clowns with a gasoline-huffing hobby? That was just courting chaos.

So when we pulled up to Bozo's house, we didn't know what to expect. Still, seeing Bozo and Finster on the ground, Mrs. Grabine standing over them with a shotgun and a growling dog? Not even on the list.

"What's going on here?" Clint asked, hopping out of the car.

"And what the fuck is that smell?" I added. Though I was pretty sure I already knew. It was the stench of something foul and fecal—and judging by the clowns' appearance, it wasn't decorative.

"I think *I* deserve an answer first," Mrs. Grabine interrupted, not even looking at us. "Considering you were just driving my stolen car. So go ahead. Explain yourselves. Or maybe Lulu and I get a little better acquainted with your face."

"You better listen, Woody," Finster chimed in. "That dog's fucking psycho. Look what she did to Bozo's—OW! What the hell, bitch? Why'd you kick me?"

"I told you, douche bag. My dog isn't a *he*. Lulu is a *she*. Get it straight. And call me 'bitch' again, I *dare* you."

As if on cue, Lulu let out a low, menacing growl.

"Sorry! I'm sorry! Just keep her away from me!" Finster whimpered.

Mrs. Grabine didn't answer. She just glared at the clowns and gently stroked Lulu's head. Then she turned, finally addressing me.

"So. Why'd you steal my car? And I want the *real* story."

So I gave it to her. The whole mess—*Irony*, The Mantis, The Seed, cops on the take. I gave her the condensed version, because we had a deadline, and the Mantis didn't strike me as the patient type.

When I finished, she took a deep breath, folded her arms, and said, "You boys are in a world of shit, aren't you? And I don't just mean the two *literal* piles on the ground," she added, nodding at the clowns.

"I'm not sure how I feel about having my car stolen," she continued. "You two seem alright, but these depraved motherfuckers?" She punctuated the thought with a sharp kick to Finster's thigh.

"Ow! What the hell was *that* for?" Finster yelped.

"General principle," she said calmly.

"I can't believe I'm even considering this," she went on. "But believe it or not, I was married once. And—"

"Who the fuck would marry you, fat ass?" Bozo blurted out.

I imagine he realized his mistake before the words even finished leaving his mouth. But if not then, he sure did seconds later—right around the time Lulu launched herself at his ear.

"Motherfucker!" Bozo screamed. "Get him off me! Get him off!"

"Her, asshole."

"We get it, Mrs. Grabine—Lulu's a her. Now please, just make her stop," Finster begged, trying to peel the dog off his friend.

"Heel, Lulu."

The dog obeyed, reluctantly, and Mrs. Grabine started walking away, motioning for me and Clint to follow. So we did, leaving the clowns writhing in the driveway.

"As I was saying," she continued, "I don't know why I'm even considering this. But here I am. Like I told you—I was married once. My husband passed a few years ago. No kids. I always wanted them, but I guess it just wasn't in the cards. So yeah… I can sympathize. I can't imagine what I'd do in your shoes, knowing my family was on the line. So despite my better judgment… I want to help. There. I said it."

"We'll take all the help we can get," I said. "But we're running out of time. We'll have to figure it out on the way. Let's hit the road—and thanks again. And, uh… sorry about the whole stealing-your-car thing."

"Don't worry about it," she replied. "I'd have done the same—or worse—to save my family. But before we go, there's one thing we need to handle. Five minutes, tops."

Clint and I exchanged looks, then checked our watches. We nodded.

Mrs. Grabine walked off toward her house, returning two minutes later pushing a pressure washer in front of her and carrying a couple of towels.

"Ain't no way those clowns are getting in my car like that," she said. "They smell like shit."

"You're right about that," Clint agreed. "Just make sure you use the low-pressure nozzle, huh? No need to blast the skin off 'em."

She nodded—barely—but the smirk on her face, and the jet-engine howl of the pressure washer, suggested otherwise.

Chapter One Hundred And Four

After Eddie killed Officer Malor, Storm ran into the corner hardware store and grabbed a hacksaw. Apparently, the store owner was either immune to the commotion in the strip mall parking lot or was an extreme capitalist who didn't mind selling to an accessory to murder.

When Storm returned moments later, they realized that sawing through the handcuff would be fruitless. Instead, they used it to cut the passenger door handle. With the handcuff now dangling from his wrist, at least Eddie was free.

"Now let's get the fuck out of here," Eddie said, hopping out of the car.

Storm followed behind, running as quickly as she could to keep up. In the distance, they could hear police sirens approaching.

"Shit! We're not gonna have time to get a car right here, babe. Let's head for the woods."

The two lovers ran across the street, with onlookers staring agape. On the other side of the road, they disappeared from sight, swallowed by the tree line. Although they were free—for the moment—their troubles were far from over. Without a car, on foot, and with the cops about to descend on the area, they had to move fast.

The woods were dense, but thankfully, not very wide. Minutes after they entered, they emerged on the other side, revealing a cul-de-sac with four average-sized, middle-income homes like you'd find in any suburb in the country. The children riding their bikes seemed unconcerned by the approaching strangers, despite one of them having a handcuff dangling from his wrist.

Eddie and Storm did finally attract attention, however, when they broke the driver's side window and climbed into Billy Magee's car.

"Hey, what the fuck, dude!" Billy's son Erik screamed. "Get the fuck outta my dad's car, asshole!"

Eddie and Storm ignored the profanity-laced protest of the ten-year-old as they worked quickly to hot-wire the car. Undeterred, the kid pedaled up beside them and banged on the window.

"Get the hell outta my dad's car, assholes!"

Eddie responded with a middle finger and a smirk. Moments later, tires squealed and smoke billowed as they tore off, leaving the kid coughing in their exhaust.

Storm grinned, glancing over at Eddie. "You're surprisingly good at hot-wiring cars. It's kinda turning me on."

"Oh yeah?" Eddie slipped his right index and ring fingers into his mouth, coating them with saliva. Then, slowly, he ran his fingers along her thigh, teasing the edge of her underwear before giving her a knowing glance.

"Damn, babe. You weren't lying," Eddie said, glancing over with a grin.

Storm let out a breathless laugh, gripping the dashboard as Eddie swerved wildly through the neighborhood. Whether it was the adrenaline or just Eddie's shameless bravado, the moment had a chaotic energy all its own.

But doing 80 through a residential cul-de-sac wasn't exactly a recipe for safe driving. As they flew past a stunned mailman and briefly bounced onto the sidewalk, Eddie yanked the wheel and slammed the car back onto the road.

"Jesus, Eddie!" Storm yelled, half-laughing, half-terrified.

"Don't worry," he said, eyes wild. "I've got this."

Eddie flipped the bird at the poor mailman as they sped off. Not that the guy saw it—he was still face-down on someone's lawn after narrowly avoiding being flattened. But Eddie laughed anyway, pleased with himself.

"You're insane, Eddie. Completely insane," Storm said, stroking his cheek. "But I love you. And your fingers? Let's just say you've got a real gift."

"Don't I know it," Eddie grinned proudly. He lifted one hand and gave it an exaggerated sniff. "Still smells yummy."

Before Storm could reply, she suddenly pointed over her shoulder. "Shit. Look. Behind us."

Eddie's smile vanished as the red-and-blue lights flickered in the rearview mirror. "Fuck," he muttered, quickly easing off the gas. "Alright, babe, just play it cool. That little punk couldn't have called the cops that fast. I was only… distracted… for like, a minute."

"A damn good minute," Storm smirked, kissing his cheek.

"Okay, okay," Eddie said, trying to stay calm. "We just cruise outta this neighborhood like normal people. No panic, no sudden moves. Then we ditch this ride, find a fresh one, and disappear. Got it?"

Storm nodded. "The sooner we swap cars, the sooner I get to see you work your magic again. Watching you hot-wire this baby? Total turn-on."

"You're not wrong," Eddie said, flashing a wicked grin. "And hey, if we make it out of this mess… maybe I'll give you an encore."

Storm laughed, her eyes wide with mock innocence.

"Promises, promises."

Chapter One Hundred And Five

Inside the Mantis' mansion, Bill Daylay paced like a man possessed. Calm never came easy to him, but now, under the looming threat of his boss's wrath, he was jittering like a jackhammer. Where the hell was Eddie Bretz? And why hadn't Officer Tulber called back? The Mantis was not known for his patience — or mercy.

As Bill fumbled his phone from his pocket, about to dial, he flinched hard when The Mantis appeared in the doorway, ghostlike and sudden.

"Jesus—" Bill yelped, dropping the phone.

"Nervous, Bill?" the Mantis asked, his voice like silk wrapped around a blade.

"No. No, not at all. Why would I be nervous?" Bill chuckled nervously. "Just, you know… pacing. I always pace. Keeps the blood flowing."

The Mantis said nothing, simply staring with those jet-black eyes, the silence pressing down like a stone slab.

Bill rushed to fill it. "I swear, I—"

The Mantis raised a hand, palm out. Bill shut up.

"You see, Bill. It's not just your erratic footwork that gives you away. Shall we talk a moment? Just us."

He slung an arm around Bill's shoulder in a gesture that might have seemed friendly — if it weren't for the ice running down Bill's spine.

"Of course. Anything you want."

"That's the correct answer. Now, tell me. Who were you about to call?"

Bill hesitated. He knew lying to The Mantis was the human equivalent of self-immolation.

"Officer Tulber," he admitted. "I wanted an update."

"Ah yes. Officer Tulber. Since Officer Malor is… unavailable."

Bill nodded, gulping hard.

"Let's hope Tulber proves more useful than Chuck. Otherwise, I fear your name might be next in line for early retirement."

The Mantis smiled without warmth. Bill's blood ran cold.

"You're correct, Mantis. Chuck Malor wouldn't be able to answer the phone — because he's dead. But I guess you already knew that."

The Mantis stopped walking. His arm slid off Bill's shoulders as he slowly turned, fixing Bill with a stare that felt colder than death.

"Watch your tone, Bill," he said, voice low but razor-sharp. "Just nod your head, yes. I really don't want to hear your voice right now, if that's alright with you."

Bill swallowed hard. His throat felt like sandpaper. He nodded.

"If Chuck is dead—and I assume you deliberately failed to inform me—then who, exactly, is searching for our elusive friend, Eddie Bretz? I'll make another assumption. You have others working on this, yes? Collaborators?"

Another nod.

"I seem to be making a lot of assumptions, Bill."

"I'm sorry, Mantis—"

The punch landed like a sledgehammer. Bill doubled over, gasping, dropping to one knee.

"I *explicitly* said I didn't want to hear your voice."

Wheezing, Bill looked up and nodded again.

"Thank you. You may rise."

The Mantis extended a hand, helping him up.

Then punched him even harder in the stomach, dropping him completely this time. Bill curled on the floor, breathless and writhing. The Mantis crouched beside him, speaking softly.

"Now let's try this again. And to reiterate—for clarity—I *still* do not want to hear your voice. Understood?"

Bill nodded from the ground.

"Good. Because I detest assumptions. And you've made me rely on far too many today, haven't you, Bill?"

Another nod.

"One assumption I've been forced to make — and it is the most concerning — is that with Chuck dead, we are no closer to finding Eddie Bretz than we were an hour ago. I realize others are looking for him now — at least I do *now*, thanks to your very belated disclosure. But it leaves me with one final question…"

The Mantis leaned in, his mouth inches from Bill's ear.

"Tell me, Bill… are you more useful to me breathing… or bleeding?"

Bill barely had time to shiver before The Mantis continued.

"Let me guess. Regardless of who you've got out there looking, no one's found Eddie yet. Correct?"

Bill nodded, swallowing hard.

"I find that… deeply disappointing," The Mantis said, his voice cold, almost calm. "And when I'm disappointed, I tend to get… creative."

Bill flinched as The Mantis placed a hand on his shoulder — not in comfort, but as if testing pressure points. His grip tightened.

"What shall we do with all this mounting frustration, Bill? You may speak."

"Please, Mantis. I'm trying. We're close, I swear. Just give me—"

"I didn't ask for excuses," The Mantis cut him off. "I asked for a solution."

He turned away and slowly walked to the far end of the room, then stopped and looked down at the floor, contemplative. When he turned back, there was a glint in his eye that made Bill's skin crawl.

"I think it's time we go for a little walk. You and I. Somewhere quiet. Somewhere private. I need to think."

"Mantis, please," Bill said, his voice cracking. "I just need more time."

The Mantis didn't respond. He extended his hand.

Bill hesitated—then, on instinct, lunged for his service weapon. It was a mistake.

With lightning speed, The Mantis closed the distance, smashing his forearm into Bill's nose with a sickening crunch. Bill collapsed to the floor, his weapon skidding away across the tile.

"You always had poor reflexes, Bill," The Mantis said, standing over him. "And now look at you."

He delivered a brutal kick to Bill's ribs, followed by a precise elbow to the side of the head. Bill crumpled fully, unconscious, his body twitching once before going still.

Finished, The Mantis slowly turned, crossed the room, and picked up the gun. Without pause, he called out, "Lawrence, would you mind coming in and cleaning up this mess?"

He raised the gun, pointed it at Bill's head, and pulled the trigger.

"Also," he added, as Bill's body lay motionless on the floor, "call Officer Tulber. I'll need a replacement—and given my mood, it's time he experienced the pleasures of the sex room."

"Yes, sir," Lawrence replied, stepping into the room, utterly unfazed by the corpse at his feet.

"And one last thing, Lawrence," The Mantis said, brushing dust from his sleeve. "I'm growing tired of calling it 'the sex room.' So uncivilized. Don't you think it deserves something… more refined?"

"Understood, sir. I'll think on it," Lawrence responded, kneeling to retrieve the corpse.

Chapter One Hundred And Six

After leaving the housing development with their stolen car, Eddie and Storm headed to the nearest Walmart. Once there, they ditched the first vehicle and quickly hot-wired another. Still in the parking lot, they did it again—swapping cars not for stealth, but because Storm insisted watching Eddie work the wires was, in her words, "deeply motivating."

They might've kept the theft-and-flirt routine going indefinitely if Eddie's middle finger hadn't cramped. Romance, as it turns out, has limits. And they really did need to put some distance between themselves and the cops. More importantly, from The Mantis.

"So, which way you wanna go, babe?" Eddie asked, shaking out his hand.

Storm thought for a second. "I've always wanted to go west. Like, I don't know… Colorado. Or Utah?"

"Colorado's cool. Legal weed, mountains, and it's about a thousand miles away from that lunatic Mantis. Utah, though? Doesn't that place have, like, a weird energy?"

"Just a bunch of dudes marrying everyone in sight. Could be worse," she shrugged.

"Could be better," Eddie smirked. "Maybe we start a dispensary in Colorado. Go straight. Ish."

Storm grinned. "As long as we stay far, far away from anyone named Mantis, I'm in."

"Hell yeah. And if we happen to meet a few new play-friends out west..." Eddie raised an eyebrow, suggestively.

Storm leaned over and tapped his nose. "No solo missions, lover boy. That broken dick of yours is strictly mine. But... if they're cute, and we're both in the mood to share? We'll talk."

Eddie chuckled, then winced, adjusting his seat. "Just gimme a few weeks. Once this busted gear's back in commission, we'll revisit the topic."

"Deal," she said, smiling as she turned up the radio. "Now drive, my wounded little road warrior. We've got a whole new life to steal."

"Now that's what I call a win-win situation," Eddie said, nodding happily.

Caught up in his excitement over a future filled with orgies, Eddie momentarily lost focus—and blew through a red light. Fortunately, there wasn't a cop in sight. Unfortunately, a black Honda entered the intersection at the same time, slamming into the driver's side of the stolen SUV. The impact flipped the vehicle one and a half times before it came to a rest on its roof, Eddie and Storm dangling upside down in their seats, held in place by their belts.

The SUV was totaled. Eddie and Storm, miraculously, were fine.

"Holy shit, are you okay?" Eddie asked.

"Yeah, I'm good. You?"

"Yep. Don't feel a thing. Even my broken cock's not acting up."

"Well, that's a blessing," Storm said with a wink. "The sooner that thing heals…".

"Just because my dick's out of commission doesn't mean my fingers retired," Eddie grinned, wiggling his hand in Storm's direction.

Still dangling upside-down in their wrecked SUV, Storm blinked a few times, trying to process the absurdity—yet she didn't stop his hand from wandering.

"Eddie, we just got t-boned and flipped. Maybe we should, I don't know, *get out of the car*?"

Before Eddie could answer, a knock on the driver's side window interrupted them. A woman crouched outside, peering into the wreckage. Eddie raised one finger in the air, signaling her to wait a moment—he was clearly in the middle of something. With complete disregard, he turned back to Storm, doubling down on his effort. When the woman knocked again, Eddie simply pointed toward Storm, as if that explained everything.

Amazed, the woman's eyes widened as she slowly backed away from the wreck. Eddie shot her a thumbs up and a cocky grin. A few moments later—when the moment had passed—he reached for the window controls and rolled it down... or technically up, given they were still hanging upside-down.

"Hey, Fat Ass. What do you want?"

Without hesitation, the woman marched over, crouched beside the window, and socked Eddie square in the jaw.

"Jesus Christ! What the hell, bitch? That actually hurt!"

She pointed a finger in his face. "Call me 'Fat Ass' or 'bitch' again and I'll show you what pain really feels like."

Turning away from him, she yelled over her shoulder, "Can you believe this asshole? First he totals my car, then he calls me Fat Ass like it's some kind of nickname. What the hell is wrong with people?"

Chapter One Hundred And Seven

I strolled up beside Mrs. Grabine, Clint right behind me, with Bozo and Finster tagging along like stray dogs.

"Yeah, you really don't want to be calling Mrs. Grabine *Fat Ass*," Bozo said, peering into the wrecked SUV. "Wait—what the hell? Eddie?!"

"Bozo? What the hell are *you* doing here?" Eddie snapped, still hanging upside down.

"Well, I'd say I'm here because some maniac ran a red light. Ring any bells?"

Eddie squinted. "Are you saying *you're* the one who hit *me?* What the hell, man? Who taught you idiots how to drive—Mrs. Fat Ass here?" he said, jabbing a finger toward Mrs. Grabine.

He really should have learned by now.

Without hesitation, Mrs. Grabine marched up and kicked him square in the face through the open window.

"Aw, come on! What the hell?!" Eddie yelled, blood already dripping from his lip. "You knocked out my damn tooth!"

"Good. I'll knock out another one if you call me *any-thing* besides my name again," she growled. "You want to run that mouth, I'll help shut it."

"Yeah, yeah. Message received," Eddie muttered, dazed.

Clint leaned in close and muttered, "Wait... *this* is the broken penis guy? Eddie fucking Bretz?"

"Sure is," Bozo said, crouching next to the busted car. "That upside-down dickhead right there, groping his girl-friend like he's on spring break? He's with The Seed. Or *was*, anyway."

"Formerly," Eddie called out, brushing glass off his arm and unhooking his seatbelt. "I'm done with them. Done with all of it."

"Then you won't mind answering for the mess you left behind," I said, stepping forward. "Everything that's happened—*Irony*, The Mantis, my family—it all comes back to you."

Eddie looked up at me, upside-down and bloodied, somehow still managing a smug grin. "Yeah, well. Life's weird like that, huh?"

And then, he recognized me.

"You son of a bitch," Eddie shouted. "This is the idiot who flushed *Irony* down the toilet! Storm, remember? I told you about some jackass who duct-taped my mouth and dumped all my coke."

Storm squinted. "Wait—*this* guy?"

"Yep. What a goddamn coincidence. Mike Rodgen, right? I never forget the name of the man who completely screwed me."

"Yeah, well, the feeling's mutual," I shot back. "But honestly, we don't have time for reunions. We've got a deadline, and The Mantis doesn't do fashionably late."

Eddie's expression darkened. "What do you mean, 'keep The Mantis waiting'? What the hell's going on?"

"We'll explain. Briefly," I said, glancing at my watch. "But you need to get out of that car first. We're already pushing it."

"Fine," Eddie grunted. "Storm, help me down, will you? I'm sick of hanging here like a damn bat."

"Unless you'd like to fondle me again," Storm teased, shooting him a smirk as she unbuckled her seatbelt and began maneuvering to help him.

"Not the time, babe," Eddie muttered, wincing. "Let's just get vertical and figure out why everyone's losing their minds."

"Hurry up! Or stay in the damn car. I don't care. Either way, we're gone in three minutes," I said, nodding toward Mrs. Grabine's battered but still-running vehicle.

After thirty seconds of fumbling with their seat belts, Eddie and Storm managed to crawl out of the overturned SUV and stagger over to where the rest of us were standing.

I don't know why I didn't punch Eddie in the face right then and there. God knows he deserved it. Half the reason I was even in this nightmare was because of him. But instead of breaking his nose, I gave him the cliff-notes version of what was going on—and our fast-approaching meeting with The Mantis.

"Well, that sucks for you," Eddie said with a shrug, like I'd just told him we were out of coffee.

"Dickhead!" I snapped. "You're goddamn right it sucks for me! It sucks for my family. It sucks for Clint's family. And a huge chunk of that suckage is thanks to you!"

Eddie held up a finger. "And Finster."

"What?"

"Finster," he repeated, pointing at the clown. "Let's not forget he's the one who stole my coke. If we're handing out blame, I'd say he's earned his fair share."

I turned and glared at Finster, who looked like he was trying to remember how breathing worked. "Fine. You've got a point," I admitted. "Nevertheless, you've got—"

But I didn't get to finish.

The sound of a cop car approaching cut me off. All of us froze, eyes darting toward the siren's echo.

That hesitation lasted all of one second.

"Get in the car. Now. We've got to get the hell out of here," I barked.

The five of us ran towards Mrs. Grabine's car, leaving Eddie and Storm behind.

"Yo, what the hell, man? What am I supposed to do?" Eddie shouted, jogging up to the car. "I can't get arrested again! If the cops grab me, they'll turn me over to The Mantis—and then I'm screwed. Literally. That guy's got a reputation, and I don't mean that metaphorically."

"Sucks for you," I said, flipping him off as I reached for the ignition.

"Wait! Wait!" Eddie pleaded, his voice climbing higher as he ran beside the car. "Come on, man. Help a brother out! If I go down, I'm done. The Mantis will throw me in that room of his and—look, let's just say it won't be pretty. Please. I'm begging you."

"And why should I do that?" I asked, staring him down. "After everything you've put us through?"

Eddie looked around frantically. "Okay, yeah, sure, I've caused some problems—but so did Finster! Let's not forget he kicked off this whole mess."

"Oh, for the love of—fine," I muttered. "But you didn't answer the question. Why should I help you?"

"Because I'll help you!" Eddie blurted. "I don't know how exactly, but I will. Whatever you need, man. Just let us in before the cops roll up!"

I stared at him for a second, then turned to Clint, Finster, and Bozo. "Well, looks like the clown car's getting more crowded."

I turned back to Eddie. "Fine. Get in. But no funny business with your girlfriend, got it?"

Eddie threw a hand to his chest. "Scout's honor."

"Pretty sure you were never a scout."

"Fair. But still—no funny business. Got it."

Chapter One Hundred And Eight

Officer Tulber was confused — and more than a little on edge. Why was *Lawrence*, The Mantis's personal assistant, the one calling him? Tulber had never spoken to the guy before. Hell, he'd never spoken to The Mantis himself. That kind of communication usually went through Bill Daylay. Chain of command, and all that.

But now, Daylay was silent. And The Mantis was summoning him *directly*. Something about that didn't sit right.

Tulber trusted his instincts. They'd never failed him. Not when they told him his wife Jean was cheating with his brother. Not when they told him to stay out of the crack house on 7th Street — a decision that probably saved his life. His instincts might've been the only honest thing left in his life.

Still, he didn't have much of a choice. When The Mantis calls, you go. Simple as that.

The mansion loomed larger the closer he got. Tulber pulled up out front, left the engine running, and just sat there — watching the house, watching his breath fog up the windshield. After a few minutes, he turned the key and stepped out.

He climbed the marble steps, his hand resting near his holster. The moment his boot touched the top stair, the door creaked open.

"Officer Tulber," Lawrence said, smiling in a way that didn't reach his eyes. "Thank you for coming on such short notice. The Mantis will be... very pleased."

That last part stuck in Tulber's mind. *Very pleased.* Three harmless words, but something about the way Lawrence said them sent a chill up his spine. It was like stepping into a room and not realizing the lights were off until the door slammed behind you.

He followed Lawrence inside, every sense on high alert.

"The Mantis is very eager to meet you, as you'll soon find out. But first, we have a small matter to resolve. This way, please," Lawrence said, gesturing toward a side room with the smooth detachment of someone offering coffee instead of leading a man into a nightmare.

Tulber followed, each step heavier than the last. *Very eager to meet you.* The phrase echoed in his head, strange and loaded. He didn't like it. He didn't like any of this.

Then he saw the chair.

"What the hell?! Bill?" Tulber rushed forward, but it was obvious from the stillness, from the dark stain on the floor, that Bill Daylay wasn't going to be answering.

"I assure you, Bill will no longer be responding to anything," Lawrence said calmly. "Now, if you would, please assist me. My back isn't what it used to be. And we do need to tidy up before The Mantis arrives."

"Goddammit, Lawrence," Tulber snapped. "I'm not lifting a damn finger. You hear me? Not one."

A soft chuckle floated from the doorway.

"Ah. So this is the Officer Tulber I've heard about," came a voice—measured, refined, and unnervingly amused.

The Mantis stepped into the room with a confident stride, hand extended, smile just a touch too wide. Tulber shook it out of instinct, but the gesture didn't end. The Mantis leaned in closer than necessary, his arm draping briefly across Tulber's back like a python testing its grip.

"Now," he said softly, still smiling, "you were saying something about not helping?"

"I..."

"Officer Tulber," The Mantis interrupted, voice silk over steel, "I don't need excuses. I need obedience. Now let me ask you—who do you think you are? Or better yet, do you truly understand who *I* am?"

"Yes, sir. You're The Mantis. I—I apologize for my attitude, sir." Tulber's voice cracked slightly, his eyes darting briefly toward Lawrence.

"Hmm. I'm not convinced an apology is quite enough. You see, I demand absolute compliance. No hesitation.

No improvisation. You *do* understand what happened to Bill Daylay, don't you?"

"Yes, sir. I do. And you'll have no issues from me going forward."

"Good to hear. Though it's a shame we still have your earlier... outburst to deal with." He turned his head. "Lawrence, thoughts?"

"Perhaps he could be shown to The Nest, sir," Lawrence said mildly.

"The Nest. Hm. Not terribly inspired, Lawrence — but I appreciate the restraint. Certainly better than our previous 'sex room' terminology. Cruder days, I guess."

"Yes, sir. It could use refinement, but it does have a certain charm."

Tulber squinted between them, confused and deeply unsettled. "Look, I've heard rumors... I don't know what you people are planning, but I —"

"Please, Officer." The Mantis stepped forward, seizing Tulber's face in a surprisingly strong grip. "Now look what you've done. You've made me raise my voice. I *hate* when I lose my composure."

He released Tulber's face and straightened his jacket. His calm returned like a closing door.

"The Nest is a place for reflection, Officer. And you, it seems, have a great deal to reflect on. Lawrence, prepare the room. I believe we'll be having a longer conversation than I anticipated."

On his drive to the mansion, Tulber's mind played through every possible scenario he could think of. His instincts had warned him something was off—and he wasn't wrong. But out of all the scenarios he considered, not one involved Bill Daylay being murdered. And he damn sure hadn't imagined being dragged off to The Mantis' so-called *Nest*, the rebranded name for what everyone else called the sex room.

No, Tulber hadn't prepared for that.

He'd told himself to be ready for anything— *anything*—no matter how twisted. But telling yourself to be prepared is one thing. Actually *being* prepared? That was another matter entirely.

"Mantis, can we wait a second? Please," he asked, trying to keep his voice even. "Shouldn't I help Lawrence, maybe? You know... with the body?" He nodded toward Bill Daylay's lifeless frame.

The Mantis smiled slightly.

"Well, that is thoughtful of you, Tulber. Quite considerate. But unfortunately, what I need to discuss with you can't wait. Bill, on the other hand, won't mind sitting there a little longer. Isn't that right, Lawrence?"

Lawrence gave a courteous nod and a neutral smile. Tulber swallowed hard.

Moments later, they arrived at the room Lawrence had ominously referred to as *The Nest*. Tulber had heard whispers about it—strange, unsettling rumors that most dismissed as exaggeration. But now, standing in the doorway, staring at the cold metal table outfitted with restraints, he realized the truth was far worse than anything he'd imagined.

It felt like stepping into a nightmare — one where the door shut behind you and didn't open again.

"Tulber, I'm sure you're aware of how I use this room. And more specifically, how I use this table."

The Mantis ran his fingers slowly along the edge of the restraints. "I don't think I need to spell it out. If you'd like me to elaborate, feel free to interrupt. Otherwise, I'll assume you understand."

He turned, expression unreadable.

"This room — this *Nest* — serves a purpose. It's not just about punishment. It's about clarity. A leader must be respected... but more importantly, he must be feared."

He took a step closer.

"Do you fear me, Tulber?"

Tulber swallowed hard. "Abso-fucking-lutely, Mantis. I'm practically shitting myself. Believe that."

"Oh, I believe you. And that's good. But relax — for now. You have nothing to be worried about."

He stepped closer, just enough to make Tulber tense again.

"But if you cross me — *even once* — we'll be back here. You and I."

The Mantis placed a hand on the table's straps, then looked him dead in the eye.

"If you disobey me, if you hesitate, if you slight me in *any* way… I promise you, this room won't just be a rumor anymore. Do you understand?"

"Yes, sir. Loud and clear. You don't have to tell me twice."

"I should hope not. Telling you twice would mean you failed the first time, wouldn't it?"

"Understood. Completely." Tulber nodded, emphatic and pale.

"Good. I won't trouble you with more about *The Nest*. I trust your imagination will fill in the gaps. Now — on to business."

The Mantis walked toward the door, gesturing for Tulber to follow.

"With Bill Daylay out of the picture, that leaves a few pressing matters. First — where the fuck is Eddie Bretz?"

Tulber opened his mouth, but The Mantis cut him off with a raised hand.

"Second… we have a meeting to attend. You'll be joining me. I'd like to introduce you to Mike Rodgen, Finster, and a few others responsible for stealing something of mine."

He paused.

"Have you heard of *Irony*?"

Chapter One Hundred And Nine

Back at the apple orchard, the car came to a stop. It had only been an hour, but it felt like a lifetime.

Sitting next to me, Clint let out a breath I think he'd been holding the whole ride.

"Well," he said, "I guess this is it, huh?"

"Yeah. One way or another, it ends here. Just gotta hope we end up on top."

"We have to, Mike. We *fucking* have to. Not for us — fuck us. I've made enough mistakes for three lifetimes. If I die saving my family, I can live with that. Well, not *live* exactly, but you get it. I just — if this goes south, I don't know, man. I don't know how I'll handle it."

"Look, Clint, we've all screwed up. That's being human. Yeah, it's a cliché, but it doesn't make it less true. I wrestle with the same shit every day. And I'm not saying that to blow smoke up your ass — although I'm sure you'd enjoy that."

He flipped me the bird, but I kept going.

"Every single day, I have to *choose* to stay in the moment. Because if I don't, I'll either collapse thinking about the past or spiral out thinking about the future. So listen to me: get your head out of your ass and get your game face on. Because I need you. *My family* needs you. And more than anything, *your* family needs you."

He nodded, eyes fixed on the windshield. "I hear you. I do. But it's hard, man. There's just so many ways this can go sideways…"

"Time out," I said, cutting him off. "Just stop. How does focusing on worst-case scenarios help anything right now? Seriously — how does that help?"

He didn't answer.

"Exactly. It doesn't. Am I scared? Of course I am. Who wouldn't be? But I'm still gonna do everything in my power to get us out of this. Not just alive — free. Free from The Mantis, from all of it.

"There's a difference between having healthy fear and being *paralyzed* by it. We don't have the luxury of freezing up. I need you at your best, Clint. Your *absolute best.* That's how we win this."

"Understood," Clint said, his tone shifting. "And before you get any ideas that your brilliant pep talk inspired me — it wasn't you. It was them."

He pointed off into the distance.

About a half-mile away, a pair of cars approached. The first — a sleek, jet-black Jaguar — I recognized instantly. The Mantis. Just the thought of him made my stomach tighten.

Close behind was a cop car.

Clint and I looked at each other and, in unison, muttered, "Fucking Bill Daylay."

I guess we hated that prick equally. Betrayal'll do that to a person. Bill had betrayed his badge, sure—but worse, he'd betrayed *us*. We hadn't seen him since the day we discovered his alliance with The Seed back at the hospital—the same day we learned about Eddie's broken dick and about how deep this whole thing really went. Remembering it made my blood boil all over again.

The cars pulled to a stop.

The Mantis stepped out first—immaculate as ever, radiating that same unsettling calm. The cop car door opened, and… it wasn't Bill.

I didn't recognize the guy by name, but I'd seen him before. One of the cops who circled the hospital parking lot, trying to track us. Clint clocked it too—we shared a look that said it all.

Corruption. It ran deeper than we ever imagined.

The Mantis approached, his stride smooth and deliberate. The officer followed close behind, posture stiff.

"Good afternoon, gentlemen," The Mantis called. "You seem… surprised. May I guess why?"

He reached out to shake our hands. I hesitated, then took it. His grip was a fucking vise.

"Let me see," he continued. "Was it the police escort? Were you expecting someone else? Perhaps... Bill Daylay?"

I didn't bother hiding the glare. "Yeah. That was the assumption. So where is he? And more importantly — how many cops do you *own*, Mantis? Just how deep does this shit go?"

"Such language, Mike. I'm not a fan of profanity," he said, still gripping my hand with unnerving pressure. When he finally let go, he turned to Clint and extended his hand.

"And how are you today, Clint?"

"Just peachy, Mantis. Living the dream."

"I'm also not fond of sarcasm. Profanity and sarcasm — both cheap tools, in my view," he said, releasing Clint's hand and beginning to pace, slow and deliberate.

"As for your question, Mike — about the extent of my reach into the police force — well, let's just say it runs deeper than you'd be comfortable knowing. But why limit myself to cops? I prefer a broad network: lawyers, judges, elected officials. Influence is a currency I spend liberally. It's just smart business."

He paused, pivoting to face us. "But enough about me. Where is my product? Where is *Irony*?"

"You'll get your answer," I replied. "Right after we see our families. Not before."

The Mantis stepped forward, closing the gap between us.

"Do you really think you're in any position to negotiate? How cliché." He turned and motioned toward his car. A man exited the vehicle, carrying a box, and approached silently. Without a word, he placed it at The Mantis' feet.

"Do you remember the movie *Seven*?" Mantis asked. "Hard to believe it's been over twenty-five years since it came out. But I digress. Two detectives tracking a serial killer inspired by the seven deadly sins—gluttony, greed, sloth, the whole lineup. It's a fascinating film."

He glanced at the box, then back at us.

"I hope I'm not spoiling anything, but considering it was released in the mid-nineties, I'll assume you've seen it. Now then—back to the matter at hand. The box," he said, nodding toward it. "Thank you, Lawrence," he added with a polite tilt of the head to the man beside him.

"Gentlemen, forgive my lapse in etiquette. Allow me to make introductions. This is Lawrence," he said, gesturing to the man who brought the box. "And this is Officer Tulber. Mike and Clint, meet the newest members of my extended circle—the ones tasked with recovering what's mine: *Irony*. Go ahead, shake hands. Be civil."

Clint and I were momentarily frozen, unsure of how to react. But Lawrence stepped forward first, calm and composed, as though none of this—none of *any* of this—was remotely out of the ordinary. So we followed his lead, exchanging quick, awkward handshakes with both him and Tulber.

"With introductions out of the way," The Mantis continued, "let's return to that movie I mentioned — *Seven*. Near the end, the killer delivers a box to the detectives. Before they even open it, he describes what's inside in a way that leads one of them — Brad Pitt's character — to realize it contains a piece of his murdered wife."

He paused, eyes glinting as he looked down at the box near his feet.

"Disturbing, yes. But memorable. So… what do you suppose is in the box beside me? Any guesses, Mike? Clint?"

"You sick son of a bitch," I growled. "If you've done anything to my wife or kids, I swear to God, I'll — "

"Stop right there," The Mantis said sharply, lifting a hand. At the same time, Officer Tulber stepped forward and drew his weapon, aiming it squarely in our direction.

"Let's skip the dramatics," The Mantis continued, his tone calm but chilling. "Whatever — or whoever — is in that box, rest assured, it's just one. The box simply isn't large enough to hold more than that. But don't get too comfortable. I still have your families. All of them. So unless you want more boxes involved, I suggest you stay calm. Understood?"

"You sick bastard," I shouted, my fury boiling over as I took a step toward him.

Before I could get any closer, a loud crack split the air. The impact knocked me off my feet. Pain seared through my shoulder as I hit the ground, dazed.

"Thank you, Officer Tulber," The Mantis said, unbothered. "That was quite proactive of you. I'm sure I could've managed him myself, but this makes a better point. Consider it a warning, Mike."

Still reeling from the pain, I pushed myself to my feet, my hand pressed tightly over the wound. Clint stood beside me, motionless. His eyes were wide, mouth slightly open—blank. Shock, no doubt. After everything—losing Amy, now facing the threat of losing his wife and son—it was more than any person should be expected to handle.

"Alright," The Mantis said casually, "let's end the suspense. Lawrence, if you would."

Frozen in place, I watched as Lawrence stepped forward and knelt beside the box. He lifted the lid with the same dispassion one might use to open a gift. Inside was the severed head of Bill Daylay.

Relief hit me like a wave. Twisted as it was, I actually sobbed—with joy. My wife and kids were still alive. For now. Bill's death, grotesque as it was, meant hope. And I felt no remorse. Not a flicker. Bill betrayed everyone. He played both sides, wore the badge while selling out to monsters. He got what he deserved.

Wiping my face, I turned to Clint. Just moments ago, he'd looked shattered. But now—something had shifted. His brow was tight, his jaw set. His eyes burned with something fierce.

It wasn't fear anymore. It was resolve.

"See?" The Mantis gestured toward the box. "I can be a reasonable man. Fair, even. When you cross me, there are consequences. Sometimes... severe ones." He gave the box a light tap with his shoe. "As Bill learned."

He turned slightly. "Officer Tulber. Lawrence. Tell me — would it not have been entirely reasonable for me to have placed one of their wives in that box? Or one of their children?"

Lawrence nodded without hesitation. Tulber followed suit, a beat slower. His eyes, however, betrayed a flicker of unease as they settled on the severed head. Still, he understood the performance expected of him. Disagreement was not an option — not if he hoped to keep his own head attached.

"You see, gentlemen," The Mantis continued, his voice smooth, "I am a man of nuance. Compassionate, even. Generous, when appropriate. I know that may sound arrogant, but I find it to be accurate."

He reached into the box and lifted Bill's head by the hair, holding it up like a prize. The lifeless eyes stared out as he turned toward me.

"Mike, this could just as easily have been your wife — Suzy, yes? Or one of your daughters. Halle. Lynn. Little Janie. You understand that, don't you?"

He turned to Clint. "And you, Clint. You of all people should appreciate the fine line between mercy and devastation. This —" he raised the head slightly higher "— this could've been your wife, Marietta. Or your boy, Tommy. Imagine that, on top of losing Amy to cancer."

"You motherf—" Clint growled, stepping forward.

The Mantis didn't flinch. "Careful," he said quietly, eyes narrowing. "Think very carefully about your next words. They may be your last."

Clint froze, his lips pressed tightly together. But his eyes said everything. The Mantis studied his face for a long second. He got the message—and smiled like it was a challenge.

"You wish me dead, don't you, Clint. The hatred in your eyes—it's almost tangible. Not exactly polite, considering the hospitality I've shown you and Mike. Aren't you the least bit grateful that this," he said, lifting the severed head with both hands, "isn't your son Tommy?"

Without warning, The Mantis turned, took a single step, and punted the head like a soccer ball. It tumbled thirty feet before landing in the grass with a sickening thud.

Clint, Officer Tulber, and I just stared, stunned by what we'd seen. Lawrence, unsurprisingly, remained calm—just another day at the office.

"Lawrence, if you would," The Mantis said, extending his hand.

"Of course, sir," Lawrence replied, placing a crisp towel in his palm.

"I'll wash properly in a moment. For now, this will do," The Mantis said, dabbing his hands with slow precision. Then he turned to me, offering the towel.

"No thanks," I muttered, confused and wary.

"No, I insist." His smile was cold as ice.

Reluctantly, I took the towel.

"Now," he said, lifting one foot and pointing it at me, "if you would."

I blinked. "What the hell do you want me to do?"

"Language, Mike. Really. It's so tiresome. Wouldn't you agree, Lawrence?"

"Entirely, sir."

The Mantis shifted his weight, still holding his foot in the air. "Surely you understand. I just punted a human head. There's bound to be some blood. A bit of hair. Maybe some... scalp. And I *do* hate dirty shoes. It's unseemly. Now—clean it. Please."

"I'm not cleaning your fucking shoe," I said, glaring up at him. "Are you insane?"

I barely saw him move. The space between us vanished in a blink, and his fist landed square in my solar plexus. I've taken hits before. Been in my share of fights. Friends used to call me a badass. But this? This was something else. A freight train. A bomb.

The pain crushed the air from my lungs and dropped me to my knees. I couldn't breathe, couldn't think—just clutched at my gut, gasping.

While I wheezed on the ground, The Mantis stood over me, calm as ever.

"Déjà vu," he said. "That's what I'm feeling. Do you know why, Mike? Let me tell you. Earlier today, Bill Daylay knelt just where you are now. On the floor, gasping. Because I punched him. And not long after that? I killed him.

"Now, the real question is—how does *your* day end? Will your head wind up in a box next? Maybe I'll send it to your wife and daughters. I could even tie it with a little bow. A family keepsake. What do you think, Mike?"

Still hunched over, struggling for breath, I forced out what I could.

"You… sick… mother—"

"Careful," The Mantis warned. His voice was soft, but full of menace.

He dropped the towel in front of me.

"You know what to do."

I looked up at him, then down at the towel. Just stared for a moment, hating everything about this. Then I glanced at Clint. He met my eyes and gave me the slightest nod.

I've always thought of myself as a man with pride. Not arrogance—just dignity. But there I was, on my knees in the dirt, towel in hand. Staring at the blood, the hair, and God knows what else clinging to the polished Italian leather of a man who might murder my entire family.

And with no options left, I did it.

I wiped the damn shoe.

"That's a good boy," The Mantis said, patting me on the head like a dog. I swallowed the urge to snap his wrist.

"Now," he continued, "back to business. Where's my *Irony*?"

I stood slowly, breath ragged but steady.

"We see our families first, Mantis. Call it a gesture of good faith. You didn't kill any of them — so for now, I'll take that as a sign you're willing to deal."

His eyes narrowed.

"You're in no position to make demands," he said. "But... I do pride myself on being reasonable. Unless, of course, you'd prefer to see what unreasonable looks like."

He turned to Clint. "And you? You've been awfully quiet. Shall I give you a demonstration?"

"No, Mantis," I said quickly. "Not necessary. And honestly — I think Clint would agree — we're grateful. Our families are still breathing. That means everything. I'm just... tired. Burned out. This whole situation — it's taken a toll."

Clint nodded and stepped in. "Same here. We're not trying to provoke anything. It's just hard, knowing the people you love are entirely at someone else's mercy. If you could let us see them — even briefly — it would mean the world."

The Mantis turned to Lawrence. "Isn't it fascinating how polite people become with the sword of Damocles over their heads?"

"Quite so, sir," Lawrence said.

"Well," The Mantis mused, "whatever your motivations, I do appreciate the shift in tone." He glanced at Officer Tulber. "Let's grant their request."

Tulber nodded and stepped away, pulling out his phone. We couldn't hear the conversation, but within moments, an SUV rolled up beside the police cruiser. The driver stepped out, opened the rear door—and in one swift, careless motion, yanked Suzy out and threw her to the ground.

I took a step forward before I even realized it.

"Easy now, Mike," The Mantis warned. "Let's not escalate, hmm?"

I bit down hard, swallowing the rage, forcing myself to stay still.

"And Tulber," he added, turning slightly. "Restrain Nicholas, would you? He does get overly enthusiastic. And there's no need for that—at least not yet."

With his hands raised in a gesture of de-escalation, Tulber walked over to the SUV. We couldn't make out the conversation, but after a brief exchange, he bent down and helped Suzy to her feet. At the same time, the driver—presumably Nicholas—opened the rear door and began ushering out the rest of the passengers.

Moments later, they were all standing in a neat line: my wife Suzy and our three daughters—Halle, Lynn, and Janie—alongside Clint's wife Marietta and their son,

Tommy. No guns were pointed at them, but the message was loud and clear.

"Snookie!" Marietta called out.

"Snookums!" Clint answered, his voice cracking. "Hey Tommy! How's my big boy?! Daddy loves you, little man!"

Even with the air charged like a live wire, I couldn't help but snort at the exchange. *Snookie and Snookums?* Jesus. I used to think that was cringe — but then again, I call Suzy 'Honey Buns' and 'Sugar Plum,' so who the hell was I to judge?"

Then Suzy's voice pulled me back to the moment.

"Hon! Are you okay, babe?"

"Yeah, sweetie! I'm good! You? Girls — are you alright?! Everything's gonna be fine! Daddy loves you! You hear me? I love you!"

Before any of them could respond, our families were quickly ushered back into the SUV. Officer Tulber and Nicholas weren't exactly rough, but there was no kindness in their movements either. Just like that, they were gone — our wives, our children, driven away in a cloud of dust. And for all Clint and I knew, that might've been the last time we ever saw them.

"As you've just seen," The Mantis said smoothly, "your families are safe. For now. But whether they remain that way depends entirely on how you answer my next question. So listen carefully."

He paused, letting the moment hang heavy.

"Where is my *Irony*?"

"It's in the back of our car," I said, reaching into my pocket and pressing the key fob. The trunk clicked open with a dull mechanical thunk.

"It better be, Mike," he replied, the amusement gone from his voice. "I'm growing tired of this little game."

Then he turned to Tulber.

"If you please."

The officer gave a curt nod and started toward the car. As he moved, I glanced skyward, subtly rubbing my ear with my middle finger. A quiet signal. Whether Finster saw it or not was anyone's guess—relying on him was never a safe bet. But right now, faith was all I had.

"Mantis, are you a fan of music?" I asked.

He cocked his head slightly. "What a peculiar question, Mike, given the circumstances. But yes, I do enjoy music. My tastes are eclectic—Tupac, country, classical, even metal. Though if I had to choose, I'd say EDM. Electronic Dance Music."

He gave a sly smile.

"It's my preferred soundtrack when I'm in the sex room."

"The Nest," Lawrence corrected, without missing a beat.

"Ah, yes. The Nest," Mantis echoed with a nod. "Thank you, Lawrence. Much more civilized. Anyway,

EDM really heightens the experience. Perhaps you'd like to find out sometime?"

"I think I'll pass, Mantis."

"That remains to be seen," he said, eyes narrowing. "Depends what Tulber finds in your trunk. But tell me — why the sudden curiosity about music, Mike?"

I shrugged. "Just a thought. Been working on a song lately. Figured I'd get a second opinion."

He gave a theatrical wave of his hand. "By all means."

I'm not tone-deaf — just tone-impaired. What I lacked in pitch, I made up for with gusto. Strumming an imaginary guitar, I belted it out:

"I don't like Mondays, no Tuesdays, no Wednesdays, no Thuuursdays…"

And with that, all hell broke loose. From the trees, Finster swung down on a rope like a deranged Tarzan — if Tarzan had been raised in a junkyard instead of a jungle. He wore a makeshift construction helmet, each side rigged with a plastic canister of gasoline, plastic tubing snaking into his nostrils and held in place with duct tape. Higher than a kite in a windstorm, Finster let out a war cry that was more wheeze than roar, gripping the rope with one hand while cradling a bag of dogshit in the other.

At the same moment, the trunk of our car burst open, and Bozo sprang out like a deranged jack-in-the-box. Without missing a beat, he flung a similar lumpy bag straight into Officer Tulber's face. The impact stunned

Tulber, who stumbled back, coughing and flailing, as the bag's contents—collected earlier from Mrs. Grabine's unfortunate yard—made a memorable impression.

"What the hell?! Get him off me!" Tulber shouted, slipping on his own confusion.

Bozo didn't answer. He launched himself at the officer like a rabid chihuahua in clown makeup, tackling him to the ground in a tangle of limbs and wild shrieks. The two of them rolled across the grass, one trying to subdue, the other trying to gnaw and flail his way to victory.

Meanwhile, Finster crash-landed in a nearby bush, dazed but delighted.

"Bozo! That was incredible, man!" he shouted, trying to stand up but promptly sitting back down. "I saw it all from the sky. You came outta that trunk like a shit missile, bro! It was beautiful."

Shocked, Tulber stumbled backward, frantically clawing at his face, trying to scrape off the feces. In the confusion, Bozo sprang from the trunk and tackled him, knocking him flat on his back. Like a feral dog, Bozo sank his teeth into Tulber's face—utterly unfazed by the fact that it was covered in dogshit.

"What the fuck?! Get the fuck off me! Get the fuck—" Tulber screamed.

But Bozo didn't get off. Instead, he doubled down. This time, he went for the throat.

Tulber thrashed, trying to push him off, but it was useless. The pint-sized lunatic in clown makeup clamped down hard, tearing a bloody chunk from Tulber's neck and shredding his carotid artery in the process. Tulber's hands shot to the wound in a futile attempt to stop the blood from geysering out. Less than a minute later, he was dead.

Still riding the high and apparently battling the munchies, Bozo didn't even spit out the chunk of flesh. For a few seconds, he chewed thoughtfully, weighing the pros and cons of human neck meat. It wasn't as rewarding as M&M's—no crispy shell, no sweet payoff—but at least it didn't melt in his hands.

Had he looked in a mirror, he might have reconsidered the snack. His face was drenched in blood, his clown makeup smeared into a crimson mask. Then again, knowing Bozo, he probably would've called it an upgrade.

"Wooooooooooo! Bozo's coming! Bozo's COMING!" he howled like a banshee.

And then—because insanity knows no ceiling—he and Finster launched into a duet:

"I don't like Mondays!" Bozo bellowed.

"No Tuesdays!" answered Finster, clawing his way out of a bush, still clutching a bag of shit in one hand.

"No Wednesdays!"

"No Thursdays!" Finster belted out, off-key, climbing clumsily back up his rope like a malfunctioning circus act. As his swing reached its arc, he hurled the bag of dog crap with all the grace of a drunken softball pitch. It smacked Lawrence square in the chest.

Unfazed, Lawrence calmly brushed it off, as though swatting away lint.

The sudden shift in weight threw Finster off balance. He lost his grip, tumbled through the air, and crash-landed with a graceless roll—coming to a stop two feet from The Mantis. Without hesitation, The Mantis delivered a swift kick to Finster's head, knocking him out cold.

Bozo, high and unhinged, sprang into action. Covered in blood and still wearing his smeared clown makeup and wild green wig, he charged forward like a lunatic in a horror movie. But for The Mantis and Lawrence, it was business as usual.

They exchanged a glance. The Mantis gave a bored wave—Lawrence's cue to handle it.

"Wooooooooooo! Bozo's coming! Bozo's coming!" the clown shrieked, barreling toward them.

Lawrence adopted a loose, practiced stance. As soon as Bozo was within range, Lawrence snapped forward with a front kick, connecting cleanly with Bozo's face. The clown crumpled mid-stride, collapsing beside his friend in a heap of limbs, paint, and bad decisions.

"Well done, Lawrence," The Mantis said, almost cheerfully. "Clearly, you haven't lost a step since your MMA championship days."

He turned to face us.

"I assume your little clown car sideshow has come to an end? Good." Then, with a glance back at Lawrence: "Be a dear and call Nicholas. Have him bring the hostages back. I'm feeling a bit… disrespected. And as you know, that comes with a price."

He gave us a cold smile.

"Oh, and have The Nest prepped. I have a feeling Mike and Clint will find it… unforgettable."

Chapter One Hundred And Ten

With the clown and my former friend Finster still lying unconscious, all Clint and I could do was wait. Our half-assed plan hadn't gone quite as hoped. Sure, Tulber was dead—that was something, I guess. But Finster's jungle-rope stunt and Bozo's banshee charge? Total disasters.

Lost in thought, I barely noticed The Mantis speaking again.

"I must say, Bozo has quite the voice. If he'd chosen a different path, perhaps he could've used it for something more... productive. But it is what it is, as they say. At any rate, I doubt he'll be singing again anytime soon." He turned slightly. "Lawrence, have you reached Nicholas, my friend?"

"Yes sir. He'll be arriving shortly."

"Very good. Now then, let's discuss the punishment." He waved a dismissive hand toward the limp bodies of Bozo and Finster. "You know what your punishment will be, don't you?"

We just stared, numb.

"Answer me or don't—it changes nothing," he con-tinued. "Your punishment, Mike and Clint, will be a pro-longed visit to The Nest. I'm getting hard just thinking about it. But that's not all. Your families, too, will face consequences. Proportional consequences, for the disre-spect you've shown. I'm afraid you'll be making some dif-ficult choices very soon."

Still, we said nothing. It was too much to take in. Would he kill Suzy or the girls? All of them? The horror of The Nest loomed, but I'd gladly endure it if it meant sparing my family. I knew Clint was thinking the same.

"Ah, here comes Nicholas," The Mantis said, pointing off into the distance.

As the SUV grew larger, my world seemed to shrink. Everything felt like it was collapsing in on itself. My heart pounded like it might burst. My thoughts were spinning, wild, helpless. And with each second, the fear only grew.

"Mantis, please," I said, my voice cracking. "Please just let them go. I'm—"

"Save it, Mike," he snapped, cutting me off. "The time for begging has passed. The time for negotiation is over. Now comes the time for action. Decisive. Complete. Ac-tion."

Time seemed to warp and drag. The SUV rolled to a stop, twenty feet away. The door opened.

Nicholas stepped out—or tried to. He staggered, diso-riented, as if the world had tilted sideways. And then, without a word, he collapsed.

All of us—Clint, The Mantis, Lawrence, and I— stared, confused.

"Lawrence," The Mantis said calmly, "please see what's troubling Nicholas."

"Yes, sir," Lawrence replied, and began walking toward the fallen man.

He never made it.

The SUV suddenly roared to life and surged forward—slamming into Lawrence and launching him through the air. He landed in a crumpled heap beside Bozo and Finster.

The vehicle didn't stop. It barreled toward us, faster and faster.

Out of instinct, Clint and I bolted for the trees.

The SUV didn't follow. Instead, it stayed its course— headed straight for The Mantis.

He didn't move. Not until the last possible second. Then, with balletic precision, he dove aside, rolled cleanly through the dirt, and popped back up, cool as ever.

The SUV missed him, spun into a wide U-turn, and came around again.

This time, The Mantis strolled to Tulber's corpse and calmly retrieved his revolver.

The SUV charged again.

But The Mantis didn't flinch. He simply raised the gun and fired.

The SUV veered sharply to avoid him—too sharply. Its driver-side wheels lifted from the ground. It flipped, tumbling side over side. One, two, three and a half rolls before it slammed to a stop—upside down.

The Mantis walked toward it slowly, still firing.

But then—return fire.

Gunshots cracked from inside the vehicle.

For the first time, The Mantis looked surprised. He dove again, rolled, and sprang to his feet—just in time to take a bullet to the back of his left thigh.

He stumbled slightly but didn't cry out. He reached behind him, touched the wound, and assessed it like one might check a sore muscle. Then, with calm resolve, he turned back to the SUV and fired several more rounds through the shattered windshield.

Moments later, it was quiet. Then came a faint, pained cry.

A woman's voice.

I knew that voice. It had to be Mrs. Grabine.

Clint and I crouched low in the woods, holding our breath. Watching.

The Mantis crouched too, slowly creeping toward the overturned vehicle, revolver ready.

"Mrs. Grabine!" I shouted. "Get the fuck out of the car! He's coming!"

The Mantis whipped his head in our direction—and fired a single shot into the trees.

"I'll be coming for you, Mike. And you too, Clint. But first," he said coldly, "I have other priorities."

Then he turned back toward the SUV.

Through the broken window, we saw movement—Mrs. Grabine, crawling out of the wreckage. For someone dubbed "Fat Ass" by Bozo, she moved with surprising agility. She hit the dirt and slithered on her belly, inching toward the woods.

"Come out, come out, wherever you are," The Mantis taunted.

Mrs. Grabine ignored him, crawling faster. If he swung wide around the SUV, she'd be fully exposed. Her right hand was useless—shot through during the exchange, thumb and middle finger broken. She gritted her teeth, pistol in her left hand. She didn't expect to hit anything—but if he got close, she'd sure as hell try.

The Mantis reached the passenger side of the overturned vehicle. He dipped down quickly to peer through the window. Then again, just to be sure. Empty.

Pressing his back against the frame, he paused, then spun around, gun raised. Nothing. Only grass bent low and a trail of blood leading into the brush.

Now in the open, he retreated behind the SUV, reconsidering.

"Don't think you've gotten away, Mrs. Grabine—whoever the fuck you are."

Then, shaking his head: "Apologies. I despise profanity. But given the circumstances—Lawrence murdered, myself shot—I hope you'll forgive my lapse."

"Fuck you," came her voice from the trees.

"Well now, that's a bit ironic," he said, smirking. "I apologize for profanity, and you double down. I also find irony in the word itself, considering *Irony*—my cocaine—is the reason we're all here. Did you know Eddie Bretz named it after his mother? Beat her to death with a curling iron. Poetic, no?"

"I repeat: fuck you!"

"Tsk. Let's be adults. Hand over my *Irony*, and I'll promise you a painless death. Relatively speaking. And that offer goes for all of you—Mike, Clint, Mrs. Grabine. You're going to die. The only variable is how."

Then—crack.

A blur behind him. He twisted too late. A baseball bat caught him just behind the ear, knocking his pistol from his hand and sending him stumbling.

"You dickhead!" Storm shouted. "I heard what you said about Eddie's mom! Yeah, she was a cunt—but *you* don't get to mock her like that. Not you!"

"Again with the swearing," The Mantis muttered, scrambling for the revolver.

Storm didn't stand a chance. She'd never seen anyone move so fast. A second later, she found herself staring down the barrel of the gun.

"Well, since you're here," The Mantis said coolly, "I assume Eddie is, too. Tell me where he is—unless you'd prefer to watch me pull this trigger."

"Oh, he's here all right," Storm said. "But if you really want to see him... go ahead. Turn around."

The Mantis kept the gun trained on her as he pivoted slowly.

"Eddie. How lovely to see you again. Despite the gun you're pointing at me. Now, drop it—unless you'd like Storm's brains to decorate the grass. And from what I've heard, that wouldn't sit well with you. Is it true? Eddie's in love with a whore? The one known for her... special technique? What was it called again? Nod job?"

"Shut the fuck up, Mantis," Eddie growled. "And don't call her a whore. Show some respect."

"My sincerest apologies," The Mantis said. "To you, Eddie. And to you, Storm. But just to clarify—was it *nod* job?"

Storm grinned. "That's the one. And yes, I'm proud of it."

"As you should be, dear. As you should be."

Eddie added, "You'd be lucky to get one, you twisted bastard."

"Oh, maybe you'd like to give *me* a nod job, Eddie," The Mantis said, grinning. "In The Nest. Formerly known as the sex room. You remember it, don't you?"

Eddie winced and reflexively rubbed his ass.

"Yeah. That's not happening again, you sick fuck."

The Mantis rolled his eyes. "Language. Always with the language. And *I'm* the sick one? You're the guy with the broken penis, remember?"

"It's healing," Storm said flatly.

"I'm sure it is," The Mantis replied. "But we've gotten a bit sidetracked, haven't we?"

He turned his gaze to Eddie.

"I'm a rational man, Eddie. Looking at the current situation, I'd call it a stalemate. I've got a gun on your girlfriend. You've got one on me. No winners in that exchange. And to complicate things further, I sense there are... others in the woods. People not exactly on my side. So let's skip the theatrics."

He lowered the pistol slightly—not all the way, just enough to signal a shift.

"I'm offering you a deal. Come back to the Seed. No strings. Clean slate. In fact, a promotion. Lawrence is dead, and his spot's open. It's yours, if you want it. And I'll even put this in writing if you need: no visits to The Nest. Ever. That *does* disappoint me, I won't lie. But I give you my word."

Eddie glanced at Storm, who gave the world's most casual shrug. Eddie mirrored it and answered, "Sure. Why the fuck not? Never liked those douchebags anyway," he added, waving vaguely toward the woods.

"Excellent." The Mantis grinned, his voice like a scalpel hidden in a handshake. "Then I believe you know what our first order of business is."

Eddie nodded. "You got it, boss."

He cupped his hands and shouted:

"Hey Mike! You hear that? How 'bout you, Clint?! And you, Fat Ass?! We're coming to get you!"

Chapter One Hundred And Eleven

That motherfucking Benedict Arnold. Goddamn traitor," I muttered. Clint nodded, tight-lipped. So did Mrs. Grabine, who crawled up beside us in the woods.

"Well. Another fine mess," Clint said. "What's the plan?"

"We've only got one gun," Mrs. Grabine pointed out. "And considering the state of my hand, one of you better take it."

"You take it, Clint. You're a better shot than me. That's about the only thing you're better at."

I tried to land it as a joke, but it went nowhere. No one was in the mood.

"We can't just sit out here forever," Mrs. Grabine said. "And I'm getting hungry. And no Fat Ass jokes, either," she warned, with a sharp look.

"Hey, it's not Bozo or Finster you're talking to," Clint replied. "We've got some manners."

"Yeah, I know. Just making that crystal clear. No more Fat Ass comments. Ever."

"Got it," I said. "Now — back to the plan."

Clint and Mrs. Grabine leaned in.

"Clint, you stay put. Mrs. Grabine, can you run? Hand's a mess, but your legs looked just fine when you bailed out of that SUV."

"Damn right I can run," she said. "I was a college gymnast back in the day."

"Good to know. You take off that way — opposite direction of the cars, away from The Mantis. Create a little chaos. Clint, every sixty seconds, fire a shot. You got ammo?"

"He does now," Mrs. Grabine said, pulling a box of bullets from her jacket. "If that's not enough, we're all fucked anyway."

"Such language," Clint said, deadpan. "The Mantis would not approve. But yeah, fuck him."

Mrs. Grabine grinned despite herself. "What about you, Mike? What's your move?"

"I'm swinging around the other side. Toward the police car. If we're lucky, there's something in there we can use."

"And? What the hell are you going to do when you get there?" Clint asked.

"Clint, if I knew, I'd tell you. Since I don't... I'll wing it."

We all looked at each other, shrugged at the same time, and laughed—just a little. It was the kind of laugh people make when they've got no clue what comes next but are too tired to panic.

Without a word, we stacked our right hands together in a rough circle of three.

"If I don't make it back," I said, "it was nice knowing you."

"Likewise," Mrs. Grabine nodded.

"Fuck that," Clint snapped. "And fuck The Mantis. We're all making it back. I appreciate the drama, Mike, but no one's dying today. We end this. And we end up on top. Period."

I smiled. "I like the attitude. And I like the mantra—if that's the right word. On three: 'Fuck The Mantis.'"

" One. Two. Three."

"Fuck The Mantis!" we shouted.

And with that, Mrs. Grabine and I took off in opposite directions, leaving Clint behind—steadying his aim, locked in, ready to raise hell.

Chapter One Hundred And Twelve

Behind me, Clint fired the first shot.

Simple plan: draw the attention of The Mantis and that goddamn traitor Eddie Bretz. Moments later, I reached the tree line. The police cruiser sat forty feet ahead—forty feet of wide open, no cover. If I moved now, I'd be an easy target. So, I waited.

Bang. Another shot rang out.

I bolted.

I used to be fast. At forty-five, I'd lost a step or three. But I was still fit enough—and lucky enough—to make it to the rear of the police car undetected. What now? Still no fucking clue.

I crouched behind the trunk, peeking through the windows. The Mantis. Eddie. Storm. All three of them stood out in the open, weirdly relaxed. Another shot from Clint kicked me back into gear. I crept along the side, heart hammering, and reached the driver's door.

Still couldn't see them from this angle. Just had to pray they weren't already moving my way.

Bang.

I slipped inside, low and quick, and shut the door without a sound. Hunched over, hidden, I waited. Then popped my head up.

There they were again—sixty feet out, just... talking. Not arguing. Not panicked. Just chatting, like they were discussing dinner plans. It was surreal.

Their casual moment didn't last.

Another shot. Eddie took off, sprinting straight into the woods.

I acted without thinking—impulse and stupidity in equal parts. I grabbed the PA mic.

"Clint! Look out!" I barked. "Eddie's coming your way!"

That did it. They all turned toward the cruiser. Including Eddie—who didn't stop running. Still charging toward Clint.

Didn't have time to worry about it. Because The Mantis raised his gun and opened fire—straight at me.

Glass exploded.

I ducked, heart slamming in my chest. Bullets ripped through the windshield, shredding the dashboard inches from my face.

And that's when I saw them: keys. Still in the ignition.

I didn't think. I just twisted.

The engine roared to life. I dropped it into drive and floored it.

I couldn't afford to lift my head, so I drove blind — turning the wheel on instinct, praying I was creating distance. The gamble paid off. Bullets shifted from the windshield to the rear window. I was headed in the right direction.

I slammed the accelerator. The gunfire slowed... then stopped.

Safe?

I risked a glance. In the rearview mirror, The Mantis leapt into his Jaguar. The engine roared. He was already gaining.

"Well... shit's about to get real," I muttered.

I floored it.

Didn't matter. Whatever engine the cop car had, it couldn't compete with the Jag. The sleek bastard grew larger in my mirror with every second.

"Fuck, fuck, fuck," I whispered, white-knuckling the wheel, rocking forward like my own momentum could push the car faster. It didn't.

Fifty feet. Maybe less.

Bullets again.

They weren't hitting close — yet — but I knew better than to count on his bad aim. Then, up ahead: the orchard entrance. Long, winding, narrow. Not ideal for a high-speed chase, but perfect for screwing with his line of sight.

I cut the wheel.

The cruiser lurched, tires squealing as I entered the winding path.

He'd have a harder time shooting now. That bought me a little breathing room. But I still had no real plan. Just motion. Just panic. Just the sound of leaves whipping past and gravel pinging the undercarriage.

And then, like lightning — an idea. A stupid, desperate, maybe-this-will-work kind of idea.

But it was something.

And right now, something was all I had.

Chapter One Hundred And Thirteen

From Clint's vantage point, he couldn't see Eddie approaching—but he sure as hell could hear him. Stealth was clearly not Eddie's strong suit.

Clint sat with his back against a tree, tense. Another rustle—closer this time, off to the right. Maybe forty feet, tops. He craned his neck for a better look but saw nothing.

He stood slowly, still shielded by the trunk. One more peek, then he'd move.

Two eyes met his.

"Hi there, Clint," Storm said with a sly smile.

"What the—how the—" Clint stammered, caught off guard. He whipped his head around to look for Eddie—

"Looking for me?" Eddie asked, jabbing him in the back.

Clint spun around, but too late. The butt of Eddie's gun met his temple, dropping him to the ground.

"Well, that was easy enough," Storm said, brushing the leaves off her pants.

"Yep. Easy as pie," Eddie replied. Then paused. "Actually, what the fuck does that even mean? Pie isn't easy. Ever try to make dough from scratch? You gotta chill the butter, fold the layers—don't even get me started on blind baking. One wrong move and boom: soggy bottom."

Storm smirked. "I love it when you talk dirty about pastries."

"Baby, you know I keep it flaky."

They kissed over Clint's unconscious body, giggling like teenagers at prom.

"This isn't exactly my idea of a threesome, babe. But I guess Clint can say he was part of one—kinda."

"I guess it does," she said, nodding in agreement.

"Ya know what, Storm? Who would've thought we'd end up here. Not here *exactly*—not with *this* douchebag," Eddie said, elbowing Clint's head for emphasis. "I mean us. You and me. After the way I treated you, tossing money on the floor after your Nod Job? So damn disrespectful. But you stuck with me. Through all of it. I don't deserve you. I really don't. One day—ahhh! What the fuck?! Get the fuck off me! Get the fuck off!"

Eddie thrashed wildly, trying to reach the figure clinging to his back. But Bozo held tight, his teeth sinking into Eddie's neck, the taste of Tulber still fresh on his lips.

With a sudden hop, Bozo leapt off, a bloody chunk of flesh clenched between his teeth. Just like Tulber, Eddie dropped, twitching for a moment before going still.

"Woooooooooo!" Bozo screamed, euphoric.

"Eddie! Eddie!" Storm shrieked, crawling toward him. "Eddie, my sweet Eddie..." She collapsed onto his chest, sobbing.

"I don't like Mondays, no Tuesdays," Bozo sang, still jazzed.

"No Wednesdays, no Thurdays," Finster joined in, strolling into the bizarre scene. "Hit it again, Bozo!"

"I don't like Mondays, no Tuesdays, no Wednesdays, no Thurdays," Bozo belted out, a grin splitting his blood-smeared face.

Storm looked up, dumbstruck. Grief-stricken or not, even she was momentarily entranced by Bozo's hauntingly melodic voice. Then Bozo coughed, gagged, and hacked up a piece of Eddie's neck, spitting it out beside her.

That did it.

With a scream, Storm launched herself at him.

"Now we're talkin'," Bozo grinned, flat on his back with Storm straddling him. Mistaking her fury for arousal, he grabbed her ass. "How's that, babe? You like?"

"Like?! You sick fuck!" she shouted, raining punches on his face until Finster rushed in, wrapping his arms around her from behind.

"Whoa! Whoa! Easy, Storm. Easy. I get it. Emotions are high. But maybe... maybe losing Eddie isn't the worst thing in the world."

Storm whirled her head around. "What the hell are you saying?"

Finster looked to Bozo, gave a solemn nod.

Bozo wiped a smear of blood from his cheek, grinned up at her, and said, "Storm... you ever consider *starring* in clown porn?"

Chapter One Hundred And Fourteen

We didn't have much of a plan—hell, barely a plan at all. But it was something. And we had one key advantage: surprise. When we split up, Mrs. Grabine and I went in opposite directions. With The Mantis tailing me and Storm and Eddie occupied with Clint, Mrs. Grabine was completely off their radar. I intended to use that.

Still driving like a lunatic, I grabbed my phone, hit dial, put it on speaker, and tossed it onto the passenger seat.

"Mrs. Grabine? You safe?"

"For now. Where the fuck are you? And what the fuck is our endgame here?"

"Working on that. The Mantis is still behind me—I think. Remember the entrance to the orchard? That long, winding road?"

"Yeah, I remember. What am I, a fucking idiot?"

"Jesus, okay. Sorry I asked."

"No, I'm sorry. My goddamn hand is killing me. I've never been shot before. And I'd really like to keep it that way going forward."

"Fair enough. Anyway, I've still got a stretch of road ahead of me. At least ten minutes, easy. And The Mantis isn't gaining on me. This road's too narrow and twisty — no way he can push it much faster than I am. Whoa — shit!"

"You good?"

"Yeah. Almost spun out. Exactly what I was saying — this road is shady as hell."

"I get it, Mike. Speed limits. Traction. Blah blah blah. Just spit it out."

"Damn, you're cranky."

"I've got a bullet hole in my hand. Sue me."

"Right. Okay, remember the barn at the entrance to this road? Left-hand side?"

"Of course I remember."

"If you head out from where you are, take a right toward the main road — it should loop you back to the barn. The S-curve in this road brings me around your side eventually. Think you can make it there in five minutes?"

"Holy shit, Mike! A little more warning would've been nice. I guess I better hustle."

"Yeah — please do. Call me when you get there and we'll regroup. This is gonna be tight."

"You wanna fill me in on the actual plan?"

"No time, Mrs. Grabine. I need both hands and all my focus just to stay on this damn road. I just saw The Mantis in my mirror—he's gaining."

"Got it. Heading out now. Be safe, Mike."

She hung up before I could respond.

Chapter One Hundred And Fifteen

A few minutes later, my phone rang.
"I'm here," Mrs. Grabine said. "Now what?"

"I'll be there in two minutes. I'm bringing Officer Tulber's shotgun. He won't be needing it anymore."

"Yeah, I guess not," she muttered.

"I'm gonna swing a U-turn and get as close to the barn as I can. If The Mantis follows, ambush the son of a bitch. Hide on the back side. And if you get the chance — kill him, Mrs. Grabine. Kill him."

"I'll do my best, Mike."

"That's all I can ask. I'm rounding the last bend. Be ready."

"You got it."

As I came out of the curve, I spotted her. She was posted near the barn, scanning the road. In my rearview mirror, The Mantis still wasn't in sight — but I could hear him. Engine roaring. Thirty seconds, tops.

I swung the cruiser into a sharp U-turn, rolled down the window, and flung the shotgun. Mrs. Grabine caught it cleanly, pivoted, and sprinted behind the barn. I was halfway out of the car when a bullet shattered the side window. The Mantis had arrived.

Crouching low, I scurried to the front of the vehicle. Another shot slammed into the driver's side—just two feet off. I had no weapon, but The Mantis didn't know that. Still, Mrs. Grabine was my only hope.

His car screeched to a halt behind me. The fact he could shoot while driving was impressive in the worst way. Now that he was parked, I had no doubt his aim would improve.

"Come out, come out, wherever you are," he sang.

I stayed crouched, inching toward the passenger side. Another shot barked overhead, slamming into the barn's façade and showering me with splinters.

Where the fuck is Mrs. Grabine, I asked myself. *Come on, come on...*

"It's really a shame, Mike," Mantis called out. "This whole situation. Officer Tulber is dead. And Bill Daylay, too—though that one's on me, I admit. I own that. But Tulber? That blood's on your hands."

Another shot punched into the barn.

"Sure, he was expendable. But still, I feel some remorse. You know what really hurts, Mike? Lawrence. He was with me ten, twelve years. And we weren't just business associates—we enjoyed each other. Vigorously. Sexually. I wouldn't call it love... not exactly. But I loved him as a friend. A friend I occasionally bent over. I'll be bending you over soon, too. In The Nest. Right before I kill you."

Another shot rang out—closer this time.

"Die, motherfucker," Mrs. Grabine growled, emerging from the side of the barn with the shotgun raised.

Somehow, The Mantis was ready. He dropped low and fired without looking. The bullet shattered her hip, sending her sprawling to the ground. Calmly, he strode over, collected the shotgun, and flung it toward the barn, far from her reach.

"Well. This is how it ends," he said, aiming the pistol at her face.

Then came the sound—faint but growing—a strange, warbling chant from the road behind us. The Mantis paused, cocking his head.

"I don't like Mondays, no Tuesdays, no Wednesdays, no Thurdays," Bozo sang, his voice distorted by the Doppler effect.

The Mantis couldn't help himself. Despite everything, he started to sway to the rhythm, even mouthed a few words along with it.

That was my moment.

I sprang from behind the car like a linebacker, shoulder-first into his ribs. We both went down hard. But he recovered fast, rolling to his side and slamming an elbow into my cheek. I felt the socket give—my vision went blurry and red.

The Mantis stood up and snatched his pistol from the dirt.

"I don't like Mondays, no Tuesdays, no Wednesdays, no Thurdays," Bozo crooned, even closer now.

The Mantis turned toward us, gun in hand, face twisted with irritation and something like amusement.

"You know I hate profanity," he said, lazily sweeping the barrel between me and Mrs. Grabine. "But let's call this what it is—a goddamn clusterfuck. You. Her. That clown with the golden pipes. Jesus, sometimes I wonder if I should've just gone into real estate. But who am I kidding? I was born for this." He spun in a slow circle, arms raised, grinning like a game show host. "This chaos? All mine."

Bozo pulled the car to a screeching stop next to The Mantis' Jag, still singing.

The Mantis turned toward him, pistol steady, eyes locked on the clown's painted face.

"Out of the car," The Mantis ordered. "You may continue singing, Bozo. In fact, you *will* continue singing until I say otherwise. But you'll also get out and lie down— right there, next to them."

And Bozo did just that. Singing as he stepped out. Singing as he strutted our way. Singing as he lay down beside us. *So this is how it ends,* I thought. Lying in the dirt beside a clown with a voice like Sinatra. At least I'd die to a lullaby.

"Who should be first?" The Mantis mused, pistol raised.

"Eeny." The barrel pointed at me.
"Meeny." It shifted to Bozo.
"Miney." Mrs. Grabine.
"Mo." And back to me.
"Looks like you're the lucky winner, Mike."

But just as he steadied his aim, the trunk of Bozo's car flew open. Storm exploded out, screaming—and hurled a bag of dogshit at The Mantis. One of the bags we'd packed earlier, now weaponized like some unholy grenade. Her aim was awful. It missed him completely and smacked me square in the stomach.

At that point, it hardly mattered. I figured I had seconds to live anyway.

"The ridiculousness continues," The Mantis muttered, firing two quick shots. Both hit Storm in the legs. She collapsed mid-charge, screaming in pain.

"I could've killed you, Storm. You know that. But I'm curious about your famous Nod Job technique. Yes, you're a woman. And yes, I'm gay. But I'm nothing if not open-minded."

He turned back toward me, raising the pistol again.

"Now—where were we? Oh right. Why did you stop singing, Bozo?"

"I don't like Mondays, no Tuesdays, no Wednesdays, no Thurdays," the clown sang, clear and beautiful as ever.

"Good. Let's finish this properly."

He spun the pistol lazily from one of us to the next like a demented carnival game.

"Eeny. Meeny. Miney…"

It landed back on me.

"Mo."

I closed my eyes. *This is it.*

I heard the shot.

But I didn't feel it.

Slowly, I opened my eyes. Checked my chest. My stomach. My legs. Nothing. No blood, no pain. I was alive.

But someone else wasn't.

Then my eyes shifted to the scene around me. On the ground in front of me was The Mantis — motionless. Standing over him, gripping the shotgun, was Finster. The same shotgun Mantis had tossed out of Mrs. Grabine's reach just moments earlier.

Still in shock, I glanced between The Mantis and the dark pool spreading beneath him. Then back to Finster. The same Finster who got us into this nightmare in the first place. But now… the Finster who had just saved my life.

In that instant, I forgot his screw-ups: the coke binges, the selfishness, all the reasons I'd written him off. Instead, I remembered the fishing trips, the late-night talks, the time he told me he loved me like a brother — and I said it right back. I remembered when he asked me to be the best man at his wedding.

I ran to him. Threw my arms around him. Vowed to myself I'd help him get clean. I'd be a better friend. I'd make this right. I held him tight, shaking, grateful, knowing it was finally over — and he'd given me my life back.

Then I thought of my family. I wanted to hold them. Run to them. Be with them. But I didn't even know where they were. I started to pull away to ask Mrs. Grabine —

And that's when I heard the shot.

Still hugging Finster, I saw the exit wound bloom between his eyes. Blood trickled down his face as he slumped against me. I held him tighter as we collapsed together, feeling his life slip away in my arms.

Chapter One Hundred And Sixteen

Several months later, I sat on the porch with my wife, Suzy. Little Janie slept in her arms as the three of us rocked gently on the swing, watching Halle and Lynn chase each other barefoot through the front yard. I was quiet, lost in thought, overwhelmed by how lucky we were just to be alive.

The Mantis died that day—using his final breath to drag Finster to the grave with him. I don't know how long I held Finster in my arms. But I do know that when I finally let go, I released more than just him. I let go of the worst parts of the past, or at least tried to.

A lot of people died that day. Eddie Bretz. The Mantis. Officer Tulber. Lawrence. Bill Daylay. And Nicholas, the bastard who drove The Seed's SUV. For some reason, his death made me smile. Maybe it was the memory of him yanking Suzy out of the car and throwing her to the ground. That image never stopped making my blood boil. Still, none of them hit me like Finster.

I thought about him a lot. About how he saved me. About how he saved all of us—Mrs. Grabine, Clint, Storm, Bozo. And indirectly, our families too. Because let's be honest: The Mantis wouldn't have stopped with us. Not a chance in hell.

Thinking of Mrs. Grabine made me smile. She'd recovered—mostly. The bullet to her hip left her with a permanent limp, but she took it in stride. The shot to her hand was minor by comparison—just a pair of puckered scars, front and back.

Somehow, against all odds, she and Bozo had become... friendly. Maybe it was inevitable. She was now managing *Clownophobia*, keeping the band alive after Finster's death. And with Bozo's voice—hauntingly beautiful, if you ignored the clown face—they were building a local following. It's a strange world.

Even Storm found common ground with Bozo. Given her background in prostitution, transitioning to on-camera work wasn't much of a leap. The real surprise was her niche: clown pornography. But she leaned into it. Hard. Cult followings bloomed in Japan, and her breakout role in *Sad Face, Smiling Vagina* put her on the radar. I've never watched it. Honestly, I'm not sure I could ever get aroused by a frowning clown—but hey, to each their own.

Their next marketing move? Comic-Con in San Diego. Between the cosplay addicts and those with a soft spot for greasepaint erotica, they figured Storm would fit right in. Who knows, maybe they'd even move a few more copies of that movie. Maybe even launch a sequel. Probably something tasteful like *Tears of a Clown, Cream Pie of Regret.*

But for me, the circus was finally over.

And I was exactly where I wanted to be.

Lastly, I thought of Clint.

Clint—the guy who kidnapped me.

Clint—the guy who, like me, would do anything to protect his family.

Given all that, it wasn't surprising we'd become pretty damn good friends. We met up about twice a month for drinks and texted daily, mostly to bust each other's balls.

Speaking of balls... the boil in my groin finally erupted. It happened during my scuffle with The Mantis, just before he almost shot me. Out of habit, I reached down to check for any new lumps. Thankfully, nothing. Clint would've loved that—would've used it as another excuse to mock the size of my dick.

As for the other wounds—the shattered eye socket, the bullet in my shoulder—they healed. More or less. Time heals all wounds, right? Maybe even the loss of Finster.

Just then, the phone rang.

"Hey, Clint," I said. "Funny. I was just thinking about you."

"Yeah?" he replied. "I was thinking about you too—but not in the way you were thinking about me, homo."

A beat.

"Not that there's anything wrong with that, of course. You just don't exactly float my boat, Mikey."

"You're a real sweetheart."

"Hey, I've got a drink in my hand."

"Same. Vodka. Delicious."

"So, how about we raise a glass?" he said.

"I'm listening."

"To Finster," Clint said.

"To Finster," I replied, lifting my glass toward the sky before bringing it to my lips for a long, slow sip.

THE END

About the Author

Mark Royer writes about clown fetishes, drug cartels, murder, childhood memories—and whatever else tumbles out of his monkey brain. His writing has connected with readers who appreciate stories that are dark, absurd, and unexpectedly heartfelt.

He's the creator of *The Ramblings of a Madman*, a periodic blog on mindfulness, depression, sex, dogs, favorite foods, and whatever else refuses to stay quiet in his head. Before writing full-time, Mark earned an obscure degree in Metallurgy from Penn State and spent years masquerading as a licensed engineer. Eventually, he left engineering to pursue his true calling: telling dark, hilarious, and occasionally unhinged stories.

Born and raised in Pennsylvania (where he still lives), Mark is the proud father of six, godfather of three, husband to an inspiring and amazing woman, and full-time Pooper Scooper to a mostly cool but occasionally annoying dog named Charlie. He's been published in several scientific journals, contributed editorials, and *No Tuesdays* is his debut novel — with many more on the way.